GHOST

MOTHER

GHOST
MOTHER

A NOVEL

KELLY DWYER

UNION
SQUARE
& CO.

NEW YORK

UNION SQUARE & CO.

NEW YORK

ISBN 978-1-4549-5282-4
ISBN 978-1-4549-5283-1 (e-book)

Library of Congress Control Number: 2024003560
Library of Congress Cataloging-in-Publication Data is available upon request.

For information about custom editions, special sales, and premium purchases,
please contact specialsales@unionsquareandco.com.

Printed in Canada

2 4 6 8 10 9 7 5 3 1

unionsquareandco.com

Cover design by Ian Koviak/The Book Designers
Cover images: Front: Arcangel: © Jarek Blaminsky (house),
© Samantha Pugsley (woman); Shutterstock.com: Sasin Paraksa (floor).
Back cover and spine: Shutterstock.com: faestock (veil), magicoven (wood).
Interior design by Rich Hazelton

For Alice

"And everything that once was
infinitely far
and unsayable is now
unsayable
and right here in the room."

—FRANZ WRIGHT, "PROGRESS," FROM
GOD'S SILENCE: POEMS (2006)

"And so, it is said, you are haunted!
My friend, we are haunted all."

—ISABELLA BANKS, "HAUNTED!" (1878)

CONTENTS

GHOST

MOTHER

1

FALLING

DOES "FALLING IN LOVE" IMPLY that you fall and keep falling or that you fall and land into love? In other words, was love a dark, vertical tunnel without end, or more of a soft, cushiony feather bed? This was what I was thinking about while I opened cupboards and peeked inside closets, trying to feign disinterest, because the truth was, as soon as I'd taken one look at the 1920s Romanesque Revival mansion on Hill Street, a crumbling, ivy-covered brick-and-stone castle, I knew that I couldn't live without it, that I was in love, that it was—or would be—mine.

Ours, I mean, naturally. Jack was with me, either feigning disinterest even better than I was, or else seriously not in love with the house. "What's this water damage?" he asked the real estate agent in a sour, put-upon tone, and I began to rehearse how I was going to talk him into it. *You dragged me out here to the middle of nowhere, at least let me choose the house.*

They discussed the ancient furnace, the faulty electrical wiring, the dilapidated roof, and then finally I interrupted to ask Al Martin, the agent, a truly important question. "What's the circus connection?"

He appeared to be in his mid-sixties, about the same age my father would be, if he were still alive, but while my father had thinning light brown hair, a champagne smile, and perfect vision, Al Martin sported a full head of fuzzy gray locks, a serious expression, and bifocals, which he now peered over to look at me.

"The what?" Jack asked.

"The listing said to be sure to ask about the house's circus connection," I told him. "So I am."

"You've heard of the Lawrence Brothers?" Al Martin asked.

I looked at Jack, but he was on the floor now, inspecting a heating grate. "We're not really from the area."

"They owned a circus, a very famous circus. Wisconsin is the circus state, of course, all the big circuses came from right here." He tapped his index finger toward the hardwood dining room floor so that I found myself gazing at his feet, as if searching for elephant dung. "It was the oldest son, I think he was the oldest, Edgar Lawrence. May have been the second oldest. There were four brothers altogether. Anyway, Edgar Lawrence built this house in 1921. It was very . . . unusual for its time. He was quite wealthy, and he didn't skimp on a thing, as you can see."

I could see, all right. From the outside, the house looked like a decrepit manor, or an abandoned château, complete with brick-and-limestone walls crawling with ivy, an ornate arched doorway, and three chimneys jutting to the sky. The front door was a large, heavy wooden monster, about twelve feet high, with iron hinges, and when Al Martin had opened it for us, I had been greeted by a sight that had taken my breath away; that is, I had sucked in my breath and had held it until I'd remembered to let it out and breathe. It was the most magnificent residential foyer I had ever seen, with a black iron chandelier dangling from above and a view of a grand wooden staircase. A quick tour revealed the downstairs alone housed a living room, formal dining room, kitchen, hearth room, library, conservatory, and two stone fireplaces.

Of course, the house was also falling apart. The beautiful pink-and-yellow Art Deco–print wallpaper in the dining room was held up by duct tape. The hardwood floors were stained, scratched, and streaky white from water damage, and a few of the downstairs windows were cracked and covered with plastic sheeting. Perhaps most distressing, in the middle of the dining room ceiling, there was a hole through which one could see up to a spare room above. Apparently, a chandelier had fallen, taking much of the ceiling with it, and no one had bothered to replace it—or patch up the ceiling/floor. A few of the walls seemed to be crumbling in on themselves, as plaster layered the damaged floors like breadcrumbs from decades of white toast. But all this shabbiness was part of the house's charm. It looked like the ancient manor home of an English aristocrat who had come upon hard times. I was falling. I had fallen. I was in love.

"Has anyone ever told you that you look like Jean Shrimpton?" Al Martin asked. In fact, quite a few people had told me I looked like the famous model from the 1960s, with her light brown hair, doe eyes, arched brows, and wide lips, but not for many years. I shrugged, though I was pleased, even as I knew the real estate agent was doing his best to sell us the house. "The first supermodel, the original It girl. You could bring back that glamour to this estate. You two must have beautiful children. Do you? Have children?"

I glanced at Jack, and this time he looked up at me and then quickly looked away. I used to say, "Not yet," but I was getting old—thirty-seven—and I was afraid that the hopefulness that statement implied would begin to result in pity. The truth was, I was a sort of half mother, a ghost mother. I had a few dead fetuses, but that wasn't what people meant when they asked.

"No," I said.

Al Martin, a real pro, simply nodded. "There are seven bedrooms."

"Seven!" Jack exclaimed.

"That's a lucky number," I assured him.

Al Martin looked uncertain, but said, "Sure it is. Of course, some could be made into studies, guest rooms. Apparently the third-floor attic was used as a ballroom as well as for circus practices."

"Well, that'd be useful," Jack muttered.

"I should also mention that the circus society is willing to let some of the furniture come with the house."

He said this as if it were a favor, but I suspected that most of the furniture would not be up to the standards of the Salvation Army's pickup truck. And yet, they were certainly up to mine. Would the society include the worn farm-style table in the kitchen? The wobbly dining chairs with their faded seats depicting ancient roses? The ornate secretary in the library with feet gnawed by hungry mice? Shabby, threadbare, damaged, I wanted it all.

"Would you like to go upstairs first or see the basement?"

Jack came over and put his arm around me, then squeezed my shoulder. He knew I didn't do basements. Was he feeling protective of me from the reference to children? Or was he simply showing Al Martin that we were a united front, ready to wheel and deal and make something happen immediately? I almost said, "We'll take it." But Jack spoke first. "I'd like to see the basement."

While the men went downstairs, I opened the back door and walked into the backyard. It was late afternoon, mid-September, one of those perfect early fall days when you feel that life is brimming with possibility. I stepped onto the brick patio, stared at the ivy growing on the stone walls, and knew: this was the house I was meant to have. I felt as if something were pulling at me, as if the house and I were both magnetized, and it was drawing me toward it. Now that I'd seen this forsaken mansion, its neglectedness calling to me like the big eyes of a regal but mangy greyhound dog at a shelter, I could not imagine living anywhere else.

The backyard was made up of a sweeping expanse of lawn with a weeping willow cradling a tire swing, and an overgrown flower garden the size and shape of a kidney swimming pool. One side yard consisted of a steep, long slope of grass leading into woods, while the other side of the house consisted of the driveway, a fence, and more woods. I remembered reading in the listing that the property was surrounded by public land. There were houses across the street, but no others on this side. Edgar Lawrence had managed to build his mansion in the middle of a forest preserve.

On a hill. Hill Street. From my vantage point, I had a view of the quaint town square with its clock tower and nearby church steeples, and the majestic bluffs beyond. I looked in all directions and realized this was the highest point around. Then I heard a sound. Water running, a current. I could hear, but not see, the river somewhere below.

I walked closer and found that the land at the back of the yard ended in a precipice, a cliff above the river. There was nothing gradual about this drop. One inch there was land, and the next inch, empty space. I had never thought of myself as having a particular fear of heights. I'd grown up on the forty-fifth floor in a penthouse apartment overlooking Lake Michigan, after all. But this drop frightened me.

I stepped back a few feet and looked out. It was strangely beautiful, to see the edge of land leading to, well, *air*. I was both attracted to the cliff and repelled by it. But something made me continue to back away and then turn and walk until I was safely in the middle of the lawn.

I heard the back door open and shut. Jack. When he came up next to me, I smiled at him. We'd met at a New Year's Eve party eight years before, on the night the centuries had changed, Y2K, at the home of a mutual acquaintance, while Prince sang in surround sound. Most of the guests had worn jeans and sweaters, but as an actor, I had always taken my costumes seriously, and I'd sparkled in a beaded silver dress, sheer stockings, and silver heels. Jack and I had sat by the fire, and he'd talked me into kissing him at 10:20 because, he'd explained, it was midnight somewhere.

"No, it's not," I said. "It's 11:20 somewhere, or 12:20, not midnight."

He had cropped hair and glasses that made him look smart and geeky and sexy and cool all at the same time, and he shook his head at me in a charmed way, as if I were very bad at math and he found it adorable.

"It's done by gradations," he explained. "It's 10:21 somewhere, and 10:22, and somewhere it's midnight, probably in Nova Scotia, which is a fine place, with hearty soup and strapping fishermen, and they're all kissing the beautiful women beside them right now."

He said it so convincingly that I half believed him—maybe he was right, maybe it was midnight in Nova Scotia—and then he leaned closer and kissed me. Eight years later, I still remembered that kiss: soft and gentle, and then a little less soft, a little less gentle. His mouth had tasted of port. I wanted him to kiss me like that now.

"Isn't it lovely?" I whispered, standing beside him, gazing out over the trees to the newly risen moon. "Listen. You can hear the river."

Al Martin's steps came up the pebbled path behind us.

"Man," Jack said, loud enough for the realtor to hear, and letting out a long, beleaguered sigh. "You'd need a fucking goat to mow this lawn."

"Jack, I loved that house," I said when we were inside the car. I was wearing a cotton sweater over a short-sleeved sundress and sandals, and I was getting chilly. I turned on the heat, which blew around cool air. Jack didn't bother to tell me to wait until the car was warmed up to turn it on, but I knew it was what he was thinking from the way he glanced at the heater and then leaned his head back in the driver's seat. I couldn't help it; I got such a psychological perk from hearing that hardworking burst.

"Yeah, it was a cool house, all right."

"Really? You liked it?"

"I mean, of course I liked it." Jack was a sincere person. I'd never thought of him as a good actor, a good liar. He had never excelled at charades. I wouldn't have suspected this poker talent, and for a moment, it distracted me from the house. But only for a moment.

"You did?"

"Yeah, I did."

"You didn't seem like you liked it. Were you just playing hard to get?"

He turned to me, as if realizing that we were talking about two different things. "But of course we can't buy it, Lilly."

"I thought you said you liked it."

"It's a cool house. Really cool. But it's falling apart. A classic money pit. You know how much that thing would cost to heat in the winter?"

"There was practically a fireplace in every room!"

"Oh, I get it, you'll lug wood into all those rooms and keep us warm that way. I suppose you'll be the one to chop down the trees, too?"

"You can order wood, you know. It's not hard. This is Wisconsin. They sell it at the gas station."

"There's water damage everywhere. Plaster's crumbling from the walls. The electricity needs to be replaced. There's a hole in one of the ceilings!"

"Think of it as an investment. We could fix it up and sell it."

"Because we're so handy, and because there are so many millionaires in Haven, wanting to buy a renovated stone mansion."

He had a point there, and I had to think for a moment. "Naturally, we wouldn't turn it around right away. But, you know, eventually, it would be an investment. Our nest egg."

"That roof is over thirty years old."

"Oh, but what about the view from the main bedroom? Looking out into the woods. And that river. I mean, Jack, it's on a river! And that staircase? Isn't it amazing? It's like it was built for a princess."

Maybe it was the wistfulness in my voice, maybe it was the word "princess." But whatever the reason, suddenly Jack touched my cheek. "You really want that house?"

I remembered that magnetized pull, making it painful to leave, as if this was the house I was meant to have. I remembered going into the nursery—the room we would use for the nursery, anyway, right off the main bedroom, with its pink roses wallpaper and view of the backyard—and I had been sure, I had *known*, I was going to have a baby in this house.

"More than anything in the world."

"You know we can't afford to pay anywhere near what they're asking."

"I could get a job."

He looked skeptical.

"Really, I'll get a job. I promise!"

He rested his forehead on the steering wheel and banged it about three times.

Then he turned to me and said, "Okay. Lowball offer. If they don't take it, we walk away. If they do take it, you get a job."

"I love you," I said, throwing my arms around him.

When I broke away, he nodded, as if to himself. "Lowball offer. There's nobody living there. It's owned by the circus society, right? They need to get it off their hands. I bet they're desperate."

We had been house hunting for three weeks, ever since Jack had landed a position at the leading digital imaging company in the Midwest, and we had fled Chicago for Wisconsin. Jack's job was to train people—radiologists, physicians, research scientists in university labs—how to use his company's software so that they could detect cancer and identify promising therapies. He was part scientist, part computer guy, part teacher, part detective, and part soldier, working on the front lines of the battle against disease. He had to travel a lot, and the most central location of his service area was a town called Haven.

Since we'd been in Haven (population 17,334, plus, now, two more), we'd gone to four open houses, had been inside thirteen homes, and had made an offer on exactly none. As far as I could tell, we were the ones who were desperate, staying in the only motel in the area that charged by the week and allowed cats, surrounded by unopened cardboard boxes and a mini fridge that could only hold a pint of milk, a carton of yogurt, and two beers at a time.

"In a normal place," I reminded him, "that house would be going for about three million."

He ignored my jab at our new environs and said, "They're asking three-fifteen. I say we offer two hundred and see what happens."

"You really think they'll take two hundred thousand?"

"They don't take it, we walk away."

We offered two even. They came back with three. We didn't walk away.

After many days of negotiating, we bought the house, and everything in it, for $279,000. More than we could afford, but in 2008, banks were lending to anyone with a 10 percent down payment and a W-2. Jack had needed to cash out some of his 401(k) to come up with the twenty-eight thousand down. (As a former actor, waitress, and teacher, I didn't have a 401(k) myself.) A bowl of Hershey's Kisses sat in the middle of the table at the closing, ostensibly to sweeten the deal. Jack, who never ate candy, popped the chocolates compulsively, pausing every so often to sign something or wipe the sweat off his brow.

Moving day was warm and sunny; the sky was periwinkle blue. I felt
ebullient, a kite billowed by the wind. Jack made iced tea with honey
and lemon, which we drank sitting on the floor of the conservatory.
The room consisted of a glass roof and glass walls, and seemed to be
in pretty good shape, with only three glass panels covered with cardboard. Olivier, our fluffy gray-and-white Persian rescue cat with his
adorable squished-in grumpy face, seemed happy as well. He lay in
the sun, belly up, as relaxed as any beach bunny lying on a towel in
the sand. "We can have a garden here," I said. "We can grow herbs,
even in winter. And a piano. Wouldn't it be great to have a piano in
the living room?" The conservatory and living room were divided by
French doors, and I could see through to the living room, which was
enormous and nearly empty.

"Do you miss it?"

"What?"

"Playing."

I shrugged. I was a depository of useless talents: music, drama,
French, Italian, piano . . . one more thing that I no longer engaged
in didn't really matter.

"Someday we'll get you one."

"I know."

"But in the meantime, we should get some chairs. Ouch." He
patted his rear as he stood, and then helped me up.

That afternoon, I was on my way down the long driveway to see if we
had any mail yet when I noticed three children lugging windbreakers
and backpacks along the road. It was a Monday in early October,
and I felt like it was a good sign that we were on some kids' route
home from school.

I'd almost reached the bottom of the driveway when I yelled,
"Hi there."

"Hi," they said back, stopping.

"You move here?" one of them asked.

"Just today," I said.

"That house is haunted," the boy said. The two girls beside him nodded.

"Oh, really? By whom?"

"A ghost."

"Yeah, a ghost," one of the girls repeated. She appeared to be the oldest of the three, maybe nine, and she spoke with a bored authority.

"Whose ghost?"

"Some lady."

"We seen her in the window at night."

"Is she a spooky ghost?"

They looked at each other, as if this were a dumb question, then shrugged.

The boy kicked a block of hard dirt a couple of times, and then they walked away.

Kids, I thought. But despite myself, I stared up at the window of our bedroom, searching, although it was broad daylight. I thought I saw something, and then realized it was just a flash of sunlight. Afternoon sun can play tricks upon the eyes.

2

NEW HOME

THE FIRST NIGHT IN OUR NEW HOUSE we didn't make love. I wasn't ovulating.

Between the six months before the first miscarriage, and the eight months since the second, our lovemaking had been cool, calculated, timed precisely to body temperature, cervical mucus, and ovulation predictor kits. It was like work, tiring and passionless, only we didn't get paid. In my twenties, I'd have thought one had to "christen" a house by having sex in nearly every room, on the floor, in the shower, on the big farm table in the kitchen. I would have thought it as unromantic as not having candles and chocolate on Valentine's Day to simply say *Good night, Good night*, and fall asleep. But that's what we did. I don't know if it occurred to Jack to do otherwise. It didn't to me.

In the morning, Jack whispered in my ear, "We own a house."

"Do we?"

"How does it feel?"

I opened my eyes and smiled. "Good. I love our house."

"Good. Because we're stuck with it." He kissed me on my forehead. Olivier meowed, stretched his legs, and immediately fell back to sleep. I took my temperature and recorded it in my fertility graph. Jack said, "I'm going to make you breakfast."

The kitchen had never been updated. It included no stainless-steel fridge, no convection oven, no triple-tier dishwasher. In fact, there was no dishwasher at all, just a working fridge, a brand-new range that the circus society must have installed to sell the place (plain white, nothing fancy), and a deep, farm-style sink. But there were gorgeous mahogany built-in cabinets that I'd fill with the Pottery Barn dishes we'd received for our wedding. They were also plain white, nothing fancy, but they were the only dishes we owned, since my family's good china (and French silverware and crystal wine glasses and just about everything else) had been sold at auction to pay off debts after my father's bankruptcy.

We sat in the breakfast nook and drank coffee (decaf for fertility-minded me) and ate eggs, buttered toast, and bacon for Jack, soy sausages for me. I'd grown up in a skyscraper with half grapefruits and cold cereal for breakfast, and the scent of that American farm-style breakfast, in that kitchen, moved me. "I can't believe that with our debt and everything, we own a house," I said.

"The bank owns it. We're just the caretakers. You remember our agreement."

"What was that?"

"That you get a job."

"Of course I'll get a job."

"Doing what?"

"Hmmm?" I said, my mouth full of soy sausage.

His lips were oily with butter. They twitched at one corner, which meant he was beginning to panic. "I said, doing what? What kind of job are—?"

"Don't worry," I told him. "I'll get a good job."

"This is a promise?"

"Scout's honor," I said, holding up three fingers, though I'd never made it past Brownies.

He gave me a quick peck on my cheek, leaving an unguent mark, and then grabbed his laptop case to go teach health care professionals

at hospitals how to use his company's software so that we could pay
our mortgage.

"I'll see you tonight," he said.

My career, such as it was, had not turned out exactly as I'd planned.
I was fifteen years old when I'd started working as a hostess at Lake
Oyster Bar, my father's hugely popular restaurant on the Magnificent Mile, where sometimes men would slip me a hundred just for
seating them at a coveted table. My dad, who'd once been a successful restaurant and nightclub owner, had always assured me that
someday I would manage his half-dozen establishments and eventually inherit them. I'd envisioned a life after college in which I'd earn
money as a successful restauranteur while acting in the city's many
illustrious theaters, maybe even becoming an ensemble member of
Steppenwolf, like Gary Sinise, John Malkovich, and Joan Allen. That
had been my dream, and I had spent my twenties working hard for it.

Then a combination of changing neighborhoods, tax issues, and
a wee bit of a gambling addiction combined with an unlucky streak
had managed to leave my father penniless. My mother divorced him,
married a multimillionaire, and moved to Aruba, from where she
occasionally emailed me Zen-inspired advice. About six months after
my father lost everything, moved in with his brother, and started
working as the manager of a seedy nightclub, he'd died.

That was over ten years ago. In the span of a few months, I'd gone
from a Gold Coast starry-eyed darling living off minimum equity
gigs, part-time waitering, and the plush cushion of my father's gen-
erosity to a starving artist barely making it in a run-down studio in
Bucktown, grief and bills piling up around me.

I threw myself into my work. I landed some of my best roles that
first year after my father's death (Viola in *Twelfth Night*, Maureen in
Rent, Maggie in *Cat on a Hot Tin Roof*), received some of my best

reviews. And it almost seemed like I was going to pull off my dreams despite, or perhaps because of, having survived the worst thing I could ever have imagined happening.

But acting is a fickle business. And as I neared my thirties, I started losing roles to the "new" talent. I needed to waitress longer hours just to keep the lights on in my apartment. By the time I married Jack, the roles I was being offered were fewer and farther between, and we both agreed that it made sense for me to do something else. I'd always been good with children, and I had fond memories of playing school with my cat, pug, and stuffed animals as a little kid, and so I earned a teaching certificate as a "backup plan."

I began to teach fourth and fifth graders while landing the occasional supporting role here and there. I'd kept that up for years, until I'd turned thirty-five, when my dreams of becoming a successful working actor had pretty much evaporated, and I'd shifted my hopes to becoming a mom. I now thought of myself (sometimes bitterly, sometimes with sweet nostalgia for all the amazing parts I'd had, all the great plays I'd been in) as an actor manqué.

So where did that leave me?

I could teach elementary school, but the mere thought made my skin feel prickly, as if I were about to break out in chicken pox. It was just so hard to be around children right now, when I wanted a child of my own so desperately. The only other practical job I'd had was as a server and cocktail waitress, and while I'd excelled at that work, making hundreds of dollars in tips a night, I was currently much too obsessed with my fertility to carry heavy trays and stay out until closing time in bars hazy with smoke.

But I needed to make money. We owned a decaying castle, we were well past our ears in credit card debt, and if I didn't get pregnant soon, we were planning on starting IVF. I decided I would pound the pavement, résumé in hand, and see what was out there, who was hiring. I walked up the grand staircase to get ready for a trip into town.

When I reached the second-floor landing, with its threadbare orange velvet divan and Tiffany-style lamp that had come with the house, I saw out of the corner of my eye that something was out of place.

I glanced down the hallway to the right. There were two closed doors on each side of the hallway—four of our seven bedrooms. All but my study was empty of everything but dust bunnies. At the end of the hallway was another door leading to the third-floor attic/ballroom. The home inspector had called this room a "death trap," with floors that were "structurally unsound." Against the home inspector's warning, Jack had insisted on seeing for himself. He'd gone up there with a sense of adventure and a flashlight and had come down ashen and pale. I clearly remembered him closing the door firmly behind him. But it stood halfway open now.

Maybe Jack had gone back up there this morning, I thought, though I couldn't imagine why. I walked down the hall and then stopped in front of the open door. I felt afraid. Then I told myself not to be ridiculous. Why should I be afraid of an open door? I hesitated, then peeked through. A narrow set of stairs lined with cobwebs. I let out a deep breath and then inwardly laughed at myself. What did I think I'd find? The ghost the kids had seen in the window at night? I closed the door shut, and the latch clicked into place.

I walked back down the hallway, past the landing, and then found myself going inside the room I thought of as "the nursery." It was empty now save for a Mission-style rocking chair that had come with the house. The chair arms, which were wide, dark-brown mahogany, were thick with dust. I needed to come up here with a bucket of soapy water and some rags and do some serious cleaning. I walked across the parquet floors and imagined this as a baby's room, with a crib, a dresser, and pictures of vintage nursery tale characters on the walls. When I stood in this room, I felt a strange mixture of wholeness and longing.

I heard something behind me and instinctively turned to the door. I let out a deep breath. It was just Olivier, standing in the doorway. "Olivier," I said, in my sweet cat-mama voice. But he didn't move. I stared at his squished-in, grumpy-looking face, his fluffy white-and-gray coat, trying to feel the usual sense of calm and amusement I felt around him, but instead I felt tense. He was crouched, with his tail wrapped around his body. His big eyes were staring at something to the side of me, and beyond me, unblinking. I turned to see whatever he was looking at. But nothing was there. "Olivier," I repeated, in a sterner voice, trying to rouse him from his hypnotic stupor. He kept staring. I took a step toward him, and he met my eyes, appearing startled, as if he'd just awakened from a dream. Then he let out a "*Hiss!*" and turned around and ran down the stairs, feline fast. *Stupid cat*, I thought. But between his reaction and the open door to the third floor, a part of me was shaken, and I decided it was a good time for me to leave the house and go job hunting, as I'd promised Jack I would.

I drove into town wearing an old pale pink and black tweed Chanel skirt suit and black pumps and parked in the town square. Planters of autumn mums and pumpkins lined the sidewalks, a scarecrow and hay bales festooned the town green, and construction paper crows, witches, and ghosts decorated store windows and proclaimed "Boo!"

I grabbed my worn leather satchel, which held a few copies of my résumé and some ballpoint pens, and walked up and down the shops along the square. I went to the bookstore, the natural foods store, and the ladies' clothing store, none of which were hiring. I avoided the taxidermist's office, the toy store, and the bank.

Inside the fancy linens shop, I fingered damask throws, Egyptian cotton sheets, and velvet-quilted pillows while I waited for the salesclerk to finish helping a young woman with a baby sleeping in a stroller, a pacifier in its little rosebud mouth. I took one look at the beautiful baby and tried not to loathe the mother with all my heart.

"May I help you?" the saleswoman asked.

"Yes, are you the owner by any chance?"

"Yes, I am."

"What a lovely store you have."

"Thank you," she said.

I detected enough of a French accent that I ventured to ask, "*Vous êtes française?*"

"*Oui*," she replied, clearly pleased.

"I'd so enjoy working here. Are you hiring?"

"No, not at the moment," she said, checking me out, and I felt satisfied that at least one person in this town would know a Chanel when she saw one, even if it was thirteen years old. "But you vould be fabulous here. Why don't you fill out an application and I vill call you if I need you?"

I did. And I felt so buoyed by the possibility of landing a job in such a nice store, with such a nice boss, and undoubtedly such a nice employee discount, that I bought a sage green chenille throw for our living room, putting it on the card.

On my way back to the car, I passed a homeless guy—the first homeless person I'd seen during my time in Haven—holding out a tin can. Beside him lay a scrawny mutt that looked like a crazy cross between a black Lab and a dachshund. The two of them gave off a sour and dank scent. They smelled like the L in Chicago at about two in the morning, not like Haven, Wisconsin, at two in the afternoon.

"Miss, can you spare a little change?"

I thought of my father. At one point he had been so rich, he had no idea how much money he had. But he could have ended up like this. I could have. Let's face it, still could. There were times when I'd felt we were one horse race, one paycheck, away from a tin can and a mangy dog and a plea for a little change. Instead, I had just moved into the grandest hovel in Haven. Besides, how could I say no when I was carrying around a chenille blanket that probably cost more than this guy had seen in a couple of months? (Never mind that I hadn't earned a dime in nearly a year.) I searched inside my wallet. I only had a fifty. I considered for a minute. And then I handed it over to him.

He looked stunned.

"I hope this buys you and your dog a few good meals," I said, trying to sound cheerful.

He stared straight into my eyes. "God bless you, miss," he said.

The blessing of a beggar is no small thing. I felt lucky and alive.

That night, our second night in the house, I dreamed that someone was giggling. The voice was a female's, but I couldn't tell if it was a young girl's or an old lady's. I was trying to figure this out when I realized I wasn't dreaming. I was awake. It was the middle of the night. A woman was laughing, a sound like falling coins. Suddenly the laughter died.

"Jack," I said, my voice somewhere between a croak and a whisper. "Jack!" I repeated, shaking him. Then I turned on the light.

"What? What?"

Without his glasses, Jack's blue-gray eyes were myopic and vulnerable, like something newly hatched.

"Someone's here, someone was laughing," I said.

He sat up in bed. "What are you talking about?"

"I dreamed someone was laughing, but then I woke up; I mean, I realized I was awake, and I still heard the laughter, and then it stopped."

Jack looked like he wanted to kill me but was too tired. "I have to leave for northern Wisconsin at six in the morning, and you woke me up to tell me you dreamed some lady was laughing?" He lay down again, curling away from me.

"I never said it was a lady."

He didn't respond. He was already asleep. I turned off the light.

3

THE MURDER HOUSE

I WAS NOT A MORNING PERSON. The following day, I stumbled to the kitchen with crusty eyes, brain fog, and the memory of a woman's high-pitched laughter echoing through my head.

I was putting on the kettle for tea when the kitchen telephone rang. "Hello?"

"Hey." Jack's voice. "What are you up to?"

He sounded curt, and I wondered if he was checking up on me, making sure I was following through on my promise. I immediately felt guilty. "Oh, you know, just . . . getting ready to . . . go job hunting again. Yes! I'm getting ready to go job hunting right now!"

I scanned the kitchen for a wall clock, but we hadn't put one up yet. The cooking stains on the walls were yellowish brown, like nicotine-stained teeth, and I thought I saw one of them, face-shaped, move, as if it were yawning. I blinked. The stain looked normal again. It was funny how your mind could play tricks on you. (*Ha ha!*)

"Listen, one of the guys here has a wife who works in the Haven school district. He told me they still have a couple of openings for this year."

I went into acting mode. I was playing the part of Model Wife, composed and not at all disoriented by lack of sleep, an unexplained open door, Olivier's staring at something that wasn't there, and the midnight sound of a woman's laughter. I was the relocated teacher looking for a new elementary school position. "Oh, that's wonderful!"

I exclaimed. (*That is*, I thought to myself, *the composed job-hunting teacher exclaimed*.)

"Wonderful?" Jack said doubtfully; he knew me well. "It'd probably be decent pay. I mean, you'd have to find something temporary to tide you over until you could get your license renew—"

"I'll take over my résumé today!" I was speaking in exclamation points.

"Lilly?"

"Yes?"

"Are you okay?"

Perhaps I was overdoing it. "Fine," I said. "I'm fine." I looked away from the stains and stared out the window, into the side yard and to the woods beyond them.

I took a deep breath, and, to change the subject, I asked Jack, "How are you? How's the drive?"

"Pretty. Lots of green, rolling hills. They could have filmed *The Sound of Music* in Wisconsin."

I kept gazing out the kitchen window into the copse of trees in the side yard. "It is beautiful here," I said.

"And it's not everyone who owns a . . . what did Al Martin call it? 'A grand Romanesque Revival estate'?" He laughed. "Okay, so it's about to fall on our heads, but still. Who would have thought? Jack and Lilly, caretakers of a grand, historic Romanesque Revival estate!"

Jack was right. It was pretty amazing for a boy who had grown up in a tract home in the suburbs and a girl who had come of age in a sterile luxury high-rise to now live in a place so rich with history. A mansion built by a circus baron. *Who was this man who had built this palatial estate?* I wondered. The question gave me an idea.

"I should go."

"All right, honey," he said. "But you know, things are looking up. I know they've been rough. But they'll get better."

I pressed my hands to my flat belly. I imagined it being round, the size and shape of a beach ball, a baby inside, kicking and swimming. I remembered the certainty I'd had that I'd become a mother here, in this house. "I think you're right," I said.

"I love you," he said.

"I love you, too."

I hung up the phone and went upstairs to get dressed.

It was a weekday around noon, and the Haven Public Library was humming with activity. Music wafted from the children's floor above, and every seat in the computer area was taken. I stood in line behind a woman checking out some new releases, an elderly couple with a stack of DVDs, and a man in a business suit carrying *Eat, Pray, Love* and a slow cooker cookbook, and then it was my turn.

"I need some help," I told the librarian behind the desk. Then I smiled awkwardly, because I realized I could have accurately used the same phrase at a psychiatrist's office. I had gone that route once before, without much success, and with much financial cost, and I really didn't want that to be my next stop.

"Shoot," she said. She appeared to be about thirty, with bright-red braided Pippi Longstocking hair and a sweatshirt with a picture of the TARDIS on it. She had eyes that flickered with engagement behind black nerdy glasses. It occurred to me that, with her artsy mien and her probable love for books, she might be the sort of person I would like to be friends with, and I pictured us having coffee at the cool café on the square or drinking a beer together at one of the town's dives.

"My husband and I recently moved here from Chicago, and we bought the—" I paused to think of the right words. "Crumbling castle"? "Condemnable manor"? Then I remembered the architectural term from the listing, which Jack had just used on the phone.

"Romanesque Revival estate up on Hill Street. 217 Hill Street. I'm wondering if there's any way to find out about the original . . ."

"Oh my God! You bought the Murder House?" Her eyes widened, and her mouth gaped into an expression that was half shock, half glee. She looked like someone enjoying a horror movie.

"The what? No, that's not . . . you must be thinking of something else."

A middle-aged woman with straight blond hair in a headband arrived at the circulation desk, and Pippi Longstocking said, "Patty, this woman bought the Murder House."

Patty appeared to be trying to hide her shock, or at least surprise. She stood stock-still for a moment, not responding, and then she smiled and said, "Don't call it that, Jess. It's her new home!" Then to me, she added, "So you're the one who bought the Lawrence Mansion?"

I was doing a timed puzzle, trying to fit all the pieces together to keep up. From the address, Jess had surmised I lived in "the Murder House," and from that description, Patty had known it was the Lawrence Mansion. What the hell was going on?

"Listen, I just moved here, and I don't know what you two are talking about."

Jess still had that gleeful shocked look on her face, while Patty seemed to be checking me out, looking me up and down, as if curious about the person who had bought the run-down mansion on the hill. Maybe I should have worn something fancier than jeans with a growing hole in the knee and an old gray T-shirt that read "I Can't, I Have Rehearsal," which a director had given me when we'd done a Sam Shepard play together. He'd had his own reasons for wanting me to be at every rehearsal, but I still liked the feel of the soft cotton T-shirt very much.

A man with a service dog approached the desk, and Patty left our conversation to help him.

"They didn't tell you about the murder suicides?" Jess asked.

"Are you sure we're talking about the same house?"

"The castle up on the hill with cracked windows covered with plastic sheeting and ivy all over the place?"

"I . . . guess?" She was describing our house, but she had it all wrong. She was making it sound as if it was abandoned, when in fact it was inhabited. By us. By me.

She cocked her head to the side, as if she were talking to a child, or someone who wasn't all there. It was a reaction I elicited a lot, even when I wasn't in shock. "Look, not to be rude, but there aren't too many castles in Haven. Is that your house, or isn't it?" she said, enunciating carefully. Maybe we wouldn't be having that beer or coffee after all.

"That's my house," I said. The words came out in a whisper.

"Well, then, I'm sorry, but that's the Murder House." I must have looked as horrified as I felt, because then her eyes softened, and she added, "Listen, all that happened a long time ago. It's ancient history. That makes it cool instead of creepy, right? Like a murder podcast! But is it true what they say? Is it haunted?"

The kids' words ran through my mind. The woman's laughter. The open door. Olivier, standing there stupefied. I leaned back, away from her and the circulation desk, almost tripping over myself, and then faked a stretch, like a cat trying to convince you its clumsy fall was purposeful. "Haunted? I don't think so. I mean, of course not. Who says that?"

"Um, everyone. I mean, not that I believe in that sort of thing."

"I can help the next person," Patty called.

"Right," Jess said. "Is there anything else you need?" She gestured behind me, and I saw that a line had formed. A few patrons carrying books, magazines, and CDs were staring at me with expressions that ranged from dumbfounded to amused, and I realized they had probably heard everything. *My house isn't haunted!* I wanted to tell them.

I turned back to Jess. "The reason I came here was to find out more about the house's history . . ."

Jess nodded, her librarian training evidently kicking into gear. She typed something into the computer behind the desk, wrote something on a Post-it note, and handed it to me: *April 15, 1955.*

"That's when it happened. I'm sure there are newspaper articles in the microfilm archive." She pointed to a glass door in the far corner of the library. "The instructions are by the machine. It's a pain, I'm not gonna lie."

The microfilm archives of the local newspaper were stored in a collection of small white square boxes, all of which were stamped with a red State of Wisconsin seal. The seal was quite detailed, with illustrations, images, symbols, people, and the state motto "Forward," which I told myself was a good omen. I would move forward, beyond this day, this moment, of finding out my house was *the Murder House.*

I searched through the boxes until I found one that was labeled "January–June 1955." Then I took the box to the chair in front of the machine and began to read the directions.

One of the many ways in which I find myself unfit to manage the world is that I am constitutionally unable to follow directions more complicated than those on the back of a frozen microwaveable dinner. I removed the canister from the box, stared at the directions, stared back at the canister of film, stared at the directions again, and then just sat there. I thought of Jack, who could assemble IKEA furniture barely glancing at the illustrations. Whenever I would ask him to do something like hook up the computer to the printer because I couldn't figure out how, he would tell me I wasn't trying, but the truth was, I had no understanding of how anything worked because I had no curiosity about how anything worked. Cars drove, planes flew, computers started and printed and took you to the internet, and if I had to explain how any of it worked, I would say it was done by magic.

I stared at the machine. A sticker read "Spool here." That must refer to the film, I thought. I put the "spool" there, and it clicked into place. I felt a wash of accomplishment. Then I noticed another sticker that read "Take-Up Reel." I looked at the directions, then placed the film under the glass plate, hooking it under a roller and into the Take-Up Reel. I turned the wheel, and an image appeared on the screen of a newspaper page. I felt quite proud of myself and couldn't wait to tell Jack about my accomplishment, before realizing I would never tell him about my accomplishment, as I didn't want him to know I was figuring out how to work a microfilm machine instead of going job hunting. I ignored that thought and turned the wheel farther to the left, which didn't work, then farther to the right, which did: the dates on the newspaper pages went from January to February. I kept turning until I got to April 15, 1955, and then I turned to the next day.

TRIPLE-DEATH TRAGEDY AT LAWRENCE MANSION!
PROMINENT CIRCUS STAR BEATRICE "BIRDY" LAWRENCE SHAWCROSS
KILLS HUSBAND, CIRCUS FINANCIER BOBBY SHAWCROSS,
THEN JUMPS OFF CLIFFS TO DEATH!
8-YEAR-OLD DAUGHTER FOUND DEAD!

I held on to the metal table in front of me for support as I reread the headline. Whatever I'd been expecting when I'd left the house to learn more about its history, I hadn't expected this. A child. *The Murder House.* I forced myself to concentrate.

> APRIL 16, 1955—Beatrice "Birdy" Lawrence Shawcross, the celebrity trapeze artist, age 28, killed her husband, Robert "Bobby" Shawcross, age 40, at approximately 9 o'clock last night before committing suicide outside their home in Haven, WI.

Police were called to the Lawrence Mansion by the property's gardener and caretaker, Lorenzo DeMarcos, age 29, who lives in the coach house. He had heard a series of gunshots before discovering the bullet-riddled body of Mr. Shawcross near the back door of the house.

Upon searching the home, Chief of Police Chip Rippmann and his deputy found the body of Amelia Lawrence Shawcross, Mr. and Mrs. Shawcross's 8-year-old daughter. The child's body, clad in bunny-print pajamas, was lying on the sofa in the living room, with no visible injuries or signs of foul play. The cause of her death is not known at this time.

Chief Rippmann then called the State Police Headquarters in Madison before he, the deputy, and Mr. DeMarcos engaged in a search of the grounds. Initially it was suspected that these crimes had been committed by outside intruders, and that Mrs. Lawrence Shawcross may have been kidnapped. However, the only tire tracks detected were those of Mr. Shawcross's blue Studebaker.

A detachment of state troopers arrived at the same time as the first newsmen. The troopers cordoned off the crime scene and continued the investigation. A single set of footprints was discovered, leading from a discarded firearm near Mr. Shawcross's body to the precipice of the cliff at the edge of the property.

Since it was too steep to scale, certainly in the dark of night, the troopers made an emergency call to the Wisconsin DNR, and a boat was dispatched to that part of the Wisconsin River.

It was nearly midnight when Mrs. Shawcross's body was discovered on the rocky riverbank, approximately ten yards from the river, wearing a white dress and one high-heeled shoe, the other shoe found approximately thirty yards down the riverbank. A preliminary examination of the body determined there was

gunshot residue on her right hand, and it was concluded that
Mrs. Shawcross shot her husband multiple times before flinging
herself off the ledge of the cliff to the rugged terrain below.

Asked about the condition of Mrs. Shawcross's body, DNR
agent Wayne Young replied: "She landed on a sandstone boul-
der. Her neck was broken, and the rest of her . . . I've never seen
a body so badly shattered. And never want to again. But I can't
imagine she suffered any."

Mr. DeMarcos recounted his experience of the night's events
to reporters in the following way: "I heard shots. I don't know
how many, 'cause at first, I thought it was just a car backfiring.
Maybe six. Seven. Coulda been eight. By the time I came out to
investigate, Bobby was already laying in the yard dead, bleeding
from every which way, and Birdy must of already jumped."

A late-night call to the home of Doctor Hal Grodin, longtime physician and friend to the Lawrence family, provided
additional information. When he was told what had happened
and asked to comment, Dr. Grodin said, "Birdy had been
suffering from anxiety and female hysteria. Head and body
aches, forgetfulness, insomnia. She was . . . unstable."

The three bodies were transported to the county coroner's
office. An autopsy will be performed on Amelia Lawrence Shawcross to determine the cause of death.

I'd had toast and black tea hours earlier, and I tasted marmalade
rise in the back of my throat. I swallowed it down and gripped the
cool table. I felt dizzy and faint.

A murder and suicide. Three deaths, one of them a child's, on
the same day, in my house. The house I lived in, the house I slept in,
the house Jack and I owned. It was terrible, impossible, horrible, and
unthinkable—and yet, apparently, it was true. I stared at one of the

photographs, a 1950s crime scene in my own backyard, complete with a smoking cop and "DO NOT CROSS" tape in front of the cliffs.

"That's my yard," I whispered stupidly.

The article was the entire front page. In the bottom right corner, there was a picture from the waist up of a beautiful dark-haired woman wearing a glitzy leotard. A perfect collarbone, a smooth expanse of skin, and a combination of features that was glamorous (dark almond-shaped eyes, full lips) and girl next door (dainty nose, rosy cheeks) at the same time: She was an impossible cross between Sophia Loren and Grace Kelly. Her smile was not really a smile, maybe a quarter-inch turn on one side. It was more the expression of the cat that ate the canary and felt no guilt at all, only a purring satisfaction.

"Why'd you do it?" I asked the woman in the photograph.

She suffered from anxiety and female hysteria. She was hysterical.

"Hysteria," from the Greek word *hystera,* which means "uterus." *Uterus, hysterectomy, hysteria, hysterical.* What a horrible, sexist word to mean that someone (some woman, for no one ever called a man "hysterical") was upset. How many times, how many people— teachers, boyfriends, my onetime shrink, my own mother—had said similar words about me? *Lilly, you just seem so . . . unstable. . . . You're too much. . . . Here's a prescription for anxiety. . . . Have you been taking your medication? . . . My God, Lilly, you're hysterical!*

But being upset didn't cause people to commit murder.

I studied another picture, which was taken at night, from a distance, probably from across the street, from somewhere near the mailbox. Three uniformed police officers and what must have been two "newsmen" were standing in front of a cordoned-off section of the front yard. Towering above them was the shadowy outline of the Lawrence Mansion. It looked glorious, awe-inspiring, foreboding.

The house I owned. The house I lived in. Where I slept.

The Murder House.

4

ENERGY

THERE WERE ABOUT SEVEN BILLION PEOPLE in the world, and most of us could be divided into four categories: Those who believed in ghosts, those who didn't, those who weren't sure, and those who, like Edith Wharton, didn't believe in ghosts but were nonetheless afraid of them. I fell between three and four. Not sure. Scared anyway.

I was too shaken after reading the first article to dig any further. I left the library and drove with the windows down, still in shock, needing to feel fresh air blowing on my face, back up the hill to the Lawrence Mansion.

I parked in the detached garage and walked gingerly over the patch of lawn where Bobby Shawcross's body had been found by the caretaker. I found myself gazing down, as if searching for blood. Then I shivered in the mild October air.

Opening the back door, I felt the same thing I'd been feeling these last few days, each time I'd entered the house after having been gone: a welcoming wash of relief, as if the house had missed me and was spreading its arms open wide in greeting. But after what I'd learned, I felt anxious and nervous as well. I stepped into the mudroom, and then walked through the hearth room and into the kitchen, where I turned on the kettle to brew some chamomile tea to calm my nerves.

As the water heated, I walked through every room on the main floor, listening for strange noises, searching for unlikely shadows. It was a glorious, run-down house, and I still felt a fierce attraction to it, but I wasn't sure what I'd have done if we'd known about its history before buying it. Would we have even gone to see it?

The sharp whistle of the boiling tea kettle startled me. I felt jumpy, rattled. I needed that calming tea. I set my ball of loose leaves into a mug of hot water, sat down at the kitchen table, across from Olivier, who was curled in the window seat, and pulled out my cell phone. I found the number I wanted and hit "call."

"Lilly Bly!" Al Martin said. "What can I do ya for?"

"It's what you could have done for me," I said.

"I'm not sure I understand. I take it you're enjoying your beautiful house?"

"My beautiful house where a woman murdered her husband and then died by suicide?"

I was pretty sure it was rare to stun Al Martin into silence, and I enjoyed myself for a few seconds, until he said, "We're not required to give out that information."

"Not required. But it would have been nice. Of course, then you wouldn't have sold the place to the out-of-town dupes who didn't know about the 'Murder House,' am I right?"

"I wouldn't go that far. It's been fifty years. I'm sure there are plenty of locals who don't know the story. And it's a gorgeous house. Great bones. So it has a colorful history. I take it educated people like you and Jack don't believe in all that mumbo jumbo, do you?"

I became very still. "What mumbo jumbo?" I asked, waiting for him to tell me some spooky tale.

"Boooo," he said, sounding like the wind. "Is there anything else I can do for you?"

"Yeah, how about let me know if there are any other murders that happened here that you neglected to tell us about."

"I can't think of any others. Unless you're planning on committing one yourself?" He chuckled. I stared at the phone. What a horrible thing for him to say. I didn't think his little "joke" was at all funny, and I hung up.

The instant I ended the call with Al Martin, the phone started ringing in my hand, making me jump. I saw on the outside of my pink flip phone that it was Jack, but still I said, "Hello?"

"It's me."

I felt relieved to hear Jack's sturdy, familiar voice. "I'm happy it's you."

I could hear him smile as he said, "You were expecting someone else?"

"No, of course not," I said, though for a second, I had to admit, I'd been frightened. But of what? Of Birdy Lawrence calling me on the phone from beyond the grave? "How's it going?" I asked.

"Fine. Busy. I have a meeting soon, but I'm back at the hotel now, eating a burger from room service. What about you? Any luck today?"

I opened my mouth to tell him about my discovery (*Guess what, we live in the Murder House!*), but then decided against it. Hadn't I begged him to buy this place, calling it a great investment, "our nest egg"? I was now pretty sure that would not be the case. I didn't want to give him another reason to regret the purchase, because, despite this setback, I still believed I would get pregnant and have a child here. And besides, I'd promised him I'd go job hunting today, which I hadn't quite managed to do.

So instead of saying, *You're not going to believe what I found out today*, what came out of my mouth was "I went to the school district office and dropped off my résumé." I was as surprised by these words as if someone else had spoken them. Then I guessed I might as well continue. "They said they'd be in touch."

"Good. Great. The sooner the better. And be sure to apply for your Wisconsin license." An edge to his voice articulated what his words did not: that he was traveling, working hard, trying to pay a mortgage for a house that I had yearned for, while I was doing . . . whatever it was he thought I was doing. Procrastinating. Lazing about. In any case, not drinking tea after a traumatic experience in the public library's microfilm room.

"I will," I said. But I was pretty sure I wouldn't. I wasn't ready to be in a room full of other people's children yet.

"Anyway, that's great you started the process," he added, in a softer, gentler tone. "Thank you."

Jack was a caretaker. He'd taken care of his alcoholic father, his migraine-ridden mother, his two younger brothers, and as soon as we'd started going out, he'd taken care of me.

After my father's death, even as I'd worked hard, supplementing my acting gigs by serving in restaurants and bars, my earnings had never matched my expenses, so I'd used credit cards to pay for everything over and above the rent and utilities for my apartment. On only our second date, Jack and I had gone back to my place and, instead of having sex, had done something even more intimate, even more marital. I had shown him my checkbook, my pay stubs, and my credit card bills, and he'd helped me make a budget and given me tips for sticking to it. And if I hadn't quite managed to take all his advice, well, that hadn't been his fault.

He had taken care of me in other ways as well. Within the first few weeks of our courtship, he'd held my hair back when I'd had the stomach flu and come to the rescue when my vintage Jag had broken down in the middle of Division. He didn't pry when I told him I preferred hauling my laundry to the laundromat on North Clark rather than going into my building's basement, and he didn't question me further when I said I hadn't eaten Chinese food since my father's death and never would again. On the days when I awakened from a nightmare about my dad (my final image of him seared into my brain while I slept) and could not get out of bed, could not move,

Jack called in sick for me and made me chicken noodle soup while I watched one Hitchcock movie after another. He took me to the hospital when I'd cut the inside of my arm on a broken bottle of Guinness Stout. He didn't believe me when I told him it was an accident. "If you ever hurt yourself again, I'll kill you," he said, and then kissed my bandaged wrist again and again. He proposed to me the night he saw me play Ophelia.

It hadn't been my first. I had been proposed to three times and engaged once before Jack. The same qualities that made me popular with the audience also seemed to make me popular with men (and some women). I had the sort of look that seemed to be compelling from the balcony, the first row, or a few inches away. I inhabited a character (including myself) fully, while maintaining an elusive, dreamy quality. At least, I assumed this was why so many men used to ask me, "What are you thinking?" or "How do you feel about me?" Jack had once told me, "You're the first girl I've had to really chase." When I replied, "I didn't know you were chasing me," he said, "That's what I mean."

We'd been married over six years now. I was thirty-seven. Too old to play Ophelia, too old to be stupid about money, too old to eat frozen dinners and refuse to go into a basement to do laundry, too old to obsess over an ancient murder-suicide instead of submitting my résumé. Too old, let's face it, not to have a job.

"Honey, I promised I'd get a job, and I'm going to," I told him, newly resolved. "Now stop worrying. Go to your meeting. Do whatever you need to do. I'll take care of the home front, okay? Tomorrow, I keep pounding the pavement." And I would. I would just also find time to do additional research on the house. I wanted to know more about its history, its inhabitants. *The triple-death tragedy.*

"You wouldn't need to look for a job, at least not right away, if we lived in a different house."

"Why would we want a different house?" I asked. "We own the grandest wreck in Haven."

He let out a breath. "Ain't that the truth."

After I hung up, I went up the stairs and stopped at the second-floor landing. I again gazed at the orange divan and the Tiffany-style lamp that had come with the place. Had they been here all those years ago? Bearing witness to what had happened? I peered down the hall and saw that the third-floor ballroom door was closed. But I still felt anxious, knowing now that terrible things had happened inside these walls. Wasn't it possible that there was still a trace, a remnant from those days? Not necessarily a ghost, but bad mojo, negative energy?

"Energy." The word made me think of something that had happened at my dad's funeral.

"Your father isn't really dead, you know," a longtime waitress at one of his restaurants had said to me.

The words shocked me, for I was the one who had found him, and I knew, if anyone knew, just how dead he was. She was about forty, with a wan face, crow's feet, and ruby red lips that showed vertical lines. Maybe she was forty-five.

"Energy," she said. "Energy doesn't just disappear. Energy remains energy."

Was that what I was feeling here? Energy? Was Birdy Lawrence still around? Was my dad?

I wished I'd asked the waitress what the heck she was talking about instead of smiling and nodding and walking away, thinking, *Nutjob.*

I walked into our bedroom, into the en suite bathroom, and gazed at myself in the mirror while I brushed my teeth and hair. I had a "look" that had helped me get certain roles back in my acting days in Chicago and prevented me from getting others. I was told I looked "fresh," "girl next door," sometimes "pretty," sometimes "too pretty," and sometimes "not interesting enough." Sometimes the directors who had told me I looked "too pretty" for certain roles invited me for a drink after the audition to discuss "my career." I admitted having been naïve enough to have fallen for that offer, not just once but three times, until I understood it was not my "career" in which they were interested.

My features were symmetrical, I guessed: wide eyes, a longish nose with an upturned tip, lips that naturally curved into a slight smile, as if I had Resting Sweet Face. Like Al Martin had recently done, people in Theater World used to tell me that I looked like Jean Shrimpton in the '60s, and so for a while I had worn my light brown hair like hers, accentuating that side sweep of hair across my forehead, blow-drying it to have that bump of volume in the back, curling the ends so that they finished in a flip. And then even more people had said to me, "You know who you look like? Jean Shrimpton!" But then I'd grown older, and people had stopped telling me I reminded them of Jean Shrimpton, or "that model from the sixties," and I'd grown out my bangs and had stopped bothering to do anything to my hair at all. Now it fell halfway to my elbows and ended in straggly split ends. How many years had it been since anyone had told me I was "too pretty"?

Of course, Jean Shrimpton had grown older, too, but I had no idea if Jean Shrimpton at age thirty-seven looked the way I did now. Shell-shocked, pale, nervous. As if she were living with "energy."

"Hello?" I whispered. "Birdy? Is that you?" I didn't really believe that Birdy Lawrence was here. I was playing, the way Flora Daniels and I used to scare ourselves with ghost stories during sleepovers when we were in elementary school.

But then I heard a faint sound. Like a radio between channels. Static. White noise. An electrical disturbance. I barely breathed, listening.

After only a few seconds, something happened. A loud static hissing, and then a dimming, and a quieting. And then the noise was gone.

I glanced around, but nothing, no one, was there. "It's just energy," I said aloud, trying to convince myself, though my heart was pounding hard. "Energy can't hurt you," I told my reflection.

Could it?

5

THE REST OF THE STORY

IT WAS 10:00 A.M. THE FOLLOWING DAY, and I was once again surprised to see the library buzzing with activity, just as it had been the day before. Near the entrance, on some well-worn chairs and sofas, a group of elderly women and one thirty-something man knitted while discussing the latest Scott Turow novel (*Knitting and Murder, Thurs. 9:30–11 a.m.* read the flyer). Two college-age girls with piercings, tattoos, and Badgers T-shirts whispered, laughed, and then shushed each other while browsing and typing on the computers. Muted laughter and music came from upstairs, where there was, according to the signs, a preschool children's puppet show called "Curious George Goes Bananas for the Library!" A poster above the circulation desk read READING IS DREAMING WITH OPEN EYES. Ever since I was a child, visiting the grand main branch of the Chicago Public Library, libraries had always evoked in me both contentment and excitement, and the Haven Public Library was no different.

The two women I'd encountered yesterday were nowhere to be seen, but a Black man with dark-brown skin, a gray beard, closely cropped graying hair, and twinkling eyes smiled at me from behind the counter. "Can I help you?"

"I don't think so. I'm just here to do some research in the microfilm archive room," I said. "Can I just go on in?"

"Absolutely. And let me know if you need any assistance. That machine is a little tricky. Do you know how it works?"

It felt good to smile and wave him off. "Old pro here," I said.

The microfilm room was empty again. I found the same box, spooled in the film, and turned the knob past the first story and various other articles. Someone named George Canon received his fifth DUI; the movie playing at the local theater was *Marty* with Ernest Borgnine; Jonas Salk had effectively cured polio with his vaccine, and both Congress and the *Haven Herald* were still celebrating the news, with some members of Congress even calling for April 12 to be a national holiday. But even this paled in comparison to the news of the triple deaths. I kept scrolling until I reached the April 17 headline.

PRELIMINARY AUTOPSY RESULTS IN: AMELIA SHAWCROSS POISONED BY FAMOUS TRAPEZE ARTIST MOTHER BEATRICE "BIRDY" LAWRENCE SHAWCROSS

I read the headline, feeling a combination of horror, sadness, and disgust. My stomach did a little turn, but I hadn't eaten anything that morning, and so there was nothing to come up. I braced myself and kept reading.

APRIL 17, 1955—The county coroner released preliminary results of the autopsy of 8-year-old Amelia Shawcross and determined that she died from a heavy dose of the poison thallium.

Chief of Police Chip Rippmann also reported during a press conference that residue of the poison was detected in a teacup found near the victim's body. The only fingerprints found on the teacup were those of Amelia and her mother, Beatrice "Birdy" Lawrence Shawcross, the famous trapeze artist formerly of the Lawrence Brothers Circus who shot and killed her husband, Robert "Bobby" Shawcross, before jumping to her death on the night of April 15.

The handgun used in the slaying, a Colt M1917, was also tested for fingerprints, and the only fingerprints found were those of Birdy Shawcross.

Pending the final police report, Chief Rippmann recounted his and the state office's interpretation of the high-profile murder case as follows: "All three of the eyewitnesses to this domestic tragedy are dead, but the evidence is clear. We believe Mrs. Shawcross—whether due to hidden malicious intent or a bout of insanity and hysteria—poisoned her daughter on the evening of April 15. When Bobby Shawcross arrived and discovered what she had done, Mrs. Shawcross retrieved her father's pistol and murdered him. She then committed suicide. While her motives will forever remain a mystery to all but God, we see no reason to explore the matter further."

"Bobby was a real cool cat," said Lorenzo DeMarcos, the caretaker of the Lawrence Mansion where the crimes were committed. "Birdy? Everyone called her stuck-up, but I think she was just lonely. Kept to herself. I think the loneliness and jealousy finally got to her, you know? She snapped like a rubber band."

A fellow circus performer chimed in with something of the same. "Everybody loved Bobby," Russian horse trainer Sylvia Saperov told the *Haven Herald*. "He friends with everybody! The circus lost a great man. And that poor, sweet little girl. I never met, but still. I just wish before Birdy would have killed her girl and that poor man, she would have killed herself. Reverse the order, you know?"

Other acquaintances of Birdy Shawcross expressed a different perspective.

Emmie Dunstan, Birdy's childhood friend, said, "She must have shot Bobby in self-defense. 'Cause I've known Birdy all my

life, and she wouldn't've killed a fly if the fly hadn't been trying
to kill her first."

Hattie Smith, who worked for the family twice a week as
their housekeeper, agreed. "I can't imagine her doing such a
thing. She must not have been in her right mind."

The closest relative to the family, Mrs. Ida Conklin, mother
of Bobby Shawcross, arrived in town early for her son's and
granddaughter's funeral. "I ain't seen Bobby in years," she said,
"but a mother never stops loving her son. I only hope my Bobby
and his daughter get justice now. I hope their evil murderer is
rotting in hell."

The funeral will be held on April 20.

Four photos accompanied the article.

The first was a picture of the living room where Amelia Lawrence Shawcross had died. Even though it was black-and-white, and
grainy, I could see what looked like gleaming hardwood floors, a
sparkling Steinway grand piano, and an expensive array of furniture
and artwork, everything in stark contrast to the bare room with the
scratched and water-stained floors we had inherited from the circus
society.

The second was a photo of Lorenzo DeMarcos, the gardener
and caretaker, standing outside the coach house (now our detached
garage) where he'd lived: baggy khakis, slick black hair, the fit build
and tanned skin of someone who works outdoors, a cigarette dangling from his lips.

The picture of Bobby Shawcross was taken in profile, from the
waist up. Bobby was laughing. Some animal draw emanated from
his eyes, his mouth, his body. He was dark, handsome, forty years
old (Jack's age), with a background of trees behind him. I could see
why a woman would want to be the source of that laughter, to be

the one that gaze was fixed on. I could understand why Birdy—why anyone—might have fallen in love with him. But why had she shot him dead?

The final picture was of Bobby Shawcross's mother, a tall woman with an angry expression and a thin, pinched face, wearing a black dress and black Coke-bottle glasses. Here was the person who had wanted the "evil" Birdy Lawrence Shawcross to rot in hell, the wrath of a grieving mother and grandmother combined into one. Had Birdy in fact been evil? But what about the friend who'd said she wouldn't hurt a fly?

I reread the article. My eyes lingered on the word "thallium." ". . . 8-year-old Amelia Shawcross . . . died from a heavy dose of the poison thallium." There was a computer for online research next to the microfilm projector. I scooted over and did a Google search.

Thallium is a chemical element. It has had medical uses, electronic uses, and even cosmetic uses (as a depilatory). Because it's tasteless, odorless, colorless, and deadly, thallium was not only useful for rat poisoning (until it was banned) but was also useful as a reliable murder weapon (hence, the reason for the ban). Because of its popularity as a murder weapon, thallium (along with arsenic) gained notoriety as "the poisoner's poison" and "inheritance powder" in the 1950s, when there was a string of murders or attempted murders by thallium through rat poison. One woman, Yvonne Gladys Fletcher, from Sydney, Australia, was convicted of killing both of her two husbands, one right after the other, with something called "Thall-Rat." Side effects from ingesting thallium include hair loss, abdominal pain, nausea and vomiting, peripheral neuropathy, cancer, and insanity. *Insanity.*

How could a mother give this horrible poison to an innocent little girl?

I went back to the microfilm station and turned the knob until I
reached the next news story.

BIGGEST FUNERAL IN HAVEN HISTORY:
THE RISE AND FALL OF A CIRCUS FAMILY

APRIL 21, 1955—Mourners, fans, and the just plain curious
descended on Haven, Wisconsin, yesterday in what was the biggest funeral in the town's history, after the double-murder and
suicide committed by Haven's most famous resident, Beatrice
Lawrence Shawcross, the former trapeze artist known as "Birdy,
the Flying Bird Girl."

Activities commenced in the early-morning hours, when
municipal workers began marking the route of the funeral procession with NO PARKING signs, and cars with license plates from
as far as New York, California, and Florida filled the parking
lot and surrounding blocks of St. John's Lutheran Church hours
before the 11:00 a.m. service.

Due to her role in the killings of Robert "Bobby" Shawcross
and Amelia Shawcross, as well as due to her suicide, the Reverend Arnold Schultz determined that the remains of Beatrice
"Birdy" Lawrence Shawcross would not be allowed to enter
church grounds. The hearse containing her coffin stood ready
at Sanderson Funeral Home, while the coffins containing the
remains of the victims, Bobby and Amelia Shawcross, lay inside
the church during the service, closed casket.

The Reverend Arnold Schultz read from Scripture and gave
a short homily. After the service, the mourners were invited to
join the funeral procession to Haven Cemetery.

An endless stream of cars, trucks, and even various circus
bicycles and mini-cars piloted by sad-faced clowns followed the
three hearses toward the cemetery. It was a scene reminiscent of

Haven's circus glory days past, when circus trucks and carriages would parade in and out of town for their summer tours, and doubtless many in the crowd felt the tragic finality of this one last unexpected and mournful parade to forever close the tent curtains on that chapter of Haven's history.

The Lawrence brothers were four American siblings who went from performing for nickels for their neighbors to creating a successful traveling circus. Edgar Lawrence, the oldest sibling, was the financial mastermind and president of the circus. John Lawrence managed and performed in the animal acts, while James Lawrence was a juggler, contortionist, and magician. Peter "Wags" Lawrence served as ringmaster until, at the age of 43, he enlisted to fight the Nazis and served in the USO.

In 1921, with the traveling circus already established and gaining a reputation, Edgar Lawrence began building the Lawrence Mansion, the scene of the grizzly deaths that took place on the night of April 15.

The house was completed in 1924. That same year, Edgar Lawrence married Anastasia, the 20-year-old snake charmer of the circus, and three years later, their only child, Beatrice Lawrence, was born.

Legend has it that Beatrice was already performing flips at 3 and flying through the air on trapezes by the time she turned 5, hence her childhood and lifelong nickname, "Birdy."

In 1939, at the age of 12, she became an immediate sensation when her solo act, "Birdy, The Flying Bird Girl," was launched. Over the course of her eight-year career, she made several television appearances, and became known for her "Birdy pirouette," "reverse suicide," and triple somersaults.

Tragedy struck the Lawrence family in 1942, when Anastasia Lawrence died in a circus accident involving a fire.

Beatrice, who was then 15, was absent from the circus act roster for the rest of that season but returned in 1943, when she began performing without a net. In 1947, with her celebrity at its peak, she married circus assistant manager Robert "Bobby" Shawcross, gave birth, and retired her act to raise her daughter, Amelia Lawrence Shawcross.

Edgar Lawrence died from a stroke in 1950, and Bobby Shawcross served as the circus's general manager until its closing in 1954, when declining ticket sales due to the advent of television and rising labor costs had finally taken their toll.

Who could have foreseen that one year later a sea of mourners, including past circus workers, Haven residents, and fans from across the country would be gathered at Haven Cemetery under such tragic circumstances for one last goodbye?

The three caskets were lowered into adjoining graves, the child's in the center. Reverend Schultz gave a final prayer that referenced both the merciful bounty and the limits of God's forgiveness.

I turned the knob several days forward, but there were no other stories. I looked around and noticed there was a printer under the counter with a label that read: "10 Cents per Copy." I found the machine's print function, printed out the news stories, placed the roll of film back in its proper place, and headed to the front desk to settle up.

The man who had offered to help me was still at the front desk. "Hi, I owe you a dollar," I told him, waving the sheets of paper I'd printed out. I fished in my bag to find my wallet and pulled out a ten. "Do you need to count my copies?"

He smiled with his whole face. "I trust you." I tried to remember if a stranger had ever said anything remotely like that to me in Chicago but could not. As he was making change, I glanced around and noticed the sign on a small easel on the counter: ASK ABOUT WORKING HERE!

My pulse quickened. I imagined standing behind this very counter, asking people if they needed help, trusting patrons to tell me the truth about their number of copies, checking out books, shelving them, maybe even helping people do research. I was good at research, wasn't I? Heck, maybe I could even keep doing a little of my own research on the side. There was still so much to learn about Birdy Lawrence, about my house. It seemed like the perfect opportunity.

He handed me a five and four ones. I thanked him and said, "Your sign says to ask about working here. Whom do I ask?" I smiled, partly to show him how friendly I was and partly because I was pleased with myself for knowing the difference between "who" and "whom," which I thought might get me in good with a librarian.

"That would be me," he said. He looked me up and down, and I was glad that I had worn my job-hunting Chanel suit instead of the holey jeans I'd worn the day before.

"I'm a college graduate, and I was a certified teacher in Illinois. I'm good at research, and I already know how to use the microfilm machine." I reached into my bag and handed him a résumé. "So, you're still hiring?"

He smiled. "We are definitely short-staffed right now, which is why I'm behind the counter instead of doing paperwork in my office. Yes, we're still hiring. One moment."

He picked up what looked like an old CB radio microphone, pressed the button on its side, and said, "Chris, please come to the front desk. Chris, you are needed at the front desk." A second later a crackling version of his words came through the overhead speaker system. "Let's sit down and talk," he said to me.

I followed him past the "New Books" and "Popular" shelves (*The Story of Edgar Sawtelle* by David Wroblewski, Oprah's latest pick;

Duma Key, Stephen King's newest); past the magazine racks ("New Dad Clay Aiken: YES, I'M GAY!" read the headline of the most recent *People*); and then down a hallway to an office. He led me inside, where he motioned to a red wooden chair in front of a paper-cluttered desk that had the nameplate CARL WILLIAMS, DIRECTOR. He slid into the chair behind the desk and looked over my résumé.

I knew it by heart, of course. Bachelor's from Northwestern University (impressive); one year of graduate school in acting (a little less impressive); a teaching certificate in elementary education (excellent) with a specialization in music (*hmmm*). Teaching experience in a Chicago public school (for only two years) and in a suburban charter school (no mention of quitting without a day's notice). Skills include fluency in French, some knowledge of Italian, and plenty of theater experience. Interests include drama and Celtic piano music.

I sounded about as useful as a daisy, I knew. There weren't many employers in Middle America who needed a former actor and teacher who spoke two Romance languages and could play *Galway Bay* on the piano, but perhaps the library might be interested in someone with exactly my combination of useless talents.

"Excellent!" Carl Williams said, looking up, proving my hopeful assumption had been right. "You have no library experience, but you seem very . . . well rounded."

I wondered if "well rounded" was a euphemism. For what? Flaky? Unemployable? But Carl Williams might be the sort who actually valued "well rounded."

"I'm afraid this job doesn't offer health insurance—"

"That's all right, I get insurance through my husband's job."

"—but there's no weekend work, just Monday through Friday, nine to five, with a half-hour lunch break, at ten-fifty an hour."

"Ten-fifty," I repeated.

"Yes," he said, "it's an entry-level job. You shelve books and other materials, check them out, assist people at the front desk."

I'd made over twice that as a teacher in Chicago, and about three times as much as a server in my father's restaurants and bars. Would Jack think that was enough? "What about fifteen?"

"I'm sorry," he said, still smiling. "Our budget is approved by the city. It's not up to me. But it is a pleasant place to work, I assure you. Of course, I understand, you're probably overqualified—"

"Okay, I'll take it," I said.

He paused for a moment, obviously taken aback by my abrupt response. But why play hardball when there was no point? And then he asked, "When can you start?"

I was excited to get going. "How about now?"

Carl Williams laughed. "I appreciate your enthusiasm, but we always start new employees at the beginning of the week. What say we start you on Monday?"

I could feel myself blush. "Yeah, okay, that sounds good."

"Monday it is. Welcome to the library, Lilly."

6

CONTENTMENT

I HAD DONE NOTHING the least bit extraordinary, and yet, I couldn't help but feel proud of myself. I had upheld a bargain, kept my promise to Jack. I had gotten a job. A job in a pleasant place with what seemed like a really nice boss.

Immediately I wanted to celebrate, and by that, I meant spend money. Too excited to sit inside a car, I walked around the downtown square. I had to admit, it was quite charming. The Greek Revival courthouse stood, stately, on the commons, with shops and restaurants surrounding it in a pedestrian-friendly square. I walked past the fancy linens shop, refusing to even glance in the tempting window, and stopped in front of the town's nicest restaurant, Peppers. We'd eaten there once, while we were living in the motel, and had enjoyed grilled salmon and a salad with pears, fennel, and walnuts, with the best crème brûlée I'd ever had for dessert. With drinks and tip, we'd spent well over a hundred dollars. I would have liked to have gone there tonight, to celebrate my new job, but I knew Jack would never agree. Thinking of our financial situation, my spirits sagged just a bit.

I kept walking, past an old-fashioned barber shop, a ladies' clothing store that featured elastic-waist pants and purple prom dresses, and the charming used bookstore where, instead of the requisite cat, a tiny, old, yappy Chihuahua held court on a leopard-print dog bed, and then I arrived at the gourmet food shop. I went inside, breathed in the scent of coffee beans, wood cleaner, and fresh herbs, and immediately felt my mood lift. Jack was coming home from his work trip later today, and I decided I would make us a celebratory dinner.

"Hi there," said the man behind the deli counter, to the left of the door. He was wearing a white apron, but otherwise did not look anything like a butcher. He was tall and thin, with a pink Brooks Brothers dress shirt, a goatee, and multiple earrings. I had seen him there before, and I smiled and said hello.

"How are you today?"

"Great," I answered. "I just got a job."

As soon as the words were out of my mouth, I regretted them. For now he would surely ask me, *Doing what?*, and I would have to tell him that I would be shelving books and checking out DVDs at the library and making less in a day than his pink shirt cost, which he wore to stand behind a deli counter. For a moment, I thought about lying. *I'm going to star in a movie! I'm the solo pianist at the Madison Opera!* But I knew that all he'd have to do was visit the library one time to catch me in the lie, which would be even more humiliating than telling him the truth right now.

"Congratulations!" he said. "Doing what?"

"Oh, I'm just the new assistant at the library." I looked down, embarrassed.

"Good for you! I love our library. I'm sure it'll be a great place to work."

"Thanks. I'm, um, just going to look around."

"You do that. And let me know if there's anything I can help you with."

I grabbed a basket and loaded up on Pecorino Romano cheese, fresh organic fettuccine, and a jar of vodka pasta sauce. I loved animals and rarely ate them, and those with big eyes even more rarely, but I knew Jack didn't feel the same way and would appreciate good meat. I walked to the deli counter and pointed to the row marked "Rib Eyes."

"Two, please."

"You're going to love these steaks," said the man, handing me the meat in waxy wrapping. "Local, grass-fed."

"And to cook them, you just . . ."

He looked at me quizzically. I tried to make my face appear professional, as if I were wondering how to cook these particular steaks because of course I knew how to cook other kinds of steaks.

"You just stick them under the broiler."

"The broiler, yes. For the, um, normal amount of time?"

Again, that quizzical expression. "Yes, nothing special. About four minutes, each side, for medium rare."

"And that's it?" His face was blank, as if he were trying to figure out what I was asking. I could feel my face grow warm, but I forged ahead. "You don't need any kind of . . ."

My voice trailed off, and he came to my rescue. "Seasoning?"

"Yes, seasoning!"

"I like to salt them before and pepper them afterward. I think the pepper can make them taste almost burnt if you sprinkle it on before."

"Yes, thank you. That is a good tip."

He smiled at me patiently, as if he were pretending we were two chefs swapping secrets, and not as if I was a thirty-seven-year-old adult who had no idea how to cook a steak. I wanted to tell him he was very kind, and I was very grateful, but I understood that near strangers don't say those sorts of things to one another, and so I merely smiled back and walked to the wine section.

I passed the whites and reds and went to the area marked "Champagne and Sparkling Wines." I stared at the bottle of Veuve Clicquot. Fifty-five bucks. I'd promised Jack I would be frugal to live in this house. But this was a cause for celebration, and I did love "*La Veuve*." We had drunk it at the bars at my father's restaurants like water. Ah, Daddy. He would want me to have this. I picked it up. Then I pictured Jack's hurt, disappointed face, and set it back. I picked up an Italian prosecco with a decent review for twenty-two bucks, put it in my basket, and went to the checkout counter feeling virtuous.

"Looks like you're having quite a celebration tonight." The man handed me a small bouquet from the flower section near the door. "Asters. These are on me."

"Thank you," I said, admiring the lovely pink and purple flowers. Like a Victorian suitor or a poet, I knew the meanings of most flowers (pink roses meant "perfect love," baby's breath meant "innocence," butterfly weed—whatever that was—meant "let me go," and so on), but the only flowers I could ever identify were roses, tulips, and daisies, a feat surpassed by most kindergartners. Asters. I wouldn't have been able to name them, but if I was remembering right, they meant happiness, or maybe it was just contentment. A better emotion than happiness, really. Steadier. More dependable. *Contentment.* Yes, I'd take that. "These are a wonderful gift."

"Small-town hospitality," he said with a wink.

I felt touched and so proud of myself I could have cried. I'd gotten a job. I'd passed on the champagne I knew, deep down, I deserved—or at least wanted. I really was acting like a grown-up, and the universe in the form of this nice small business owner had rewarded me with these flowers. The total cost came to just about what I'd make my first day on the job, almost the same amount that it would have cost to eat out at Peppers, I realized. It went without saying I didn't have that much cash, so I handed the man a credit card. I left the store with my packages, feeling happy and proud, and (since I'd promised Jack I would under no circumstances use my credit cards), at the bottom of those two emotions, just a pinprick of guilt, so small I could barely even feel it.

*   *   *

By the time I parked my car in the detached garage and walked across the driveway into the house, it had started to rain, and when I unlocked the heavy fortress-like door and stepped into the foyer, I heard a distressing noise. From somewhere nearby, a drip sounded, alarmingly steady and strong. I walked through the foyer, the dining room, and into the kitchen, where I set my bags on the counter. Olivier was pacing around his food plate, though it was only three in the afternoon. He meowed, and I shushed him, and then listened. I followed the dripping noise through the mudroom and into the living room, and could not help myself from muttering, "*Merde! Merde! Merde!*" to the empty room. (Somehow saying the vulgarity in French made me feel better, as if the calamity were happening to someone else.)

For there, in the center of the large, nearly bare room was a small but growing puddle that was spreading into a white-stained, already-damaged section of the hardwood floor. Clearly this had happened before. Rainwater dripped into the puddle and then splattered.

I called Jack, but his cell phone immediately went to voice mail.

I closed my eyes and told myself that when I opened them, the problem would be gone, but I knew it wouldn't be, because I could still hear that infernal drip.

I went to the kitchen and grabbed a roll of paper towels and three large mixing bowls. I cleaned up the water and set down a bowl underneath the leak. When that bowl filled up, after about ten minutes, I replaced it with another one.

To take my mind off the trouble in the living room, I decided to concentrate on dinner. I ignored the hole in the ceiling and set the dining table. I put taper candles in my family's silver candlesticks that had somehow missed being sold at auction and placed the asters in a plain glass vase. *Contentment*, I reminded myself. I chilled the prosecco. I tidied up the kitchen, did the dishes, and every so often replaced the bowls in the living room. At some point, in the late afternoon, it stopped raining. I left one empty bowl underneath the leak, just in case. *Contentment.* Back in the kitchen, Olivier meowed and wrapped himself around my ankles, then meowed louder, insistently, as if he were starving, so I fed him. When he finished eating, he curled up in the window nook and went to sleep. I petted and kissed him on his soft head, while he quietly purred. Then I cooked the pasta, which I kept warm, or tried to, in a baking dish, and made a salad with romaine lettuce and tomatoes, which were all the vegetables we had. I was searching through the pantry for salad dressing ingredients when I heard the door open and Jack yell, "Ho-ney, I'm ho-ome."

I set down the olive oil, hurried to the door, and hugged him. Anyone watching would have assumed we'd been teleported from the 1950s. "What's all this?" he said, peering into the dining room. Yes, there was a hole in the ceiling, with new plaster falling like crumbs every day, and yes, the wallpaper was held up with duct tape, and yes, the chairs were beat-up antiques that were now frayed and faded, with threads drooping from the rose brocade fabric seats, but the table was set, and I was somehow managing to play a real spouse who knew how to cook a real meal.

"I made pasta. I'm almost finished with the salad dressing. All I have left is to broil the steaks."

"Broil the steaks?" he repeated. "You . . . cooked?"

I'm sure I was positively beaming. "And I got a job."

He pulled out a dilapidated chair and sat down. I noticed he sat daintily, planting his feet on the floor, careful not to put all his weight on the seat, as if afraid it would crash beneath him. "You got a job?"

"At the library. It doesn't pay much."

"How much?" His face was so hopeful, so proud, it just about broke my heart.

"Ten-fifty an hour, forty hours a week. I'm sorry," I added quickly. "I know it's the salary of a high school lifeguard, but—"

"No, no, that's great. Four hundred twenty a week. That's almost seventeen hundred a month. That'll really help."

I felt like a schoolgirl awarded a gold star. "I bought champagne, well, no, prosecco to celebrate."

His face turned grim. "How did you pay for all this?"

"I put it on the credit card."

"I thought you weren't going to do that anymore."

We'd had this talk a million times. Since Jack and I had been married, I had tried to be good. But to me, that meant buying twenty-two-dollar prosecco instead of fifty-five-dollar Veuve Clicquot, whereas to Jack, it meant drinking water.

"Well, I was, I mean, I am. I am trying not to use the credit cards anymore. But I wanted to celebrate tonight." I stood behind him, rubbing my hands over his chest and leaning down so that our cheeks were pressed together. His were warm and stubbly and smelled like fast-food coffee and soap. "And by celebrate, I mean celebrate." I kissed the corner of his eyelid, the tip of his ear.

"You mean . . . ?"

"Yes. By celebrate I mean"—I sucked in my breath and said, mock-sexy (for there was no way to say this and actually sound sexy)— "I'm ovulating."

"Ah," he said, squeezing my arms and pulling me closer. "So, it's my body you want. Go ahead. Take it. Use it. I'm all yours."

I did. And afterward, I was so tired from not having slept well the last few nights, and Jack was apparently so tired from having been on the road all day, that we both fell asleep without dinner, the candle wax dripping on the table, the pasta congealing in its dish, the salad dressing half made, and the thirty-dollar steaks spoiling on the countertop, until Olivier gnawed them to the bone.

7

JUMP

THE NEXT MORNING, while I was making myself tea in the kitchen, Jack walked into the room, dressed and ready for work, and asked, "Why is there a bowl on the living room floor?"

"Oh, that's for the leak."

"The leak?"

I poured hot water into a *Urinetown* mug and dropped a bag of decaf Earl Grey into it. The smell made me feel a little nauseated, which I thought might be a good sign. Weren't morning sickness and sensitivity to scents the first signs of pregnancy? "It rained yesterday," I explained.

He left. I dunked the tea bag a few times, tossed it into the trash, and added honey. Then I sat at the kitchen table, sipping my tea and reading the morning's *Haven Herald*. In local news, Jenny Decorah was going on to county finals in the middle school spelling bee. In national news, the Head of the Federal Reserve announced that the recent US financial crisis was threatening to send the world into a recession, and in international news, the War on Terrorism was continuing, with fatalities in Afghanistan, Islamabad, and north of Pakistan.

Jack returned. "There has to be a hole in the roof, and it's got to be pretty big to cause that kind of water damage. Why didn't you tell me?"

"Pour yourself some coffee, sit down. I forgot. And it stopped raining. It's supposed to be sunny now all week." I pointed to the weather graph in the newspaper. There was a heat wave coming, with a high of eighty on Saturday. Proof. In terms of the leak in the roof, I didn't know if the problem was big or small, but my instinct was to minimize it, so as not to prompt Jack to say, once again, "If we lived in a different house . . ." Besides, after reading the news, I felt lucky that we had a roof over our heads at all, even if it was leaking.

Jack stared at me for a second, as if trying to figure out what my motivation was. Then he seemed to give up. He sighed, poured himself a cup of coffee, and sat down across from me. "I guess you're right. I'll take a look at it this weekend. There's nothing I can do about it right now. Crap. I hope I can patch it myself. We can't afford a new roof."

"The roof is fine," I assured him, though of course I had no idea about such things. "I'm sure it's just that one leak. It's not like I needed to put mixing bowls all around the house."

"This is your standard for 'fine'? Mixing bowls only in the living room?"

"Yes, that's my standard," I said. "Now tell me about your trip."

"It was good," he said, and then started talking about his meetings and presentations. I heard the words "enhanced mammography," "three times the resolution of old images," "reduced percentages of false negatives," and "save lives." It was all very wonderful in the abstract and all very confusing in the details. I asked him about something I could understand. "How was the hotel?"

"The hotel. 'Hotel' might be a fancy word for the Sunshine Inn of Eau Claire, but I'll tell you one thing. The roof wasn't leaking."

I ignored this jab at the house. My senses seemed highly tuned. I could listen to him while also listening to Olivier breathe and purr in the mudroom (all that contraband meat had apparently worn him out), while also listening to the refrigerator hum. I could taste precise notes—citrus, bergamot—in the tea. I could feel the honeyed hot liquid slide down my throat and settle into my stomach. My skin vaguely prickled. I was pregnant this time, I was sure.

Which would be a slight miracle, but that didn't deter my certainty. Our insurance didn't cover fertility treatments, but it did cover infertility diagnosis. After numerous tests taken by both of us (Jack's tests, apparently, had been more fun than mine: his involved porn; mine involved needles), it had been determined that Jack's sperm were healthy and numerous, while my eggs were lazy, elderly, and sparse—or at least, that's what I inferred from the diagnosis "Irregular Ovulation." I had been prescribed a drug to make me ovulate, which I was supposed to take for no longer than a year (so, until April). After that, the plan was IVF, and I'd already picked out the fertility clinic we would go to in Madison, about an hour's drive from Haven. But IVF was expensive ($15,000 per cycle) and had only one-in-four odds of success. My father's daughter, I didn't mind those odds. A scientist, Jack did. But if I was pregnant now, we wouldn't need to worry about that. And I really felt like I might be.

"I think it happened, Jack," I blurted out. "I think that egg and sperm united while I slept."

"Maybe that's why you were snoring."

"What?"

"Your body was working hard."

"I wasn't snoring."

"As loud as a steam train!"

"Shut up!" I batted him in the arm with my newspaper.

"Ouch!" he said, laughing. Then his eyes grew serious. "Don't you think you should wait like, I don't know, a day or two, to get your hopes up?"

"Too late. My hopes are up." They always were during the two weeks each month between ovulation and my period. I rubbed my tummy, wondering if I was pregnant, hoping the pregnancy would take, that nine months from now (July, a month for fireworks, lake swimming, and watermelon), we would be welcoming a new baby into the world. "This time, I think it's really happened."

He gazed at me with pity—sympathy and sorrow at the same time—and then he squeezed my hand. I let out a sad little laugh. "You think that sounds pathetic, don't you?"

He measured his words carefully. "I think it sounds like you're getting your hopes up. And I worry for you when you do that. But I also think it's natural."

Jack had been happy during my first pregnancy, cautious during my second, and extra cautious bordering on pessimistic ever since, always choosing his words carefully and trying not to say the wrong thing. He was an outsider, whereas everything was happening to me, inside my body. I knew I should be cautious, too, but I couldn't help it. The anticipation of being pregnant again galvanized me with hope.

He stood. "I've got to go to work."

"Already?" I tried to look seductive. I hadn't brushed my hair yet, but at least I'd brushed my teeth, and I was dressed. I tossed my tangled hair over my shoulders and pouted my dry, chapped lips. "We could seal the deal, just in case."

He kissed me on the forehead. "Be good," he said. "Don't open the door to any UPS workers today, okay?"

After he'd left, my mind wandered to my mother, as it did whenever I hoped I might be pregnant. We had what was known as a "toxic relationship," meaning that at some point she'd started treating me like I was poison, and her neglect had in turn induced terrible side effects.

For no reason I could fathom, my mother had gradually rejected me, until, by the time I'd become an adolescent, she'd wanted nothing to do with me, like a mean girl in middle school. And the more distant she'd become, the kinder my father had been to me, which only made my mother grow more distant.

I still got an occasional Zen-inspired email that she sent me from her life of luxury in Aruba, but I hadn't seen her in person for years.

As deeply as I yearned for a baby, I also wondered, *how would I be able to be a good mother, when I hadn't had one of my own?*

And if I was pregnant now, and if I did finally carry to term, would my mother and I stay estranged? Or would she visit, offer to stay for a week and help out, like a real mom? The idea made me smile, it was so unlikely—and shudder, it was so strange and unpleasant.

My father had also abandoned me. By dying. But that was a place I couldn't let my mind wander to.

So instead, my mind jumped to the next worst thing I could think about. Birdy Lawrence, the killer of her husband and her own child. Her *child*. That was the part that was beyond my comprehension. Because while I knew that people killed their spouses every day, the idea of someone killing their child was unthinkable. Abhorrent. Repulsive. And it had happened right here, in this house.

I needed some air. I slipped on my slides and stepped out into the backyard. I walked past the willow tree cradling the old tire swing, past the kidney-shaped garden with its overrun decaying flowers and thriving weeds, and kept walking until I got to the cliffside. I stared down the height of a four- or five-story building into the Wisconsin River below. The river made a lovely sound as it washed and tumbled over the rocks at the cliff's edge. The current was calm and gentle, the river apparently in no hurry to get to its final destination (the Mississippi, Al Martin had said). You couldn't say the same thing about the drop. There was nothing calm or gentle about that. If it wasn't quite a ninety-degree angle of imposing reddish-brown dirt mixed with jutting rocks, straight down from where I was standing to the riverbank below, it was close.

How could you ever let a child play alone out here in this yard?
This was a deadly accident waiting to happen if there ever was one. I
would have to talk to Jack about putting up a fence. Wrought iron,
maybe, unobtrusive and sturdy. That is, if I was in fact pregnant . . .
if I ever carried to term . . . *if, if, if* . . .

I closed my eyes and again thought of Birdy Lawrence, of her
terrible fall to the rocky ground somewhere below here. I thought I
heard a voice inside the river—that is, I thought the river was trying
to tell me something—but I also knew that was silly. Still, I listened
carefully, trying to make out words. It was like trying to remember
a dream from which I'd just awakened; I knew it was there, but I
couldn't access it.

After a few minutes, I turned around and began to walk back
toward the house. I was a good seventy yards away when I suddenly
felt a creeping sensation of discomfort. Something was out of place.
I had the strange feeling of being exposed, of being watched, as if I
were alone onstage in an empty theater and someone had sneaked
onto the balcony.

The street wasn't visible from here. The cliffs were behind me,
and there were woods on both sides of the property. I peered between
the trees but didn't see anything out of the ordinary. Then I glanced
up at the house and felt a rush of panic-driven heat. For she was
there, in the window of the second-floor nursery. *Some lady.* Birdy
Lawrence. Or was it? Really, it could have been anyone . . . anything.
A shadow in the glass. The shadow was visible for a brief second, and
then it was gone, as if whoever or whatever it was had seen me look
up and then had pulled away. I stood on the grass, trembling.

Despite my body's reaction, I told myself that whatever I'd
seen had probably been Olivier, or a trick of the light. (Those were
the words I said to myself, "a trick of the light," and I liked the
way they sounded so much that I whispered them aloud, not once

but three times. *"A trick of the light, a trick of the light, a trick of the light."*) I decided to go investigate. I entered the house, closed the back door behind me, went around to the foyer, and listened. I didn't hear anything. Even though I knew the odds that an intruder was slinking around the house were low, I checked to make sure that the front door was dead-bolted (it was), that the downstairs windows had not been tampered with (they hadn't), and that I had my cell phone in the back pocket of my jeans (I did), just in case.

I slowly tiptoed up that grand staircase onto the second-floor landing. I stopped again but heard nothing. I walked quietly to the nursery, or rather, I tried to walk quietly, but the floorboards sighed with my weight every time I took a step.

The door to the nursery was ajar, and I pushed it open. I half expected Olivier to come darting out of a corner, but there was nobody—nothing—in the room, save for the Mission-style rocking chair. I went to the curtainless window. It was dingy and needed washing. I inspected the windowsill for pawprints or other signs of feline mischief, but all I noticed was a thick layer of dust.

I turned around, and the rocking chair seemed to beckon to me with its comfort. I sat down in it, slowly rocking back and forth, facing the window, my hands on my knees, telling myself that I must have been seeing things. The window had been rather far away from where I'd been standing, after all, and maybe the sunlight combined with the old, dirty window had caused some sort of ripple effects. (*"A trick of the light."*) Or maybe I'd been imagining things. Maybe I'd imagined someone peering at me; maybe I'd imagined a shadow. Maybe an increase in a "wandering mind" or an "active imagination" was another symptom of an early pregnancy, along with sensitivity to scents and nausea. I did feel a little queasy and foggy in the head. Maybe hormones were to blame. That was what I told myself, anyway, so that I could feel better, function, get on with my day. *It's just hormones, Lilly!*

I was about to push myself up using the wide wooden arms of the chair, when I noticed something in the dust on the right arm. Some lines and curves. I leaned closer, and saw they were letters. And not just letters, a word:

JUNP

What did that mean? And then I realized, the third letter wasn't an "n"; it was an "m."

JUMP

JUMP. JUMP? Who had written those letters? How long had they been here? I tried to remember if they'd been here when we'd come to see the house with Al Martin, when we'd tagged along at the home inspection, when we'd closed. And if they hadn't been here before we'd moved in, then the only person who could have written them since then was Jack. But why would Jack write "JUMP" in dust on an armchair? Was it a joke, a trick, a message? Jack was not a practical joker. Maybe it was a message. Maybe he'd written a message on the arm of the Mission-style rocking chair in the nursery because . . . well, why? Why would he write "JUMP"? I took my phone from my pocket and went to "Recents."

I rang his cell phone. Straight to voice mail. I called his office phone. No answer.

Then I received a text.

In meeting.

Did you write JUMP in dust of rocking chair in spare bedroom?

WTF? In meeting

Please answer

NO

I flipped close my phone. So it hadn't been Jack, and judging from how clean the letters were, I found it hard to believe that the word had been written before the closing. Well, if it hadn't been Jack, who had it been? Who had written that word?

I thought of what I'd been doing just before I'd felt eyes on me, before I'd seen the shadow, before I'd come upstairs. I'd been at the cliffs, thinking of Birdy Lawrence, of her jump, of her *JUMP*, and imagining that the river was trying to tell me something. But maybe it was Birdy Lawrence who'd been trying to tell me something. What had she been trying to tell me? Something that I hadn't been able to understand, and so she'd written it on the chair of this rocker? *JUMP.*

Or had it been *JUMP!* . . . ?

A command.

I stopped rocking to and fro. My heart pounded, and my breathing became shallow and rapid. I was cresting into a panic attack. How many times in my life had I considered making a (metaphorical) jump? Had the ghost of Birdy Lawrence intuited my . . . history, my . . . inclinations, and that's why she'd commanded me to JUMP, so that I would experience the same fate she had?

My breathing began to steady, for as soon as I thought this, I knew it was ridiculous. In fact, I said the words aloud: "You're being ridiculous, Lilly. You learn that the woman who lived in this house and murdered her family jumped off those cliffs, and now you think she wrote a message in the armchair for you to JUMP!" I re-examined the marks in the dust. They certainly seemed to spell "JUMP," but maybe I was just seeing things.

To assure myself that there was no ghost, that I was just being silly, I said aloud, in a normal voice, as if I were talking to one of my students who had written something in marker on the walls, trying not to sound too accusatory, "Birdy Lawrence? Did you write 'JUMP'?"

I closed my eyes, so I could hear better. The word "JUMP" appeared before my lids. Was it indeed a command? Or a fear? A riddle? A coincidence? I knew that's what Jack would call it. "*Olivier just scratched some markings into the dust*," he'd say, believing it was less likely for a ghost to write a message than for a cat to spell a word.

I opened my eyes, continuing to listen. Silence. *You're being silly*, I told myself. *Silly Lilly*. How many times had I been called that in my life? But sometimes the name was justified; sometimes I was being silly. "Those markings probably just look like a word," I reassured myself. "What you thought was a specter was really just a trick of the light."

A trick of the light. A trick of the light. A trick of the light.

8

HOME IMPROVEMENT

WHEN JACK CAME HOME FROM WORK, he asked me what my texts were about. I dragged him into the nursery and pointed. "Look at these letters," I said.

"I don't see anything."

I peered down at the arms of the Mission-style rocking chair and saw that he was right. The letters, even much of the dust, had been rubbed away. "They were here! The letters were here. They spelled 'JUMP.'"

"Well, maybe Olivier climbed up on the chair and what you thought were letters were just, you know, cat marks."

Just as I'd supposed. "And I guess he rubbed them away, too?"

"Exactly." He smiled and put both hands on my shoulders. "Who do you think left a message to you in dust? A robber? An entity? Maybe poor Olivier is possessed, huh?"

Olivier had been acting strangely, I wanted to say, but I let it go. The word "entity" did sound absurd when Jack said it aloud.

"Isn't it more likely that it's just your active imagination?"

I hated it when he talked to me like that, like he was the teacher and I was a fourth grader. I considered telling Jack what I'd been hiding from him, that we lived in "the Murder House." But I decided that telling him wouldn't convince him that there had been real letters there, not cat marks, and besides, he'd want to know how I'd found out. *I did some research the other day. Oh, you mean the day you told me you took your résumé to the school district?*

"You're probably right," I said.

The next morning was Saturday, and we'd agreed to spend the day making home improvements. It was sunny, humid, and warm. The lawn was overgrown and brownish-yellow, and the flower beds were filled with weeds and leaves from the previous autumn—or maybe from the last fifty autumns. I was no gardener, but even I could tell that the place was a real mess.

"I'm going up on the roof," Jack said. "Hold the ladder for me, will you?"

I questioned the idea of holding ladders because the action seemed like such a formality. Would I really be able to steady all six feet of Jack if he slipped? But I did so until he made it safely to the roof, a container of spackle in his hands.

Then I found an ancient bamboo leaf rake in the detached garage and started raking the areas around the driveway.

"Lilly?"

"Hmm?"

"What are you doing?"

"Raking."

"I can see that," Jack said. "But why?"

"Just doing some cleanup, getting ready for fall." I tried to sound as if I knew what I was talking about, as if I wasn't a thirty-seven-year-old woman who had held a rake a couple of times in her life.

He was sitting on the peak of the roof, the jar of spackle in his hand. I had to shield my eyes to see him. He didn't look happy, from what I could tell.

"Let me rephrase. Why are you raking when we have a list of about twenty-five necessary things to do? I thought you were going to touch up the paint on the windowsills."

Jack was right, of course. That had been the plan. The paint on every windowsill was chipping, and it gave the house a forlorn, neglected appearance. Some might even go so far as to say *creepy*. Jack had gone to the local hardware store, picked out the exterior "saddle brown" paint, bought the scrapers, the brushes, and the paint trays, and we'd agreed that today we would tackle the first-story windows. Except I'd awakened this morning no longer thinking that was a good idea, and so had decided to take on the messy yard.

"You can't expect for me to paint now."

He tilted his head to the side. "I can't?"

"In my possible condition?"

I could see, even from my spot twenty feet below, that he was closing his eyes, undoubtedly concentrating on not throwing the jar of spackle at my head. It was warm, too warm. I felt cranky and sweaty, and I could practically see the steam coming off Jack's skin, a mixture of anger and heat. Finally, he said, "You have got to be kidding me."

"I'm not going to breathe in paint fumes. And I'm not going to scrape off lead-based paint. Not when there's a chance I might be pregnant. The first three months are the most important to the fetus. Everybody knows that."

I began raking around the shrubs, making a neat pile in the yard.

Jack said, "Lilly, stop." I didn't. He yelled, "Lilly, stop!" I did. He said, "What you're talking about is a zygote that may or may not exist, and if it does, is about sixteen hours old. If it does exist, it will be days before it is even a blastocyst, much less an embryo, much less a 'fetus.' If it does exist, it's smaller than a grain of rice, well shielded in protective blood and tissue. We're outside, so any paint fumes you might possibly breathe in are negligible. Do you know how many women don't know they're pregnant at this stage, who drink alcohol, snort coke, paint entire rooms indoors with minimal ventilation, and NOTHING HAPPENS?"

I felt calm and powerful having this argument with Jack while he was on the roof and I was on the ground. I thought of setting the ladder in the dirt and driving around town for a couple of hours. The idea made me smile. "You think that because you're a stupid computer guy, you know everything. But every fertility book I've read says this is a crucial time. Once again, this just shows that you're not as committed as I am to starting a family."

"I might be a stupid computer scientist, but you're a raving lunatic."

The words hung in the air. They were too close to the bone to be said that lightly, and apparently Jack knew it. "I mean . . ."

"No, fine, whatever. I'm a raving lunatic. And you're a perfectly sane computer geek who wouldn't know a normal human emotion if you found it in your hard drive. If you want to paint, go ahead, but this raving lunatic is raking."

"Lilly . . ."

I returned to my work. After a half hour or so, Jack asked me to hold the ladder for him so he could come back down.

"Not until you apologize," I said.

Even from where I stood, I could see him roll his eyes. "I'm sorry I called you . . . a name."

"Not just that, for everything."

"I have a mobile phone in my pocket. Do you want me to call 9-1-1? Now go to the ladder and hold it for me."

His voice was breezy. I could hold the ladder, or he could call for emergency services; it was up to me. I held the ladder. He came down. He drove to the hardware store and came back with more supplies to repair the roof, as well as a bag he handed me that contained gloves and a face mask, which I took to be part olive branch, part dangling carrot. I held the ladder for him while he went back up on the roof, and then I put on the gloves and face mask and used a small scraper to scrape the paint off the window frames while I tried not to breathe. I scraped slowly, resentfully. We didn't speak. At one point I went inside, made myself a sandwich, and then spent an hour scrubbing the nursery, another chore not on the list. Then I went outside again and scraped off more paint, slowly, partly out of resentment, and partly so no flecks would fly through the air and seep through the mask and land in my lungs. At the end of the day, Jack called for me to hold the ladder for him again, and I did.

"Well, I think it's patched. It's certainly not a permanent fix, but I don't think we'll need to set bowls on the floor when it rains. How'd you do?" His face was sweaty, sunburned, and enthusiastic.

I gestured to the windows in the back of the house.

"What the . . . ?" Jack said.

"Naturally, I wasn't about to stare upward and get lead-based paint in my eyes."

"So instead of completing any single window, you just scraped the bottom panel off of each one?"

"Not quite each one. I got to four of them."

Jack let out an exhausted sigh. "Were you making a point?"

"I didn't want to do the windows! If you had let me finish raking, at least something would look good!" I gestured to the yard, where there were mountains of leaves. "Instead, our baby is probably brain-dead and the house looks creepier than ever." I marched away, leaving the scraper, gloves, and face mask outside for Jack to deal with.

For the remainder of the afternoon and evening, we did our own thing. Jack made a pot of cold gazpacho and worked on his laptop. I organized my study and then lay in bed reading *What to Expect When You're Expecting* for the hundredth time. Our truce came when he

brought me a bowl of chilled soup in bed, and I said, "Thank you."
He started to leave, and I added, "Wait." He sat on the edge of the
bed, beside my knees.

I thought of the divide between us: the space between a computer
scientist who cannot fathom anything he believes to be irrational, and
an ex-actor/pianist/teacher—or, more to the point, a possibly haunted
lady with three dead fetuses—who did not want to breathe in toxic
fumes as long as there was a chance she might be pregnant. It was difficult to cross that divide. But I had to try.

"I'm sorry," I said. "I think I overreacted."

He smiled. "Maybe a little."

I brought a spoonful of soup to my mouth and swallowed. "The
soup is tasty."

"I'm glad you like it."

"Are you sorry, too?"

"Yes, I am," he said, and he looked sorry. "For what it's worth, of
course I don't think you're crazy. And I shouldn't have pushed you to
do something you weren't comfortable with. I know how important
this is to you. Being a mother."

"Thank you. I'll get to the pile of leaves tomorrow." That was
something we'd always been good at in our marriage. Saying we were
sorry. Accepting apologies. Jack had often told me that was something he loved about me, that I didn't hold grudges, that I was able
to forgive and move on. Not that he'd—not that either of us—had
ever done anything unforgiveable. I'd learned that lesson from my
father, I guessed. *Water off a duck's back* had been his motto. Until it
hadn't been.

That night, I dreamed of the ghost of Birdy Lawrence. She was wearing a white dress, appearing so ethereal as to be nearly transparent.
She had the same features as in the newspaper picture, those same

dark eyes, that same cute, upturned nose, the same sultry mouth, rosy cheeks, hard clavicle. Her white dress was mid-length, short sleeved, and insubstantial. I approached her, as if we knew each other. There was no setting, no scenery, just the two of us in some airy realm, greeting each other like old friends.

Then she spoke. "I want my baby," she said, in a sweet, offhanded voice. I was suddenly terrified. I trembled so hard I could no longer stand and fell to my knees, helpless and shivering. "I want my baby," she repeated, in that same sweet voice. I was so scared, I couldn't run, couldn't move.

"Where is my baby? Where is my baby? I want my baby."

9

NEW JOB

ON MONDAY MORNING, I woke up excited about starting my new job. The truth was, I worried I was going a little stir-crazy cooped up in this enormous old house, and the anticipation of being around people and helping them made me feel competent and sane. I picked out a librarian's costume from my closet: white three-quarter-sleeve blouse tucked into a navy pencil skirt with a wide leather belt and a tan cardigan tied over my shoulders. I slicked my hair into a proper bun with bobby pins and applied light pink lipstick and mascara. I looked like Bunny in *Desk Set*, or Dr. Barbara Gordon in *Batman*, or possibly even Marian in *The Music Man*: an honest-to-goodness librarian.

I went downstairs and found Jack busy on his laptop at the kitchen table. He kissed me goodbye on my way out. "You look terrific, honey! Break a leg out there."

I arrived right on time. Carl introduced me to everyone. Jess, the red-braided Whovian (now wearing a Star Trek T-shirt), gave me a half smile, half smirk when Carl introduced us and said, "We've met." Patty (who was wearing a different headband than the day before, this one pale green, to match her twinset) was an assistant, like I would be. So was Chris, a young man in his twenties with an eyebrow ring and a silver lip stud. Arjun, fiftyish, plump, and stylish in black Converse sneakers, was the children's and young adult librarian. Carl pointed toward a room with glass windows and said, "We won't bother Eleanor right now, but she's been here longer than any of us. If you have any questions that we can't answer, chances are Eleanor can."

I saw the profile of a gray-haired woman busily typing at a computer.

"Chris, I'd like for you to show Lilly around and begin training her," said Carl. Then he turned to me. "Chris'll take care of you from here, Lilly. Come see me if you need anything. And welcome," he added with a sincere smile.

"Thank you," I said.

Chris turned to face me. He was taller than I was by about two inches, and had blondish curly hair and perfectly straight white teeth. His parents had obviously spent a small fortune on orthodontist bills, and it occurred to me that there were all kinds of hidden costs when it came to raising a child.

"Okay. The first thing you do when you come in is punch the time clock. Eleanor is kind of like a librarian, and kind of like an HR person and accountant. She's the one who signs our paychecks. And if you forget to punch in one day and you go to her and say, 'Hey, Eleanor, I forgot to punch in, can you write it down for me?' she will not be happy. The first time, she'll let it slide, but the second time? Forget it. Like, what you don't want to do is get on Eleanor's bad side."

"So, should I punch in?"

"I don't know, are you like, starting now?"

As far as I knew, job training counted as work. "I think so," I said. I couldn't help but smile. "Where's the time clock?"

He showed me the time clock, right outside the conference room, positioned just where Eleanor could see, and then gave me a tour of the library, explaining all my responsibilities as we went.

At one point, as he showed me how to properly shelve the DVDs, he said, "So, like, can I ask you a question?"

"Sure."

"Why are you working here?"

·   I laughed. "Why are you working here?"

"I'm still in school, and it's better than McDonald's. You?"

Maybe it was his sympathetic eyes and fresh face, or maybe it was because I didn't have any friends here yet, but I told him the truth. "I'm an elementary school teacher—well, I was, but I don't want to do that anymore." (I spared him from adding, *Because I don't want to be around other people's kids, when I so desperately want one of my own.*) "And I'm not really trained to do anything else. I used to be an actor. I studied acting and music and French in school, but there aren't a lot of jobs for actors and musicians and French speakers around here. My husband has a good job, but we bought a really big, expensive house"—(I didn't say, *Because I desperately wanted to live there as I was sure it's where I'd become a mother*)—"and so I had to get a job. Also, you know, it's important to work, so you don't, you know . . ." My voice trailed off. I was going to say, *Go crazy*, but instead I said, ". . . have too much time on your hands. And I like books. I like puppet shows. I like knitting and murder." (*Or at least, books about murder.*)

If he was surprised by my confessional outburst, he didn't show it. "A teacher, that's cool. I bet you'd be good at that. You seem passionate, like my third-grade teacher Mrs. Tanaka. She was always going off about things, and sometimes she'd say, 'Okay, kids, put away your books. We're going outside to collect bugs!'"

I smiled at the memory of telling "my kids" we were going to put on a play. Then I thought of not showing up for work after my second miscarriage, and I stopped smiling.

Chris was a competent tour guide and instructor, and my tour and training session lasted over an hour. When we finished, I worked on shelving books until lunchtime. Bending down low, reaching up high, sometimes standing on a step stool, sometimes sitting on the floor, I began to think that my pencil skirt and low-heeled pumps hadn't been such a great idea. At 12:30, Patty came over and told me it was time for my lunch break. I hadn't thought to bring a lunch, so I walked to the café on the corner, where a sandwich and salad cost me over an hour's worth of work. I felt tired and my legs hurt, but I was excited when I returned to the hustle and bustle of the library and got back to work.

An older man asked me for a good book to read on feminism, and I gave him a few suggestions. A young woman asked me how to figure out the cycles of the moon, and since Jess, the librarian, was on a conference call, we looked up the information together. Arjun, who worked on the upper level in the children's and young adult section, came downstairs to welcome me to my first day on the job with an oatmeal cookie left over from their YA LGBTQ book club discussion group. "Cookies," he said. "The way I see it, cookies are the real perk to working here, and paychecks are second, amirite?" I was enjoying myself.

At about four in the afternoon, there was a lull in the action. I had shelved all the return books and had helped everyone in line at the circulation desk. Now the lobby was empty. Patty was stuffing envelopes with lost notices. I stood there for a moment, wondering what to do next, and realized this was my opportunity to learn more about the Lawrence murders.

"I'll be right back," I told Patty.

"Sure," she said.

I went to the computer center, an open area behind the circ desk that housed six computers at individual workstations. A college-aged woman was using one of them. She glanced up at me and then went back to whatever she was doing.

"I work here," I told her. "Let me know if you need any help."

She didn't respond.

I sat down at one of the stations and Googled "Lawrence Mansion Murders." Several hits popped up with brief summaries and references, but there was nothing that told me more than I already knew. I tried "Haven Wisconsin Lawrence Haunted House." The first thing that came up was a site for haunted houses in Wisconsin, which I clicked on. The website was black and red and populated with haunted house GIFs, lightning rods, and a listing of nearly a hundred haunted sites in alphabetical order. I scrolled past allegedly haunted cemeteries, restaurants, bars, hotels, secondhand shops, theaters, and houses all across the state, until I came upon a picture of our house with the following description:

> **The Lawrence Estate, Haven, Wisconsin**
> An apparition of a female figure, dressed in white, has been spotted in the windows of the upper floors of the Lawrence Estate at 217 Hill Street in Haven. This house was built by circus impresario Edgar Lawrence in 1924 and was the site of gruesome events in the 1950s, when Edgar's daughter and famed trapeze artist Birdy Lawrence murdered her husband, poisoned her daughter to death, and then flung herself off the cliffs in the backyard. Reports say the figure appears to be looking out the window. Witnesses have reported hearing creaking stairs and footsteps, as well as moaning and crying from as far away as down the street. The house is now owned by the Haven Circus Society. Tours are no longer given.

"What the . . . ?" I said aloud. The woman looked up at me, shook her head, and went back to browsing. I hadn't heard creaking stairs, moaning, or crying, but I had heard laughter, and I had seen a figure of a woman in white at the window. Or at least, I thought I had. Was I really living in a freaking haunted house? With the ghost of Birdy Lawrence?

I spent the next few minutes down a rabbit hole, clicking on various sites, not learning anything new, until I landed upon the obituary of Police Chief Chip Rippmann (". . . a long and distinguished career, which included solving the notorious Lawrence Mansion murders"), which gave me an idea. It had been over fifty years since the murders, but maybe others involved in the investigation were still alive. Maybe they would talk to me, tell me about what had happened, why Birdy Lawrence had done what she had. Maybe they would know something that would help me figure out if I was really living with a ghost in a haunted house.

I knew I couldn't be here forever. I quickly typed in the names. I found that Doctor Hal Grodin, housekeeper Harriet "Hattie" Smith, and friend Emmie Dunstan were all deceased. Then I typed in "Lorenzo DeMarcos, Haven, WI." There was only one entry. The white pages. Not only was he still alive, but he was living on Hill Street, just down the road from us. I was in the middle of calling his number on my cell phone when a voice said, "Hey, Lilly, what's up?"

I pressed "end" and turned around. It was Jess, her dyed red hair in pigtails, her closed-lipped smile forced. "Oh, hi, Jess. I was . . ." My voice trailed off as I vaguely waved at my phone. "Um, doing a bit of research for . . ." I thought it might be pushing it to add the words "a patron," and let my voice trail off.

"Okay, well, just so you know, we don't allow personal calls during work hours—"

"Of course, I was just . . ."

"—when there's a long line at the circ desk. I'm going into a meeting, but Patty could use your help."

It was an odd feeling to be reprimanded by someone several years younger than I was, wearing a Star Trek T-shirt, and I felt my cheeks become warm. The young woman at the other computer was listening and smiling what I took to be a *Busted* smile. "Sure, I'll go there right away," I said, putting my phone in my pocket and hurrying to the circ desk, which had suddenly become crazy busy.

Patty was checking out books while talking into the library phone cradled into her neck. She shot me a look that said, *Where have you been?* or *Thank goodness you're finally here!* or maybe just, *Asshole!* (if she ever thought that word, which was hard to imagine). I whispered, "Sorry," and then announced to the line of eight or nine people who were waiting, "I can help the next person."

Maybe it was for the best, I thought, as I checked out guidebooks on Disney World to an excited mom and her two young sons. I would show up on Lorenzo DeMarcos's door, unannounced.

10

BATH TIME

WHEN I GOT HOME FROM WORK, I was exhausted, both physically and mentally. Jack wouldn't be home for an hour or two. I decided to wait until tomorrow to visit Lorenzo DeMarcos and instead focus on some much-needed self-care. I fed Olivier and went upstairs to take a bath.

I loved our en suite bathroom. Well before our contemporary obsession with indulgence and luxury, somehow Edgar Lawrence had had the wherewithal to create a haven of sybaritic peace. There was a black-and-white-tiled floor, a claw-foot tub as well as a separate shower, a linen closet with ample storage, double sinks with copper waterspouts in the shapes of swans, and, that symbol of anti-Puritanical European acknowledgment of the animal nature of the body, a bidet. I had only tried to use it once, and it had sputtered, stalled, and finally splashed a fountain of water all over the floor. Now it held a potted fern.

But the claw-foot tub was a treat. I reached for the old-fashioned spigots and turned on the hot water full blast while barely adding any cold water at all. The water was as hot as I could possibly stand. I inched myself in. My skin was becoming bright pink, like a lobster boiling to its death. I washed my face and then laid my head back and relaxed. I closed my eyes. The back of my neck began to sweat. I rested my hands on my stomach as the water rose to my neck. I soaked for a while and then wondered if a baby was brewing in there, below my hands. And then I screamed.

"Anhh!" A high-pitched wail.

I stood up as quickly as I could and sat on the edge of the tub.
"Idiot, idiot, idiot!"

For of course, you were not supposed to take a hot bath if you
were pregnant. Any temperature above 100 degrees Fahrenheit could
cause a miscarriage. I knew this fact. I had read it in dozens of books
and on dozens of websites, dozens of times. I had simply been so tired
I had momentarily forgotten.

I turned off the water and unplugged the drain. I didn't want
a lukewarm bath. I didn't want anything to remind me of a bath. I
would shower in the morning, before work.

Why had I made such a mindless mistake? Becoming a mother
was the most important thing in the world to me. I wished I had
protected the baby (zygote, blastocyst, whatever), if there was a baby
(zygote, blastocyst, whatever). It was only a few days old, if it existed,
and already I was a terrible mother. What was wrong with me?

I put on a pink cotton camisole and panties and crawled into
bed. The water finished draining out of the tub. After a few seconds
of silence, I heard the spigots turning on again. That was odd. Maybe
I'd left them on. I got out of bed and returned to the bathroom. I
could hear the water running, but I could see it wasn't running. It
sounded distant—*there, but not there*. I paused a moment, staring
at the old-fashioned spigots, trying to figure things out. I couldn't.
I went back to the bedroom and listened. Clearly, a bath was running. This time I went down the hall, to another bathroom on the
same floor, where there was a sink and a shower. Nothing. I went
downstairs. Neither the kitchen nor the bathroom tap was open. I
saw Olivier, who was curled in the crook of the armrest of the couch,
and went to pet him, but he meowed uproariously and ran away.
Evidently, I was giving off some kind of crazy mojo-juice with which
Olivier wanted nothing to do.

I went back upstairs, crawled into bed, and listened for the running water sound, but it was gone now. "It was just your imagination," I told myself aloud so that I could hear a voice, even if it was only mine. "You're stressed out. You're tired." *Unstable, anxious, hysterical.* "Pull yourself together, Lilly," I added. But instead of feeling pulled together, I felt pulled apart. Spiraling. I thought of my father, and then (as I always did when I found myself spiraling), I remembered the last time I'd seen him. I pictured his body, and then worked hard to get that image out of my mind. *No, no, no.* I pulled the blankets up to my chin and reached for a book on my nightstand. I wanted to get lost in words to take my mind off things. *A Fertility Doctor's Guide to Getting, and Staying, Pregnant* would be too depressing tonight. I put it back and picked up my current Agatha Christie. I read a few sentences, trying to lose myself in the world of the Belgium detective creating order out of chaos, but it was no use; my senses were being pulled back into the world around me, into the world of the house, of late-night female laughter, shadows, and cryptic messages written in dust, and now, phantom sounds streaming from distant water pipes. The world of Birdy Lawrence?

Then I heard a different sound. It wasn't water running; it was water splashing. I got out of bed and walked toward the bathroom, and the closer I came to it, the clearer I could hear the noise. I stepped into the bathroom and listened. The sound was still distant, but it seemed to be coming from the bathtub, an arrhythmic splashing, as if someone had drawn a bath, was now in it, and was splattering water while soaping up, or swinging their legs up and down.

The bathtub was empty. I kneeled directly in front of it and ran my hands along the porcelain sides and bottom, which were still wet from my bath. The sound stopped. I felt a chill, perhaps from the cold of the porcelain, or perhaps from something else, and stood.

I turned away from the tub, toward the mirror, and gripped my hands on the marble countertop. I bent my head down, breathing in, breathing out. It had been a long time since I'd felt like all my screws were on completely tight, but this situation was different. There was a rope, a tether, tying me to this world—the rational world, a world in which there was no sound of water *there, but not there*—and that rope was becoming thin and frayed. I wanted to get back to the other world, the real world, a world of logic, sanity, rationality, but I didn't know how.

I felt like I couldn't breathe. I was beginning to panic. I opened the bottom drawer of the vanity, looking through my box of medications. My hands were shaking, like an alcoholic going through withdrawal searching for their gallon of cheap vodka, as I sifted through all my bottles of prescription and over-the-counter drugs. There was an herbal remedy for sleeplessness that had never worked. There were over-the-counter medications for allergies, nausea, and headaches. There was my prescription to make me ovulate regularly. And there, in the back, were my anti-anxiety medications, which the shrink had prescribed, and I had taken, at various times, trying to get the dosage and the medication right. *Eureka!* I picked them up, my hands still trembling, and became immediately devastated by their lightness. All three were empty. All three were expired. I rattled them in my shaking hands and threw them back in the drawer. I pressed my trembling fingers to my eyelids, willing myself not to cry.

I wanted these drugs. I wanted them now. My onetime shrink had always told me if "things became too much" to check myself into the nearest emergency room, and if I couldn't manage to get myself there, to call 9-1-1. I had chuckled and shaken my head and said, suavely (that is, I had tried to be suave, not a Bond girl but a female Bond, Sean Connery with long hair and a short skirt), "I can assure you, that won't be necessary." But while I spoke and languidly crossed my legs, I thought, *How can he tell I'm this bad off? Pull yourself together, Lilly! Your insides are showing!* And: *Okay, note to self, get yourself to the nearest ER. If you can't get yourself there, call 9-1-1.* This had been news to me. I had thought if things got bad enough, I would need to arrange to go to a sanitarium, like in *The Magic Mountain*, and while the idea had been immensely attractive, I knew I could never afford it, with my cheap insurance. The idea of an ER had sounded not only affordable, but also appealing in a deservedly dirty way. I imagined being left out in an unclean hallway while Chicagoans with real emergencies received treatment in small windowless rooms and nurses half-heartedly searched for a bed for me, the white girl for whom "things were too much."

I took a deep breath and told myself I was not at the point at which I needed to drive myself to the Haven Hospital emergency room. I did not need to see someone whom I could ask to refill these medications, which I should not be taking while trying to get pregnant, and who would want to know why I needed such powerful meds. "Because there may be a ghost in my house!"

"A ghost, huh? Why do you think you're being haunted, Lilly? What is truly haunting you?" I knew any halfway decent therapist would say.

That was the problem with psychiatry, in my opinion. Everyone wanted to *talk, talk, talk,* and nobody would just give you drugs.

I stared at myself in the mirror, telling myself, "It's okay. You're okay." But I didn't look okay. I had washed my face in the bath, but a faint ring of mascara still hung underneath my eyes, giving me a bruised appearance. My complexion was pasty and pale. Crow's-feet were creeping around my eyes. The number eleven furrowed between my brows. I was pushing forty, hoping for what they called a "geriatric pregnancy." I was starting to look like that waitress at my father's funeral.

I took a deep breath, let it out. I gazed in the mirror beyond myself, to the side of my reflection, into some great unknown. "Birdy?" I asked. "Is that you?" I thought of her last night on earth, the blood from the gunshot wounds on her husband, the blood from the fall off the cliffs. "Were you trying to . . . cleanse yourself?"

The silence then felt solid, like the silence before a tornado.

And then I felt an icy hand wrap around the back of my calf, as if someone or something was grabbing my leg with a frozen glove.

I screamed.

I shook my leg, shaking off that icy cold grip.

And then I ran.

I ran out of the bathroom, through the bedroom, down the stairs, into the foyer, and out the front door. I stood there, shivering on the front porch. I wasn't wearing slippers or a bathrobe, and I was cold, but I didn't want to go back into that house, not even to get my car keys to drive far, far away.

It was after seven o'clock. The sky was darkening, but the street-lights were on, and I could see a man walking his dog on the sidewalk below. "Hello!" I called, without thinking, I so badly wanted to hear another human voice.

He stopped and looked up at me. He was elderly, with graying hair and a stooped back. "Hello!" I repeated. I wanted . . . what? To ask him about the ghost? To invite him to stay the night? To ask him to call 9-1-1 because I'd felt an invisible icy grip on my leg?

His dog barked at me, and I startled. I couldn't see the dog well, but the bark was mean and angry. The man stared at me, and, since he was standing directly under a streetlight, I thought I could see that his stare was not friendly. I was suddenly aware of being in my pink camisole and matching pink panties under our porchlight. I must have looked like a so-called floozy or a crazy person, trying to chat up strangers in this skimpy outfit so late at night.

The man yanked on the leash and the dog stopped barking, and the two of them began to walk away. I watched them go down the street until they disappeared down the hill.

That's when Jack pulled into the drive.

I had no choice. I told him everything. I showed him the newspaper articles and then told him what I'd experienced, reminding him of the laughter I'd heard on that first night, and explaining what I'd seen in the nursery window before I found the word "JUMP" on the arm of the rocking chair. I told him about Olivier's seeing something I couldn't, and about the door to the third floor that had mysteriously opened on its own. Finally, I told him what had just happened, the bath sounds leading to the icy grip on my leg. He listened without interrupting. When I finished, he didn't say anything for a couple of seconds, and I wondered if he was considering calling the nice men with the white straitjackets. I mean, saying it all aloud, it did sound mad, even to me.

"Lilly, honey, calm down," Jack finally said. "It's okay. Everything's okay. The water sounds were probably just your imagination, and there must be some reason for the cold sensation on your leg."

"Like what? Why would I feel that?"

"Could have been cold water from your bath or the tub. Could have been a draft from the HVAC system. There are no such things as ghosts. Just keep reminding yourself of that, okay? There's a logical explanation for everything, even if we don't always know what it is."

We were sitting on the couch in the living room. I was wrapped in the chenille blanket, and he was still in the khakis, light blue button-down shirt, and sport jacket he had worn to work. He looked tired, and it occurred to me that he was dealing with a lot of stress— from working long hours at a new job, from our financial situation, and now this.

"It's my fault," he said. "I should've done a better job vetting this place. Let's face it, we never should have bought it to begin with, but if we were going to buy it, I should have made sure we weren't stepping into a complete nightmare. I've been kicking myself . . ."

The way he said it made me realize something. "You knew," I said. "I mean, before I told you, you already knew this was 'the Murder House.'"

He looked away from me. "Not until recently. I found out Saturday when I went to the hardware store. The guys there got a real kick out of it . . ."

"And you didn't tell me?" I had found out even before he had, and I hadn't told him either. But I was still shocked he would hide something like that from me.

"Of course I didn't tell you."

"What do you mean? Why not?"

"Because I knew you'd freak out!"

I wanted to disagree, but I couldn't. I was pretty much freaking out.

"I contacted a lawyer to find out if we have any recourse with the realty company or the circus society, since they failed to disclose a material issue, but apparently, we don't. We'll just have to sell it at a loss . . . maybe to someone who wants to open up a haunted house," he added with a grim smile. "It is what it is."

"No," I said.

"No, what?"

"We're not selling it."

"You want to stay here? You were just out on the porch in your underwear, too scared to step inside. I thought we'd be going back to the motel tonight."

"Yeah, okay, I panicked. You're right. I learned about the murders and then freaked out. But I just need to come to terms with the fact that this is an old house, and there are going to be creaks and groans, but that really, there's nothing to be afraid of."

I was telling him what he wanted to hear. The truth was, I was certain I hadn't imagined the icy grip on my leg. I was pretty sure there was not "a rational explanation for everything." And yet, I still felt as connected to the house as I ever had. I believed there was a reason that we were—that I was—here, and that we needed to stay. I still clung to the hope that Jack and I would have a baby in this house, and that we'd fix up the Lawrence Mansion to its former glory. Running away to some newly constructed home and forgetting that all these mysterious events had ever happened didn't feel like an option.

"Are you sure?"

How can anyone be sure of anything? The only things I was sure of were that there were secrets hidden in this house, secrets I needed to uncover, and that I wanted to have a baby more than anything in the world. There was a six-day window around ovulation when one could become pregnant. This was day five. I crawled over to Jack, straddled him, wrapped my arms around his neck, and gently bit his lower lip.

11

THE GARDENER

LORENZO DEMARCOS'S MID-CENTURY BUNGALOW looked like it had
once been charming but had long ago fallen upon hard times. The
concrete steps were cracked and corroding, the white paint was in desperate need of a power wash, and the front door had been replaced
with what looked like the cheapest, ugliest door one could possibly
find at Menards. We owned the two eyesores on the street, he and I,
only mine was of course a much grander dump than his.

When he answered my knock, the following day after work, I
immediately saw the resemblance to the newspaper photo: same
olive skin (now lined with wrinkles), same slouched swagger (now
coupled with a stoop), heck, same white T-shirt, for all I knew, but
I also saw another resemblance. This was the man I'd said hello to
just the night before after my bathtub scare, the one who had been
walking in front of the house, the one who had glared at me, the
one with the angry dog. And in fact, I heard some muffled barking
now. Then I saw a tan dog—some sort of terrier/pit bull mix, was
my guess—leap onto a couch that was visible through the front window. It barked at me, baring its teeth, leaving slobbery spit marks on
the glass pane.

"Yeah?" Lorenzo DeMarcos said, stepping onto the front porch
and closing the door behind him.

I turned my gaze away from the dog and looked into the man's
wary eyes. His head was cocked, and he was frowning, staring back

at me suspiciously. "Um, hello," I said. "My name is Lilly Bly. I live in the house just up the street. The Lawrence House."

"I know," he said. "I seen you."

His voice was like sandpaper, a smoker's voice.

"I just have a few questions for you. Do you mind?"

"I don't take in no visitors."

"No, of course not," I said, glancing at the dog in the window, who was barking louder now. "I wasn't suggesting . . ."

"Shut up!" Lorenzo DeMarcos yelled. The dog suddenly stopped barking and jumped down, out of sight. I was fine staying out on the porch.

"I'd like to talk with you right here, if you don't mind," I said, and then continued, not giving him a chance to say no. "I understand you were the gardener and caretaker at the time of Birdy Lawrence's death. You were there . . . when it happened. Right?"

"What da ya wanna know for?"

I summoned my inner Vivien Leigh as Scarlett O'Hara and smiled in a way that I hoped was disarming, that I hoped was willful and feminine, but from his fixed frown, I could tell my rendition wasn't working. I stopped smiling and sighed. "I'm just curious. My husband and I bought the house recently. I'm trying to learn a little about its history."

"It was in the papers back then, everything I seen."

"Yes, I read that. I read that you lived in what used to be the coach house and that you were there at the time of the deaths. Please. I'm sorry to bother you, but I'd really appreciate it. Can you tell me something about the owners, Birdy and Bobby?"

Even I could hear the urgency in my voice. I gazed at him pleadingly. I wanted him to understand that this was a matter of life and death: that my well-being depended upon my finding out if I was really living with a ghost or possibly going insane. And if I really was living with a ghost, I needed to know more about her so that I could drive her out of there, or put her to peace, or at least understand her. I didn't want any more ghostly words written in dust or phantom baths or spectral grips on calves. He had been there the night of the deaths; he had seen . . . well, I wasn't sure what, but I knew he'd seen her husband's body. And he had lived with them—or behind them, anyway. Perhaps there was nothing he could possibly say to help me. But perhaps there was.

He sighed and looked heavenward, or in his case, at the moldy overhang of the front porch. When he spoke, it was in a bored, singsong tone, as if he'd told the story a million times in the past week alone, although the incident had happened some fifty years ago, and surely not many people had come banging on his door to hear the tale since then.

"I heard some shots, okay? When I come outside, I seen Bobby laying on the grass. All bloody. There was a gun right next to him."

"Why do you think Birdy did it?" I asked, trying to make my voice gentle.

Lorenzo DeMarcos looked down the street toward my house. "I think Birdy was lonely, and the loneliness made her snap. People called her stuck-up. I'm not saying that was true or not true, but one thing's for sure, she didn't mix with the regular folks or the circus performers like Bobby did. He got along with everybody." I noticed that this was almost exactly what he had said in the newspaper article, as if he were an actor who had learned his lines fifty years before and still remembered them. "And Birdy didn't like Bobby mixing with other people either," he added.

The way he said that last sentence, I thought the words "mixing with" implied something unspoken.

"Did Bobby mix with . . . other women?"

"Bobby was not a one-woman man, if that's what you're asking."

"Yes, that's what I'm asking," I said, trying to erase all judgment from my voice.

"Anyone who was to get involved with Bobby shoulda known that. A charming guy like that? He ain't gonna be faithful to a gal like Birdy forever, I don't care how rich or beautiful she was. And she was plenty rich and beautiful, let me tell you. A real looker, and loaded."

"Did you ever hear them fight?"

He shrugged. "They had their problems."

I lowered my voice and asked cautiously, "Did he ever hit her?"

"What? No, nothing like that. Bobby woulda never. They just argued."

"What'd they argue about?"

"Normal stuff. Money issues. Bobby's going out. The stuff married couples argue about, okay?"

"So they never, like, talked about getting a divorce?"

"You young people think divorce is the answer to everything. This was the 1950s, young lady. People didn't get divorced at the drop of a hat. Besides . . ."

I could see in his dark eyes, which appeared clouded and far away, that he was remembering something he wasn't sharing. "Besides what?"

"Besides nothing."

"Please, Mr. DeMarcos."

"Don't you have to run home and cook dinner for your husband or something?"

I let the sexist comment slide. By my calculations, he was around eighty years old. I wasn't about to try to teach him the ways of the twenty-first century, and I wasn't about to get into an argument with him. "I read that Dr. Grodin called Birdy 'unstable.' When do you think Birdy's . . . instability began? Was she always unstable?"

He looked away, as if he didn't want to meet my eyes, and dug his hands into his pockets. I wondered if he was searching for his cigarettes, as he seemed agitated when his hands came out empty. "Dunno. I only worked there since the June before. The guy who worked there before me quit. I met him the day I got offered the job when he was moving out of the coach house."

"Do you remember his name?"

"Lady, I'm eighty-two years old. No, I don't remember his name! I'm lucky if I can remember my own damn name. I do remember he was a family member, though. I think he mighta been a nephew. I remember, when I asked him why he was quitting, him telling me that things hadn't been the same recently. He just didn't want to live there and work there no more. I remember, 'cause I felt kind of . . . suspicious, you know? Like should I take the job or not? But Bobby took good care of me. And if he had, well, certain errands for me to do, he always paid me extra for those, in cash."

For a man who could barely remember his "own damn name," he certainly seemed to remember quite a lot. I pictured him back then, in his khakis and white T-shirt, his black, greased-back hair, doing "errands" for Bobby that perhaps his predecessor, Edgar's nephew, had been uncomfortable with, getting tipped for his trouble in cash, riding around in a two-toned '50s Chevrolet, a cigarette dangling from his lips.

"What about Amelia, the child?" I said softly. "Why do you thi—"

"I ain't talking about her," Lorenzo DeMarcos said abruptly.

"I'm sorry, I wa—"

"This interview, or whatever the hell this is, is over."

With that, Lorenzo DeMarcos turned around, went into his house, and slammed the door behind him.

I didn't need to be Hercule Poirot to understand that he knew a lot more than he was telling.

12

GENEALOGY

OVER TIME I'D LEARNED THAT the trick to acting, and lying, was to believe what you were saying. I'd learned it was a good idea not to create too elaborate of a story, not to back yourself into a corner, but simply to cover your tracks, just in case.

"I have a sore throat," I told Chris, in a scratchy voice, when I punched in at the library on Wednesday.

"Bummer," he said.

"The clinic can get me in at eleven. You know, just to make sure it's not strep?"

"Oh." He was looking at me with a confused expression, his brows furrowed, as if he wasn't sure why I was telling him all this. "Um, good idea, I guess?"

"Can you cover for me?"

Relief spread across his face: I wasn't asking for sympathy, merely a favor. "Oh, yeah, sure."

We moved away from the time clock and went to the main area together. Chris shelved books while I performed various duties at the circ desk. I checked out books to patrons, helped with the copy machine, and called someone who had left their driver's license as a bookmark in Cormac McCarthy's *The Road* in the outside book drop. I tried to clean a book on climate change that seemed to be soiled with dog poop. I used rubber gloves, Clorox, did my best, and then put it in a plastic bag in the "Damaged" box for Eleanor to deal with later.

At ten to eleven, I went up to Chris and said, "So, I'm going to
go now. Hopefully it won't take too long."

"Are you gonna punch out, or . . . ?"

"I'm thinking this will be my lunch break."

"Yeah, okay, got it."

"I just wanted to let you know in case I'm, like, a few minutes
late." I smiled at him, stroking my throat for good measure. "Thanks."

The historical society was only open during my work hours (Monday through Friday nine to five; closed from twelve to one), so
I couldn't go there before or after work or over the noon hour. I
walked inside the pink Victorian house and was met in the foyer
by a Latina woman. She was about fifty years old, with a graying
brown bob, boot-cut jeans, and tortoiseshell glasses over wide-set
brown eyes.

"Hi there," I said.

"Good morning. Welcome to the Historical Society. I'm Carmen. Do you need help with anything? Or did you come to just look
around?"

I glanced at the displays of old dresses and suits on mannequins,
architectural drawings, and arrowheads behind glass. "Help," I said.
Realizing how that sounded, I added, "I mean, I'm here for help, not
to browse." Then I smiled, starting over. "My name's Lilly Bly. My
husband and I bought the Lawrence Mansion on Hill Street, and I
wonder if you might be able to tell me about the family?"

"You bought the Lawrence Mansion?" she repeated.

Here we go again, I thought. Well, at least she hadn't called it *the
Murder House*. "Yes, we just moved in last week."

"I saw the 'For Sale' sign had been taken down. Wow. It's an amazing house. But I mean, that history, right?"

"Yeah, well, we didn't know the history when we bought it."

Carmen sighed, shaking her head. "And of course, the circus society didn't exactly print the headlines on the brochures. So, now that you know about that, what else do you want to know?" She gestured to a room off the foyer, and said, "Come into my office, please, sit down."

Carmen sat behind an antique oak desk, while I sat in a purple velvet armchair facing her. I ran my fingers over its soft arms as I said, "I met the caretaker who lived in the coach house when it happened. Or what was once the coach house. Now it's our detached garage."

"Jeez, that guy's still alive? He must be a hundred years old."

"Actually, he's only eighty-two, and still sharp as a tack. He told me he inherited his job from Edgar Lawrence's nephew. Well, he thought it was probably a nephew. I checked online, but without knowing anyone's names, I couldn't find anything. I wonder if you knew who that might be, or if he's still around?"

The crow's feet at the outer corners of Carmen's eyes crinkled as she thought. "I believe we did some genealogy research on the Lawrence family a few years ago." She went to her computer and did a search, and then something came noisily out of the printer.

"This might tell the story. There were four Lawrence brothers. Edgar only had Beatrice. 'Wags' never had any children. But John and James both had several kids," she said, showing me the page.

"Only two of the nephews are still alive," I said.

"Or were as of 2002."

"Right. Well, the caretaker was a man, that's for sure, so if he was Charles or James Jr., and if they're still around, and if they still remember anything, I guess I'm in luck."

"Hmm," she said, as if she didn't like the sound of those odds. "Anything else I can help you with?"

I felt a bit sheepish asking her this, but I forged ahead anyway. "You wouldn't know how I could get my hands on Beatrice Lawrence's medical records, would you?"

Lawrence Family Tree*
*LAST UPDATED 2002

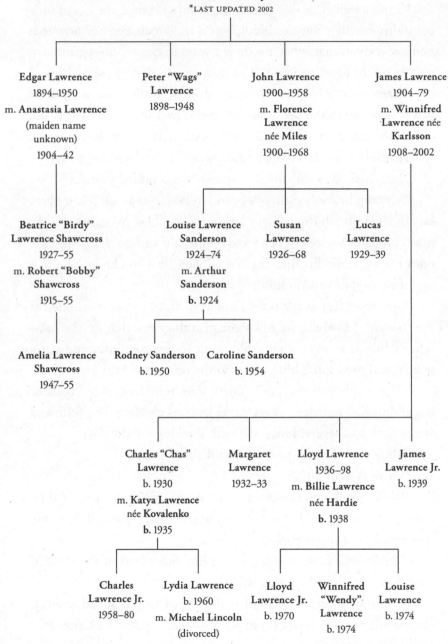

Edgar Lawrence
1894–1950
m. Anastasia Lawrence
(maiden name
unknown)
1904–42

**Peter "Wags"
Lawrence**
1898–1948

John Lawrence
1900–1958
m. Florence
Lawrence
née Miles
1900–1968

James Lawrence
1904–79
m. Winnifred
Lawrence née
Karlsson
1908–2002

**Beatrice "Birdy"
Lawrence Shawcross**
1927–55
m. Robert "Bobby"
Shawcross
1915–55

**Louise Lawrence
Sanderson**
1924–74
m. Arthur
Sanderson
b. 1924

**Susan
Lawrence**
1926–68

**Lucas
Lawrence**
1929–39

**Amelia Lawrence
Shawcross**
1947–55

Rodney Sanderson
b. 1950

Caroline Sanderson
b. 1954

**Charles "Chas"
Lawrence**
b. 1930
m. Katya Lawrence
née Kovalenko
b. 1935

**Margaret
Lawrence**
1932–33

Lloyd Lawrence
1936–98
m. Billie Lawrence
née Hardie
b. 1938

**James
Lawrence Jr.**
b. 1939

**Charles
Lawrence Jr.**
1958–80

Lydia Lawrence
b. 1960
m. Michael Lincoln
(divorced)

**Lloyd
Lawrence Jr.**
b. 1970

**Winnifred
"Wendy"
Lawrence**
b. 1974

**Louise
Lawrence**
b. 1974

She seemed taken aback, and now that I had said the words aloud, I understood why. Interviewing the nephew was a bit of a lark but going after someone's medical records sounded personal and creepy. "Medical records are difficult to get ahold of due to privacy issues. You could try calling the doctor's office or hospital where she was treated, or the state archive's office, but without proof that you're related to her and need them for your own medical reasons—well, it won't be easy."

"I see."

"May I ask what you're doing with all this information? I mean, you seem more curious than the average new homeowner."

More obsessed, I knew she meant. What was I supposed to tell her? *Oh, just trying to figure out if a ghost lives in my house or if I'm going insane.*

"Curious, yes," I said. "I've become quite interested in Haven Circus history since we moved here."

"Aha!"

"Aha?" I repeated. Had I been found out?

"You're thinking about writing a book, aren't you?" she said enthusiastically, smiling.

"Oh, well," I said, noncommittal.

"I get it, you don't want to talk about it quite yet. Well, I think that's exciting."

The grandfather clock behind her struck once on the half hour. Eleven thirty. I knew I should be getting back to work and stood. "Thanks so much for your help," I said, grabbing the paper from the desk and putting it in my bag.

She handed me her card: *Carmen Alvarez, Director, Haven Historical Society.* "Let me know if there's anything else I can do. Welcome to Haven, Lilly. And good luck on that book you may or may not be writing!"

"Thanks again."

She walked me to the door. I got as far as the large, wraparound porch, decorated with mums, pumpkins, and gourds, when Carmen said, "Oh, and Lilly?" and I stopped and turned back.

This time it was her turn to have a sheepish expression. Her head was cocked to the side, and her cheeks were flushed. "Of course, I don't really believe in such things, but a few times a year we get people coming in here who have driven by your house, or who have heard the history, and they want to know, 'Hey, the Lawrence Mansion, is that place haunted?' And I have to add, in terms of my heritage, well, many people, even some of my relatives, are convinced that the spirit world exists. My grandmother tells stories of ghosts she's seen and talked to, her sister, her first husband. . . . I mean, to her, they're not even scary, they're just, like, relatives she still argues with, you know?"

I imagined Carmen's grandmother yelling at her dead sister for gripping her calf, and I did my best to smile.

She smiled back at me, shaking her head. "So anyway, I have to ask you, crazy as it sounds, is that place haunted?"

I felt like this was a trick question. On the one hand, here was someone who may have been open to hearing all about the supernatural incidents that had been happening to me. Maybe someone in her family—her grandmother, for example—could even help me figure everything out. Maybe her grandmother would know how to talk to a ghost and put her to rest, so that I could live in the house in peace. On the other hand, Carmen was the director of the historical society, a professional woman in tortoiseshell glasses, and the idea of confiding in her made me anxious. Hadn't she said she didn't really believe in ghosts?

So I just stood there, trying to figure out how to answer, when Carmen laughed and said, "I'm sorry, listen to me. Forget I said anything. You must think I'm seriously loopy to ask such a question."

"No, of course not. I mean, I'm happy to tell you." Carmen stood in the doorway while I leaned against a column on the wraparound porch, facing her. "An old house like that, it creaks and leaks and moans, there are mice crawling around spelling words in the dust, the bidet spurts out streams of water as if it's possessed. . . . But for everything that happens, I'm sure there's always a reasonable explanation."

I was acting now, of course, playing the part of the New Homeowner writing a book about the Murder House. I think her name was Jane. Capable and competent, she was a multitasker, not just a writer but also a renovation pro. She was diligent, thrifty, and competent. Never suffering from anxiety or self-doubt, she accepted the world and its challenges with composure. She was a good wife and worker, and the only reason she ever lied was to spare others from trouble. On occasion she heard some strange noises, saw some strange things, but she never gave any of these sensory aberrations more than a moment's thought. There were bound to be unusual sounds and sights in an old house. They were caused by creaking wood, scurrying mice, and dripping leaks. Not ghosts. Jane the New Homeowner was sure of that. The play or movie in which I was the lead was a wacky comedy, after all. Something like *The Ghost and Mrs. Muir* or *Blithe Spirit,* if not quite *Scooby-Doo.*

Carmen smiled. "Thanks for humoring me. Sounds like you have a project on your hands."

I did one of Jack's *whatcha gonna do* gestures, arms out to the sides, palms raised, that squinch of resignation on my face. "You can say that again."

13

TWO CEMETERIES

IT WAS PAST 11:30, which was when my lunch break was over, and I had to get back to work. And if I'd gone the same route I'd taken to get to the historical society, I would have. But instead, I took a side route to circumvent a leaf-collecting truck, and as I did so, I happened to drive by the cemetery and felt compelled to stop. That is, I felt as if I wasn't the one driving, but as if someone else were at the wheel, pulling me through the gates.

Haven Cemetery was a typical Midwestern cemetery, with the poor folk noted by mere headstones, and the richest, most prominent figures in town remembered by towering white angels and marble family blocks. I supposed the Lawrence family would be easy to spot, and was I ever right.

The cemetery was large—several acres, some developed, others still empty—with green undulating slopes and valleys. At the top of the highest hill was a circus wagon carved from stone; on its broad side read LAWRENCE FAMILY. I was half surprised I hadn't seen it from the road—or from the highway three miles away, for that matter.

I parked the car, grabbed my navy peacoat from the passenger seat and put it on, and then walked up to the monument and paused. Beneath the circus wagon, on the ground, were over a dozen headstones. Edgar Lawrence and Anastasia had a double plot, with their birth dates (1894 and 1904, respectively) and death dates (1950 and 1942). To the right of this plot was Beatrice's. Her headstone read:

Beatrice "Birdy" Lawrence Shawcross
Beloved Mother and Daughter
b. 1927–d. 1955

I wondered who had paid for her headstone, who was the executor of the will? Who had decided she was a "beloved mother and daughter"? (And not, I noticed, "beloved wife"?) Maybe one or both of her surviving uncles, James and John. They had apparently still wanted her buried in the family plot, and they had wanted to acknowledge that her father had loved her—that wasn't strange—but also that her daughter had. Her daughter, whom she had murdered. Amelia was beside her:

Amelia Lawrence Shawcross
Beloved Daughter and Granddaughter
b. 1947–d. 1955
An Angel in Death as Well as Life

And there was Bobby, on the other side of Amelia. It occurred to me that, back in the 1950s, usually a wife was buried in her husband's family plot, but in this case, the entire family had been buried in the Lawrence Family plot, even the philandering son-in-law. His gravestone merely read:

Robert Shawcross

There were no dates given, as if the uncle (or whoever had made the decision and payments) hadn't wanted to spend the extra money for an additional line.

I kneeled in front of Beatrice's grave, wishing I had flowers. I didn't know if her spirit was stuck in my house (her house), or if it could travel, but I knew that cemeteries were powerful places. Wherever bodies were, wherever bones were, there was supposed to be a special sort of "energy," and so I cleared my throat and spoke, hoping she could hear me.

"I guess you know who I am. I'm the woman who lives in your house. I know we're not the handiest people in the world, but I promise you, we'll try to take good care of it. We love it. I love it. Even now, when it scares me, I can't imagine living anywhere else." I paused for a moment, listening. A leaf blower sounded a long way off, like a mechanical whisper in the wind. "I don't know what caused you to do the things you did, but I want you to know, everything is okay now."

Of course, this wasn't the least bit true; I had no idea if "everything" was "okay." I thought of my father. Was "everything okay" with him? Or was he haunting the basement of my uncle's rented duplex in Rogers Park? Was some troubled woman at his gravesite, telling him she was going to take good care of the place?

"You can rest in peace now," I said. "That's what you want, isn't it?" I felt silly and self-conscious. How did I know what she wanted? How did I know she was truly here, listening, that she wasn't just a bunch of decomposed bones helping to create a rich ecosystem for worms? How did I know I wasn't simply talking to worms? (Was my father nothing more than worms now? I didn't want to—couldn't—believe that.)

I took a deep breath and forged ahead anyway. It was time to get to the point.

"The thing is, Birdy . . . Ms. Lawrence . . . if you can hear me, I want to ask you to quit scaring me. I'm doing what I can, you know, to find out what happened and, well, release you or whatever, but that whole bath thing, your grabbing my leg like that? It freaked me out. And the word in dust and . . . everything. So, I'm asking you to give me time. And peace. Can you do that? I want to put you to peace, too."

I wasn't the most religious person in the world, but I wasn't stupid. I knew that prayer was as much about listening as talking. So I shut my mouth and waited. I waited for a long time. I thought of

Birdy jumping off that cliff. I hoped she'd died quickly, immediately. I thought of my father, of how he had looked when he'd died, swollen and bulging, and I shook that image out of my head. I thought of my dead babies. My dead . . . whatever they were. I remembered my first miscarriage. I'd been nine weeks pregnant and crampy and had called in sick to work. Jack had asked if he should stay home, too, but I'd told him not to be silly.

"Everything is okay," I'd said, but of course, I'd said it more to myself than to him, because deep down, I think I knew something was wrong. About midmorning I went to the bathroom and out it came. I had fished it out of the toilet with a slotted spoon. It was nine weeks old and looked like little alien tissue. But I still loved it. I called my doctor to ask her what I should do with it. My doctor wasn't available, but I spoke to a physician's assistant who said she was sorry for my loss. She explained that miscarriages were very common, there wasn't a need to test it, I could dispose of it. She asked if I was bleeding heavily. I thought of the word "dispose." I already couldn't remember the question, but I said, "No." She said to come in if I started to. *Started to what?* I wondered. Dispose? I hung up the phone and stared at my dead baby, at its gel-like, wormy body, its little arm buds. The word "dispose" rang in my ears. No, not rang—buzzed. I felt like a bee had crawled inside my ears and was buzzing and buzzing until I thought I would go crazy. *Dispose. Dispose. Dispose.* I thought of flushing the remains down the toilet, like a dead goldfish. I thought of throwing it into the trash, like a used coffee filter. Finally, I realized I didn't need to "dispose" of it; I could bury it. The word "bury" had a permanent feel, a hard thud in the chest, which was what I needed. But where?

Not in the backyard. Jack and I were merely renting the house we lived in, a teardown in a fringe neighborhood. I wanted to bury it in a place where I could visit, years later, or every day for the rest of my life.

I tried to call Jack at his work, but he didn't answer. I didn't think I could sit in the apartment, with the dead baby, all day by myself, waiting for him to come home. So, I put it in a plastic baggie, pulled on a hoodie, grabbed my purse, and carried it in my sweatshirt's pocket to find a peaceful resting place.

Our neighborhood was no Lincoln Park, where I'd lived when my father was alive. I had taken for granted the million-dollar town houses with their inlaid cabinets and vaulted ceilings. I had taken for granted the magnificent park with the lily pond and zoo, the lovely tree-lined streets busy with boutiques, restaurants, and cafés. I still frequented those shops sometimes, with my credit card, but you couldn't pay rent with a credit card, and so Jack and I were living in the best place we could manage, a place where the windows had bars on them.

In this neighborhood was one tiny park, about three blocks from our apartment. It was the size of an elementary classroom, and consisted of some swings, a rusty metal slide spray-painted with graffiti, a sandbox filled with hypodermic needles, and a square of dead grass. I walked there, slowly, stopping every so often to rest my hand on a bus bench or a mailbox. There were no trees in this neighborhood, no shade, no wrought iron park benches on which to sit. And then I glanced around, perusing the options, the baggie moist in my sweaty hand inside my pocket, although it was March, and cool. It occurred to me that perhaps I was bleeding heavily, and suddenly I felt weak. I sat down on the patch of brown grass and put my head between my knees, breathing in and out. Cars and buses whizzed by, spewing exhaust and loud revving noises. I knew that one of the cars could stop at any time and someone could get out, someone who would not have my best interests at heart, but I couldn't move. I felt empty and numb.

I wanted my daddy. I wanted my mommy, the mommy I'd had, or had thought I'd had, anyway, when I was four or five. Most of all, I wanted Jack.

Where should we bury the baby? I imagined asking him, and then I knew: the cemetery. Of course. I wanted to talk to him, but I could picture my cell phone on the kitchen table where I'd left it after calling the doctor's office and then Jack. I wanted to go to the cemetery with him, but I didn't think I could manage backtracking to the house, calling him, and then walking back this way and then some if he didn't answer. I felt a gush of blood leave my body; the pad I was wearing felt heavy and full. I knew I couldn't make it across town to the cemetery where my dad was buried, but I wondered if I could make it to the nearest one. Where was the nearest one? I felt disoriented and dizzy. I thought about trying to figure out where the nearest cemetery was, and then taking a bus or the L to get there. The very idea sounded impossible, like trying to take the Red Line to the moon. I took out my wallet and found a twenty. Good. I would take a cab and worry about how to get home later.

As I waited at the curb to hail a cab, a white guy with a goatee and no hair leaned out the passenger window of a Trans Am and yelled, "Fuck me, bitch!" and then sped by. I wondered if he'd have yelled that if he'd known what was in the baggie inside my hoodie's pocket. If he'd have known that the pad I was wearing was full and heavy with blood. Would I still be a bitch by whom he wanted to be fucked? The idea made me feel powerful, not scared. I was beyond anyone's desire or hate.

A cabbie pulled over, and I got in and told him to go to the local cemetery. He asked me if I was okay. I was surprised by his prescience. "Why do you ask?"

"You look kind of pale," he said, and I could see he was concerned, whether for me or the back seat of his cab, I wasn't sure.

"Funeral today," I said by way of explanation. Through the rearview mirror, I saw him take in my unwashed hair, my faded Northwestern hoodie and yoga pants, and then nod and pull back into traffic. He was a cab driver in a city of three million; this was surely not the most unusual fare he'd ever had.

The short drive cost twelve dollars. I handed him the twenty, and then, worried perhaps that I had stained the back seat of his cab, told him to keep the change. He dropped me off at the front entrance. I walked unsteadily down the asphalt path. I was sweating and didn't feel well. My legs were heavy and weak.

I had never been inside this cemetery, although now that I was here, I knew I'd driven by it several times. It was not a rich person's cemetery. There weren't many trees, and the asphalt path was cracked. The headstones themselves were mostly modest, with the occasional winged angel or tall cross scattered among the graves, most of which were overrun by crabgrass.

A shady tree with large, protective boughs was farther down the path, and I walked there slowly. When I finally arrived, I sat down. The tree was an oak, which symbolized strength, family, endurance, wisdom—everything I could possibly need.

I took the baggie out of my pocket. I'd been imagining the life inside me as a chubby-cheeked Gerber baby, but this looked like an alien hatched prematurely from an egg. I didn't love it any less. If anything, I loved it more, the way I'd always been drawn to the sickly runts of any litter.

It was then I thought of the one I'd aborted. He or she had been even older than nine weeks, even closer to looking like the picture on the side of the baby food jars, but of course, I hadn't buried that one. It had been "disposed" of, and for the first time, I wondered what that meant. Had they thrown him or her into the trash? Flushed him or her down some drain that led into a sewer?

Where was that baby now?

Where is my baby?

Where is my baby?

I want my baby.

Suddenly, I felt a familiar twinge of regret that crested into a wash of despair that was overpowering. I had "disposed" of my first baby, had lost this one, had lost my father, had lost my mother—although she wasn't dead—and Jack seemed like someone I barely knew, like a stranger. I no longer wanted to be alive.

The thought of killing myself, however, seemed like too much work. I decided to just lie there until . . . well, until forever. Then I would join my father. The thought made me happy. It would be good to see him again, and I knew he would understand, if anyone would, why I no longer wanted to live. Yes, he would understand that too well. I wondered how long it would take if I kept bleeding. I supposed it wouldn't take long. But first I had to bury my baby.

It wasn't quite spring yet, and the ground was still hard, having been frozen only a couple of weeks before. I searched in my purse for anything I could use as a trowel, and found my set of keys, which would do. I had to move away from the roots of the tree a bit, but I finally found a place soft enough to dig a shallow grave. I didn't look as I set the baggie into the hole and covered it with earth. I put my keys back into my purse and lay down underneath the tree, using my purse as a pillow. I felt tired and weak.

A warm, calm feeling came over me, and suddenly I understood, with a pleasant, comforting certainty, that this had all been a bad dream. I was still pregnant. I was in a beautiful house with the man I loved. My father was holding court in the living room, telling a story about a horse he'd bet on, a long shot that had come in first. Rich, earthy smells came from another room. Sautéed mushrooms, maybe portabellas. I lay in a warm feather bed, my head on the softest pillow. I thought, *Just a few minutes ago I'd believed everyone I loved was dead. But that was just a bad dream. Silly Lilly!*

*   *   *

I woke up in a hospital room. An IV pinched my arm. Later I would learn that I had lost too much blood and had passed out, that an elderly widower had seen me and found a groundskeeper, and that they had called an ambulance; now the doctors were preparing me for a D&C. But I didn't know any of that yet. All I knew was that I was cold and tired, that I'd lost two babies, that my father was dead, that we lived in a run-down house in a dangerous neighborhood— *Fuck me, bitch!*—and that Jack loved me, and I loved him, and so I was going to have to live.

I never told Jack half of that. I told him I had gone to the cemetery to bury the fetus, "so that we can visit it every day."

Neither of us ever set foot in that cemetery again.

14

HARD WORK

WHEN I RETURNED TO THE LIBRARY, I saw that there was a line at the circulation desk, and that both Chris and Eleanor Sawnhorn were checking out items for patrons. My stomach did a nausea-inducing somersault, for Eleanor almost never worked the circ desk. To save time, I didn't even bother to go to the staff room to put my bag in a locker and hang up my coat, but simply stuffed them into a bottom shelf, beside the lost and found box. "Hello, Eleanor, hello, Chris," I said in my most professional voice.

Chris turned around, said, "Hey," and then shrugged, as if to indicate there was nothing he could do about whatever had happened or was about to happen.

"I'm filling in for you," Eleanor said, her words precise and clipped, a voice like Katherine Hepburn's. Eleanor stood only about five feet tall in sneakers, but she was a formidable presence. I remembered Chris's warning. *Like, what you don't want to do is get on Eleanor's bad side.*

"Thank you," I said. "I'm sorry. They were backed up at the doctor's office, and then naturally I got behind a tractor, and . . ."

She waved me off. I stopped talking and just stood there while Eleanor continued to help patrons until there was a lull. Then she grabbed something from beneath the desk, took a pen from the pen and pencil holder, turned to me, and said, "This time sheet confirms you had a two-hour-and-fifteen-minute lunch break. Please initial here." She smiled at me with forced politeness.

Two hours and fifteen minutes? I hadn't wanted to check my cell phone or my car clock on the way home, and the amount of time seemed impossible to me. *Merde!* My cheeks were hot, and I suspected they were red as beets. I initialed the time sheet.

"I'm sorry," I said. "It won't happen again."

"You can tell that to Mr. Williams. He'll want to see you when your shift is over. Which won't be long now." She peered at me with her small, perceptive bird's eyes, nodded once, and then left.

"Oh, man," I said to Chris when she was gone. He was standing beside me, wearing a My Chemical Romance T-shirt and khakis, trying to tape together the cover of a bodice-ripper that pictured a busty woman in a purple dress and a shirtless man carrying a sword. Both the cover and the dress were ripping apart in their respective middles. "I think I'm on Eleanor's bad side now."

"Sorry," he said. "I tried to cover for you, but the desk got crazy busy."

"It's not your fault. My appointment took longer than I thought."

He looked up from the paperback and asked, "How are you feeling?"

He was gazing at me with concern in his kind eyes. He was so nice; I felt bad for having lied to him. A high school boy approached the desk to check out the *10 Things I Hate About You* DVD, a film about lying with a happy ending. "Better," I said.

When my shift was over, I knocked on the open door of Carl Williams's office. He looked up from his computer, smiled, and said, "Lilly! Good afternoon. Please, come in."

I felt like I was stepping into the principal's office, but he was certainly the most amiable principal I'd ever had. He motioned for me to sit down.

"Lilly, you've been with us for a few days now, and I just want to check in with you, to see how everything's going."

Carl took a sip of something from a Banned Books mug (organic fair-trade regular coffee was my guess), and waited, his eyes friendly behind his glasses. I almost told him that I was exhausted, that I was depressed about having probably ruined my chances for pregnancy, that I was being haunted by the town's most famous murderer/suicide, and that I was embarrassed about having been reprimanded (however rightly so) by Eleanor Sawnhorn.

But I wanted to appear professional, and so I took a deep breath. I became the fetching single mom supporting her chronically ill son who truly needed the job and was capable and upbeat to boot. "Great!" I said, enthusiasm oozing from my voice and tenderness coming from my sad but optimistic smile, or so I hoped. "Everything is going great!"

"Um, well, I'm glad to hear that," he said, his voice uncertain. "I like you, and I'd like for this position to work out for you."

I sat up straighter. "Is there a chance that it won't work out for me?" I asked.

"No, no, of course not. I mean, well, not exactly. Well, perhaps. You know, Eleanor can be a bit . . . fastidious with the time sheet. And the thing is, you've been forgetting to punch in and out. And today you were gone for over two hours at lunch. And I just want to make sure that . . . you know, we need to keep pretty tight control over your hours. Like I said, it's the city that pays your wages. They like clean records. That's all."

"I'm sorry about today. I had a doctor's appointment. I told Chris I was going, but . . . it took longer than I expected."

"I hope everything is okay?"

"Yes, fine. Well, it isn't strep, anyway. That's why I went in. I wanted to make sure I wasn't contagious, that I wouldn't infect anyone else," I said, trying to sound like a responsible coworker and employee of the city. "I should have called when the appointment dragged on, but . . . my cell phone died. I apologize. It won't happen again. And I will try to do better with the time sheet, I promise."

He smiled and stood up, telling me our meeting was over. "Thank you for being so understanding, Lilly. I'm glad everything is going well. Have a good night, and we'll see you tomorrow, okay?"

"Sounds good," I said, smiling brightly, or what I hoped was brightly, and hurried out of the room, out of the library, and into my car. I was already halfway home when I realized: I hadn't punched out.

The following day, a Thursday, I concentrated on my duties and was rewarded with an uneventful time at the library. Jack was already home when I pulled into the drive just after five. I suspected he was still worried about me from Monday's "episode" and had somehow arranged to get home earlier than usual.

Needless to say, I had no intention of telling him about my visit to the historical society and cemetery or about my struggles at the library. I shifted into "acting normal" mode, prepared to prove to him that I wasn't going over the deep end.

I stepped inside the house to the scent of something earthy and spicy simmering in the Dutch oven. It reminded me of all the times he'd cooked for me in Chicago, and my heart felt full for Jack then. He was such a hard worker and good caretaker, and I was such a . . . "dreamer" was the word my father had often used. ("This country is built on dreams, honey, don't let anyone ever tell you different.") Even so, I had also worked hard. I'd spent over half of my life waitressing, auditioning, acting, teaching. It had only been since the last miscarriage that I had, well, lost my motivation.

I found him in the kitchen, stirring what looked like chili with one hand, and holding a clipboard in the other.

"That smells good," I said, giving him a hug. "What's with the clipboard?"

"Hi, honey. Just putting together a short list of some of the things it would be nice to get fixed. I mean, over time. We can't afford to do any of this right now, but, you know, if we save up, or if I get ambitious . . ."

"Let me see." I grabbed the clipboard out of his hand and read his list.

> Kitchen: floorboards, paint, new hardware. Dishwasher?
> 1st floor bathroom: broken tile, leaky faucet.
> Windows throughout or just the cracked ones?
> Living room: paint, get fireplace working.
> Dining room: *fix hole in ceiling!*

It was amazing how easy things seemed when you put them in a list. "Totally manageable, right?"

"Oh, yeah, no problem," he said, laughing. Then he asked, "So how was work?"

"Excellent!" I'd punched in five minutes early, focused on my responsibilities, and remembered to punch out. This wasn't the highest bar in the world, but still, if I were being graded on improvement from Wednesday, I would give myself an A+. "What about you?"

"Good." He looked up at me, a concerned expression on his face. "But remember, tomorrow I leave for that trip to Minnesota and the UP. I'll be gone for about a week. It's not something I can cancel, but I want to make sure . . . I mean, are you going to be okay, here by yourself?"

Jack's work required him to travel a lot, but I'd forgotten about this trip. A week! Here by myself, to learn more about what had happened, to continue my research, without having to worry about his telling me that everything I was experiencing was all in my head.

The idea made me shiver, with a mixture of dazzling excitement and jittery anxiety, which I tried to mask by nodding vigorously. "I'll be fine," I said.

When I got home from work on Friday, I fed Olivier, and then ate a bowl of cereal for dinner while I browsed the online white pages for every Charles, Charlie, Chuck, Chas, James, Jim, and Jimmy Lawrence in Haven, Wisconsin.

At about seven o'clock, when I thought the good people of Haven might have finished eating, I started making phone calls. I was intent on finding the nephew of Edgar Lawrence who had worked for the Lawrence family before Lorenzo DeMarcos.

My first call was to Charles and Doris Lawrence.

"Hello?"

"Hello, is this Charles Lawrence?"

"If this is a salesman . . ."

"No, this is Lilly . . ."—I decided not to use my last name and simply trailed off—". . . and I'm doing some research on Birdy Lawrence."

"On who?"

"Birdy Lawrence. Her given name was Beatrice. The trapeze artist?"

"Look, are ya trying to sell me something, or ain't ya?"

I took a deep breath and raised my voice. "You wouldn't happen to be related to Beatrice Lawrence, would you?"

"You don't need to holler," he yelled back. "Why? Did we win something?"

The next calls didn't go much better. Charles Anthony Lawrence claimed he wasn't related. Chuck said I had the wrong number. Neither Charlie D. Lawrence nor C. and K. Lawrence were home. I left messages, asking them to call if they were relations.

I then moved on to the Jameses, the Jims, and the Jimmys, where I experienced more of the same.

It was nearly nine when I finished calling everyone on my short list, and my mind turned to Jack, and the house.

I'd been frustrated with Jack's unrelenting logic and his always-right attitude, but I also knew I probably hadn't been fair to him. Buying this place when we couldn't afford it had been my idea. I'd agreed to get a job and reduce my spending to live here. And we'd talked about fixing it up—well, as much as we could on our shoestring budget and without any home renovation skills. Instead, I'd gotten a low-paying job at which I was not even excelling, had reduced my spending some but not enough, and had done nothing to fix up the place.

I rose from the kitchen chair and walked around the first floor, until I found Jack's clipboard with the list of home improvement projects sitting on top of a built-in cabinet in the living room.

Except for "paint," Jack's list was mostly practical rather than aesthetic, and I didn't pretend I could fix a leaky faucet or patch a five-foot hole in the ceiling. But there were other things I could do. A couple of the biggest eyesores were the scratched and water-stained living room floors, and the deteriorating wallpaper in the dining room. I added to Jack's list: "Refinish living room floors" and "Take down wallpaper and paint dining room walls." I stood in the living room, examining the floor, thinking. I would have loved to make it look like it did in those newspaper pictures back in the fifties.

I went to the kitchen, scooped up a willing Olivier with one hand and my laptop with the other, and took them upstairs to bed with me. Then I went online to see how hard it would be to refinish the hardwood floors myself. The answer appeared to be: very. Article after article said that this project was best left to the professionals, but they were too costly for us to afford. Even doing it myself wouldn't be cheap—that is, if I rented a floor sander. Renting a floor sander would cost hundreds of dollars and create enormous amounts of dust for me to breathe in, and every blogger and article author recommended it; using an electric hand sander would be inefficient, impractical, and difficult. But we owned a hand sander, and it was stored in the garage, not the basement, and using one would apparently be much less dusty. I watched a tutorial on YouTube. The no-nonsense woman wearing goggles and a tank top exposing buff arms whose channel was called "Get Her Done" made it look easy. Oh, I knew it would be harder for someone like me—someone without the goggles, the buff arms, or the do-it-yourself know-how—but it wouldn't be impossible. Would it?

I petted Olivier's belly and imagined Jack's face when he came home from his trip and found the floors sanded and refinished.

"Who did this?" he would say. His face would be grim at first. "Did you hire someone? How much did this cost? You know we can't afford—"

"Shh," I would interrupt, putting my finger to his lips. "I did it. All by myself. It barely cost a thing."

He would be so proud of me. His eyes would positively glow with love and respect, and his cheeks would flush with amazement. "You!" he would say.

"Me," I would agree.

And what about Birdy? "Look, Birdy," I would say, "look at your floors, returned to their former glory!" It was hard to imagine what would happen next. But surely, she wouldn't grab my calf with her icy hand. Whatever peaceful thing a ghost did to her house's new inhabitant, that's what Birdy would do to me.

Leave me in peace, perhaps.

Or cohabitate with me in peace. Anyway, it was worth a try.

*   *   *

Saturday morning, I went to the home improvement store and bought all of the supplies the online articles suggested—sandpaper to fit our electric sander, goggles, more N95 face masks, painter's tape, utility cloths, plastic to cover the furniture and vents, environmentally-safe varnish—and, as long as I was there, cereal, pistachio nuts, milk, cat food, and other groceries and household items, putting everything on the card. When I got home, I covered the furniture and vents in the living room with the plastic, while Olivier watched me, curious. I taped the plastic to the walls and the furniture to keep it from drifting away.

My plan was to spend Saturday and Sunday on the sanding. Jack's electric belt sander had a dust catcher, and if I opened the windows, kept an oscillating fan going, and wore a face mask, I didn't think I would breathe in too much dust, exposing my possible baby to any potential toxins from the old floors. I'd vacuum up the dust Sunday night and varnish the floors during the week, after my shifts at the library. By the time Jack returned a week from Saturday, they would be gorgeous.

But as the YouTubers and article authors had warned, hand-sanding turned out to be harder than it looked. My progress was slower than I'd expected. Much slower.

By 2:00 p.m. on Saturday, after four hours of steady work, I felt like my right arm was about to fall off, and I found I'd made about a five-foot-by-five-foot dent in what must have been at least an eight-hundred-square-foot living room. I took a break to have an apple and peanut butter for breakfast/lunch, which I ate on a folding chair, looking over my progress, and felt dejected.

Rome wasn't built in a day, I reminded myself. Actually, as my fourth and fifth graders and I had researched, it had taken about 1,200 years to build the Eternal City. But I wasn't building Rome, or even the Colosseum, just sanding a floor. That comparison made me feel better, and I got back to it.

This time I used my left hand, and as I worked, I began alternating hands when the soreness in one arm became unbearable. Every hour or so, I would go to the outside trash bin, carefully empty the dust bag, and take a short break before working again. Occasionally, I treated myself by replacing the worn-down sandpaper belt with a fresh one.

By early evening, I'd doubled my morning's work. I was *Getting Her Done!* After feeding Olivier and eating an organic frozen dinner, I decided that I needed to rest my aching arms to have the strength for a good long day of work on Sunday. I took a shower and then went to bed and read my Agatha Christie novel for a while. I was happy when Olivier came into the room and snuggled up beside me. I lay on my side, with Olivier curled into my chest, and I read with my book over him. His fur was a warm blankie, his purring a soporific lullaby. I fell asleep by nine.

I woke up in the morning to Olivier's paws poking at my cheeks. I squinted open my eyes and gazed into his squished-in face. He was looking at me with his "feed me" expression.

"You hungry, sweetie?" I cooed.

He jumped off the bed and meowed at me, as if to say, *Come on already.* I checked my phone: 11:00 a.m. I'd slept for fourteen hours. I had to pee, badly.

I went to sit up, but I couldn't. Something was holding me back, and I panicked for a moment before realizing it was nothing otherworldly, just good old-fashioned bodily pain. Every limb in my body ached. My arms were killing me. My back wouldn't move. My neck had a crick in it. My fingers were stiff and sore. Everything hurt.

I rolled onto my side, bent my knees, swung my feet over, held on to the bed, and raised myself up. I felt 137 years old.

I hobbled to the bathroom. Then I managed to get myself downstairs, feed Olivier, who was by now meowing frantically, and make myself a cup of tea. I took my tea into the living room, excited to survey my progress from the day before. *What the . . . ?* I stared at yesterday's "accomplishment" with astonishment. My body felt as if it had been hit by a truck for *this*? For this uneven patch of ugly light yellow that was maybe the size of a classroom whiteboard?

I wanted to cry, but I didn't have the energy.

Instead, I finished my tea, picked up the electric sander, and got back to work.

15

THE EMBRACE

I GOT MY PERIOD MONDAY MORNING and called in sick. I felt terrible. I don't mean physically—though I was just as sore as the day before, and crampy—I mean emotionally, mentally. Spiritually. I felt abandoned. I felt lost. I felt like I wanted to die.

I lay in bed all morning, thinking again about my abortion, or, as I often put it inside my head, "something that happened to me." But whom was I trying to kid? For I had been the one to schedule the appointment, hadn't I? The appointment hadn't "happened to me." I'd met with someone . . . I didn't know her role, exactly. Counselor? Nurse? Receptionist? She'd had the mien of a warm, maternal mom with a soft belly and compassionate eyes. She'd asked, "Have you given this plenty of thought and you're sure that this is what you want to do?" in a quiet, understanding tone.

I was twenty, a sophomore in college. Manuel, a senior philosophy major who was also a stoner in a rock band, was my first serious boyfriend. When my father asked him how he planned to make a living, the only time they'd met, Manuel had said, "A what?" But as soon as I saw him, from the audience in a smoky room, watching him play his guitar, his thin hips loose in his jeans, a dreamy expression on his face, and he turned to look at me and then kept looking—at me! Out of all the girls in that room!—I felt like I'd been punched in the gut. When they finished playing, he came over and we yelled in each other's ears for a few minutes until we gave up and started making out, right there in the club. We then spent six months together studying, discussing Sartre, watching movies, eating pizza, driving downtown to hear bands and see plays. Six months of my going to his gigs and his running lines with me, and then ogling at me as I'd played Pegeen in a miniskirt and crop top in *The Playboy of the Western World*. Six months together having the sort of fast, clumsy sex one has when one is twenty and cannot keep one's hands off the other person, until my diaphragm apparently didn't do its job and I found out I was pregnant. I loved him. Or at least, I thought I did. But I wasn't about to marry him and raise a kid with him, even if he asked, which he didn't.

I was in college. I hadn't wanted to be pregnant. I hadn't wanted to have a baby. I hadn't wanted to tell my dad.

When the kind woman asked me if I'd given the matter plenty of thought, I'd told her "Yes."

I had the abortion the following day. Manuel didn't come with me; he had a gig in Ann Arbor. My roommate Casey came instead. She drove me back to our dorm room, where I slept for a while and then worked on my European History paper. Something about the development of textiles. I had to stop every so often to hurry into the bathroom down the hall to vomit.

Now, lying in bed in my pajamas, I started to feel that prickling of shame and regret I'd felt ever since my first miscarriage, that feeling that my miscarriages and periods were some kind of punishment for my abortion. I knew the idea was ridiculous. I believed in safe and legal abortions. And I didn't fault my younger self for making the decision she'd made. But thirty-seven-year-old Lilly wanted to create some sort of impossible time machine that would magically protect them all: her younger self, her unborn baby, and current Lilly who wanted a baby of her own so badly.

I spent the morning under the covers feeling sick.

At some point, I got up and went downstairs, without bothering to get dressed. I fed and watered Olivier, cleaned out his litter box, made myself tea, and grabbed a few graham crackers and some Advil. Then I went upstairs to my study and sat in front of my computer with my tea and toddler's snack. I wanted to get my mind off everything. I checked my email and found in my inbox many "special discounts" from home stores, clothing stores, bookstores, drugstores, and pet stores. I did need a few toiletry items, so I clicked on the link for the drugstore site, and immediately felt better. I was reading product reviews, checking out the clearance section, putting items in my cart—shampoo, moisturizer, shavers, organic hand soap, lavender-scented laundry detergent, an eye shadow called "Bad to the Bone"—everything we needed, and some things we really didn't need. I felt focused and calm. Comfort washed over me the way a rush of contentment must wash over a drug user after a hit.

I looked at my cart one last time and then used the express checkout, but a message came up saying my credit card was declined. I checked the number and expiration date, and entered it again. Same thing. I tried another credit card. And a third. Those were all the credit cards I had. I stored the items in my cart, logged out, and called the 800-number on the back of the first credit card. A computerized voice asked for my credit card number and the last four digits of my social security number. I listened to the new balance: $10,342.10. Our limit for that card was ten thousand. We were over. Well over.

I did the same thing for the second card. A terrible fear lurched in my stomach because I knew that card had a higher limit. Twenty thousand. Surely we weren't over that limit? But then the voice gave me the new balance: $20,118.00.

The third and final card was my oldest one, and the balance had always staggered near the top of the $12,000 limit. I knew it would be over, and it was, by about two hundred dollars.

I wrote the numbers down and did some quick math: we had to pay over six hundred just to get under our limit again.

Jack was going to kill me. I'd like to say that our financial instability was the thing that bothered me the most, that I was worried for our future, that I was terrified we would be headed for bankruptcy, or even divorce, that Jack would leave me once he found out what a neurotic wife I truly was. But really, what bothered me the most, at that moment, was that I wouldn't be able to buy the things from the online drugstore that were in my cart. I started imagining a future without credit cards, and I began to panic. Jack gave me seventy-five dollars a week every Friday for food, gas, and incidentals, which I usually spent by Monday. What if I was at the checkout in the grocery store and didn't have enough cash? What if I was about to run out of gas? How could I live without credit?

A voice inside my head said, *Well, you're going to have to, aren't you?* It was a new voice, strict and unfamiliar. I hated it.

I lay down on the hardwood floor of my study thinking about how I'd been hoping to buy a nice wool rug for this room, and now I couldn't even afford the most plastic-feeling polyester one at the big-box store by the highway. After my father had gone bankrupt, he'd had to sell everything, even our furniture. My mom had pilfered a few items before divorcing him, including a Persian rug I'd always loved. It was antique, threadbare in spots, old money. Of course, there wasn't an ounce of old money that ran through any of our bodies. My mother had been a poor girl from Springfield who had cleverly seduced my father (or been swept off her feet by him, depending on who told the story) when she'd worked for him in his first restaurant; my father had come from a long line of bootleggers and card sharks, and he, for a while, anyway, had known how to turn everything he touched into gold. But my mother had ambitions, pretensions. She'd wanted to be accepted by the Lake Forest country club set, and so had hired a designer to make our Michigan Avenue penthouse look WASPy. I knew it wasn't real WASP. I'd gone to prep school with plenty of kids who had gazed a little too long at Daddy's shiny Rolls and Mother's ostentatious jewels, the slightest smirk on their boarding school faces, and who would have grinned over our marble Italian statues, if they'd ever been inside our home. (I had known better than to invite them.) I had been to enough of their places in the city and to their weekend "cabins" on lakes or rivers in Indiana and Wisconsin to know that our interior tried too hard, that even the antique Persian rug hadn't looked truly authentic in the library with the hardcover editions of leather-bound books that were never opened, except by me.

I had received much of my education in that room, which had been furnished with books designed to show off that you cherished first editions, that you read "The Classics," even though I was the only one who had ever cut the pages, and I'd only managed to get to a small percentage of them. The books had sold at auction, used to pay off back taxes. The collection had brought in over three hundred thousand dollars. My father had been quite pleased.

Then my mind went, as it often did when I thought of old possessions, to my Jag. My 1974 Jaguar XKE had been a present from my father when I'd graduated from Northwestern. It had been much more than a means of transportation: it was a symbol of my dad's belief in me, his pride in me, his extravagant love for me.

Which was why it had been so hurtful when Jack had made me sell it ten years later.

My back was hurting on the Persian-rugless hardwood floor, and so I got up and walked toward the bedroom. Olivier was pacing around the hallway. I picked him up and set him on the bed. He meowed his protest, but I rubbed his white, soft tummy until he was calm. Then I curled up under the covers, my feet next to his warm body.

I closed my eyes, telling myself that it was all a dream. My father had never gone bankrupt, I had no credit card debt, my mother hadn't abandoned me, my father had never done what he'd done, had never died, Jack wasn't gone all the time, I hadn't sold the Jag, I hadn't gotten my period, I'd never had an abortion, I'd never had an abortion, I'd never . . . And if I went to sleep, I would wake up and find that the world was once again whole. Silent tears ran from my eyelids past my temples to the hair above my ears. Why couldn't I get pregnant? Why couldn't I carry to term?

Where is my baby?

Where is my baby?

I want my baby.

"I want my baby," I said aloud. Hearing the words, the truth of them, surprised me into silence. I stopped crying. I said the words again, this time more quietly, barely a whisper. "I want my baby."

Then, two things happened at once: the floorboards creaked by the foot of the bed, and Olivier, who had been sleeping there, next to my feet, suddenly leapt up as if he'd been violently jolted. He meowed loudly, and then he began hissing, his back arched like a Halloween cat, his tail curved down, his fur electric, meowing and hissing at something I couldn't see.

The floorboards creaked again, and then Olivier leapt off the bed and ran out of the room and down the stairs.

That's when I saw an indentation appear in the comforter at the foot of the bed. I was lying on my back, and I quickly scooted my body away from the indentation, away from whatever Olivier had been hissing at, until my back pressed against the headboard. I used my feet to push myself up to a half-seated position, with my head and shoulder blades raised over my pillows, and my legs spread, heels dug into the bed, ready to push away whatever was crawling toward me.

The indentations in the comforter crept closer—*hand, knee, hand, knee, hand*—until what looked like a hand pressed down between my legs, and I found I couldn't move my feet or any part of my body at all. I was paralyzed with fear, unable to do anything but watch as the horror came closer. Something—someone—was now nearly on top of me, as if crouching, two indentations beside my waist, two between my legs, and this something or someone had to be some sort of . . . apparition, phantom, spirit, disembodied soul, specter, phantasm, something unholy and undead. A *ghost.*

"Birdy Lawrence?" I whispered. "Is that you?"

Or at least, I thought I whispered those words. I meant to whisper them. But they may have only been breaths, croaks, for I'm sure I was too petrified to speak.

I felt something touch me over the comforter, an icy pressure, on top of my stomach, *on top of my womb.* And then I felt two icy arms wrap around my waist.

Tears rolled down my cheeks as I realized I had said, "I want my baby," and now, Birdy Lawrence, who had borne and then killed her daughter, was embracing me, her frozen head perhaps lying on my empty womb, her snow-cold arms wrapped around me. Was she mocking my barrenness with her ghostly hug?

I was so terrified that without volition or will, warm urine left my body and spread through my thin pajama pants all over the sheets. I could feel it beneath my bottom, beneath my legs. I could smell it, a sharp, pungent scent.

"My God," I prayed/swore. "Why are you doing this? Please. Please. Let me go! Stop scaring me!"

And just like that, I felt released. The pressure—the frozen embrace—was gone. Birdy Lawrence was gone. I found myself lying there, in my puddle of piss, alone.

*   *   *

I threw off the covers, stripped the sheets, and hurried into the bathroom. I removed my clothes and wiped myself with a towel. Then I quickly got dressed and rushed down the stairs. I did not want to be in this house, did not want to sleep here tonight; I would check into a motel. I searched all around for my keys, and the longer I couldn't find them, the more frantic I became. My heart was pounding. I could feel the hairs prickling on the back of my neck. The keys weren't in my purse, in my coat pocket, or on the table in the foyer. I went into the living room, ripped the plastic sheeting off the couch, and tossed the pillows onto the dusty floor. The keys weren't on the couch. (But of course they weren't! I had driven the car five times since I'd covered the couch with plastic sheeting!) I walked back into the foyer, looking under shoes and boots, and then realized: I couldn't go anywhere anyway. I didn't have any cash and could no longer use my credit cards.

I pressed my head against the heavy, ridiculously tall front door, feeling deflated and trapped. I thought of all the stupid things I had wasted my credit on, everything from the chenille blanket and uneaten steaks of the last few weeks to a Dolce & Gabbana faux leopard-print coat of years before, which I'd bought for fifteen hundred dollars, worn three times, and then had left in a taxi cab at two in the morning in Bucktown on my way home from a play I'd seen to support a friend who'd beat me out for the lead. Where was that coat now? Who was wearing it? And why had I foolishly wasted my money on it, when what I really needed was about eighty dollars for a night in a Motel Six?

I called Jack. No answer. I left a message. "Jack? Call me as soon as you get this."

It was not quite five in the afternoon, but I nonetheless went into the library, where we kept the bar cart as well as most of our books, and perused our collection of booze. It was unimpressive. Two bottles of red wine, one white, a bottle of gin, one of vodka, and one of tequila. Neither of us was much of a drinker. I decided on the gin. I poured about four shots into a tall water glass, splashed some tonic on top, and then walked into every downstairs room and turned on every light, calling Olivier, who was nowhere to be found. My voice echoed in the huge, barely furnished rooms as I called his name. I ended up in the living room, where I tore the plastic sheeting off the TV, lay on the couch, turned on the TV, and sipped—make that guzzled—my drink. I watched a sitcom. Or rather, my eyes stared at the screen while a sitcom was on, but I couldn't concentrate. When the phone rang, I jumped.

"Hello?" I answered, my voice cracking.

"What's the matter?" Jack asked.

I laughed. I didn't drink often, and it occurred to me that I hadn't had anything to eat except for a few graham crackers all day. I felt tipsy. "Oh, that's funny," I said.

"Lilly?"

A ghost just pinned me to the bed, and I peed my pants! I wanted to yell. Instead, I said, "I got my period today, that's one."

A silence, then, "I'm sorry."

"Uh-huh. Then I found out we've maxed out all our credit cards. That's two."

Jack generously let slide the pronouns "we" and "our."

"That's not possible," he said.

"Yep. It is."

"Have you been drinking?"

"Yep. I have. I am. But I didn't get to number four yet."

"You mean number three. Or is there more?"

"Whatever."

"How much maxed out, Lil?"

"Six hundred something dollars total over the limit."

Silence. Then Jack said, in a frightened, little boy's voice, "How am I going to pay that?"

"You mean we don't have six hundred something dollars?" My voice was slurred. Even to my ears it sounded like, *Sis-hunger-ing dollars.*

"I mean, I already pay over a thousand each month just for the minimum charge. Now I need to pay six hundred above that? On top of this mortgage? I was going to raise your allowance once your paychecks started coming in, but now . . . well, forget it."

I glanced at the TV, where a commercial for a children's charitable organization was on, and I thought of the time I had seen a similar commercial and had immediately signed up to send $150 a month to "Feed the Children." That was seven or eight years ago, and Jack had long since canceled that and other automatic donations, including those to save orphaned elephants and abused shelter dogs. The world was filled with hungry children, threatened elephants, and abused dogs, all of whom needed my money, but I had spent it on chenille blankets and uneaten steaks and Dolce & Gabbana faux fur coats and eye shadow called "Bad to the Bone." (Or at least, I had tried to spend it on eye shadow called "Bad to the Bone" but had not. That was a pyrrhic victory if ever there was one.) For a couple of seconds, I thought I was going to puke. Then the feeling passed.

"I'm sorry," I said. I meant it, too. I took a long swallow of my drink. It burned the back of my throat, a nice, penitential feeling.

"What's number three?" he asked quietly.

But I couldn't possibly tell him now. It would seem crazy to him, or perhaps a lie, the sort of stunt a has-been actress would pull on a day she'd maxed out three credit cards: *A ghost scared Olivier and crawled into bed with me. It grabbed me around the waist. I was so scared I peed myself!*

"Never mind," I mumbled. *Nayermine.*

"You sure?"

I took a deep breath. "I promise not to use the credit cards again."

This time Jack laughed. It wasn't a pleasant sound. He sounded like a B-actor villain. "That's about fifty grand too late of a promise," he said. "Even if you wanted to, you can't use them now."

"I know." Then I added, "I love you."

There was a long pause, and in its silence, I could feel the tenuousness of the bonds that held us together. The intense passion of our early years. How he hadn't been able to keep his eyes—or hands—off me. The way we used to make each other laugh. The desire to be together all the time, so that we'd miss each other even during a normal day at work. But something was changing. Or had things been changing for years, and I was only now realizing it?

"I love you, too," he finally said.

"You aren't mad at me?"

"I am . . . devastated."

There was nothing to say to that. We said goodbye and hung up.

I took the last swig of my drink, clumsily tipping the glass so that a few drops of bitter alcohol dribbled onto my chin. Then I set down the glass and pulled that stupid chenille blanket over me and curled into it. I thought back to the incident upstairs. *What if I'm going insane?* I wondered. *What if I created the whole production to take my mind off my debt, and my . . . worse-than-debt?* If this were true, if I were making up all this ghost business, then I really ought to see a shrink. I had seen one after my father's death and had never managed to tell him what happened, why I was there, but he had prescribed a couple of different medications for me just the same.

Did Jack's insurance cover therapy? And if it did, could I bear talking to someone about . . . everything? I knew I could not. And I also knew I still felt strongly about not taking unnecessary medications, now that I wanted to conceive.

To conceive. The thought, the words, exhausted me. Would I ever drum up the energy to try "to conceive" again?

Besides, I didn't believe that what I'd experienced was insanity. No, it wasn't my mind playing tricks on me. It wasn't my "active imagination." Everything I'd experienced, everything I'd seen and felt, had been so real. It was Birdy, the murderer, the suicide. *The ghost.*

I closed my eyes and, exhausted, fell asleep immediately.

I dreamed of Jack kissing another woman. They were standing together, holding each other, caressing one another. I grabbed Jack's arm. "Stop that! What are you doing? Why are you kissing her?" He looked down at me. "Lilly, what are you talking about? I'm not kissing anyone. You're imagining things. You know, you've been acting a little crazy. Maybe you should get some help." He went back to their embrace, and I pulled him away. He shook his head at me, all concern. "Honey," he said, "I think there's something wrong with you."

16

THE FLYING BIRD-GIRL

"HOW ARE YOU FEELING?" Jess asked as I was punching in.

For a moment, I had no idea what she was talking about. How could she possibly know about my troubles? Was she talking about my impending bankruptcy, my haunted house, or my aborted hope of being pregnant? And then I remembered I had called in sick the day before. "Oh, better," I said. "I had stomach issues, and . . ." I was trying to think of whether I should say "throwing up" or "vomiting" when it occurred to me that, when lying, it was better not to overexplain, and I let my voice trail off.

Jess had bright eyes and chubby, pink cheeks, which, along with her graphic tees that depicted Disney fandom or sci-fi geekdom imagery (today she wore a Yoda shirt), gave her the look of a trusting child, although she didn't appear to trust me. "Um, that's good," she said, clearly unconvinced, and then walked into her office.

I decided I needed to be more careful. I went to the circulation desk and got to work. I shelved books, assisted patrons, placed DVDs and CDs back into their proper cases, and helped a young boy use the copier, which I remembered to charge him for.

"Are you a librarian?" a teenage girl asked me while I checked in books at the counter. She had cropped blue hair, a ring through her nose, and a Hello Kitty shirt.

"I'm just an assistant. But maybe I can help you. What do you need?"

She pushed a stack of papers my way. "I'm supposed to do a high school senior research project on global warming."

I glanced over the assignment instructions. "It says here that you need to pick a side, decide if global warming is a scientific fact or an unproven theory."

She titled her head like a pug who wasn't quite sure what the words meant. "Yeah, see, I don't know how to do that."

I turned to Chris, who was busy with another customer. "Mind if I help this patron?"

"Go right ahead," he said, without looking up from his screen.

I led the student to the computer area. We sat side by side at two different computers. I showed her how to search for information and then verify to see if it was reliable or not, my many years of expensive formal education finally coming in handy for something. Once she got going, I looked around the room. It was eleven in the morning on a Tuesday in late October (why wasn't she in school?), and there were three other people in the computer area, all of whom appeared to be self-sufficient and busy.

I opened my computer's browser and typed "ghosts" into the search bar. The info that came up was something any fifth grader who had ever trick-or-treated would know. I typed in "paranormal investigations," and finally, "paranormal investigations Wisconsin." Bam. There was a paranormal society that did investigations right in this county.

I asked my high school senior how she was doing. "Ugh, fine," she said. I chose to ignore the "Ugh" and focus on the "fine." I copied the email address, went to my account, pasted it, and sent the paranormal investigators a quick email:

To: ghostfinderswisco@gmail.com
From: Lilly_Bly@yahoo.com
Subject: Request for Info

Dear "Ghost Finders":

I live in an old house that I suspect might be haunted. Lots
of weird incidents that I can tell you more about. Right now,
I'm just requesting information. What do you do and how
do you do it? How much does it cost to "remove a spirit
from the premises"?

Thank you, Lilly Bly

    I felt ridiculous writing the email, but I hit "send" just the same.
Then I went back to Google, and this time I typed in "Birdy Lawrence" and received several hits. The archived newspaper articles of the
murders behind a paywall (which I'd already read for free on microfilm, thanks to the American public library system, of which I was
now a proud employee). A short Wikipedia entry containing information I already knew. Links to vintage circus posters selling on eBay.
The Haven Circus Society site, which outlined a brief history of the
Lawrence Brothers circus, and which concluded with a plea for donations. (*I already gave*, I thought, thinking of our down payment and
mortgage.) A grainy black-and-white five-second clip of Birdy doing a
perfect triple somersault on the trapeze, while audience members held
their collective breaths, gasped, and then roared with applause. And
a small picture icon that led to an image of Birdy's appearance on an
early television show called *The World in Your Home*.
    I clicked on the link and was suddenly staring at a photo of
a teenage Birdy Lawrence. She was strikingly beautiful, clad in a
bodysuit lined with black beads and feathers, her face made up with
black eyeliner and red lipstick, her eyes staring fixedly at the camera.

Her expression displayed a mixture of sexuality, anger, and sadness. I thought of the teen girls on Disney shows just before they went into rehab.

The heading read:

Birdy, the Flying Bird-Girl: A year after the death of her mother, this 16-year-old is flying high without a net!

Who was this person? This teenager who performed death-defying trapeze acts (including the triple somersault I'd just watched) without a safety net? I remembered reading that Birdy's mother, Anastasia the Romanian Snake Charmer, had died in a circus fire when Birdy was only fifteen.

What had happened between the Birdy of this photograph and the Birdy who had murdered her family and then jumped off the cliffs in our backyard? Did Birdy's breakdown have something to do with her mother's horrible death? Was that why Birdy had become "unstable"? "Anxious"? "Hysterical"? *Evil?* Had the death of her mother triggered something in her that had eventually driven her mad?

Had the abandonment of my mother triggered something in me? The sort of "instability" that led me to imagine a ghost pinning me to the bed? Or, to put it another way, the sort of "instability" that had led me to become the sort of person a ghost would pin to the bed?

At fifteen, sixteen, a girl needs her mother more than ever. I know I had.

"What are you doing?"

I looked up, disoriented, as if I'd been awakened from a dream. It was Jess, and this time her bright eyes and pink cheeks didn't look young and friendly and open, but angry. One hand rested on her hip; the other gestured toward my computer, at Birdy the Flying Bird-Girl.

"I was just helping . . ." I'd been about to say ". . . this girl do research," but when I turned to gesture her way, I saw that she was gone. How long ago had she left? How long had I been sitting here?

I turned back to Jess and continued in a shaky voice, "There was a student here doing a research paper. I was helping her until just a minute ago."

"Lilly, please. You don't need to make up stories. There was nobody here."

"Yes, there was." My hands were unsteady as I closed the web page and then stood up. It was shocking to be called a liar. Of course, I was a liar, but not in this case, so her accusation seemed maddeningly unjust. "She was a high school senior, doing a paper on global warming. I saw the assignment. I helped her. You can ask Chris."

"But there was no one here. And we don't allow personal web surfing or whatever when you could be helping patrons, you know?" She shook her head, clearly disappointed in me. "I'm sorry, but I'm going to have to tell Carl about this."

For someone who had seemed so cool, she sure took the tattle-telling part of her job seriously. "I was only online for a minute, after I had finished helping her," I said quietly. "If you'll excuse me, now that she's gone, I'm going to get back to the circulation desk."

"That is an excellent idea," Jess said as I walked past her.

I arrived at the circ desk, which was crowded with patrons. It was nearly noon, lunch break hour, always a busy time at the library. Chris was at one of the computers, while Eleanor Sawnhorn made copies for a man who stood watching her, tapping his feet, seeming to be in a hurry. "Hello, Lilly," she said, in her patrician voice, her smile not really a smile.

I took over at the other computer. I was flustered and made silly mistakes. I checked in a book to the wrong account. I charged someone five dollars instead of fifty cents in overdue library fines, and the patron—a man named Mr. Watkins, a sweet, talkative regular—accused me, in a loud, teasing voice, of skimming off the top for my own lunch money. He was joking, but it was clear that both Jess and Eleanor heard (it was clear that everyone on the entire main floor heard), and not a soul laughed. The more mistakes I made, the more nervous I became, until I could feel myself perspire in my long-sleeved light-blue denim shirt. I only wore natural, unscented deodorant, not wanting any unnecessary chemicals in my body if I became pregnant, and the deodorant really only worked if I didn't sweat. Now I could smell myself, a sour, acidic scent, vaguely reminiscent of middle school locker rooms and cheap taco sauce. I rolled up the sleeves, exposing my cutting scars from the bad old days after my father's death, not caring if anyone noticed, and dabbed at my forehead with a Kleenex from the box on the counter.

When the rush died down, and Chris and I were alone, he gave me a sideways grin and said, "Dude, what was that about?"

I didn't know which weird thing he might be referring to. Was he talking about my cutting scars, my sweaty underarms, or my making ten million mistakes in twenty minutes' time? "What?"

. "That run-in, or whatever, with Jess. She seemed pissed."

"Oh, that," I said, relieved. "You know that girl I helped? When she didn't need me for a minute, I did a little research of my own. Jess caught me. And what's worse, she never saw the student, so she thought I just went over there by myself when the circ desk was busy. She said she was going to report me."

"Oh, man, bummer."

"Where'd she go, anyway?"

Chris was looking at me blankly. "Who?"

"The girl!"

"What girl?"

"The high school senior with the blue hair and the Hello Kitty shirt."

He laughed. "I don't know who you're talking about but sounds like my kind of girl. If she comes back, point her out to me, will ya?" His face grew grave as he added, "I mean, I'm just kidding. I would never date a high school girl. Even if she was eighteen."

My smile was forced. "You didn't see her?"

He shook his head. "Nope, but before you went over to the computer center, I was helping some guy deal with a lost CD he claimed he returned. Actually, he said someone stole it. Jethro Tull. Who's gonna steal a Jethro Tull CD? Anyway, pain in the butt. Kind of kept me busy for a while." Just then, a man came up to Chris and asked him where the Egyptology books were, and Chris led him away. I just stood there, my hands on the smooth, mahogany desk, that forced smile still on my face.

That afternoon when Carl called me into his office after my shift again, he was a little less twinkly. "Jess told me what happened today," he said, sitting behind his desk. He hadn't stood when I'd entered the room, hadn't motioned for me to sit, both of which I took to be a bad sign. "And I'm sure you wouldn't say you were helping a patron when you weren't, but regardless, Lilly, we can't allow you to be on the internet for personal reasons when there are patrons waiting for help at the circulation desk. I'm sure you . . . you know. Understand?"

"Of course."

He let out a sigh and leaned back in his chair. "So, with those lost couple hours, and the time clock, and the personal calls"—so Jess had told him about that, too—"and now this, I'm afraid I'm going to have to give you a warning. If anything like this happens again in the next couple of weeks, we're going to have to let you go. I'm sorry."

I shook my head and went into acting mode. "Don't be, Carl. I understand. I'm not exactly used to all the rules here, and it seems that some people here would rather catch me breaking them than helping me learn."

Carl Williams looked embarrassed. His brown cheeks flushed with a pink undertone, and his eyes gazed at a point on the tip of my forehead, which I recognized from my theater days as a way to reduce anxiety. "The thing is, Lilly. I mean, everyone probably assumes that you know the rules, like don't leave for over two hours without asking a supervisor for permission to be gone for that long, or don't do personal research when there's a line of patrons at the counter. I mean, we don't have to tell most of our adult employees stuff like that. Do you understand?"

Now it was my turn to be embarrassed. I was thirty-seven, but I felt seventeen.

"Thank you, Carl, I have to go now."

I hurried to the door and left. Probably that was another understood rule: when you're leaving a meeting, tell your boss goodbye. Or maybe even wait to be excused. Don't just dash out the door and practically run to your car to bang your head on the steering wheel in shame.

But I'll give myself credit for one thing: at least before I'd gone into Carl's office, I'd remembered to punch out.

17

THE NEPHEW

IT WAS WEDNESDAY, AND JACK was still in the Upper Peninsula. After work, I stopped off at the store to buy my usual organic frozen dinner, and for the first time, checked the price. They were five to six bucks a pop. I often ate one for dinner when Jack wasn't home, and I sometimes brought another to work to eat for lunch as well. That meant I probably spent about forty bucks a week on organic frozen dinners alone, which suddenly seemed like a certain path to bankruptcy. I went to the generic section instead. The dinners were filled with chemicals, but they were also less than half the price, and since I wasn't pregnant, what was a little MSG in my mac and cheese? I had a crumpled five and some pennies in my pocket from my weekly allowance to get me to Friday and no access to credit. I felt less virtuous as I realized: I didn't have a choice.

I went home and microwaved my dinner. Olivier came up to me and rubbed against my legs. This was unusual; he always seemed to be hiding somewhere nowadays. I bent down and stroked his adorable furry gray head with its squished-in face. "You're back to your old self, huh, lover boy?" I crooned. He meowed, letting me know he was hungry. I gave him some food, refilled his water dish, and was about to sit down with my heated dinner when my cell phone rang.

"Hello?"

"This somebody named Lilly?" a man asked.

I set down my fork. "Yes?"

"This is Jim Lawrence."

I held my breath for a moment and then remembered to breathe. "Oh. Mr. Lawrence. Hello, this is Lilly Bly."

"You said to call if I was a relation."

"Yes. Thank you for calling. And are you?" I stood up, searched for paper and a pen.

"Was my first cousin."

It took me a moment, but then I thought I understood. "Birdy Lawrence was your first cousin?"

"I'm the third James in a row. Never had kids myself, but I can tell you, if I had? I wouldn't a called him James. Gets mighty confusing. Anyways, my dad was brothers with . . . I'm drawing a blank, can't think of his name. Birdy's father?"

I was so excited, I began to pace. "Edgar?"

"That's it. There were four Lawrence brothers. My dad was the youngest."

"James, yes. And your mother was Winnifred."

"Everyone called her Winnie."

"This is wonderful! Thank you so much for getting back to me, Mr. Lawrence."

"You can call me Jim."

"Jim. Thank you."

"So, what's this all about?"

"I recently moved into her house. Into Edgar Lawrence's house. And for right now, I'm just doing research, trying to figure out the history."

He let out an impressed whistle. "By, golly. 'Scuse me for saying this, miss, but you must be loaded."

I was so much the opposite of loaded, I didn't know whether to laugh or cry, and out came a noise that sounded like some sad mixture of the two. I murmured, "No, no, not at all. We're finding it trying, actually, to live here. But we love the house."

"I used to go there," he said quietly. "We all did. I was just a teen when . . . when it happened. Then it was abandoned for a long time, between the time when . . . well, between the time when no one lived there and the circus society bought it. My dad and his brother John owned it, but they didn't do much to it. Kind of a spooky place back then."

"We're trying to take good care of it," I assured him, though I didn't know whether this was true. Was the mess I was making in the living room an example of care—or neglect? "Do you remember her?" I asked him gently. "Do you remember your cousin Birdy?"

"A glamorous trapeze artist like that? A woman like that is hard to forget. But I didn't see her much growing up. Before my Uncle Edgar died, we went up there a few times for Christmas parties, and they came to some family gatherings, but after his funeral? Never. I never saw her again. And I was only ten or eleven when my uncle died, mind you."

"What was she like?"

"Beautiful. Glamorous. But also, I don't know. Not what you'd call a party girl. She always had a book of some sort with her, and that was unusual in our family. We don't come from a line of bookworms. Doted after her husband, and then doted on her baby after she was born."

"Amelia."

"I believe she was named after Miss Amelia Earhart. Course I was only a boy when Amelia was born, but that's what I remember hearing."

Of course, I thought. A gifted trapeze artist, a flyer, would name her daughter after the greatest female aviator—the greatest flyer—who had ever lived.

"How did you all . . . take the news?"

He let out a blow through both lips. "We were shocked, all of us, but especially my brother. It hit him the hardest. Not that he talked about it much. It was the town's great tragedy and our family's great shame. But Chas? He wasn't quite the same after it happened."

"He was the caretaker," I guessed aloud.

"Yes, ma'am. Hired to live in what was the coach house back then and take care of the estate. I don't think Uncle Edgar wanted someone outside the family to do the job. He worked there for, oh, I don't know, musta been a good four or five years. Even after Uncle Edgar died, oh . . . what was his name? Birdy's husband . . ."

"Bobby Shawcross."

"That's him. Bobby Shawcross kept Chas on. For a while."

"Do you know why your brother left?"

Jim Lawrence laughed. "Miss Bly—"

"Lilly, please."

"Lilly, you're asking me to go back into ancient times. No, I can't remember why Chas left that job. I can't remember if he got fired or if he quit. All I know is, by the time Beatrice went mad and killed her family and herself, I was glad he wasn't working there anymore."

"Yes, of course," I said. "Your brother, Chas. He was older than you. Is he by any chance still alive?"

"Chas is seventy-eight. He's alive and well enough physically, but unfortunately, he has Alzheimer's."

"I'm so sorry to hear that."

"Thank you. He's living in a nursing home now. His wife Katya had to send him there about four years ago. His Alzheimer's was getting too bad. And with his particular dementia, well, he can't always remember Katya, or his children, or his grandchildren, and he certainly can't remember what he ate for breakfast, or who the president is, but the 1940s? The '50s? You have a good chance of hearing stories from those days. I visit him every now and then, and he still has a thing or two to say about the War, or our childhood, or his goofy brother who wanted to be the nurse when we played army, even if he can't always remember that I'm the one he's talking about."

"Do you mind my asking the name of the nursing home?"

"Golden Oaks, right here in Haven."

I wrote the name on a piece of paper and tried to remember the family tree. "Any other living family members?"

"Chas and Katya had two children. I'm sorry to say the boy died of a drug overdose in his twenties."

"Oh, how awful. I'm sorry."

"Lydia's almost fifty. Has two grown-up kids. Our brother Lloyd had three kids, but he moved out west before they were even born. Like I said, I didn't have children myself. I'm what they used to call a 'confirmed bachelor' and what I now go ahead and call gay. I'm sixty-nine and just came out fourteen years ago."

"Good for you," I said, smiling. "I imagine that wasn't easy. In a small town."

"I'm not sure it's easy anywhere at fifty-five, but it was worth it."

I felt a surge of warmth for him then, for his bravery, and his ability to open up like this to a stranger, but before I could say anything, he added, "I sure do wish you luck on your project, or whatever it is you're doing."

"Thank you, Jim. I enjoyed talking to you. If you'd ever like to meet in person, I'd love to hear more about you and your family."

"I will keep that offer in mind."

I had a lead! Chas Lawrence. And if he couldn't remember many details, maybe his wife or daughter could. I brought my laptop to the kitchen table and typed their names into Google while I nibbled on my now-cold mac and cheese. Apparently, Chas had had nothing to do with his family's circus, as far as I could tell, though his Ukrainian wife had been a horse trainer and equestrian performer there, and Chas had managed to profit off its name. He had owned a hardware store, Circus Hardware, which seemed to have been a vibrant part of the community until it had closed in 2000. I found his daughter Lydia on Facebook. She had frizzy reddish hair streaked with gray and a warm smile. I searched through her posts until I found one of her, her two twenty-something children, and an elderly couple posing in front of a Christmas tree from the previous December. The man was in a wheelchair and had silver hair and blue eyes. The woman standing beside him was wearing leggings, a sparkly sweater, dangly jewelry, stage makeup, and red hair so thick and perfectly coiffed I guessed it was a wig. The couple must have been Chas and Katya. The caption of the post read: "All I want for Christmas is time with family. Wish granted!"

After I finished browsing, I quickly checked my email, and, among the offers from online stores, which I ignored, I found a message I'd been waiting for:

To: Lilly_Bly@yahoo.com
From: ghostfinderswisco@gmail.com
Subject: Re: Request for Info

Dear Lilly,

Thank you for contacting Ghost Finders Paranormal Investigators. We are sorry to report that, due to funding problems, we have pretty much shut down. But we do have a psychic who used to work for us who still does some home visits. If you let her use any findings for a book she's working on, she waives her usual fee of $75/hour. If you agree to those terms, or if you are willing to pay her fee, please contact her at the number below. We wish you luck on your ghost busting!

Bob at Paranormal

More good news: a free consultation! What did I care if she used her findings for a book that may or may not get published, and if it did, Jack would never read? All I had to do was make sure she came to the house when Jack wouldn't be home, a feat that would be easier to schedule than not. I felt good. I was making progress.

18

GOLDEN OAKS

I DROVE TO THE NURSING HOME at nine in the morning on Saturday, to be on time when visiting hours began at 9:30, so that I'd be back before Jack got home in the early afternoon. I wore dark blue denim trousers, a crisp white blouse, an Italian merino wool V-neck sweater, and my wool peacoat, to look nice, like a real visitor.

I turned on an alternative station (Panic! at the Disco), switched to classical (Bach), then to Top 40 ("Love Story"), my fingers desultorily tapping piano keys on the steering wheel as I drove what ended up being only twelve minutes to get across town.

Chicago had numerous neighborhoods, some distinguished by economics, some by the cultural or ethnic background of many of its residents, others for the "vibe," and still others by the work or leisure for which the neighborhood was famous for. The city was too big to be divided by something as simple as railroad tracks. In Haven, on the other hand, it was easy to understand the expression "on the wrong side of the tracks." Railroad tracks crossed the town north to south. On one side of the tracks were the nicer houses, restaurants, and stores; on the other side were the more run-down houses, a few dive bars, and a couple of tire shops. There were exceptions to the rule, of course, but the Golden Oaks Nursing Home was not one of them. It was on the south side of the tracks, in a neighborhood with parched lawns and chain link fences, a small liquor store, and a dry cleaner with a neon sign with missing letters: DR LEAN RS.

The nursing home itself was one-story, faded yellow, fronted by an asphalt parking lot. A single struggling, skinny oak tree poked out from a strip of lawn between the lot and the building.

I parked and went inside. The walls were institutional beige; the floors were off-white and tan linoleum in swirl patterns evidently meant to evoke Italian marble, but with all the chips revealing the concrete underneath, I don't think anyone was fooled. A sign on the wall read WELCOME TO GOLDEN OAKS NURSING HOME and pictured a glorious oak sprouting golden yellow leaves, a sharp contrast to the skimpy tree outside.

I waited in the reception area for a couple of minutes, and then a young woman, who appeared to be nineteen, maybe twenty, walked around the corner and stood behind the desk. She didn't greet me, ask if she could help me, or apologize for being late. In fact, she looked irritated to see me there, as if I had interrupted something important.

"Hello," I said. "I'm here to see one of your . . . patients?"

"Residents," she corrected me. She had brassy platinum hair with dark roots and chipped black fingernail polish, which she now picked at, bored, while I continued.

"Yes, residents. Chas Lawrence?"

She met my eyes, a suspicious expression on her face. "What do you want to see him for?"

The question took me aback. What did I want to see him for? Was this a professional question from the training book, or simply a nosy one from a rude teenager? I decided to err on the side of caution.

"I'm a distant relation." I smiled politely, the sweet Midwestern girl next door doing her familial duty.

"Hmm. The only family we know of is his wife, his daughter, his grandkids, and his brother. And you ain't any of them."

"Like I said. I'm a distant relative. Now, may I see him, please?"

"If you're that distant, he ain't gonna know you. But you can try. But it's only 9:15. Visiting hours start at 9:30."

"Seriously?"

"Look, lady, we got rules here. We've got to concern ourselves with security, you know. Here, sign in. And let me see your ID."

I signed my name and address on a coffee-stained sheet of paper in a binder, and showed her my ID, which she scrutinized, as if I were a terrorist in a J.Crew peacoat ready to plant a bomb in a run-down nursing home.

"217 Hill Street?" she said. "You live in the Lawrence Mansion?"

"Yes," I said, not bothering to be bashful about the word "mansion," and glad she hadn't called it "the Murder House."

"Jeez, I guess you are related." She looked me up and down. I was glad I had brushed my hair, worn lipstick, and dressed in a nice outfit. Of course, this was the minimal effort made by most women my age every day, but it felt good to look presentable while a teenage girl with chipped black nail polish and a bad attitude judged my fate. "Okay, you can go in early. Room 110. That way," she said, pointing. "It's on the left."

"Thank you." I walked down the corridor. The walls along the hallway were covered with hip-high scuff marks presumably made by the black rubber tires of wheelchairs. I glanced into rooms and saw many elderly people still in bed. Every room seemed to have a TV on with the highest possible volume. In the hallway, the sounds of game shows mingled with cooking shows and even the occasional Saturday-morning cartoon. Then I came to a quiet room, and I slowed. Room 110. The name to the side of the door read MR. CHARLES "CHAS" LAWRENCE.

The door was ajar. I knocked. No answer. I stepped inside.

There, sitting at the foot of a bed, was an elderly man in a pale blue dress shirt and navy sweatpants. His silver hair was thinning, and his complexion was ruddy and wrinkled, but in his face, I could still make out the same blue eyes and straight aquiline nose from Lydia's Facebook page.

"Mr. Lawrence?"

I walked closer. "Mind if I sit?" Again, no answer. I sat in the chair across from the foot of the bed. He was wearing clean white tennis shoes that hadn't seen much, if any, outdoor action, and white sports socks. Apparently, someone had dressed him for weekend visiting hours, and I wondered if Katya or Lydia would be here soon. I didn't know if that was a good or bad thing: Would I be able to interview them, too, or would they mind my coming here, unannounced, without their permission?

"Mr. Lawrence? Chas?" I repeated the name more forcefully, and he looked up.

I extended my hand. "My name is Lilly Bly," I said. "I live in the Lawrence estate. On Hill Street? Your Uncle Edgar's house? I came to talk to you about Beatrice Lawrence."

He didn't shake my hand. He didn't move his fingers from his lap; they were long and thin, with manicured nails. Our knees were merely a few inches apart. He smelled like old wet newspapers and sour cabbage. Someone had dressed the elderly man, and evidently filed his nails, but I wondered when he had last been given a shower or bath.

"Beatrice?" I repeated. Then I changed course. "Birdy," I said more loudly. "Birdy Lawrence?"

"Fly away, Birdy, fly away."

I paused and stared at him. He had a kind of smile on his face. It was just as I'd been told; it was clear he was suffering from some sort of dementia.

"Yes, Birdy," I repeated. This time, when I spoke, I made sure I enunciated clearly and projected by breathing from my diaphragm, as if to reach the audience in the middle of the theater, if not the far back. "I understand you were the caretaker there, at Birdy's home, and I'm wondering if you can tell me what you remember about her. And Bobby Shawcross."

"Bobby?" The name seemed to trigger something in him. He frowned, and his blue eyes suddenly became alert.

"Yes, Bobby Shawcross."

"I won't do it, Bobby," he said. "I won't!"

I sat back, startled by his sudden vehemence. What wouldn't he do? What was he remembering? *Okay*, I thought. *We're doing improv now, and I'm going with it.*

"You have to, Chas," I told him, making my voice as low and steady as I could.

"I won't! It isn't right. It isn't right! Birdy is my cousin."

"Forget about Birdy."

"She's my cousin!"

"Let me worry about Birdy. You worry about . . ." I let my voice trail off because I had no idea what we were talking about. Lorenzo DeMarcos had said that he didn't mind doing "certain errands" for Bobby. Maybe Chas had. Lorenzo had also said that Bobby was no "one-woman man." Maybe Birdy's cousin wouldn't—what? Bring flowers to Delores? Deliver a cheap locket to Maria? Go shopping for lingerie for Betty and then deliver the sexy, silky items to a hotel, where Bobby would meet her an hour later?

"What won't you do, Chas?" I ventured to ask.

"You know what I won't do, Bobby."

"Say it."

"No!" he shouted, and then he began to cry. His shoulders shook, and his eyes ran with tears. A Kleenex box was on the table beside me, and I handed him a couple of tissues, which he took. Then I stood up, setting a hand on his shoulder, which was bony and frail underneath his dress shirt.

"What's going on?" a voice said.

I turned and saw a nurse, or a nurse's assistant, or an attendant—someone wearing a smock covered with bright yellow happy faces—except the middle-aged Black woman wearing the happy face shirt wasn't smiling. She was scowling, and her expression said what her words did not, which was that she didn't make enough money to deal with this shit.

"I'm sorry," I said.

"Why'd you go and upset Mr. Chas?"

"I didn't mean to."

"What'd this lady upset you about, huh?" she asked Chas Lawrence, coming in and rubbing his back. "You okay, Mr. Chas? Huh? It's me, Gloria, you can tell me." He had stopped crying and handed me his dirty tissue. I looked to Gloria, but she looked back at me, like, *You made him cry, you deal with his dirty Kleenex*, so I threw it in the trash, and then used the hand sanitizer attached to the wall.

"I guess I'd better be going," I said.

"Sounds like that'd be a good idea," she said.

"I'm sorry."

"Mm-hmm."

"Goodbye, Mr. Lawrence," I said more loudly. "It was nice to . . ."—I was about to say "meet," which would have blown my cover—"see you."

And then, just when I thought he couldn't surprise me any more, he started to sing: "*Alouette, gentille Alouette, Alouette, je te plumerai . . .*"

I stopped at the door.

"*Je te plumerai la tête, je te plumerai le bec . . .*"

It was nothing personal. He had a song stuck in his head, that was all. The name "Birdy" had reminded him of a childhood song about a lark. That was it, I told myself. But the way he sang about plucking off its feathers gave me chills. And when he got to the next line . . .

"Et le cou, et le cou, et le cou, et le cou . . . !"

I felt dizzy by the troubling repetition of the word *cou*, or "neck," like a needle stuck on a record, as if the needle knew just how to get to me.

"That's it, you sing if it'll make you feel better," cooed Gloria. "I didn't know you could sing French so good."

Neither of them was paying any attention to me anymore. I muttered, "Goodbye," but I'm not sure they heard—or cared. I hurried down the hall, out of the nursing home, and into my car. On my short drive home, I tried, without success, to get that accursed song out of my mind:

I will pluck your feathers off, I will pluck your head.
I will pluck your beak, I will pluck your eyes, I will pluck
    your neck.
And your neck! And your neck! And your neck! And your neck!
And your neck! And your neck! And your neck! And your neck!
    Oh . . .

19

INSULATION

"LILLY? LILLY!"

Jack was standing over me, a glum expression on his face. It took me a while to figure out what was happening, to understand that after returning from the nursing home, I must have fallen asleep on the couch, and that Jack was home from his trip and mad about something.

"What the hell?" he said.

I wiped the drool from my mouth and chin, smoothed back my hair, and sat up, lowering the chenille blanket down to my waist. My first reaction was to feel guilty for taking a nap, but that emotion was immediately replaced by annoyance. "What the hell, what? I haven't seen you all week and you wake me up to yell at me?"

"I'm sorry. I'm not yelling. I just want to know what's going on."

"What are you talking about?"

He made a sweeping gesture with his arms. I looked around the living room, seeing it as if through his eyes. Plastic sheets were in balls on the floor. The hand sander and sandpaper were just lying there. And the paltry area I'd sanded looked horrible, chalky white, uneven, and altogether worse than if I'd left it alone.

"Oh, this. It's a work in progress," I said.

"But what is the work in progress, exactly?"

"I'm finishing the floors. Obviously."

"With a hand sander?"

"Yes."

"Good God, I'd never do that myself. I mean, do you know what you're doing?" he asked, rubbing his cheekbones with his fingers, in a gesture of fatigue.

"Yes, I know what I'm doing. I'm following the instructions on 'Get Her Done.'"

"Get 'Er Done," he repeated. "Okay. Well. So, you're going to see this through, right?"

I wanted to be angry over his condescending tone, but I had to admit that there was some precedent for his comment. A few years before, I had bought a "vintage" desk for $200, planning to sand it down and repaint it. But I'd gotten busy and ended up setting it on the curb outside our rental in Pilsen with a sign that read FREE. I imagined Jack trying to figure out how he was going to finish the floors on top of his heavy workload and all his traveling.

"Don't worry. I'm going to see this through."

"Because I don't have time to—"

"I know."

"I'm not sure you realize how difficult this is, that's all."

I wanted to say, *I know exactly how difficult this is*. Instead, I said, "I'm going to finish the floor." I felt impatient. I didn't want to think about the floor. I wanted to figure out what Lorenzo DeMarcos and Chas Lawrence were hiding. What Bobby Shawcross had asked Chas to do that half century ago. And I wondered how I'd find out, especially with Jack around . . .

He'd only been home for a few minutes, and already I wished he were gone.

"Hey," he said, leaning down and putting his hand on my shoulders. "Sorry, I'm glad to see you." I didn't tell him I was glad to see him, too. He kissed me on the lips. Then he asked, "Where's the mail?"

My stomach lurched. "On the dining table," I replied.

We went to the dining room, where Jack sat on one of the rickety chairs and began opening bills, while I stood across from him.

"That's one of the credit cards," he said. I didn't know if he was talking to himself or to me, so I said nothing. "About what we thought. Water, that's lower than I expected." I felt proud of myself then, for not using too much water, like most Americans, who were so wasteful. Of course, I knew our low water bill was due to the fact that I had never run the washing machine, which was in the basement, but instead washed most of my clothes by hand in the tub or (once) at the laundromat, and also because I almost never cooked, and so didn't need to wash many dishes, but still. It was something. "The propane bill. Now this'll be interesting, I have no idea what to expect." The home inspector had explained to us that this house wasn't heated by natural gas but by propane, which was pumped into a tank in our backyard by someone from a propane company, who came by every so often in a truck and filled the tank up with a hose. It seemed exotic and old-fashioned to me, and I couldn't imagine that anything that sounded so technologically primitive would be expensive. "You've got to be freaking kidding me!" Jack said. But maybe I was wrong.

"How much?"

"Six hundred."

"Six hundred . . . dollars?"

"No, six hundred pesos. Yes, dollars!"

"For the week?"

He gave me an exasperated look. "For the month. It's bad enough, though. It's not like it's January! My God, we just can't afford to live in this house. We need to sell this damn thing, even if it's at a loss."

I felt my pulse quicken. The idea of no longer living in the Lawrence Mansion filled me with panic. This was where I was going to become a mother, I was sure. If I gave up now, I didn't know how I'd pick up again. And from where? Some cheap double-wide on the wrong side of the tracks in Haven? Maybe near the Golden Oaks Nursing Home? I tried to remain calm. "We could do things to make the heating less expensive," I said.

"Do things," he repeated, as if I'd actually said something useful, as if it hadn't occurred to him we might do something. "We could close off some rooms. Turn off the vents and close the doors. All those upstairs bedrooms."

"Sure. And we could put stuff on the windows," I added. "Plastic stuff."

The circus society had put "plastic stuff" on two windows that were cracked, but I had seen houses with plastic sheeting (or whatever it was called) on all the windows to ward off the cold, and they looked so ugly that I assumed the sheets must work; otherwise, no one would use them. "For insulation," I said, using a word I hoped sounded scientific and official. But as I said it, I was reminded of its other meaning. "To insulate" was also to isolate. I shook the thought from my head and went on. "And, um . . . maybe we could patch up some drafty spots. For insulation," I repeated, for good measure.

"Plastic sheeting, window insulation. Patching," Jack repeated. "Okay, right, that might help."

I was still panicking, but my heart wasn't beating quite as fast as it had been. I knew I had to convince Jack we could save money without moving, and it seemed I was doing an okay job of it.

Jack finished going through the mail, but there were no more bills, only coupons I was too lazy to use and a postcard from his peripatetic brother who was roaming around Asia, trying to make a documentary. I knew it read:

Thailand is awesome!!! Might stay here forever!
Ha! You should visit!
Cheers!!!

—*Josh*

Jack read it, glanced at the picture (a heavenly beach, paradise), and sighed. I knew his sigh was part judgment, part envy, for his youngest brother's irresponsibility, good fortune, and sophomoric use of multiple exclamation points, and I felt a wave of pity for Jack then, the inveterate caretaker.

"Okay, you ready?" he asked, standing up.

"Ready?"

"To go to the home store. Let's buy some window insulation kits. And . . . patching stuff."

"Oh, we're doing that now?"

"I only have a day and a half at home. I'm driving to Indiana on Monday. And let me tell you, whatever work asks me to do, whatever overtime they need me for, I can't say no. Not with that stack of bills in there. Not unless we want to get rid of this money pit."

"No, no, fine, I'm ready."

We stopped at Culver's and grabbed a ButterBurger for Jack, a fish sandwich for me, and a couple of orders of fries. I felt happy, or at least normal, driving to the home improvement store, eating my sandwich and the salty, crinkly fries, gazing out the window at the jack-o'-lanterns on porches and the paper ghosts hanging from trees. Halloween was only a week away. We were like any normal couple, going on any normal errand. Except that Jack was tapping his fingers on the steering wheel, as if to music, when the radio wasn't on.

"You okay?" I asked.

"Sure, yeah. Just thinking about my brother. Must be nice to be in Thailand," he said.

Both of Jack's parents were dead. One of his brothers played in a band and lived with his boyfriend in San Francisco. Josh, his other brother, was single and traveling the world. I wondered if Jack ever regretted being the responsible one.

"Do you wish you were in Thailand?" I asked, but what I meant was, *Do you wish you had a different life?*

"On the beach, eating fish, drinking . . . whatever they drink in Thailand. Sure, why not?" He was smiling a faraway smile, as if imagining himself there.

"Am I in the picture?" I asked. I meant to say the words playfully, but they came out like an accusation.

He glanced at me. "Of course you are. What would Thailand be without you?"

What would Thailand be without me? Freedom, I guessed. Freedom from debt, freedom from obsessions over babies, houses, and ghosts, freedom from responsibility. I couldn't blame Jack if his words sounded perfunctory and if his smile was strained.

We spent the entire rest of the day and the following one working on the house. Jack affixed the plastic sheeting to almost all the interior windows with double-stick tape, and then I used a blow dryer (per instructions) to shrink-wrap the sheeting onto the window, my expensive ionic hot pink appliance finally coming in handy for something, as I was usually running too late to use it on my hair. I applied tacky rope caulk to the drafty spots around the doors, and Jack sealed holes on the outside with a sort of insulation in a spray can that looked as amateurish as it sounded. When we finished, the house may have been warmer and better insulated, but it also looked a good deal worse than when we'd started. The sheeting on the windows made me feel claustrophobic and made everything outside appear blurry, and from the street below, the house looked creepier and more run-down than ever. But I didn't complain. It was all my fault.

In the evening, we went around to the unused upstairs bedrooms, closed the vents, and then closed the doors. When Jack began to close one of the two heating vents in the nursery, I asked, "What are you doing?"

"What does it look like I'm doing?" he said from his spot on the floor.

"Not this room," I said. My desire to use it for a baby's room was so strong, it was painful. Closing off this room felt like closing off my dream for a child. "Let's leave this room alone."

He finished, stood up, and looked at me. I was standing in the doorway. He was across the room, but I could clearly see his expression. It said: *Okay, so we're going to have another irrational conversation, fine.*

"We're not using this room right now. Therefore, we need to close the heating vents and close the door. It's as simple as that." He was a dad, speaking to an eight-year-old, patient and calm. He went over to the second vent and closed that one, too.

I wanted to say, *Don't you "therefore" me!* But I didn't want to lose the argument by getting "overly emotional," *unstable, hysterical.* Instead, I said, "I just don't feel it's good luck, to seal off this room. It's like saying that we're sure we won't have a baby in this house."

"Listen," he said, standing up again, and just by that one word, I could tell that his patience was wearing thin, "you're the one who drove us into credit card debt, who kept using the cards even when we couldn't afford it. You're the one who wanted this house, 'more than anything in the world,' quote, unquote. So I'm not the one turning off the vents and closing this door—you did that. If closing this door is bad luck, then so be it. That was your choice."

I was stung into silence. What he said was true, but it was a cruel thing to say, and a cruel way to say it. He walked past me and went to close the vents in the room with the hole in the floor.

Later, we ate generic frozen pizza while watching *Buffy the Vampire Slayer*. It was satisfying to watch a teenager slay the forces of darkness while fighting high school cliques. It seemed both harder and easier than trying to battle heating bills, ghosts, and the sometimes bitter loneliness of marriage.

20

THE JAG

IN BED, JACK FELL RIGHT TO SLEEP. But I just lay there, listening for something I never heard, waiting to feel something I never felt. I thought of Jack's closing off the nursery and wondered whether we would ever open it again. I remembered that original sensation I'd never shaken, the certainty that I would have a baby in this house. Had I been wrong? I thought of all my dead babies. The aborted one. The first miscarriage, buried in that run-down Chicago cemetery. The second miscarriage, which my doctor had tested. It had been a boy "with no abnormalities." I always thought of him as a five-year-old looking like a miniature Jack, with neatly trimmed hair and hipster glasses, *and no abnormalities*, but of course, he must have looked like the first miscarriage, a sort of bloody alien worm with little arm buds and a too-big head. I wondered now, in bed, where he was. The doctor had "disposed" of him, I supposed. I had been too bereft to argue, too hardened to think I should bury the fetus in a cemetery where I could visit it "every day." People said to me, "I am sorry for your loss," and they were kind to say that; they were right, it was a "loss," but somehow I always heard it in my head as "I am sorry for your lost," which seemed even more accurate. My babies were not just a loss but also lost. They were lost. I had lost them.

Where is my baby?
Where is my baby?
Your baby is lost.

I want my baby.

I was going to a dark place, and to stop myself, my mind took a quarter loop and I thought of other things I had lost, less important things, objects. I thought of my faux leopard Dolce & Gabbana coat. It was so soft and well fitting, with silky bright pink lining and deep pockets. I was certain I would never own a coat that nice again. I thought of the first diamond earrings my father had ever given me, lost on a sophomore year ski trip. Were they still on that mountain in Colorado, buried in a forever snow? The first note a boy had ever slipped me, in seventh grade, asking me out on a date. I had accepted, and his mom had driven us to a movie theater (*Indiana Jones and the Temple of Doom*) where we'd held hands greasy with popcorn. We'd never gone out again, but I'd kept the note tucked away in a desk drawer, until both the note and desk must have been lost to some bigger and better new bedroom furniture set.

I thought of Tiffany, a summer-at-Interlochen best friend, and the necklace she'd given me, a locket with an engraving of a theater mask on the outside, a picture of the two of us together on the inside, as Sandy (me) and Rizzo (her), the parts we'd had at camp. What had happened to that necklace? What had happened to Tiffany? She moved to California the day after her high school graduation to try to "make it" in Hollywood. I received a letter from her about two years later, asking me for money. Mad at her for not getting in touch with me until she'd needed cash, I never wrote her back. I spent years looking for her on TV shows and in movies, staying until the end of films to read the credits, to make sure I hadn't missed her, but I never saw her, not once. By the time I turned thirty, I would have sent her every dime I had. Was she married with kids in the suburbs? Was she still alive? I had this terrible feeling that she'd overdosed. Though, as far as I knew, she had never done drugs in high school. As I lay in bed, Jack breathing rhythmically beside me, I had a crazy, late-night daydream of driving cross-country to find her, to make sure that she was still okay, and somehow in this daydream (nightdream), I was driving my old Jag. That was another thing I'd lost.

I had never owned a car until I'd graduated from Northwestern, when my father had taken me to a car lot in the North Shore of Chicago that specialized in European models and had told me to pick out anything I wanted. It had taken me about three seconds to gaze around and fall in love. I'd never been a car person. I didn't know a Ford from a Dodge, an Audi from a Volvo. But as soon as my eyes fell upon the dark green 1974 Jaguar XKE, with its sleek, feline shape, its buttery leather interior, its open-air coupe-ness, I knew I had found my car.

"That one," I said.

"You have good taste," the car salesman said.

"Expensive taste," my dad said.

"Oh, is it too much?" I didn't know what "too much" would be, but I didn't want to be greedy. I bit on a cuticle and turned to my dad, worried, but he was smiling.

"It's fine. It's beautiful. Let's take her for a test drive."

We drove down Lake Shore Drive with the roof down, whizzing by the mansions, my hair whipping in the wind.

"You know how you know you've found the perfect car for yourself?" my father asked. Although the roof was down, he didn't need to shout. The car was as quiet as a cat purring softly in its bed.

"How?"

"You just do." He smiled at me, a warm, paternal smile, happy with me, with the car, with the sun and wind, with life.

My dad's face was sunburned and freckled from golf. He had smoked for over thirty years and had just turned fifty-two. Although he spent his working hours in nightclubs and dinner-only restaurants, he had a sort of outdoorsy, Robert Redford–like mien, which was part of his charm, and undoubtedly part of his success. Patrons loved him and financiers trusted him. I didn't know if he and my mother still loved each other, but I had never seen him flirt with another woman, and he worked with plenty of them. He was a man's man—gambling, golf, horses, poker, Johnny Walker—and he always smelled like leather.

But he was also moody. If his horse came in, it was champagne on the house; if it didn't, he was sulky and morose, short-tempered. I'd seen him slip busboys hundred-dollar bills, and I'd seen him fire them for breaking a single dish. And, to be sure, he was not entirely aboveboard when it came to money. He was not above cooking the books, cheating the IRS, paying illegal immigrants under the table, holding high-stakes card games in back rooms. He had said, "I gotta call my bookie" so often during my childhood that I'd thought his best friend was a man who had earned his nickname because he so loved to read. No, my father was not perfect, as my mother would be the first to say, but I loved him with an animal instinct that was like breathing: he was my dad.

Back in the lot, the suave car salesman in the Armani suit asked us how we liked it.

"It runs nice," my dad said. "How much?"

"Fifty-five."

My father whistled through his teeth.

"It's in mint condition. Completely original. We don't replace the engine with a Chevy engine, like they do down the street."

"Fifty-five hundred?" I asked. I really did know nothing about cars. The two men looked at me funny.

"Fifty-five thousand," the salesman said, as if I had insulted his only child.

"Oh my gosh, Daddy, we can't . . . I mean, I don't need—"

"Excuse us, Lilly. We'll be in the office."

"Would you like some champagne? Espresso? A bite to eat while you're waiting?" the salesman asked me.

"I'll just take a stroll around the lot, thank you," I said.

My father turned to the salesman. "Shall we?"

The salesman gave him a little bow, and they walked away.

My father had told me he'd be paying for my car in cash. Was it possible that he'd brought over fifty thousand dollars in cash to the car lot? Had a horse come in? Had some backroom deal come through? Or had he simply made a withdrawal from a bank account which stored the legitimate earnings from his restaurants, clubs, and investments? Had he paid full price (that was hard to believe) or had he whittled the salesman down to some reasonable amount? And what, exactly, would that have been? Fifty grand? Forty-five? I didn't know. I didn't ask. All I knew was that my dad left the office alone and tossed me the keys.

We left my dad's BMW in the lot (he told the salesman he'd have one of "his guys" pick it up later) and drove home together in the Jag. I knew that you were not supposed to equate expensive gifts with love. I knew that it was foolish to think, *My dad must really love me to spend fifty-five grand on a car for me.* I knew that it was sentimental to mix up the smell of the car with the smell of my dad. But I couldn't help it; I did all those things. At one point, driving down 90-94 back into the city, the lanes Sunday empty, the late May dusky air cooling our faces and hair, my dad touched my hand and said, "You worked hard, honey. I'm proud of you." My dad had never gone to college. To him, a theater degree from Northwestern wasn't useless— it was impressive. My late nights memorizing scripts and attending rehearsals weren't frivolous—they were extraordinary. The fact that I'd had to study endlessly to earn C+s in Intro to Biology and Calc I were not signs of left-brain stupidity but badges of determination and industry. He was proud of me; he believed in me; he loved me. Those feelings were a part of him, a part of me, and a part of the 1974 Jaguar XKE.

*   *   *

The Jag was fast and sublime, and there were quite a few men who'd asked me out in those early years just for a chance, I was sure, to ride around in that car (though of course I never let any of them in the driver's seat). But it was nearly constantly in need of repairs. It was fragile and temperamental, a horse who sometimes won the race and sometimes collapsed before leaving the gate. When my father had been alive and solvent, he'd paid for all the repairs, knowing I couldn't afford them on my waitressing and acting earnings. After he'd died, I'd kept the Jag in a garage most of the time, like a fancy threadbare dress I was afraid of wearing out, and had taken the L everywhere. When I got the job at the charter school, which was in the suburbs, I began driving it again to work, and it kept breaking down. When it needed a new catalytic converter, I called Jack from the foreign auto repair shop and told him the news.

"How much?"

"Three grand."

"No."

I didn't have a cell phone back then. I was using the auto shop's phone, and the receptionist was sitting a few feet away, pretending that she wasn't eavesdropping. I said quietly into the phone, "What do you mean, no?"

"I mean we can't afford that car anymore. A few times a year it needs a major repair. We spend about five thousand dollars a year just maintaining that thing. You're going to have to sell it and buy something practical."

I don't think I'd ever missed my father more than I did at that moment. I don't mean his money, I mean him, his *joie de vivre*, the way he understood me. If Daddy had been alive, we would have sold the shirts off our backs, been without a home and lived in the Jag, but we would never, ever have sold that beautiful car.

For a moment, I felt angry at my father. A heat in the head, behind my eyes. And then the feeling disappeared.

The receptionist busied herself with papers. "Not the Jag," I hissed into the phone. "Please, Jack, anything but the Jag. I'll sell my jewelry! I'll give blood!"

"You still need a car, one that won't break down every few months. I'm telling you, it's done. See what you can get for it. Call me back."

Something inside my heart shifted then. Something inside me became cold and indifferent. My mouth tasted of prunes. I asked to speak with the mechanic. The receptionist—a tall, put-together brunette wearing (if I wasn't mistaken) a Helmut Lang pantsuit with an asymmetrical jacket (this was quite an upscale auto repair shop that looked after my Jag)—went to get one. The man who returned was Franz (I knew all the mechanics there), a fifty-something German with glasses who looked like a professor going to a Halloween party in a mechanic's uniform. My voice did not break as I asked him how much I could get if I traded it in for something "more practical." He checked the Blue Book and said, "Well, you will not get the top of the range, not with the work it needs. Beautiful car, ya, but it needs a good deal of repair. What is that joke? You know why British drink warm beers? Because they have Lucas refrigerators."

He was smiling. I looked at him blankly. He stopped smiling and continued. "I'd say ten, maybe eleven."

I had no idea what he was talking about. "Ten, Eleven what?"

"Thousand," he said matter-of-factly. "I would say $10,500, ya?"

"$10,500. For my Jag?"

He nodded, untroubled. "If you are looking for something practical, I have got really decent Toyota I can sell to you for twelve, so would be only fifteen hundred after trade-in. The reliability on that thing is awesome."

"A Toyota," I repeated. "For my Jag."

He tilted his head to the side. It occurred to me that perhaps he was beginning to think I was mentally impaired. He spoke slowly. "Ya, it is Toyota Corolla, highly reliable car. You want to see?"

Beige, two doors, low to the ground, the car had no style, no personality, no self-awareness of its aesthetic. I came close to crying but did not.

"You want to go for test drive?"

"No, that's okay. I'm sure it's fine."

Again, he looked at me like I wasn't all there. "So, you are interested?"

"Can I put the fifteen hundred on my credit card?"

"Sure, ya, we can do that."

"Okay. Fine. Let's do it."

We went back into the shop, and I handed him my Visa. He said, "Beautiful car, that Jag. But is better for you not break down so much, ya? You will like this Toyota. I won't see you so much in here. Not so good for me, ya, but will be much better for you."

I drove home in the Toyota Corolla. It was noisy, and the car smelled like pine air freshener. I was wearing a skirt, and the cloth seats felt itchy on the back of my thighs. I pulled into the little drive of our rented brownstone. Jack *ooh*ed and *aah*ed like he really admired it. He hugged me and told me I'd made a great decision. But it hadn't been my decision, and I hadn't hugged him back. And from then on, it was hard for me not to see him in this light: he was the man who had made me sell my Jag.

Where was it now, that sleek, feline '74 Jaguar XKE? Who was driving it? Did they love it as much as I had? Did they understand that it was a gift of love between a parent and his only child? Did it still smell like my dad?

For of course, that's why I'd loved the Jag so much: not because it was beautiful, or an icon, or because it could reach 150 miles per hour, or because Enzo Ferrari had called it "the most beautiful car ever made"—but because my dad had given it to me.

My dad. That was my greatest loss, of course. I thought of the word "lost" and then the word "found." *Lost and found.* For I had been the one who had found him. In the basement. Where, of course, he had not died of a heart attack. That was just another lie I told myself so that I could fall asleep at night.

I turned away from Jack and curled into a little fetal ball, tucking the covers up to my chin and curling my fists into my neck. If I had slept like this in the womb, I couldn't remember, but it felt familiar to me and comforting, like a time just before birth, or perhaps, just before death. I nearly sucked my thumb.

"My father had a heart attack and died before he got to the hospital." That was the lie I had told others so often that it had become not something I'd made up but almost a truth, the way a woman will shave a year or two off her age and then not quite remember how old she is.

But that wasn't true, either. No, if I was being honest with myself (and curled up in a ball, in the dark, in the middle of the night, I was always honest with myself), I never forgot how my father died.

Instead, I merely channeled the Lilly who had once been a talented enough actor to play Honey in *Who's Afraid of Virginia Woolf?* at one of Chicago's prestigious theaters, whenever I said the words: "My father had a heart attack. He died before he got to the hospital." I made my voice and expression fetching and a little vulnerable but not at all self-pitying, so that the people I'd told this to (Jack, for example) felt that I was terribly brave. A good performance, all in all.

Those were the words Jack had said, when I'd told him about my father, about his "heart attack," about how I'd tried to rush him to the hospital, but it had been too late.

"You are so brave."

I turned over and gazed at him. He had stubble on his cheeks and smooth eyelids, through which I saw tender veins. There was so much between us. No, I wasn't thinking about the Jag and the dead babies and the crippling mountain of debt; I was thinking about the five inches of air and the tough, protective skin that separated his dreams from my thoughts. I thought of waking him, of telling him the truth. *Let me tell you the truth about how my father died.* But more than being afraid of saying the words aloud—and I was terrified of saying the words aloud—I was afraid of his reaction. That he would be furious at me for lying to him all this time. *Do I even know you?* he would say. *Why didn't you tell me the truth? How could you keep something like that from me?* And: *What else have you been lying to me about?*

For when we had first told bits and pieces of our life stories, I had not known that Jack and I would get married, that eight years later we would still be together, and he would still believe that my father had suffered a heart attack and had died on the way to the hospital, because I had never told him anything different.

And after all this time, how could I tell him anything different now?

21

THE HORSE TRAINER
AND THE PSYCHIC

IN THE MORNING, JACK AND I met in the kitchen, which smelled like coffee and ancient, cold house, a scent like old books. Outside, the temperature hovered in the thirties, and inside, the air seemed to struggle to reach the thermostat's setting of sixty-eight degrees. I was wearing a black wool skirt, a thick green sweater, tights, and boots, and I was still cold. Jack was wearing jeans and a long-sleeved shirt and looked perfectly comfortable. "Good morning," he said, handing me a mug of coffee.

"Thanks." I took a sip and then dropped a piece of whole wheat bread into the toaster. While the bread was toasting, I put out fresh food and water for Olivier, who was sleeping in the window seat. It was eight o'clock and barely light outside.

"About yesterday," Jack said. "I don't want to leave all week on a bad note. We're good, right?" I thought about the nursery and the vents. I couldn't read his expression. He was leaning against the island, sipping his coffee, gazing at me with . . . what? He looked neither angry nor sympathetic. His face, with its unlined forehead, high cheekbones, and peaceful blue-gray eyes, seemed as neutral as Switzerland.

The toast popped up, and I put it on a plate. "Sure," I said, trying to be as Swiss as he was. My fighting style had always been "avoidance." "We're good."

"You gonna be okay here by yourself?"

He seemed less concerned than the last couple of times he'd left, and I wondered if he was getting sick of worrying about me. For my part, I was more excited than ever for him to be gone. Not only because it meant I could proceed with my research, but also because I'd been emailing back and forth with the psychic, and we'd arranged a free consultation for Tuesday afternoon. The farther away Jack was from that event, the better. "I'll be fine," I said. "Don't trouble yourself about me. Have a good trip."

He poured the rest of his coffee into a thermos, added more from the French press, and kissed me on the forehead. "You too, honey, have a good week. And don't worry, we'll get through this, one way or another."

Then he left, leaving me to wonder what he'd meant by "one way or another" (what was one way? What was another way?) and also "this." Our financial problems? Our marital issues? Our differing positions over the heating vents in the nursery? Well, at least the latter was easily remedied, now that Jack would be in Indiana. I marched upstairs, went to the nursery, and opened up the vents. And then I backed out of the room, pleased with myself.

At the library, I was immediately reminded that this was the week leading up to Halloween. Most of the staff members on the main floor were assigned a decorating task to complete between our other duties, and mine was to create a scary books display using classic books (as opposed to true crime thrillers, which was Patty's job, or horror movies, which was Chris's). I made a banner that read FEAR NEVER GOES OUT OF STYLE and attached it above my table of classic scary novellas and novels including *The Turn of the Screw*, *The Haunting of Hill House*, *Beloved*, *The Shining*, the *Xenogenesis* trilogy, and *Rosemary's Baby*, as well as collected ghost stories from Scotland, Mexico, and Japan. I arranged the books around black feather boas and raven figurines with beady red eyes while trying not to think about my own ghosts and what had become, in recent years, a dreaded holiday. (All of those adorable kids dressed up in adorable costumes made my stomach hurt as badly as if I'd eaten too much Halloween candy.)

In the afternoon, while I checked in books at the circ desk, Arjun brought me a sugar cookie in the shape of a ghost, and said, "Today in book club the kids wrote *Twilight* fan fiction with Edward and Jacob as lovers. I have to say, the whole thing makes a lot more sense that way."

I laughed. "More cookies?"

Arjun had thick, dark eyebrows with gray strands, heavy-lidded eyes that always seemed amused about something, and a mustache and beard he was already growing out for "no-shave November." He rubbed his stubble now and stared at the white frosted cookie on the napkin in my hand. "Honestly, I'm not sure if that's supposed to be Edward or a ghost."

I took a bite. I hadn't eaten much of my toast, and I'd only had pistachio nuts and an apple for lunch. I had to resist stuffing the entire rest of the cookie into my mouth. "Thank you," I said. "It's delicious."

I spent my evening half-heartedly sanding the floor while wondering how I could find out more about what Chas Lawrence had refused to do for Bobby Shawcross. It felt like I'd been close to a breakthrough, maybe just a few words or minutes away from solving some critical mystery of this house, of its past, but then Chas Lawrence and I had been blocked by the ravages of the disease of his mind, by his trauma, and possibly by the kind attendant who had come to soothe him. Should I go back there? Try to visit him again? Or was it possible that he'd told someone else what had happened between him and Bobby Shawcross, someone close to him (his wife?), before he'd lost his memory? I went to the phone directory and found the number for C. and K. Lawrence (was that them?) and punched it into my cell phone.

"Hello?"

"Hello," I said. "Is this Katya Lawrence?"

"Yes, speaking." Katya's voice was melodious—I could imagine her addressing the horses she'd once trained in this gentle, singsong voice—and her accent mild. I pictured Midwestern farms rolling into golden Ukrainian plains and an occasional spiky castle. "May I help you?"

"I hope so. My name is Lilly. I recently moved into your husband's family's estate. The Lawrence Mansion? I'm doing some research on—"

"So, it was you."

"Excuse me?"

"He was still agitated when I got there. Gloria told me some relative came and made him cry. Who are you? Why would you do such a thing? What are you thinking, making an old, sick man so upset?"

My mind raced to come up with some sort of response that would smooth things over so that she would tell me what I needed to know. "I'm sorry, Mrs. Lawrence. I was doing a little research on the house I recently purchased, and I thought your husband might be able to answer some of my questions. He seems like such a kind man. I never meant to upset him."

"He really is kind man," she said. "But claiming you are relative? What was that about?"

"I never said I was a relative, just that I lived in the family house," I answered, thinking quickly. "They must have misunderstood. They aren't very well organized there, are they?"

There was a pause. Perhaps both of us were picturing the young girl who could barely be bothered to come to the front desk. "Those people," she said, angrily blowing the *p*s, and I imagined she'd had some run-ins of her own.

"I would have been glad to check in with you before I went, but I hope it's not too late now? To ask you a couple of questions?"

"What kinds of questions?" she asked, and I could hear the suspicion in her voice. "What did you ask Chas that got him so upset?"

"Well, I'm sure you know that your husband worked for his cousin Birdy Lawrence and her husband Bobby Shawcross when he was a young man."

"Yes, of course. Before the tragedy."

"That's right. I was wondering about their . . . relationship."

"Relationship?" She made the word sound dirty, and I knew I had to get to the point.

"Did you ever hear your husband talk about something Bobby Shawcross wanted him to do?"

"Whoa," she said, as if I were one of the horses she'd trained fifty years ago. "You have no right to dig up past like that!"

"I'm only trying to und—"

"Listen here," she said. "That was difficult time in my husband's life. His first cousin committed murder and suicide. Can you imagine? It was something he never wanted to talk about. Not to me, not to anyone. So whatever Chas heard, whatever he saw, you can forget about bothering him again. I don't want you stirring up these emotions in him. Understand?"

"Yes, ma'am. And again, I'm sorry . . . ," I began, but Katya had already hung up.

I stared out the kitchen window that faced the backyard. It was getting dark. I felt bad for upsetting Katya, bad for upsetting Chas, who really did seem like a nice man, and, I had to admit, bad for myself. For I had some questions that needed answering, and now I didn't know how they would be answered. But "one way or another," I'd have to figure it out.

*   *   *

On Tuesday after work, when the doorbell rang, I opened the door to find a woman about thirty years old, with straight blond hair and blue eyes, wearing a salmon suit and beige pumps standing on the stone porch. I didn't know what I'd expected, but the woman in front of me looked like a junior real estate agent or a fresh, young news anchor, not a woman who sent spirits to the other side.

"Ricarda Heller," she said, extending her hand. Shaking it, I noted her firm grip, soft skin, and trim pink nails.

"Hi, I'm Lilly Bly. Come on in."

During our email exchange, we'd set a date and time for her to come over, and I'd agreed to allow her to use any findings for her book, but I hadn't told her anything about the house's history. Of course, she could have looked it up, as I had, or perhaps, as someone in her line of work, she hadn't needed to. She probably knew this was "the Murder House." I also hadn't told her much about my experiences, just that I'd felt a "presence" and wanted to understand more about it. Now, with her standing in the foyer, cocking her head to the side as if she were a prospective home buyer listening for a clanking pipe, I felt silly.

"I'm probably just imagining things," I said.

"No, you're not." If her appearance was that of a sorority girl, her voice was steely and certain, the voice a knife would make if it could talk. "These kinds of places get their reputations for good reason. Violent death always leaves a mark. And I can already feel it. . . . There is definitely a presence here. A complicated presence. I sense confusion, desire, darkness."

I felt uncomfortable. It seemed as if we were starting already, still standing in the foyer, beneath the black chandelier. I had assumed we would begin by sitting down and chatting over tea. Engage in some sort of paranormal foreplay. "Umm, you mind my asking how this works?"

"My former colleagues had equipment. I don't. I use my mind. The main activity of the presence is upstairs. Am I correct?"

Without waiting for an answer, she walked past me and up the stairs, her heels clicking on the wood, and I followed. I thought she'd walk into our bedroom, where a ghost had taken a bath, gripped my leg, and wrapped its arms around my waist, but she surprised me by walking straight through the open door of the nursery. She stood in the middle of the room, set down her bag, put her finger to her lips, and closed her eyes.

I followed her lead and squinted my eyes shut for a moment, trying to feel something otherworldly, but I just felt chilly. I didn't know if that was because a ghost was near, or because it was an evening in fall. After a few seconds, Ricarda opened her eyes, and I noticed that her blue irises had a design around the pupil, like a snowflake. When she spoke, her voice was icy as well. "There is a presence here. Someone died in this house, then couldn't leave. They shouldn't be here. And they want something from you. Something you can't give. Something you must not give. It's important that you understand that."

Goose bumps traveled up my arms. But while Ricarda's words sounded ominous, they were also a bit generic. *Someone died in this house, then couldn't leave.* Surely, this could be the description of any ghost. I thought Ricarda Heller would need to do better than that to get her book contract, but what did I know?

"Okay, sure, I understand," I said.

"There are terrible secrets in this house," she said.

I thought of *Hamlet*. *There needs no ghost come from the grave to tell us this.*

"I see a skull and crossbones, but there's something strange about the skull. It has . . . it has . . . ears? Mouse ears? Rat's ears? I see a room, a dark room . . . stairs. You don't want to go in this room, but you must. You're in terrible danger here, Lilly."

This small blonde in the salmon pink suit was beginning to freak me out. "What do I do?" I asked, more quietly than I'd intended.

"Short of packing up and leaving, which would be a solid option, there's only one thing you can do."

"What?" I whispered, and then waited while she reached into her leather satchel.

"Smudge."

She grabbed a bundle of wrapped herbs from her satchel. "I'm sure you thought we'd be smudging sage today," she said, giving me more credit than I deserved, "but that's cultural appropriation. I'm not Native American. My ancestors are from France and Scotland, which looks about where yours come from, too?" I supposed she was referring to my light brown hair, my pale complexion. I thought of myself as a mutt, plenty of crossbreeding on both sides, and there very well might have been some Scottish and French in me, sure. I gave Ricarda Heller a noncommittal half nod, half shrug. "Therefore, I brought wild lavender. It's an herb our ancestors would have used, and it has calming, healing, and circulatory properties, so it really moves energy throughout the house."

"You've done this before? And it's worked?" I could hear the hopefulness in my voice.

She gazed at me with those steely blue eyes. "This is not my first rodeo. Open the window, please. We want the spirit to be able to leave." I did as I was told. Cold air entered the room. I wrapped my cardigan tightly around my chest and hugged my arms together while Ricarda took a hot pink Bic lighter out of her skirt suit jacket pocket and lit the bundle of lavender. I breathed in the scent and felt calmer.

"Repeat after me," Ricarda said, and then, as she spoke, she walked around the room, waving the smoldering bouquet of lavender. "I command any negativity . . ."

"I command any negativity . . ."

". . . any low spiritual energy . . ."

". . . any low spiritual energy . . ."

". . . any malevolent beings and spirits . . ."

". . . any malevolent beings and spirits . . ."

". . . within this space to leave and go to the light . . ."

". . . within this space to leave and go to the light."

"You are not welcome here."

"You are not welcome here."

"I command you to leave! Go to the light! Cross to the other side!"

Ricarda's eyes were squinted shut. One hand was waving the wild lavender while the other arm curved above her head. She looked like a Broadway performer or a Pentecostal preacher. After a while, she opened her eyes and said, "Lilly?"

"Oh, um, what was it again?"

She repeated the words to me, and I said, "I command you to leave. Go to the light. Cross to the other side."

"Very good." She set the lavender on the windowsill and then stood by it for a few seconds, her eyes closed. When she opened them, she said, "I usually feel something when the spirit goes out the window. But this time . . ." She shrugged.

"But this time?" I repeated.

Ricarda closed the window, retrieved a camera from her bag, and took a few shots with a flash. "I expect I'll see orbs when I develop these. There is a spirit in this room. A spirit with a dark past. A complicated spirit. Cloying and needy. I sense sadness, anger. Trauma. It isn't safe for you here." She put her camera in her bag, looked me in the eye, and said, "I'm sorry. I've done everything I can. Some spirits just don't want to leave." With that, she walked down the stairs.

I trailed after her. "Wait," I called. "What do I do?"

She opened the front door and stood in the entryway for a moment, her back to me. "You need to get out of here, you need to move, you need to save yourself." She turned around, and then, in a gentle, kinder tone, with a sad expression in her eyes, the expression of a bartender pouring a drink to someone who's just shown them their sobriety chip, she said, "But you won't."

With that she walked down the mossy stone pathway, got into her Subaru, and drove away.

22

HALLOWEEN

YOU'RE IN TERRIBLE DANGER. They want something from you. It isn't safe for you here. You need to save yourself.

For the rest of the week, these warnings floated in and out of my mind, as I went through the paces of my day-to-day life. Sleeping fitfully, waking, getting ready, going to work. Coming back home to my beautiful, cavernous mansion. Feeding Olivier (and, when I remembered, myself). Wandering through the nearly empty rooms, trying to sense the entity that the psychic believed resided with me, the entity that wanted something from me, that was putting me in danger. But everything was quiet and still. Perhaps too quiet.

Friday was Halloween, and I arrived at the library to find my coworkers dressed in costumes. Chris was a zombie, Jess was Superwoman, Arjun was Professor Snape, Patty was Belle, and Carl was the Black Panther comic superhero. Eleanor, in a red layered skirt and peasant blouse, announced that she was a gypsy, until Carl took her aside. I watched him speaking to her, smiling, touching her shoulder. She went into her office, and when we saw her again, she had ditched her headscarf and told us she was a flamenco dancer.

"Dude, awesome, I love flamenco music!" Chris said, and Eleanor blushed, pleased.

I was wearing black jeans and a T-shirt I'd found at the local

Goodwill. The shirt pictured a bowl of cereal, with words that read, in bloody orange font, "Cereal Killer."

I struggled through the day of excited kids and their doting and stressed-out parents and came home depressed and exhausted. I called Jack in his hotel room in Indianapolis as soon as I got back from work. "Can you come home?" I asked.

"When?"

"Now?"

"Now? What's up?"

"It's Halloween. I didn't think about being here by myself on Halloween, and . . . I'm scared."

There was a silence, and I was reminded, as I often was, of how difficult it must be to be married to me. How you couldn't just say whatever you were thinking—"You're crazy!"—for example, but always had to choose your words carefully, so that things (craziness, for example) wouldn't get completely out of control.

"What are you afraid of?" he finally said, in a voice sweet and calm, as if he were talking to a sensitive child.

How could I possibly answer that question? I was afraid of everything, from being haunted by Birdy to fearing I was going insane to having to hand out candy at the door to little kids. And then something occurred to me.

"I don't have any candy."

"That's what you're afraid of?"

"No, I'm just saying, I don't have any candy."

"So, turn off the lights."

"We're going to be *that* house?"

Now Jack sighed into the phone. "What do you want me to tell you, Lil? I'm in Indianapolis, nearly four hundred miles away. I can't exactly rush home to greet trick-or-treaters. Either go to the store and buy candy or turn off the lights."

Both options felt terrible and paralyzing to me.

"We never handed out candy," he continued. "You know, my mom with her migraines, my dad drunk and asleep. My brothers and I were always out trick-or-treating, or later, going to parties. Nothing bad ever happened. Kids just skipped our house."

What did he mean by *Nothing bad ever happened*? What bad things were supposed to happen? "By bad you mean, like, you know . . . ?" I couldn't quite say the words aloud: *Ghosts came?*

"I mean our house didn't get egged."

"Oh my gosh, that's a possibility?"

"No. That's what I'm telling you. Kids don't do that. They're too busy going to the next house and the next one. Have you ever seen kids trick-or-treat with eggs? That's like, from the fifties or something. I'm telling you, just turn off the lights. Everything will be fine."

It had not occurred to me that anyone would egg our house if I didn't have candy, and I focused on that, on that "trick" kids would do if you didn't give out a "treat," instead of focusing on the undead, and the idea motivated me.

"I've gotta go. I need to go get candy."

"Honey, are you gonna be okay?"

"Yes, I'll be fine," I said, and pressed "end."

I went to the quick mart at the gas station and bought a bag of fun-size Snickers, my childhood favorite. Then I rushed home, turned on the porch lights, and sat in the dining room, so I could see anyone who came to the door through the window. I tried to read my library book while I waited, but I felt jumpy, unable to concentrate on Chandler's detective, on the Santa Ana winds, the femme fatale, the hardboiled prose. Trick-or-treating had started at four, when I was still at work; I didn't get the candy until close to six. By seven, no one had come to the door.

Then, through the plastic sheeting on the windows in the living room, I thought I saw movement outside. I ripped open the tape along the side of one of the windows, peeked through the opening, and saw three children coming up the long driveway. As they came closer, I made out a ballerina, Spider-Man, and a bloody zombie nurse. They got about halfway up, then stopped. I hurried to the door with the wooden bowl of fun-size Snickers in my hand, ready. I waited. The door was a large, heavy, wooden thing, with only a tiny stained-glass window, the door of a medieval castle or fortress, and I really couldn't see out. I opened the door, closed it behind me so Olivier wouldn't escape, and stood on the porch. "Hello?" I called. My heart was beating fast. "I have candy!" I yelled. I took a step closer. One of them (the ballerina?) squealed, and then the other two joined in, with half-terrified, half-gleeful screams. They ran down the street, away from me, from my bowl of candy, from my haunted house. I wondered if they were the same kids I'd met the day we'd moved in. (*Yeah, a ghost. Some lady. We seen her in the window at night.*) I wondered if they'd go to school the next day and tell their classmates about how brave they were to trick-or-treat at the creepy Lawrence Mansion, the haunted house, *the Murder House*, where there was not only a ghost, but also a witch! Offering them candy!

I went back inside, turned off the porch light, and decided to call it a night. Upstairs, while brushing my teeth, I gazed into the mirror. A disturbing feeling crept over me, that it wasn't me in the reflection. The reflection looked like Lilly, but I couldn't help but feel that she was wearing a mask. Those weren't my eyes, staring back at me blankly, hollow, without expression. Were they?

I shook my head, trying to get rid of the strange sensation. I splashed water on my face and looked up. The mask was gone. I was once again there.

23

THE MIDDLE OF THE NIGHT

WHAT WAS HAPPENING? Why was I hearing music? I grabbed my cell phone off the nightstand and saw that it was 2:33 a.m. Why was I hearing music at 2:33 a.m.? I listened carefully and realized it was Perry Como, singing "Don't Let the Stars Get in Your Eyes," a song from the 1950s my dad had loved.

I sat up and turned toward Jack's side of the bed. Empty. I was groggy and tried to figure out what was happening. It was Halloween night (or, to be exact, the morning of All Saints' Day), a Saturday. Jack wasn't supposed to be home until the afternoon.

So why was Mr. C's smooth baritone voice coming from what sounded like the living room?

I got out of bed. I was wearing thin owl-print cotton pajama bottoms and a white tank top. The middle-of-the-night air was chilly, and I slipped on a cashmere cardigan and wool socks. As I walked down the stairs to investigate, the music grew louder. Perry Como was singing about his sweetheart, whom he hoped wouldn't stray while he was away, because she was the only one he'd ever love. It was an upbeat, danceable Western song, out of place in the dark house in the middle of the night.

Before I reached the foyer, and could see anything, I yelled, "Jack?" For even though Jack wasn't supposed to be home, why else would Perry Como be playing unless Jack was playing him? The sound was loud, clear, but slightly grainy, as if it were coming from a record player (which we didn't own).

I stepped off the bottom stair, into the foyer, and gazed to the left. In place of our empty, tattered living room was a gleaming, vibrant space—the *Haven Herald*'s mid-century version of our living room. The decor was a combination of tasteful old money (Edgar's leftovers?) and 1950s hipster (Bobby's influence?). The hardwood floors were pristine, glossy, and scattered with large, expensive antique Persian rugs. There was a green sofa, and a Scandinavian-style circular wooden and glass coffee table (our coffee table, the same coffee table that had come with the house, though this one looked brand new), on which sat a ceramic ashtray shaped like a hand. Two round orange armchairs flanked the fireplace and faced a TV console that didn't stand on anything but was its own piece of furniture, the shape and size of a large cabinet. An eclectic combination of paintings hung on the walls, some abstract expressionist, some realistic oils of landscapes with horses, a few sketches, and one portrait of the Lawrence-Shawcross family, which was mounted above the fireplace.

But all this was background. What was truly shocking was that they were there, right in front of my eyes, come to life, so to speak. It was *them*: Bobby, Birdy, and Amelia. I could see them as clearly as I could see living souls, as clearly as I had seen the patrons and my coworkers at the library the previous afternoon.

Bobby Shawcross lay on the couch, his legs stretched out in front of him. He was wearing a black-and-white short-sleeved shirt and khaki-colored slacks with a crease down the front and small cuffs at the hem, just above his tan-and-white shoes. He was smoking a cigarette, and occasionally tapped the ash into that hand-shaped ashtray. I could smell the smoke, feel it fill my lungs.

You're hallucinating, I told myself. *You're dreaming*. It was the middle of Halloween night, after all. I'd had a hard day, a hard week. And just a few days before, the psychic had come to the house. Clearly, the stress had taken a toll on me. I pressed my fingers against my temples and willed the illusion to go away. But even as I did so, I could still hear the music, feel the smoke inside my lungs, see the humans and Persian rugs in front of me. Everything and everyone were still there, as clear as the phenomenal world.

Bobby continued to recline on the couch, while Birdy and Amelia danced while holding hands, their socked feet gliding on the gleaming hardwood floor.

Birdy spun Amelia, dipping her so low that for a moment, Amelia's hair touched the floor. Both Birdy and Amelia wore white blouses; Birdy wore hers with black high-waisted, slim-fit capri pants that came down to mid-calf, while Amelia wore pink stretch pants and a headband in her hair. Mother beamed down lovingly at daughter while they danced, and daughter gazed up lovingly at mother. I watched them dancing, smiling, laughing, gazing. And even through my haze of confusion, it occurred to me to wonder: *How was it possible that Birdy could (would?) murder this child?*

I felt shaky and nauseated, not able to understand what was happening, but also curious and fascinated, as if I were an invisible member of an audience watching a play unfold before me.

The song ended. Birdy went to the record player, picked up the needle, and set it on its stand. She tucked the record in a sleeve and put it away. Then both she and Amelia collapsed in the two orange chairs by the fireplace. Bobby sat up, stubbed out his cigarette, and walked across the room.

He put his hand on his wife's shoulder. His face was handsome, chiseled, concerned. "It's time for your tea."

"Oh, I'm so hot! We worked up a sweat, didn't we, Butterfly?" she said to her daughter, who nodded and smiled. "Just some water would be nice. Thanks, Bobby."

"I'll have some water, too, please, Daddy."

Bobby's smile was accommodating, as if he aimed to please. "Sure, sure, two waters coming right up. But I'll also get you some of your tea, Birdy-boo. Doctor says it's good for your nerves." A slight drawl in his voice reminded me not so far south to be of Mississippi swamps, but more like Oklahoma plains. "I'll add some ice cubes to cool it down, how's that?" he said as he walked right past me, in the foyer, through the dining room, into the kitchen.

"Mommy, what's wrong with your nerves?" Amelia's big brown doe eyes were wide with love and worry. She had full lips, like her mother, and shiny brown hair, the same dark shade as both of her parents'. She was beautiful and innocent, and my heart broke for her, knowing what everyone in the scene playing before me did not: that she would be dead before she reached the age of nine.

Her mother smiled a sad smile, as if she had seen too much of the world and was tired. Her dark almond-shaped eyes didn't move along with her mouth. "My nerves are fine. I just have some pins-and-needles that make it hard to sleep. Nothing for you to be concerned about, dear. Dr. Grodin prescribed valerian root tea to help."

"Does it taste good?"

Birdy laughed. "If you put a sugar cube in it, it sure does!"

Bobby returned with a tray filled with two glasses of water and a mug, which he set on the coffee table. He handed Amelia one of the glasses of water, and he handed Birdy the mug. "I loaded it with ice and put a sugar cube in it, just how you like. Should be refreshing."

She took a long drink and said, "That is refreshing, thank you."

"Sure, honey," he said, his voice exuding uxorious concern. "Now, listen, I'm gonna go out. You girls be good, hear?"

Both Birdy and Bobby looked like movie stars. Bobby oozed charm and charisma. He emanated an aura of a tomcat leaving to go on a hunt, track a scent, and see what female feline he could meet. Birdy reminded me of a model in an ad for a 1950s perfume, with her sultry mouth, cute, upturned nose, and former athlete's elegant physique. She was poised and calm as she listened to her husband say the words that must have turned her stomach.

"Do you have to go, Daddy?" Amelia asked. "Why don't you stay home with us tonight? It's almost time for bed."

"That's why you won't hardly miss me. Mommy'll run you a bath and read you a story, and before you know it, it'll be morning and I'll be tickling you awake." He leaned down and kissed her all over her cheeks, and she giggled, reluctantly at first, and then as if she couldn't help herself.

He turned to Birdy. If he were an actor, I'd have said he looked like he was trying not to appear uncomfortable. He stuck his chin out, haughty, but he jangled his keys in his pockets, nervous. "Hey," he said. "Can I get a twenty off you?"

She sipped her tea, as if she hadn't heard him. Then finally she said, "I just gave you a hundred two days ago. Who'd you spend it on?"

"It ain't like that. Me and the boys. We just gambled a little. For fun."

"And tonight?"

He stood up straighter. His eyes peered into hers, deep and wronged. "Why you gotta be like that? Can't I just have a twenty for gas and a little booze?"

"You know, you could always get a job."

"Get a job." He shook his head. "Or I could sell one of these rugs."

"You're not selling my family heirlooms. My father worked very hard for them."

"I worked hard, too," Bobby said.

"And I'm sure you will again, someday. Someday soon, I hope. Then you won't need to ask me for your spending money. That will be nice for both of us."

"I will get a job, sweetheart, but in the meantime?"

She didn't look at him as she said, "My purse is in the mudroom."

He went to the mudroom and came back waving a fifty. "Thanks, darlin'. I appreciate it." He walked over to Birdy and kissed her on the cheek. "I won't be home too late. But you don't need to wait up."

"Don't worry," she said. "I won't."

He looked toward the foyer, as if he'd heard something (me? I stepped back, out of sight, just to make sure), and then he must have put on a new record, because I heard a woman's voice. The song was slower, less danceable. The lovely voice reminded me of a warm pink bubble bath as the woman sang about being awake but still dreaming.

Bobby walked into the foyer no longer wearing his shirt and khakis of only moments before, but a royal blue suit. When had he had time to change? I leaned against the coat closet, as if to let him pass and exit out the front door. But then something astonishing happened: Bobby met my eyes. I turned my head in either direction, even though we were out of eyesight, and probably earshot, of anyone in the living room. He was looking directly at me—directly into my eyes. I felt fear form in my stomach and radiate out, to every limb, every hair, every pore. My arms tingled with goose bumps. He came closer and set his palms on the closet, one hand on either side of my shoulders. His chest and face were inches away from mine, and I could smell the smoke on his breath. "Hey, beautiful," he said.

"You can . . . see me?"

He laughed, showing movie-star-white teeth. He took his hands off the closet beside me, twirled my hair with one hand, and put the other hand on my shoulder. I could feel it there, as if he were a real human, a real man. His hand was warm, large, and strong. "I can see you as you are, and I can see you as I'd like to see you. Know what I mean?" The hand that was on my shoulder fingered down the side of my body, grazing the side of my breast, my waist, until it landed on my hipbone. Then the other hand joined its opposite, and both of his hands squeezed each of my hipbones. I could feel my body jut out to meet him; I could feel myself become wet, even with my fear. "Lordy! What I'd like to do to you when there ain't nobody around," he said, his voice deep and sexy, a midnight radio voice. "When my wife is gone, and when your husband is gone." He grabbed me, pressing me against him, so that I could feel his erection, big and hard beneath his pants. One hand was on my ass now and one was wrapped around my back. I couldn't get away if I'd wanted to. And truth to tell, I didn't want to.

The singer on the record was afraid to close her eyes, afraid that, if she dreamed, she'd discover this thrill was just an illusion.

Bobby smelled of cigarette smoke, whiskey, and something like sulfur and metal.

"What are you going to do about your husband? Huh?" he whispered into my ear.

The space between my legs was throbbing as his hardness pressed against me. I felt dizzy. What was he talking about? "What do you mean, what am I going to do about my husband?" I whispered back.

The hand that was on my back crept over and cupped me over my pajama bottoms. He was clutching me against him hard. My God, it felt good. I wasn't thinking about Birdy or Amelia in the next room, or Jack, working hard for me in another state. I was only thinking about this man, being naked with him, having him inside me. He kissed my neck, pushing down my sweater with his lips, and then his kisses became tiny little bites. I closed my eyes, tilted my neck to the side for more.

"There are lots of ways," he said.

"What?" I barely managed to ask.

He was now nibbling on my ear, pressing his erection against me. He stroked my breast just barely over my tank top, squeezing it hard, and then softly brushing my nipple, and then squeezing it hard again. I was throbbing. I wrapped my arms around him, one hand on his back, the other on his ass.

The singer wanted her lover to pinch her, to prove that she was awake. She couldn't believe that he was truly hers.

"It'd be nice if we was together, and he was . . . gone. You'd like that, wouldn't you, baby?"

I tried to concentrate on what he was saying. What did he mean by gone? Was he telling me to leave Jack so that I could be with him?

"You want me to leave my husband?" I said aloud.

I opened my eyes—and when I did, I saw that Bobby had disappeared. I was trembling. Slowly, I peeked around the corner to see the living room. Birdy and Amelia weren't there. The 1950s living room was gone. Patti Page singing "With My Eyes Wide Open, I'm Dreaming" had stopped. It was just me, standing in the foyer of my enormous, empty, run-down house, my heart pounding, my pulse racing, the space between my thighs still throbbing, alone.

24

THE DAY AFTER

I WOKE UP AT TEN, immediately remembering, and then trying to understand, what had happened in the middle of the night. It must have been a dream or hallucination. That was the only explanation for it, wasn't it?

But I found it hard to believe I'd been dreaming or hallucinating that scene. It had been too real. Lying in bed, I touched myself where Bobby Shawcross had touched me, starting with my shoulder, moving down my side, stopping at my breast, and then cupping myself, feeling a dried stickiness in my pj's where they had once been wet. There were ghosts. They were living here. I had seen them. I had touched one of them. He had touched me.

And when I went into the bathroom, in the mid-morning light, with the sun streaming through the windows, I saw shocking proof.

Two purple marks bloomed on the left side of my neck, little bruises, little love bites, made by my demon almost-lover, my ghost almost-lover, Bobby Shawcross. It was a relief, in some way, to see them, for it meant I couldn't have hallucinated him. Them. Could I have? But my relief soon turned to despair as I wondered, *How will I explain these marks to Jack?*

I covered my neck with concealer and then foundation and blended in the makeup until the dark purple spots disappeared. Then I brushed my teeth and got dressed, choosing a turtleneck from my closet, hoping the marks wouldn't show.

*   *   *

I closed the door to the nursery so Jack and I wouldn't have an argument about my opening the vents and keeping the door open while he was gone. Then I fed Olivier, cleaned his litter box, made myself tea, and sat at the kitchen table while he purred beside me in the window seat.

"Lilly?"

It was Jack's voice. I went into the foyer, where I found him setting down his bag and taking off his wool coat. We gave each other a kiss and a hug, and I guess I lingered with the hug, because he said, "Hey, you okay?"

"I'm glad to see you."

"I'm glad to see you, too." He broke away and looked at me. "Sure you're okay?"

"Let's see. I survived Halloween. It should be smooth sailing from now on, right?" I gave him what I hoped was a cheerful smile.

But apparently, he saw through it. He wiped my hair away from my face and held my cheeks between his hands. I knew it was supposed to be a loving gesture, but my face felt claustrophobic and trapped. "You can tell me what's going on, you know."

I gazed into his cool eyes behind his hipster glasses. Was that true? Could I? He was my husband. He loved me. I loved him. I felt my vulnerability tense up into a ball in the back of my throat, and I forced myself to let it go. I took his hands away, so I could speak, and I held them. "I just feel . . . I mean, I love this house. I feel connected to it in ways I can't explain. But I think it might be haunted. I feel like—like I really saw them last night. The people who once lived here."

He let go of my hands, emitted a deep breath, and walked into the kitchen. I followed.

"Jack?" He didn't answer. "You told me to tell you what's wrong."

He turned on the electric kettle and brought down the instant coffee from a cabinet. "I love your imagination, I do. The way you can become different characters on the stage, inhabit different people. The way you have so much empathy for other people, for animals. I love that about you. It's an endearing, childlike gift. But this is getting to be too much. It's like you're losing touch with reality. This isn't a play. This isn't a story. You're telling me you're seeing ghosts. Do you know how . . ."—he paused, as if thinking better of saying a "certain word" out loud—". . . that sounds?"

I felt broken, and my voice was gravelly when I spoke. "You asked me what's going on. You told me I could tell you. So I did. I knew I shouldn't have. I knew I couldn't . . ."

"Couldn't what?"

"Couldn't trust you with the truth."

"The truth? This is not 'the truth.' This is you spending too much time alone, too much time reading and fantasizing about a murder that took place fifty years ago! This is—" He stopped himself short.

"What? Insane?"

The kettle boiled. He scooped instant coffee into a mug, poured the water over it, and stirred. "Not healthy," he said. Then he turned toward me and took my hand. "Honey, listen. Do you think you should . . . talk to someone?"

"A shrink."

"A doctor, a therapist. Someone. I have excellent insurance with my job. I know it would be covered."

"And tell them I believe I'm being haunted."

"Well, sure. Or whatever you want to talk about. I know you haven't had the easiest time. With . . . everything."

His eyes were compassionate. His face looked tired. Was that from working late hours and driving all afternoon from the middle of Indiana, or was it from coming home to a wife who said that she was seeing ghosts? Well, at least I hadn't told him about the hickeys. "I'll think about it," I said.

"There's no shame in getting help. If you have a physical illness, you go to the doctor. If you're having anxiety, or hallucinations, you get help for that." The speech sounded unlike him, and I wondered if he was quoting from a talk HR had given to him when he'd been hired, or from something he'd heard on NPR as he drove across the Midwest. "Right?"

"Of course. It's just . . ."

"Just what?"

How could I explain to him that I was more certain than ever that I was being haunted by actual ghosts? What I needed was a ghost-buster, not a shrink.

She suffered from instability and anxiety.

"I know you stopped taking your medication when you started trying to get pregnant, but I also know you don't need to. There's plenty of that type of medication you can take while trying to con-ceive and while pregnant."

Taking the drugs while trying to get pregnant was only part of the issue. I'd never told him how flattened-out they'd made me feel, how unlike myself. Then I remembered how badly I wanted—I'd needed—to take something like Valium or Xanax recently. Maybe I could just take the calming meds without the other ones.

"I love you," Jack said.

He set down his mug, put his hands on my waist, and kissed me, tenderly, on my lips. He had a thin layer of stubble on his cheeks, as if he had last shaved the morning before. He smelled like flannel and coffee and Jack-neck. My own lips and body responded.

"Want to go upstairs and . . . take a nap?" he asked.

It occurred to me that he was asking me to make love with him right after he'd told me I should see a shrink; he had always found my *instability* appealing. Maybe he was the one who should see the shrink, I thought bitterly. I could point this out to him, tell him he didn't understand me, that he was patronizing me, that he was getting turned on by what he took to be my *instability*, that I didn't need to talk to someone, *that there were real fucking ghosts in the house!* But what was the point? I knew he would deny everything, and I was just sane enough to know I would only sound more insane than I already did.

I thought about how this was the real racket they sold you about marriage, adulthood, life: how lonely you would be most of the time.

But my body was willing enough, so I said, "Sure."

While we were making love, I fantasized I was with Bobby Shaw-cross. I imagined his dark wavy hair, his cheekbones, his strong hands touching my breasts, the throbbing space between my legs. I imagined him hard, pressed against me, inside of me. I imagined it was Bobby on top of me, that my arms and legs were wrapped around Bobby's back. It was the hottest I'd ever been. And then I wasn't fantasizing anymore. Bobby and Jack began to wobble in and out. Sometimes Jack was making love to me, sometimes Bobby. When I came, the eyes I was gazing into—they were Bobby's.

"What the—?" Jack said when we had finished, lying side by side on our backs. He was sweating, breathing hard. "You were on fire."

You always are, baby, another voice said.

"I always am, baby," I said.

25

KEEP IT TOGETHER

JACK AND I WERE IN BED, facing one another for a moment, and it seemed to me that he was gazing at my neck. I panicked. "Don't look at those, they're gross," I said, and then regretted it. I should have just ignored them, gotten up, and put on my turtleneck. What was wrong with me?

"Don't look at what?"

"My . . . bug bites."

"Bug bites? In November?"

Jack turned away, put on his glasses, and then turned toward me again, but by then I was already getting dressed.

"They're nothing, forget it."

"Let me see them. If we have bugs in the house, I want to know."

He walked over to me while I was standing there in my panties and inspected my neck. I had no choice now but to stand by the diagnosis of bug bites, and I was planning on saying that I thought they were due to some kind of spider, hoping the Google search that would inevitably follow would back me up, when Jack said, "Those red marks?"

I had thought they were purple. "I guess so."

He looked closer. "I don't know if they're bites or scratches or what. Have you been scratching?"

"Yes, yes, I've been scratching."

"Well, put some cream on and stop scratching."

I slipped on my bathrobe and went into the bathroom. I turned on every light and inspected my neck. The bites were pale, nearly healed. What was there could have been fading hickeys or old mosquito bites that had been scratched.

On the one hand, it was a relief that Jack and I didn't need to get into a fight about why there were bites on my neck that may have been caused by the undead, the living, or a spider; on the other hand, it was troubling that they had faded so quickly. Had I truly received a couple of love bites? Or if I hadn't, were the ghosts of Bobby Shawcross and those of Birdy and Amelia as real as they had seemed, or had I just dreamed or imagined the scene?

I felt like I was going crazy. I felt like I was going to cry. I sat on the edge of the claw-foot tub, squeezed my head in my hands on both sides of my face, to keep it all together, and then I rocked a little, back and forth. I felt comforted and insane.

I heard Jack say, "Jesus, are you okay?" and realized I hadn't closed the door.

I turned to face him. I wasn't about to tell him the truth, which was *No, I'm obviously not okay.* I had tried the truth earlier and it had gotten me nowhere.

"I'm fine," I said. "Just a little headache. I'm going to take a shower."

I stood up, closed the door, and took a hot shower. "Keep it together, Lilly," I said quietly, while the water ran. Then I started singing, "Keep it together, together, keep it together," while I washed my hair, used conditioner, and scrubbed my face. I felt a little better. I toweled off, dressed in fresh clothes, and even blow-dried my hair. I looked in the mirror and saw there was a reflection staring back at me. A real, human reflection, with pale, dry skin and sunken eyes. I felt my cheeks with my hands, and the woman in the mirror felt her cheeks with her hands. This was me. Lilly. I was still there. Keeping it together . . . more or less. I went downstairs.

*   *   *

While we were sipping coffee and herbal tea in the kitchen, we heard a loud noise in the dining room, as if a book had fallen. "What now?" Jack said, going to investigate. Olivier was curled in the window seat beside us, and while his ears pricked up at the noise, he didn't even bother to run away, so I supposed the noise didn't portend anything otherworldly. Those ghostly machinations never seemed to happen while Jack was around.

"Shit!" he yelled from the dining room.

But I could have been wrong. "What is it?" I asked, not really wanting to know.

"This house!"

I set down my mug and walked into the dining room, wrapping my cardigan tightly around my waist. There, on the dining table, was a chunk of plaster the size of the Oxford English dictionary, with about a hundred plaster crumbs surrounding it. I looked up at the ceiling. Another speck fell into my eye. I stopped myself from swearing and discreetly tried to rub away the plaster with my sweater sleeve.

"What happened?"

"More of the ceiling fell onto the table," Jack said. "I was hoping we could pay someone to fix this. It's too big a job to do ourselves. But that's not going to happen now."

I bit my cuticle. By "now" I knew he meant *now that we are overdrawn on all our credit cards and need to get out of debt before we go bankrupt.*

Jack was wearing jeans and a flannel shirt. A hole was growing in one of the knees—not because he thought this was stylish, but because the jeans were probably eight years old. He ran his fingers through his hair and then left them on his neck. "I guess I'm going to have to reinforce it as a temporary fix. I need to go buy lumber." He turned to me and smiled. It wasn't a happy smile; it was the smile of someone who has had a joke played on them and was trying to be a good sport. "Okay, so much for relaxing before I leave for work on Monday, right? I'm gonna go get started."

"Do you need help?"

"Nah."

"Are you sure?"

"Honey, whatever you weigh, even if it's ninety-nine pounds, I'm not sure the floor up there can take both your weight and mine. As it is, I'm going to spend three-quarters of my time trying not to fall through the hole myself. It's just better if I do it alone."

"I wonder if you should wear your bike helmet."

"Damn," he said, "that's not a bad idea."

"Then you might survive the fall without brain injury."

"Whereas I'd still be able to work with a broken back, right? Maybe from the hospital bed over Skype?"

"Sure. But brain dead you're useless to me." I turned toward the living room. "Well, if you don't need me, I might as well keep working on the floors."

That was how we spent the next day and a half: Jack reinforcing the dining room ceiling with two-by-fours and plywood while I continued sanding the living room floors. It was slow going. I wore a face mask and opened all the downstairs windows halfway for ventilation. Although it was now November, the temperature had crept back up to the low fifties. If Jack was bothered by my keeping the heat at sixty-eight degrees and the living room windows open partway, he didn't say anything.

By the afternoon of the second day, Jack had finished boarding up the hole, and we both hoped it would prevent any new craters of plaster from falling until we could afford to truly repair it. My sanding had now grown so that about a quarter of the living room floor was done. I shut the windows and reapplied the plastic sheeting to the bottom edges and vacuumed up most of the dust. Jack stood in the foyer and gazed out over the living room floor as if he were looking at something he didn't like but couldn't do anything about: a traffic standstill due to an accident, for example. He opened his mouth, closed it, and walked away.

After dinner on Sunday, Jack fell asleep early, while I lay in bed, listening for anything out of the ordinary.

"I'm sorry," I whispered. The words came out of my mouth unwilled; I didn't know to whom I was apologizing. To Jack, who was asleep, for fooling around with and sort of making love with a sexy ghost who had seemed to suggest I leave him? Or to that ghost's undead wife, whom I had betrayed while she'd been in the next room? "I don't know what came over me," I added. But that wasn't true. I knew very well what had come over me: Bobby Shawcross. And even as I was apologizing, I was yearning for him to come over me again.

After a few minutes of lying on my back, listening carefully, I thought I felt a presence, thought I heard a breath. I waited, half hopeful, half afraid. Out of the corner of my vision, I saw movement, and startled—and then let out a deep, relieved breath. It was Olivier, slinking into the room.

"Olivier, come here, kitty, kitty," I cooed. He jumped onto the bed and curled right beside me. I turned off the light, exhausted from my hard work, his rhythmic purrs lulling me to sleep.

I dreamed that I was back in that room, in that scene, in the 1950s. I stood in the foyer, peering into the living room. There was the same couch, the same chairs, the same floors, the same rugs, the same art.

It was darker this time. Only a single light shone, the light above the piano. Someone was lying on the couch. I knew who it was without looking. I couldn't look. Didn't want to.

The fear burrowed inside me the way I imagined cold would be inside you if you fell through the ice into a freezing lake. I shivered uncontrollably.

Birdy came in from outside, from the backyard. She was wearing a white dress and one shoe. Her dress was covered in blood, her neck was broken, tilted to the side, hanging to the right. Her face was bruised and bloody. She was dead, but not dead.

She went to the lifeless body of Amelia on the couch and staggered to sit down. She struggled to hug her daughter with one arm, the other flopping uselessly beside her. She labored to shake her, to wake her up. Then, her neck still dangling to the side, she looked around the room.

"Where is my baby?" she said. "I want my baby. I want my baby. Where is my baby? I want my baby."

I awakened and sat straight up in bed. My forehead was raging hot, while the rest of my skin ran icy cold. I was drenched in sweat. Jack was still asleep. Olivier was gone.

I checked my cell phone. 3:46 a.m.

No way was I closing my eyes again.

I went downstairs, turned on the TV, and watched the news. The presidential election was coming up the next day, and pundits speculated about who would win, given the current financial crisis and other issues. I tried to concentrate on what they were saying instead of my dream. When I heard Jack go into the kitchen at five, I met him there. He was showered, dressed, and making instant coffee. He smiled when he saw me.

"You didn't have to get up so early. But that's nice of you. I wish I didn't have to be away for such a long stretch."

I squinted at him, trying to understand what he was talking about. But if he was accusing me of being nice, I wasn't about to correct him. I smiled back and said, "Well . . ."

"I put the name of the hotel and the flight info on the fridge."

I went to the fridge and saw Jack's neat block letters on an index card:

HOLIDAY INN SAN FRAN GOLDEN GATEWAY Front Desk
415-441-4000
MONDAY Nov 3: United #3816 Madison (9:20 a.m.) to
San Francisco (2:05 p.m.)
    (1 stop Denver)
MONDAY Nov 17: #1451 San Francisco (4:15 a.m.) to
Madison (11:28 a.m.)
    (1 stop Denver)

BELLAMY 608-355-3801

And then I remembered that Jack was flying to California for a multisite installation of his company's software at a Bay Area hospital system. He'd told me about his travel plans months ago and about how this job was one of the biggest contracts his company had ever landed, and that the regional reps were participating to cover all the work involved. He'd told me—and I'd forgotten.

Now, staring at the index card, at the departure and arrival dates, I felt a momentary sense of buoyancy at the thought of not having Jack around for two full weeks, but then the giddy feeling was soon replaced by something like concern. Anxiety. Two weeks alone. But not alone. Not alone at all.

Perhaps sensing my nervousness, Jack wrapped his arms around me, and I breathed in his scent. Soap and wool. He always smelled so good. "You gonna be okay?"

I had no idea whether I would be okay, but I said what I always did, which was, "Sure, I'll be okay."

He broke away and looked into my eyes. His own eyes were steady and concerned. The eyes of a caretaker about to leave their charge for a fortnight. "There's a phone number on the fridge, too. That's the number of a family doctor one of my coworkers recommended. Dr. Bellamy, right here at Haven Physician's Group, is supposed to be excellent. If you need anything, just call that number, okay?"

"When did you arrange this?"

"What do you mean?"

"I mean, did you talk to this coworker before our talk on Saturday? When you suggested I see someone? Or did you text your coworker since then?"

Jack averted his eyes. "What difference does it make?"

"I'm just wondering."

"I didn't want to leave you without giving you the name of someone to call. Is that wrong of me?"

"What did you tell the coworker?"

"I asked for the name of a good doctor."

"Did you tell her—it is a her, isn't it?—that I was losing it? Or how did you put it?"

Jack sighed. "Yes, it's a her. Of course I asked a woman coworker for a recommendation for a doctor for you. I told her that since I would be gone for two weeks, I thought it'd be a good idea to give you the name of someone to call. Are you sure you're okay?"

I shook my head and tried to smile. He was right. I was being paranoid. I was thirty-seven, and I should have a doctor. It was good of Jack to find one for me. Not that I would make the appointment.

"Yes, I'm sure. Thank you," I said.

We kissed goodbye, and he left.

26

THE WALLPAPER

I TOLD MYSELF I WASN'T GIVING UP when I decided to postpone my work on the hardwood floors. I would get back to them eventually, but for now, they seemed so far from the grandeur of the smooth, polished floors of my vision, that I couldn't muster the energy to continue. Instead, when I came home from the library the day Jack left for California, I roamed the house, nibbling on some almonds, Buena Vista Social Club playing in the background, searching for a project I could actually complete while Jack was gone. I stopped in the dining room, struck by the glorious mess. Now that the ceiling probably wouldn't fall on my head, what about attacking the wallpaper and painting the walls? I ran my fingers over the tiny yellow flowers and bronze stems on the pink background. The wallpaper had clearly once been gorgeous, but it was nearly ninety years old. Chunks of it were missing or torn, and what was left was faded and patched together with duct tape. Yes, I thought. This was it. This would be my next project.

For the next two weeks, after my shifts at the library and on weekends, I worked on the wallpaper, making steady if hard-fought progress, taking only occasional breaks—to go grocery shopping, take brief naps, and once, to vote for America's next president, the first African American president in history, one who promised change, pledged universal health care, and read poetry. Some of the wallpaper came off easily, but most of it I had to spray with a mix of vinegar and hot water, scrape at with a putty knife, and ultimately dig at with my

fingernails, which became cracked, broken, and ragged, the fingernails of a witch in a spooky house.

While I worked, scraped, and dug, I began to hear things. Voices.
Dim, staticky. Like a radio in the backyard. *I won't do it, Bobby!* . . .
It's time for your tea. . . . *Mommy, what's wrong with your nerves?* . . . I
tried to drown out the voices with music. But no matter how loudly
I played Nina Simone or Tony Bennett or Rihanna, the other voices
made themselves known.

Every night, I would go to bed exhausted, my neck, back, and
fingers aching, but I'd just lay there, unable to sleep. I would think
of Chas Lawrence, in the Golden Oaks Nursing Home, wondering
what riches lay tapped in that locked mind. I would think of Birdy,
Bobby, and Amelia in the living room—*their* living room—mother
and daughter dancing, Bobby bringing Birdy water and valerian root
tea before begging for money so he could go out carousing, and then
Bobby and I in the foyer. My mind playing the night's events over and
over again. Often my stomach would growl, and I'd realize I'd forgotten to have dinner, but I was too tired to go downstairs to the kitchen
to make myself something to eat. I was afraid of dreaming, and so I'd
lay awake, hungry and aching, filled with anxiety about both falling
asleep and having another nightmare, and also about not falling asleep
and being exhausted the next day.

Sleep-deprived, I made stupid mistakes at work. One day I filed
two dozen DVDs in the Books on Tape section before Jess, of all
people, caught my mistake. The next morning, I made change for
a twenty instead of a ten for overdue fines, an error that wasn't discovered until the end of the day, when we were ten dollars short in
the till. In the afternoon, I checked out an R-rated DVD to a minor,
which I found out when his mother called to complain on the phone.
(Fortunately for me, Patty fielded the call, and she sweet-talked the
mom, who was in her Zumba class, out of filing a complaint.)

GHOST MOTHER211

Another day, I tripped while carrying an armful of books to the New Book display shelf, so that half of the brand-new books I'd been carrying went spilling all over the floor, causing a ruckus that both Carl and Eleanor witnessed. One Friday in mid-November, I spent my lunch break in my car, the engine running with the heat on low to keep me warm, eating a peanut butter and raspberry jam sandwich and then dozing until my cell phone alarm went off. I hit "snooze" and then fell back to sleep again, so when it went off the second time, I hurried into the library after my break nine minutes late, without bothering to inspect my face in the sun visor mirror of my car.

When I arrived at the circulation desk, Chris was helping a patron check out a dozen *Car and Driver* magazines. After she was gone, he asked, "You okay?"

I didn't know what he was referring to—my being nine minutes late after lunch or my having made mistakes all week long—so I responded to both by saying, "I haven't been sleeping well. Why?"

"You seem kind of preoccupied, and . . ." He looked down, embarrassed. ". . . I guess you might want to go to the bathroom?"

Oh no. I tried to imagine what outward manifestation of my inner turmoil was showing.

I didn't say anything, just immediately left the circulation desk, went to the employee bathroom, and looked in the mirror. So, this was what I got for trying to make an effort. For that morning, my eyes had looked so tired that I had worn eyeliner and mascara to make them appear more awake, to make them "pop," as the magazines put it, and I had forgotten all about this beauty trick during my car nap, when I'd apparently smudged my face while using my arms as a pillow against the door of the car and then rubbed my eyes upon awakening. For now, looking in the mirror, two black raccoon eyes stared back at me. Also, raspberry jam covered my mouth, which made me look as though I either didn't know how to apply lipstick or I'd ravenously eaten something bloody.

I splashed my face with water, then took a scratchy brown paper towel from the dispenser on the wall and rubbed it all over my eyes and mouth, then took another one and dabbed it on my eyelids until they were dry. I looked in the mirror. There were two faded shadows encircling my eyes. I repeated the process. I looked in the mirror again. My eyes were now red from all the rubbing with the rough paper towels, but they were no longer black raccoon eyes. I looked sleep-deprived and allergy-ridden but not socially unacceptable. I returned to the circulation desk.

"Thank you," I said.

"*No problema.*"

"It's been a rough week," I said, and then a woman I knew as Tricia White Eagle began to approach the circulation desk.

"November's rough," Chris said. "Unless you're a football fan."

"Are you a football fan?" I asked him.

"No. Are you?"

"No."

Tricia White Eagle set the newest Jodi Picoult novel in front of us and smiled. "Go, Packers!" she said.

That night, I finally finished scraping the last of the wallpaper off the dining room walls. The plaster underneath the paper was off-white and bumpy with age, wallpaper glue, and possibly asbestos.

I cleaned the floors and furniture, threw the old wallpaper away, and put the tools back into the garage. I was scrubbing the dining room walls with soap and water and thinking about all the progress we'd made—the living room floors still needed quite a bit of work, sure, but the dining room walls were nearly a clean slate, and the dining room ceiling was patched and probably secure—when I noticed something. It was about three feet off the ground, written in pencil.

HELP

I immediately dropped my soapy rag and put my hand to my mouth. I had taken down the wallpaper on this particular place on the wall (the northeast corner, away from the windows, closest to the living room and stairs) a few days ago, I was sure. When had this been written? Had it been written decades ago, and the wallpaper had been covering it up, and I had simply missed noticing it? (But how could I have missed it?) Or had it been written minutes ago, while I had taken the tools to the garage? And who had written it?

The letters were in all caps, with handwriting that was a little shaky. The pencil was harder and darker in some places than others, as if the writer were struggling to keep a steady hand. I instinctively went to grab a pencil to erase the word, and—ever the teacher—reached for one behind my ear. I inexplicably found one there. Why did I have a pencil behind my ear? Then I remembered using the eraser of the pencil to rub away at some stubborn bits of wallpaper at one point. Had the ghost borrowed my pencil and written the word? Or (and this was even more concerning) had I written the word in some cloud of amnesia I could no longer remember? Whose shaky, unsteady penmanship was this?

Who was crying out for HELP? The ghost of Beatrice Lawrence Shawcross—or me?

27

WHAT WAS IN THE ATTIC

ON SATURDAY, TWO DAYS BEFORE Jack would be coming home from San Francisco, I woke up and peed onto the familiar dipstick that would tell me if I was pregnant. I set the stick on the counter, pulled up my pajama pants, and brought my hands to my stomach. I thought of how my life would be different if I were pregnant this time, and if the pregnancy took. I would quit my job at the library and stay at home, resting in bed with Olivier purring beside me, since I was at such a high risk of miscarriage. Jack would stop traveling as much. He would take care of me, make me hot soup and casseroles. I would never eat cereal for dinner again—or at least not for the next nine months. Maybe my mother and I would even reconcile. Once she found out she was going to be a grandmother, she would call and apologize for not being there for me, for abandoning me. "But I'm here for you now," she would say. "Just when you need me most."

I begged, as I always did, "Please let me be pregnant, please let me be pregnant, if I'm pregnant I will try not to ask you for anything ever again." That was my bargaining chip. The only one I had. I was a child, saying that if she only got a Lite-Brite/an Easy-Bake Oven/a Barbie Dreamhouse/a puppy, she would be happy forevermore. But I had to insert the word "try" in there, because, as every parent knows, the bargain would only hold until the child wanted the next thing. And just like the parental figure I was bargaining with, I knew that would be me. That I would break my promise as soon as it came time to ask God/Goddess/the Universe to keep the baby healthy, to keep them safe as they walked to school/drove a car/went away to college. "Pretty please," I added.

I walked through the bedroom and into my walk-in closet, where I pulled on leggings and a hoodie, and then I returned to the bathroom and inspected the stick. Negative. Not pregnant. I threw it into the trash.

I sat on the toilet and rested my head in my hands. I felt too devastated to cry. My self-pity took a well-known turn: *Why are you such a failure? Why can't you do something any seventeen-year-old can accomplish in the back seat of a car? You'll never be a real mother. Jack had it right. You're a lunatic who can't save a penny and who thinks she's being haunted. You should go jump off a cliff.*

I sat up straight. It wasn't as if we didn't have a death-defying cliff in our backyard. "Should I really go jump off that cliff?" I whispered aloud.

A large *thwap!* sounded, like a chair being dropped to the ground. I went back into the bedroom and looked around; nothing was amiss. I went into the nursery. It was empty, save for the rocking chair, which was still. I went into the room with the hole in the floor, which Jack had now boarded up with plywood and two-by-fours. It was just as he'd left it. I backtracked to the upstairs landing and looked down the hall to the "wing" of the house we rarely used, the hall that led to my study, the three spare bedrooms, and the third-floor ballroom. Everything was quiet, and all the doors were closed. I went downstairs.

Everything looked normal, and Olivier was nowhere to be seen. I noticed his water dish was nearly empty. I filled it, and then searched in the fridge for something to eat.

Of course I wasn't going to jump off the cliff.

But as I was eating my "breakfast" (a cup of tea and the last of the leftover Halloween candy—I wasn't pregnant, so why be healthy?),

Olivier tore into the kitchen, meowing his head off, raced around my legs, then darted away, as if he were being chased by a Doberman or, I thought dramatically, the Hounds of Hell. I set down my mini-Snickers bar and crept out of the kitchen and went into the foyer, gazing up at the black chandelier and then up the grand stairwell, wondering where he'd come from, what had happened, not really wanting to know, and wanting to know desperately, both at once.

I stood still, listening. *Knock, knock.* The noise came from somewhere above. It was faint but clear. My legs felt weak, and I held on to the carved wooden banister. I put one foot on the lowest stair, then stopped. I wished I'd had a dog then, a steady, reliable collie like Lassie or a brave German shepherd like Rin Tin Tin who would come with me to investigate, not a useless, overly dramatic Persian cat frightened out of his wits, forcing me to face my darkest fears by myself.

Knock, knock. It was a little louder this time, more urgent, as if someone were getting tired of standing outside the door. The door. I turned around, went to the front door, and opened it. A woman wearing a coat and hat was walking her two fluffy white dogs on the street, but there was no one else around. It was getting cold. I closed the door.

Knock, knock. I went to the garage. Nothing but my old Toyota. I went to the back door. A crow pecked at something on the ground in the backyard. Crows were smart, bewitching birds, and, as everyone knew, symbols of death. I also knew that in Roman times, they were seen as harbingers of murder, and according to certain Native American folklore, crows were regarded as messengers between the living and the dead. I stood there, waiting to see if this one had anything to say, but it just kept pecking. I shivered. Then I went back into the foyer and stood underneath that imposing black chandelier. *Knock, knock.* The sound was coming from above, not from outside. I had no choice. I walked up the stairs.

At the top of the landing, I paused and listened. I didn't hear any-thing for a while. Finally, I said, "Birdy? Is that you?" There was no reply, no sound. I wished I could say I felt relieved by this, but some-how it only increased my fear. "Bobby?" I waited. No answer. Then . . .

Knock, knock. The sound was coming from above. I looked back down that empty hallway and let out what could only be called a gasp. For the door at the end of the hallway, which had been closed just a few minutes ago, was now open. Not just a crack, but open wide, as if to welcome me into that gaping darkness that led to the third-floor attic.

The home inspector had warned us not to go up there until we had a contractor come out. "The ceiling is dripping with asbestos, and the floor is ready to go. It's a death trap. You could kill yourself just by trying to stand on it." I think it was then that he'd cocked his head and asked us, "You sure you want to buy this house?"

It was deranged for me to even contemplate going up there. But that was where the knocking was coming from, I was sure. The knocks were beckoning me. The door was open just for me. They were invi-tations. By what? By whom? What or who was inviting me into that "death trap"?

You don't have to investigate, I told myself. I was standing in the middle of the hallway, my body cold and my forehead and hands clammy and moist, and I reminded myself of every scary movie I'd ever seen. I remembered that feeling of frustration when the heroine (for weren't the brave, stupid, curious people in these movies always girls?) left her world of safety and ignorance to go *investigate*, to go determine what the *knock* was about, and in doing so got herself hurt or killed when what she should have done was ignore the noise, walk away, and leave the house.

But the brave, stupid, curious heroines never did that, and nei-ther could I.

I walked quietly to the end of the hall and stood before the opening. It was only about five feet high, and I had to duck my head to
walk through. I stood at the bottom step. The stairs were wooden,
painted white, the paint chipped, the wood splintered. I was glad I
was wearing rubber-soled slippers. A faint light was coming from
above, and a musty, chemical smell wafted down. My heart was
pounding. I waited. I heard another knock. It was a single knock,
gentle, as if Birdy wanted to let me know where she was, wanted to
coax me up to her. *Knock.* I took a deep breath. "Okay," I said, "I'm
coming." And I walked up the dozen or so winding stairs to the top.

The attic, which had once been used as a ballroom, spread out in
front of me like the reception venue for Miss Havisham, unchanged
for hundreds of years. The walls and ceiling, which appeared to have
once been white but were now a faded grayish beige, were crumbling
with what was undoubtedly asbestos and lead paint. The wooden
floors were buckled and warped, probably from years of leaks that
had been patched but never completely sealed, and covered in detri-
tus, dust, and mouse droppings. There were cobwebs everywhere, in
every corner, dripping from the hanging chandelier and along the
windowsills. The air was freezing; one of the windows had a sizable
crack in it. The others were so grimy that the light coming in was
dark and muted, as if it were dusk.

It was the scariest room I had ever seen.

I put one foot on the floor and heard a creak. *Help,* I prayed. I
was becoming quite devout. I set down my other foot. I didn't crash
through to the second floor, and for that, I breathed a sigh of relief.
I looked around. There were built-in cabinets that lined one whole
side wall. Suddenly, a knock came from the cabinets, and I jumped.
The floor creaked but held.

I didn't know anything about warped floors that were about to
cave in, but I knew from childhood trips to the skating pond that

ice was thinnest, most dangerous in the middle, so I instinctively stuck to the perimeter. I walked slowly, softly, trying to bear down as little weight as possible. It was freezing in the room—I could see my breath—but my hands and forehead were still clammy. I felt febrile. I finally made it across the room to the built-in cabinets. They must have been lovely, once upon a time, with their alternating glass and wooden doors and their beaded beveled glass knobs. Now the wood was rotting in places and the glass was warped and cracked.

I stood still, waiting for a sound, but none came. I let out a heavy breath and opened a wooden cabinet door. Nothing. I closed it and went to the glass door beside it. I put my hand on the knob, ready to open it, peered through the glass, and then jumped back, my heart pounding so hard my ears hurt. I put my hand to my chest, caught my breath, and peered back inside. It was a dead something—a mouse, or maybe even a rat. There were only bones and bits of fur left, so it was hard to tell. My stomach lurched. I kept going. I opened the next wooden door, my heart racing, and again found nothing but empty, dusty shelves. The glass door beside that one revealed the same. I was beginning to feel calmer and also a little relieved. *You were just hearing things*, I told myself. *Oh, Lilly, you and your imagination!* I said this last line to myself brightly, as if I were a wacky aunt in a play.

But of course, I didn't really believe it.

I opened the final wooden door. Again, nothing but dust and droppings. I closed it, thinking that was the end of that. But then . . . *Knock, knock.* The knocking sound seemed to be coming from the cabinet I'd just closed. I found it hard to stand, hard to breathe. I opened the door again. This time, instead of just looking straight ahead, I ducked my head inside and looked up. I felt very scared and very brave. I saw something on top of one of the wooden crossbars. A splash of red. I grabbed the thing and held it in my hands: red tweed with a black square in the right lower corner and the words

PHOTO ALBUM in all caps. Remarkably, there were no droppings on the album, no visible nibbles. Besides being dusty, it appeared undamaged.

I looked around the room. I stood still and listened. There were no more knockings. I took a deep breath and began my careful journey back to the door. At the doorway I passed through very cold air, like a cold spot in the middle of a lake. I breathed deeply, stepped carefully down the winding stairs, and closed the door behind me.

Then I hurried to my bedroom, dusted off the album with a T-shirt from the floor, and curled back into bed, clutching the album, my heart still pounding and my blood still ringing in my ears.

28

MEMORIES

THE COVER PAGE DISPLAYED A handwritten single word in cursive:

Memories

It was an old-fashioned album, the kind with brown paper and glued photos. I carefully turned the page, which was labeled *August 1947*. Was this Birdy Lawrence's handwriting? I traced the letters with my finger, feeling the bumpy roughness of the old paper.

The first several pages were filled with wedding photos. Bobby standing at the altar beside a minister. Birdy walking down the aisle, a veil draped over her face, a bouquet of white roses in her hands, her elbow held by a dour-faced older man, whom I recognized from my research as her father Edgar. Bobby's lifting Birdy's veil, their lips joined in their first married kiss, the minister smiling behind them, Edgar still frowning.

The reception had been held in a stately park, with a large expanse of lawn, a garden blooming with flowers, hundreds of guests, and a band playing on what looked like a driveway in front of a coach house. But not just any driveway; not just any coach house. I studied the photographs more closely and realized this was our driveway, our garage which had once been a coach house. Our garden, our lawn. The reception had taken place right here, in the backyard.

The last wedding picture was blown up to fit the size of the page. Birdy is standing casually on the patio near the house. Her wedding gown has a sweetheart neckline, long sleeves, and an A-line skirt that shows off her waist. The veil—held up by a thin satin band around her forehead—flows over her long, abundant hair. It is said that all brides are beautiful, but Birdy could be a model in a bridal magazine, with her brilliant dark eyes, her wide, pink lips, and her hourglass figure. Her breasts are large, almost swollen. She looks older than the striking teenager in *The World in Our Home*, more mature—and gorgeous.

Bobby is standing beside her, wearing a black suit, and gazing into Birdy's eyes as if she's the only woman in the world. I know that expression. It's the way he looked at me.

Next to them, sitting in a folding chair, is Birdy's father, Edgar Lawrence. He's staring directly into the camera, his eyes squinting and his jaw hard and set, angry and grim. Why? Perhaps he doesn't approve of the groom, Bobby Shawcross from Oklahoma, who began his career as assistant bill poster in the Lawrence Brothers Circus (as I recalled from my research).

The next pages are from January 1948, and they're filled with baby pictures. January 1948—just six months after the wedding. So Amelia was conceived out of wedlock. Maybe that's why Edgar was so dour. Though he's smiling broadly in a picture of him holding the newborn Amelia, grandfatherly pride in his eyes.

As the pages continue, Amelia grows. She's sitting on her mother's lap in a clown outfit for *October 1948, Amelia's First Halloween*, mother and daughter both laughing at whoever is taking the picture. (Bobby?) She has her arms around a friend in the picture titled *Summer 1949, Amelia and Ginnie*, two toddlers wearing smocked floral dresses and eating ice cream cones. Underneath *Amelia, Bobby, and Flopsie, June 1950*, Amelia and Bobby are riding a beautiful elephant. Bobby is holding Amelia's waist with one hand and waving with the other, while Amelia grasps onto the pommel of the saddle with both hands and turns her head to smile at the camera with delight.

And then comes a page dated *October 1950*. There is no photograph, only a large card tucked between the pages. I picked it up, examined it, and saw that it was a funeral card. On one side was a color picture of Edgar Lawrence in profile. His hair is still brown, his eyes bright blue, his cheeks rosy; he's sporting a handlebar mustache. I recognized the image from Lawrence Brothers circus posters I had seen online. Above his picture were the words:

In Loving Memory

Edgar Nathaniel Lawrence (1894–1950)
Beloved Father, Grandfather, Brother, and Circus Master

I turned the card over and read the memorial prayer:

"When I am dead, my dearest"
By Christina Rossetti

When I am dead, my dearest,
Sing no sad songs for me;
Plant thou no roses at my head,
Nor shady cypress tree:
Be the green grass above me
With showers and dewdrops wet;
And if thou wilt, remember,
And if thou wilt, forget.

I shall not see the shadows,
I shall not feel the rain;
I shall not hear the nightingale
Sing on, as if in pain:
And dreaming through the twilight

That doth not rise nor set,
Haply I may remember,
And haply may forget.

I read the poem twice, and then tucked the funeral card back in its place.

The following pages showed evidence of what appeared to be a happy family. Birthdays, Christmases, vacations, dances. A picture of Birdy and Amelia doing handstands back-to-back, Amelia's heels pressing against her mother's calves, their hair brushing the earth. A photo of Bobby pushing Amelia on the tire swing in the backyard, both wearing black top hats and red bow ties. Another one of Birdy and Amelia sitting on a blanket in the grass, a body of water and blue sky in the background. Amelia is wearing a red-and-cream two-piece bathing suit with ruffles at the top and at the hips. Her brown hair is wet, tangled, and hanging down her back. Birdy's in a white strapless one-piece with ruching on the sides, something Marilyn Monroe would have worn, that shows off her feminine figure, her cleavage, her thin waist, and wider hips. Her hair is coiffed, dry, flowing down her shoulders. She's wearing red lipstick and smiling at her daughter with amusement and adoration, and Amelia is gazing back at her with a child's innocent love. Or so it appeared to me.

I felt it then, first in my chest and then spreading out to every cell in my body: longing. These photos reminded me how badly I wanted to be a mother. I wanted my daughter to gaze at me the way Amelia was gazing at Birdy.

I turned the page.

May 1954

Something has changed. The mood of this photo is different. Bobby and Amelia are in the back seat of his blue Studebaker, the same car that was in the crime scene photos. They're staring out the

same back-seat window—Amelia must be sitting on Bobby's lap—
and smiling, but something is off about their expressions. Bobby isn't
smiling with his eyes, as if the person behind the camera (Birdy?) has
commanded him to say, "Cheese!" and he's politely obeying. Amelia's
smile is exaggerated, clownish, but it's a scary-movie clown's smile.
Her eyes appear startled. Her lips are drawn back, teeth clenched
together. She's pretending to smile.

Then I noticed the driver, who is saluting the camera, his index
finger and middle finger at attention against his navy chauffeur's
cap. He is smiling, too, only his smile seems to be sincere. Sympathetic, even. He has a buzz cut barely visible beneath his hat. A fine,
straight nose. Piercing eyes. A kind, friendly expression, and a smooth,
unwrinkled face. He's young. By my calculations, Chas Lawrence is
only twenty-four years old.

So he was still working for them, back in May, but not for much
longer. Lorenzo DeMarcos said he took over in June and that the
reason the guy before him had quit was because "things hadn't been
the same recently." What hadn't "been the same"? What had happened recently, to put these fake smiles on Bobby's and Amelia's faces,
to make Chas suddenly quit? And, more to the point, what had
changed so that less than a year later, everyone would be dead?

There were two blank pages at the back of the album. I thought
that was it, that the photo with the Studebaker was the last photo, but
then I noticed that between the last page and the inside back cover,
tucked inside the spine, was a Polaroid. I picked it up and held the
white frame between my fingers. The glossy photo was cracked. But
I could still see the people in the image clearly. Amelia and Birdy are
sitting on the couch in the living room, clutching each other tightly.
Amelia is staring blankly at the camera with her big, brown doe eyes,
as if she's been awakened from a dream in the middle of the night. A
dream, or perhaps a nightmare, eyes wide, trying to adjust, trying to

figure out what is happening. Birdy's cheeks are red with some sort of rash. Her once abundant hair is now receding, patchy in places, and thin all over. Her cheeks are gaunt, and she is staring at the camera with a haunted expression on her face. There is no date, no heading, no title to this photo, but if I had to give it one, I would have guessed it would have read something like:

March 1955, The Lawrence Mansion Living Room,
Haven, Wisconsin. The End Is Nigh.

29

PRETEND YOU'RE HAPPY

I DIDN'T KNOW IF IT WAS THE NEWS of my not being pregnant, or finding the word "HELP" on the dining room wall, if it was my strange, erotic vision of Bobby Shawcross, or the discovery of the photo album and all that it implied, but I was feeling exhausted, disoriented, and something bordering on depressed. *Unstable. Anxious.* The cold weather and the shortening days didn't help. I'd gone from hardly sleeping to sleeping a lot, and it was difficult to tell what day or time it was.

But according to the wall clock in the lobby of the Golden Oaks Nursing Home, it was 11:45, and since the sky was gray rather than black, I knew it must be a.m. The temperature outside was in the low thirties, but it was warm inside. I took off my gloves, while leaving on my coat and pink beanie as a sort of disguise. I was hungry, and the scent of bad coffee and something pungent and meaty (meat loaf?) wafted in from the dining room, making my stomach growl. But I had used the last of my weekly allowance to partially fill up my gas tank on the way here, and I didn't have a dime in my wallet to pay for anything the cafeteria nursing home might be selling.

I stood behind a large fake potted plant in the lobby, my back to the reception desk, where the platinum-haired young woman with the chipped nail polish from my previous visit was of course glued to her post this time. I was certain Katya Lawrence had put me on some no-entry list after our talk on the phone, or at the very least, that I would be stopped and questioned, and I couldn't risk being turned away. Not until I'd had one more chance to try to uncover what was buried in the frayed pathways of Chas Lawrence's long-term memory.

Every so often, I peeked over my shoulder and around the plastic fronds of what I believed was supposed to be a paradise palm, but so far, she hadn't moved. Her seat was firmly planted in a stool, her face gazing down at her phone.

The entrance doors swung open behind me, bringing in a whoosh of cold air and a young couple, who gave me a curious glance and a smile. I smiled back and then squinted out into the parking lot, as if I were waiting for someone while pressing myself into the faux palm tree. The couple walked to the receptionist, who said, "Hi!" in a warm tone. They talked pleasantly for a minute, and then the girl actually led them down a hallway. Apparently, she could be nice and helpful when she wanted to be. In any case, the reception desk was empty now, and the coast was clear.

I walked quickly and confidently through the lobby, attempting to look like I knew exactly where I was going, which I did. I was glad to find that the hallway to Chas's room was deserted. I went to his door, which was wide open, peeked into his room, and saw that it was empty. I thought for a moment. That meaty smell. It was probably lunchtime. Maybe he was having lunch in the cafeteria.

I pulled my beanie over my forehead to better conceal myself, walked back down the hallway, and then turned left and nearly ran into a wheelchair occupied by a very old woman. "Excuse me. I'm sorry," I said.

She said, "Uhhhnnnn."

I glanced around. She was right in the middle of the hallway, blocking traffic, as it were, though I was the only other person nearby.

"Do you need help?" I asked her.

She groaned harder. Just then, a nurse, or maybe a nursing home attendant, walked toward us. I was sure that between my coat, hat, and scarf, the only parts of me that were visible were my eyes and the top of my nose, and anyway, despite Katya's warning, despite her telling me to leave Chas alone, I knew it wasn't as if the nursing home had a "Wanted" poster of me in the break room. I ventured to say, "Excuse me?"

The attendant, a white, muscular woman in her forties, with a name tag that read "Tenny," stopped and said, "Yes?"

"Hi," I said, "this lady . . ."

Tenny shook her head. "That's Betty Albertson. You can't do much of anything for her. Wherever she is, she groans. So, if that's where she wants to be, she can stay there. She's not in anyone's way." I thought she was in everyone's way, especially someone in another wheelchair, but I didn't argue. Tenny leaned down and shouted in Betty Albertson's ear, "You wanna stay here or you wanna go to your room?"

This time the groan sounded less like "Uhhhnnnn" and more like "Ahhhnnn."

"See? She said 'stay.'"

With that, Tenny kept walking. I turned back to Betty Albertson. Her hair was white and thin, so that I could see her scalp, pinkish-white and dotted with sunspots. Her hands were resting on the wheelchair, and they too were covered with spots, and protruding blue veins. "Okay, I'm going," I said. "You take care now."

But I paused for a moment, wondering about Betty Albertson, about her life. Had she been married? Had children? Had they abandoned her? If I never had a child, and Jack died before me, or divorced me for being a *raving lunatic*, would this be how I would end up?

I didn't have time to linger. I quickly walked down the hallway, following the scents of sweet, spicy meat and coffee, and ended up at the cafeteria.

The walls were institutional beige, like the rest of the place, with about two dozen cream Formica tables and twice as many black vinyl chairs. The floor was old linoleum, peeling away in places, but it appeared clean, as if it had recently been mopped. There were fifteen or so people in the room, all residents, which surprised me, given that it was a Sunday. I would have thought there would be visitors here, having lunch with their parents or grandparents, but then it occurred to me that the families might be coming later, after church perhaps. Would Katya and their daughter Lydia be coming? The thought made me nervous, and I felt myself flush underneath my hat, scarf, and coat in the warm air of the nursing home.

I spotted Chas Lawrence—his silver hair and upright posture— sitting alone at a table. I walked over to him and said, "Hi, it's me, Lilly, again. Mind if I sit down?"

I sat without waiting for a reply and examined his tray. I was right; it was meat loaf I'd smelled. A half-eaten plate was there, along with soggy green beans, a roll with too much butter or margarine on it, and a parfait glass of red Jell-O, which he was now spooning into his mouth. He was wearing a white dress shirt and navy sweatpants today, and those same perfectly white athletic shoes. He smelled better than the last time I'd been here, like a strong, antiperspirant soap. Perhaps Sunday was shower day.

I ventured to take off my hat and scarf. They really kept the place heated, and I was sweating. I ran my fingers through the hair around my scalp to air out my head and plump up my hair, but my fingers immediately got tangled. Then I took a deep breath and gazed at Mr. Chas Lawrence.

"I don't know if you remember me," I said, "but—"

"Fly away, Birdy, fly away."

I smiled, a little startled. "Yes, that's right. I came here to talk about Birdy. And Bobby Shawcross. I've learned a bit more about them since I saw you. I know you lived and worked in their coach house. I don't want to upset you, but I wonder if you could tell me about them?"

He opened his mouth and guided the spoon with the red Jell-O in carefully. It was terribly suspenseful, especially given the white dress shirt. No Jell-O spilled. I went on.

"Do you remember anything about them, Mr. Lawrence? Do you remember what Bobby asked you to do? To your cousin?"

I realized that although I was trying to talk gently and kindly, I was also speaking loudly, as if he were deaf. Well, maybe he was. He wasn't exactly a young seventy-eight. I glanced around. The other people in the room didn't seem to notice. I unbuttoned my coat. I eyed the half-eaten roll but resisted. However, there were three packets of saltines on the table, left, perhaps, by the previous soup-eating occupant, and I tore open a package and ate. My stomach was instantly angry for more. I ate another packet. Chas Lawrence was looking at me. "I left too early for breakfast," I explained. "Do you mind if I have the last one?" He didn't say anything, so I ate the last two crackers. I had once gone to fancy private schools and had driven a car that cost as much as some people's houses, and now I was in a run-down nursing home in Haven, Wisconsin, stealing crackers from the elderly. It was my own damn fault, of course, but that didn't stop me from thinking, *If Daddy could see me now . . .*

"Mr. Lawrence, can you tell me about the time, in the 1950s, when you were living in the coach house at your Uncle Edgar's estate? Please? I really need to know what happened there."

He was gazing at me blankly. I'd heard that people suffering from dementia were often triggered into remembering the past by music, and so I began to sing him "Pretend" by Nat King Cole. It was a melancholy song about pretending to be happy when you're not, so that you actually do find happiness and love. (These days, we would have called it "Fake It Till You Make It.") It was recorded in the early 1950s, when Chas, born in 1930, would have been about twenty-three.

Even though the song wasn't meant for my vocal range, my singing seemed to please him. He looked faraway and joyful as I sang.

When I had finished, thinking of the last time I'd been here, I went into improvisation mode. "Mr. Chas Lawrence, my name is Lilly Bly," I said, in a strict, clipped mid-century Lois Lane news reporter voice, "and I'm with the *Haven Herald*. The year is 1955. Dwight D. Eisenhower is president. The Korean War is over. Jonas Salk has just created the polio vaccine. And I'm sorry to say that your cousin Birdy Lawrence is dead, and so is her husband Bobby Shawcross, and their daughter Amelia." He was gazing at me, listening intently. "Now I promise to keep your name out of the papers, don't worry, but it's imperative that you answer one question for me. When you worked for Bobby Shawcross, he asked you to do something for him, something that probably involved your cousin Birdy. What was that? What did he ask you to do? And by the way," I added quickly, thinking of his saying, *I won't do it, Bobby, I won't!*, "you were right to refuse him, of course." I had no idea what we were talking about, but I didn't want him to cry again.

He met my eyes, and his own eyes grew darker, angrier. "You promise to keep my name out of the papers?"

"I promise."

"I've never told this to anyone before."

"It's off the record."

He nodded, his face serious and grim. "Bobby wanted me to steal the prenuptial agreement," he replied. "The one at the lawyer's office."

"The prenup?" I didn't know what I'd been expecting—do favors for girlfriends, lie to Birdy, maybe even help Bobby pilfer her money—but steal a prenup? I hadn't even known there were prenups in the 1950s. The idea seemed so modern. But then, it shouldn't have surprised me that wealthy people had always had a way of making sure their wealth was protected.

"Uncle Edgar insisted they sign one. After he died, Bobby found one of the copies in the house."

"He wanted the other copy," I confirmed. "And he . . ." I trailed off, hoping Chas would finish the sentence for me.

"He threatened me. My girlfriend worked at the lawyer's office. He said that only I could do it. Only I could get the key and do it. He threatened to fire me if I didn't. I needed that job. I . . ."

"So, you stole it?" I asked softly.

Tears began to well up in Chas Lawrence's eyes. "I would never have done anything to hurt Birdy, or her little girl. Never. I refused to steal it. Bobby fired me."

"Well, that's good. You did the right thing."

He shook his head. "You don't understand."

Chas wasn't actually crying, but his emotions were still making me nervous. I didn't want a replay of what had happened before. I looked around the room. One attendant was helping a woman eat. Another was wheeling a resident away. No sign of red-wigged Katya. I buried my head a little closer to him. "What don't I understand?" I asked, hoping my voice sounded gentle.

"I shoulda done it, I should have stolen that prenup for him."

"You did the right thing," I repeated. "What he was asking was illegal, unethical."

He kept shaking his head. "If I'd a done it, they'd still be alive today."

My body was hot under my coat, but something inside me grew cold. "What do you mean?"

"My cousin and her little girl. If I'd a done what Bobby wanted, my cousin and her little baby would still be alive today." Chas Lawrence looked up and away from me and reached for his water. It took him a long time to bring the glass closer to the edge of the tray, and then sip the water through a straw. I grew thirsty watching him. I waited until he had finished. He smacked his dry, chapped lips, while a bit of water dribbled down his chin. I wanted to help him, to dab at his chin with a napkin, but I feared it would be undignified, so I resisted.

Instead, I asked, "What do you mean? Why would they still be alive?"

Chas looked at me, but his eyes were cloudy and confused. "Alive? Yes, still alive. What's your name again, dear?"

"It's Lilly."

"Yes. My daughter. You're my daughter. I remember now."

I gazed at him, recalling his brother Jim's warning that Chas couldn't remember what he'd had for breakfast or much about his wife or family, but that I had a chance of hearing stories from his youth. Was it some kind of purgatory, being trapped in a mind that was occasionally lucid but most of the time foggy and confused? Was he aware that something important was missing? Or was he simply oblivious to the blank spaces where memory and recognition used to be?

I squeezed his hand. *Lydia, Lilly.* They were easy enough to confuse.

"I'm so glad you came to see me," he said, smiling. He really did seem glad.

"Of course, Dad," I said. He was seventy-eight, about ten years older than my father would have been if he were still alive. I rested my other hand on top of his. It was hairless, smooth, and cool. "It's so nice to see you," I said.

"My daughter Lydia," he said in a raised voice, as if he were introducing me to other residents.

A few of them glanced our way, including the attendant helping one of the residents eat.

"I'd better go." I stuffed the saltine wrappers in my pocket, leaned down, and kissed his cheek. It was creamy soft and smelled like shaving cream. "Goodbye, Dad."

As I walked through the lobby, my coat unbuttoned, my wool scarf draped loosely around my shoulders, my pink wool beanie stuffed inside my pocket with my gloves and the empty saltine wrappers, I noticed that the platinum-haired girl was back at the reception desk. She looked up as I walked by. "Excuse me?" she said. "You didn't sign in." I kept walking, head down, shoulders up. "Hey, ain't you . . . ?" she called.

I was already out the door.

30

ONE MORE CHANCE

WHY WAS JACK'S CAR IN THE DRIVEWAY? His flight was supposed to arrive the next day, on Monday, and I'd just talked to him the day before. He hadn't said anything about taking an earlier flight. I grabbed my bag, took out my phone, and checked to see if I had any missed calls or texts. Nothing.

It wasn't like him to surprise me, and truth to tell, it wasn't a pleasant surprise. He would want to know where I'd been. Maybe I could say I'd been out to the lake. That's what normal people did on a Sunday, didn't they? But when the temperature was in the thirties? And when I was wearing stacked-heeled boots? I could say I'd gone to the pharmacy to refill my ovulation prescription. But I was coming home empty-handed.

I sighed, got out of the car, and went into the house. I couldn't think of a good enough lie, which meant that I would just have to see what came out of my mouth on the spot, a dangerous proposition indeed.

"Lilly! What are you doing home so early?" Jack walked out from the kitchen, wiping his hands on his jeans. He came to the foyer and gave me a hug. Then he stepped back. He had a worried expression on his face that I didn't understand. I hoped he wasn't going to nag me about the floors, which were neglected, only one-quarter sanded, or the dining room walls, which were still bare and needed to be painted. At least I'd erased the word "HELP."

"What are you talking about? I should be asking you that. I didn't expect you until tomorrow."

He was wearing jeans and a V-neck sweater with a couple of moth holes around the hips. His hair was longer than usual, and his glasses were smudged, and underneath them, his eyes were tired and dry. He was working hard, too hard. He was also giving me a funny look, which I didn't understand. "What?"

"You expected me tomorrow? But the flight itinerary I left you said that I'd be flying into Madison this morning."

"No, it said that you'd be flying in Monday morning."

As soon as the words were out of my mouth, my heart began to pound, and I was hit by a hollow sensation in my stomach.

He didn't need to say it, but he did. "Today is Monday, hon."

Then he seemed to see what I was thinking, because he ran his hands through his hair and let out a deep, beleaguered breath. "Tell me you knew that."

"Somehow, I thought it was Sunday. I got my days mixed up. I didn't go into work!"

"Call them. Call them right now. Tell them what happened. Tell them—"

"I can't!" I walked into the living room and sat on the couch because I felt like I might faint. When was the last time I'd eaten anything but the saltines? It was the afternoon now. The day before at five? Six? When I'd had a bowl of cold cereal? "You don't understand. Carl told me that if one more thing like this happened, he was going to let me go. This was it. This was the last thing."

"One more thing? How many things have there been?"

"I don't know. I haven't been sleeping well."

"You'll have to go in, talk to him."

"My God, I can't."

"You have to."

"So humiliating! Like a twelve-year-old." Jack was glaring at me. "All right, fine, I'll do it."

"Wait."

I thought he was going to let me stay. Instead, he said, "I don't think you brushed your hair today. And you . . . you might want to brush your teeth."

I ran my fingers through my hair. He was right; it was thick with knots. I went upstairs into my bathroom, stood in front of the mirror, and brushed my teeth and hair. I looked haggard and pale, but at least my breath was fresh, and my hair was no longer tangled. Apparently, these were my new standards. I rushed downstairs and into my car without bothering to say goodbye.

Carl actually seemed pleased to see me. Now that he knew, in his mind anyway, that I was fired, dealing with me would undoubtedly be easier.

"Come in, Lilly," he said. "It's good to see you. We were worried. I hope nothing happened?"

It was like an improv suggestion; I couldn't let it pass. "I'm afraid something did happen," I said. "I'm sorry I didn't call, but I want you to know, I had a good reason for not coming in today. My grandfather is in a nursing home, and he had a fall. I went to visit him this morning. I meant to call from there, but then, seeing him, I just forgot about everything else."

"Oh, dear. I hope he's all right."

"Yes, he's much better. When I left, a nurse was taking him to therapy," I added, hoping the detail would give the lie a ring of truth. "I got here as soon as I could."

He tapped a pencil on his desk. I wondered if I should tell him the name of the nursing home, but what difference would it make? Carl didn't care about the name of the nursing home or whether my grandfather was going to therapy. Or even why I had a grandfather living in a nursing home in Haven, when I'd just moved here from Chicago. He only cared that I hadn't shown up for work and hadn't called, undoubtedly leaving my colleagues in the lurch and the Haven Library patrons waiting impatiently for someone to help them. Thinking about these people—whom I had worked with and served, whom I had gotten to know and like—I knew I was going to miss them. I didn't want to lose this job.

"I would really appreciate another chance," I said, gazing at my lap. I didn't want to see his face. I could almost hear him thinking.

Finally, he said, "I'm sorry, Lilly, I just don't think this is going to work out."

I nodded, still not looking at him.

"I'll have Eleanor mail you your last check."

I didn't move.

"Good luck to you."

Finally, I looked up into his sympathetic but disappointed eyes. I'd let him down. I couldn't say thank you, couldn't speak; I was afraid I would cry. I just nodded and left the room, left the library—for good.

When I got home, I found Jack in the kitchen, working at his computer, a pot of water on the stove. "Well?"

I shook my head.

He came over and hugged me. His sympathetic hug surprised me. "I'm sorry," I said. "I'll get another job, right away."

"Did you ever hear back from the district?"

"The . . . ?"

He broke away, holding me at arm's length. "The district. Did you ever apply for a teaching position there? Did you ever apply for a Wisconsin license?"

I shook my head.

"So, you lied?"

Had I? I couldn't remember now. It seemed like so long ago, the day I'd told him I was working on my résumé, when I'd found out about Birdy Lawrence instead. I sat at the kitchen table. I was so tired. "I didn't mean to."

"Where were you this morning?"

"I went for a walk."

"In your car? Where?"

Where had I said I was going? "Umm . . ."

"My God, are you lying about that, too?"

"I—"

"Where were you today?"

His face was so angry, as if he were waiting for another lie.

"Fine. I was at a nursing home. I didn't tell you because I thought you'd be mad."

"What the hell were you doing in a nursing home? What was worth getting fired for, Lil?"

"I was doing research on my . . . you know. On Birdy Lawrence."

"Good God."

His eyes were angry and stern, and beneath that was something else. Disappointment? Despair? Disgust? "I'm not sure how much longer I can handle this."

"Handle what?"

"This!" He gestured his arms to include everything. "This house. Our financial troubles. You lying to me. You spending all your time and energy worrying about someone who lived here fifty years ago. I need . . . I need a break."

I gazed out the window, into the backyard, toward the cliffs, at Birdy's fate. Why did Chas Lawrence think she and Amelia would still be alive if only he had stolen the prenuptial agreement? He'd said there had been two copies, one at the lawyer's office and one here at the house, which Bobby had found. That was over fifty years ago. Even as I worried about what Jack was saying, about our marriage, I couldn't wait to figure out what Chas Lawrence had been talking about, why he believed that his stealing the prenup would have saved his cousin and her daughter's life.

"You want a separation," I said. It wasn't a question.

"I don't know." He sat down across from me, put his head in his hands. He took off his glasses and rubbed his eyes. "I love you," he said into his hands. "I'm just not sure I can live like this anymore. We need to sell this house."

"I can't. Not yet. Not until . . ."

He put his glasses back on and gave out a bitter little laugh. "Until when? Until we're bankrupt? Until our marriage falls apart? When?"

Until I solve the mystery. Until I know that Birdy is at peace. Until I have a baby here, like I'd always felt I would. I remembered that certainty I'd had, that this house was where I would become a mother. I couldn't believe I'd been wrong, that it wasn't meant to be.

Finally, I met his eyes. "Can you give me another chance?" These were the general words I'd used just a half hour or so before, with Carl Williams. I hoped they worked better this time.

"I'm not going to do anything rash. But things have got to change around here. And fast."

He stood up, went to the cupboard, and took down an economy-sized box of Ramen noodles. I was shocked by this symbol of our poverty, but also pleased. I was so hungry I felt weak, and the thought of a huge bowl of noodles sprinkled with packets of flavored chemical mix sounded mouth-watering. "Can I have some?" I asked.

"Pork, chicken, or beef?"

"It doesn't matter," I said, trying to be easy and agreeable, and hoping the packets didn't contain actual animal products.

He dumped a few bags of noodles into the pot.

I went up to him, my cheek resting against his moth-eaten sweater. "I'm sorry."

"I know," he said, and then he pushed me away, holding me at arm's length. His eyes weren't angry anymore, only sorrowful. "I'm just not sure it's enough."

Jack left for Champaign-Urbana the following morning. As soon as his car pulled away, I went into the kitchen, put on the electric kettle for tea, and tried to clear my head. "What's so important about the prenup?" I muttered aloud, walking back and forth in front of the counter, rubbing my fingers over my temples in the classic form of someone trying to think, waiting for the water to boil.

That's when I heard it. Someone calling my name. It was barely audible, and I couldn't tell if the voice belonged to a man, a woman, or a phantom. *"Liiiiilllly."* Olivier came from out of nowhere to stand in front of the door to the basement, arch his back, and *hiss*. The call grew louder and more apparent, as if it were trying to drown out Olivier's hissing. *"Lilly . . . Lilly . . . Lilly . . ."* It was the house communicating with me, I knew. And I felt my heart drop as I realized that this time, the sound wasn't coming from above; it was coming from below. From the basement.

The basement.

The basement.

The effing basement.

"Please not the effing basement," I prayed/swore.

But there it was again: *"Liiiiilllly . . ."*

I remembered the words of Ricarda Heller: *"I see a room . . . a dark room . . . stairs. You don't want to go in this room, but you must. You're in terrible danger here, Lilly."*

I went to the basement door and threw it open. Olivier howled a screechy *meow* and ran away. I stared into the dark abyss, switched on the light, and looked down the stairs. I closed my eyes. When I opened them again, I realized I was crying angry, terrified tears. For I understood: the answer was down those stairs, and if I wanted to find out what had happened and why, I was going to have to confront my worst fear.

31

THAT BASEMENT

MY DAD HAD NOT KNOWN I WAS COMING. That is the one sentence, the one truth, that has kept me relatively happy and sane all these years, although I am no poster child for either happiness or sanity. My father could not have known my washer was broken. He had not known I was coming over to my uncle's house that morning. Therefore, he could not have possibly imagined that I would be the one to find him.

My uncle was single. Unlike my father, he'd never had a Midas touch, had never owned restaurants and nightclubs and racehorses, had never been hailed as one of "Chicago's Most Interesting Success Stories" in a major glossy magazine. They'd had humble beginnings, my dad and his older brother Lenny, and while my father had soared high above those humble beginnings, my uncle had simply moved a few blocks over. He lived in a working-class neighborhood in Rogers Park.

For as long as I could remember, my uncle had been touchy about money. He came to our penthouse every Christmas, with his first wife before she'd died (car accident), then his girlfriend (before she'd broken up with him), then his second wife (who had left him), and then alone, and in all those years, he had never exchanged a present with my dad. I had seen my father try to give him quite a few gifts, but Lenny would never accept them. Once, I overheard my father hiss, "For God's sake, Len, this'd make all the difference in the world to you, why don't you just take it?"

"I'm not taking no handout from my kid brother" was the angry reply. "Now put that damn money away."

So perhaps my uncle had felt somewhat vindicated, maybe he'd experienced a little schadenfreude, when his little brother had lost everything, every penny he'd ever earned, and his wife of twenty-some years, and had asked if he could move in with him.

I had moved from Lincoln Park to Wicker Park since the bottom had fallen out, about eight months before. My small studio apartment was on the third story of a run-down building. It had a stacked washer and dryer, but one day the washer wouldn't fill with water. I'd scheduled a repair, but I knew it would take days, and I needed to wash my waitressing uniforms for that night's shift.

Rather than going to the ratty local laundromat, I decided I would drive to my uncle's in Rogers Park. I hadn't seen my dad in a few days, anyway, and I wanted to spend some time with him. I called first, but nobody answered. I figured my uncle was out, and my dad was still asleep.

It was eleven in the morning. My father was working as the night manager at a restaurant, and I knew he wouldn't need to be at work until three or four. My uncle did odd jobs, so there was no telling what his schedule was from day to day, but I didn't really care if he was home or not. It was a small house, on a block filled with small houses, a few feet away from each other and lined with chain link fencing. Trucks on blocks stood in driveways. Dogs choked on chains. Two neighbors nodded to me as I parked my Jag on the street and walked up to my uncle's house. They were big, burly Russians, and they stood outside smoking and arguing about something in a language I recognized from cold war movies and a private after-hours club owned by a friend of my dad's, where we used to go for blini, caviar, and vodka, and to listen to a man sing traditional songs in a low register from the chest while playing the balalaika.

I shifted my laundry hamper to my hip and knocked on the door. Nobody answered, so I used my spare key and walked in.

The house was not tidy—it never was—but my uncle and father did not own enough stuff for it to be cluttered. There were dirty dishes in the sink, newspapers on the floor of the bathroom, with possible jobs circled in red ink, racing forms on the kitchen table, and a half-eaten donut on a plate attracting flies. "Dad? Uncle Lenny?" I hollered.

Nobody answered. I cracked open the door to my dad's room and saw that the bed was made, and no one was there. I was disappointed, but I knew I'd be staying for a while, until my clothes were clean and dry, and I figured my dad had gone out to the store or something, and I would see him soon. I went to the basement door and opened it.

The basement drew in water, which no one ever bothered to clean up, and so it had a damp, musty smell. I had been down there before, to get light bulbs, and I knew there was a worktable with some tools, as well as the washer and dryer. The steps were narrow and rickety, and so I walked carefully, staring straight down, over the laundry basket. I felt no sense of dread or premonition. I was thinking about not falling. I was thinking about the dishes in the sink, how it would be nice if I did them before my dad got home. I was thinking of my stomach, of what we would eat for lunch. I wondered if I should scrounge around my dad's and uncle's fridge or wait for my father to get home and suggest we walk to the taqueria on the corner. Going out to lunch with my dad was hit-or-miss in those days. Sometimes he would put a good face on things and enjoy the cheap tacos or fast-food burgers we could afford, and sometimes he would become tearful, lugubrious, and apologize for his bankruptcy, telling me I deserved better, declaring that he could never forgive himself for putting me through this, that he was a terrible father, a failure as a man. And I would have to comfort him and tell him not to be silly, that I didn't care about any of that, that I loved him and we would get through this, while a part of me was silently blaming him for whatever had caused this disaster—carelessness, shady dealings, dishonesty, a bad luck streak . . . who really knew?—and then feeling guilty for blaming him. It was hard to predict which sort of lunch we would have. I decided that maybe we should just stay at home and make sandwiches.

That was my last thought before I got to the bottom step, turned the corner, and looked up.

There is a small window in the basement, but it is sunny and light outside, and so the first thing I see is a silhouette. A body, a neck to the side, a rope. A chair is kicked over, turned on its side. I am not aware of dropping the laundry basket, but my hands are free, and I bring them to my mouth. There is no part of me that is close to screaming, to running away. As if in a dream, compulsion forces me to take a few steps forward. In front of me are brown leather loafers, tan socks, tan dress slacks, and a navy polo shirt. Somewhere it registers that my father chose this outfit. The arms are bulging, like the Incredible Hulk's. The hands are to the side, unclenched. My eyes move up to the neck. I have never realized what a fragile piece of the human body the neck is until this moment, when it is simply dangling there, to the side, about to fall off. Finally, I look at the face. I say "the" but of course it is a "my." It is my father's face, and it is swollen and red, with the tiniest tip of a black tongue protruding out of his mouth. His eyes—my father's eyes—are open. They are hazel, dilated, and staring, but even I can see that they are dead, unseeing eyes, no longer windows to the soul but just body parts, like the eyes of a swollen dead fish.

Still, something compels me to save him. I give the scene a wide berth and go to the toolbox on the wooden worktable. My hands are shaking terribly as I paw through a hammer, a wrench, dozens of nails, three screwdrivers, until I find an old rusty box cutter. I go back to my dad, to the chair. I go to right the chair and notice that there, on its underside, is a spider's cocoon. It is then that I pause to vomit. I vomit on the concrete floor and a little bit on my shoes. Leftover shrimp fried rice covered in soy sauce I'd reheated in the microwave before my morning shower. I wipe my mouth on my shirtsleeve and continue.

I upright the chair and stand on it. I am very close, only inches from my dad. He no longer smells like leather and tobacco and Scotch and Jaguar cars. He smells like sweat and urine and shit. Bile rises into my mouth, but I do not want to vomit over the smell of my father, and so I swallow it down. My throat burns. I am behind my dad, so that I'm staring at the back of his head, with its thinning brown hair that appears to be recently trimmed, and his neck, which is swollen and wrinkled. I bring the box cutter to the rope and realize I am going to have to lift my dad a little to cut the knot. He was never fat, but he was not exactly skinny, either, and he is heavy, and it is difficult for me to touch him, his cold body, his corpse. I realize I can't do it, that I will have to saw through the rope without cutting his neck as best I can. I say out loud, in a strangely normal voice, "Don't worry, Daddy, I'm going to get you down from here," and I cut the rope with the rusty box cutter a few threads at a time. I don't know how long it takes me. But I think that maybe eternity cannot be half as long.

I'm almost done, just a few more loose threads to cut, when my dad falls, and because I am unprepared, the chair and I fall with him. I fall on top of him and then roll to the side. I have fallen on my hip and my left hand, both of which now ache and sting. I am right beside my dad. His face is not his face. It is a swollen, red, horror movie face, with a dark scar, a dark line, around his neck. Our faces are just a breath away from one another, though of course only one of us can breathe. I think it is then that I pass out. I only know that at some point I awaken, on the cold basement floor, the scent of my own regurgitated Chinese food around me, my dad's open eyes a few inches away.

I run. I run up the stairs and out the door, and once I'm outside, I see one of the Russians there, now watering his lawn, and ask him to call 9-1-1.

"Yeah, sure, 9-1-1," he says, rushing into his house to use his phone. After a few seconds, he yells to me through the open screen door, "What is your emergency?"

"My dad! My dad . . . had a heart attack!" The lie comes out unbidden, unwilled, unplanned. I don't know what my motivation is, except that I cannot say the real words aloud.

"Next-door neighbor had heart attack. Come quick!" he yells into the phone.

I thank him and run back to my uncle's house and wait inside, leaving the door wide open, a couple of flies buzzing in and out.

When the paramedics come, in about five minutes, I am unable to speak but simply motion to the basement. Two of them rush down the stairs with a stretcher, while another, the driver, tells me I can ride with them in the back of the ambulance. I grab my purse, follow her through the back, get in, and wait for my dad.

The paramedics are not rushing when they come out. They slide the stretcher clunkily into the back of the ambulance, where I am crouching, not crying, comatose. A white sheet is pulled over my father's head.

One of them—youngish, white, with shaggy blond hair—talks to the driver, and then says to me, "Heart attack, huh?"

The other says, "Looks like she's the one that needs help." He's Black and older, with a goatee.

"Busted our asses to get here."

"You got somewhere else you got to be?"

"Could be people having real heart attacks right now."

"Yeah, there could be, and there could be people who need a little compassion right now."

This silences the younger man, and we ride the rest of the way in quiet, the siren of the ambulance painfully absent.

The next days passed in a blur.

I had to plan the funeral by myself. My uncle said he couldn't handle it. Implying, I guess, that I could.

I picked out a nice coffin for my dad. Solid cherrywood. The service was closed casket. I put everything on my credit card. Fourteen thousand six hundred dollars.

Many people came to the funeral—friends, cousins, and just about everyone in the Chicago restaurant business—but my mother was not among them.

I don't know what my mother did that day, the day of my father's funeral.

I told everyone my father had died of a heart attack, and as far as I know, everyone believed me.

One of the people who came was Ricky, a bartender at one of my dad's nightclubs I'd known for years. He gave me two white pills and handed me a flask of single malt Scotch to wash them down. "Ativan," he said. "You know how people at funerals say tell me if you need anything? Well, you need these." I swallowed and drank. He took the flask, tipped it toward me, and said, "To your dad. Who was fucking awesome."

I spent the rest of the funeral numb, calm, and a little dizzy.

I don't know what happened to Ricky. If he's still a bartender, if he's still alive, if he's still going to funerals, a good Samaritan handing people Ativan and flasks.

I wore a black Marc Jacobs dress. I spilled whisky all over it at the reception, took it to the dry cleaner's the next day, and never picked it up.

I don't know what happened to that dress.

I don't know what happened to my laundry hamper of clothes. I simply didn't show up to work, and in a week or so, I got a new job, at a different restaurant, so I would never need to see that uniform again.

I don't know what my boss thought.

I don't know what my uncle did with those clothes, whether he left them in the hamper at the bottom of the stairs in the basement.

I never went back to my uncle's house.

My uncle was at the funeral. At the reception afterward, he drank a lot and didn't eat. He said, "If you need anything . . . ," his voice slurring and trailing off, as if he couldn't imagine how to finish the rest of that sentence. If I needed anything—a father figure, money, a home—both of us knew my uncle was not the person to call. Both of us knew that if I needed any of those things—and I needed all of them—I was screwed.

I don't know what happened to the leftover Chinese-food vomit, whether my uncle cleaned it up.

I don't know what happened to the chair, whether anyone ever sat on it again.

I don't know if the spider cocoon hatched, but I assume it did. I assume that hundreds of baby spiders spilled out one day, alive and well, ready to explore the world of the basement.

I don't know what happened to the rope.

I don't know what happened to the Lilly who went into the basement.

But I know that the Lilly who walked out was a different Lilly. She was someone who had gone into a basement to do laundry and had found her father dangling from a rope and had needed to cut him down with a rusty box cutter.

She was damaged, broken, an angel of death with clipped wings.

She was someone who understood that she hadn't been enough to keep her father alive.

32

THIS BASEMENT

I HELD ON TO THE BANISTER and placed my right foot down the first step. I was still wearing the silk pajama bottoms with the frayed hems and the old Star Wars T-shirt I'd slept in, a pair of wool socks, and my rubber slides. The shoes creaked on the wooden stairs. The stairs were flimsy, the kind in which you could see through each slat. With my right hand, I held onto the handrail; with my left, I held on to my heart, to keep it from leaving my chest. My throat was dry, and my head was pounding. I thought of the irony of having a heart attack on the stairs on the way down to the basement. *Just like her father*, everyone would think.

"Lilly . . ."

The sound was clear and deliberate.

I took another step. And another. As I neared the bottom, I paused, because with one more step, I'd be able to see what was around the corner of the stairway, and I had to brace myself and my pounding heart for that sight.

It wasn't as if I believed my father's body would be there, hanging from a rope. And it wasn't as if I believed his spirit would be haunting this basement, three hundred miles away from the basement in which he'd died.

No, if I had to name what my fear of basements was about, I would have said it was like being confronted by the dementors in the Harry Potter books, those demons who suck every last bit of joy out of you, who glory in your despair, and who feed on your worst fears. It was about feeling bereft, alone, and unloved. About being unworthy of love. About being broken.

Standing on that splintered wooden penultimate step, I felt the full force of my mother's abandonment. Of Jack's loving some version of me that wasn't real, a pretty face with a pretty body on a stage, underneath bright lights. Of knowing I hadn't been enough for my father to want to stay alive.

Perhaps worst of all, I feared that I was no longer capable of loving, truly loving, anyone, including myself, that I would be incapable of loving the way a parent needed to love a child. That I would make a terrible mother, just like my own mother. That if I ever did have a child, they would be broken. Unhinged. Just like me.

Which led to the real dementor-sucking reason why I was so afraid of basements. Why I was sweating now, and shaking, and holding onto the banister so hard my right hand was pounding and then becoming numb. Because taking one more step down, I could already see the materials I would need. The wooden stepladder propped next to Jack's shelves of tools and supplies. A high enough ceiling. The supporting crossbeam on which I could easily string the rope that was coiled on the top shelf, or perhaps that orange extension cord that was plugged into the shop vac. Either of these objects would almost certainly get the job done.

And they called to me their siren call: *It would be so easy. You can leave all this pain and lovelessness. Just go ahead and join your dad. You know you want to.*

"*Lilly . . .*" It was just a whisper now.

I stepped onto the cold concrete floor. I felt the cold seep up through the rubber soles of my slides, through my wool socks, into my feet, and then spread throughout my body. I hugged my arms around me. I glanced around the dimly lit cavernous space and immediately noticed the washer and dryer in a corner, two white units that didn't look all that different from the ones in my uncle's basement. I hadn't eaten yet, and I felt bile rise from the back of my throat into my mouth. I swallowed it down.

What little light there was emanated from a fluorescent strip above the washer and dryer, but I could see that there were bare bulbs in the ceiling all over the enormous room. I searched around for a light switch and found one without a plate on it on the wall at the foot of the stairs. I flipped it on to reveal what must have been about five thousand square feet of open concrete expanse.

Heating ducts, wiring, and water pipes ran along the exposed ceiling, which was dripping with abandoned, dusty cobwebs. I thought of the spider's cocoon in the Rogers Park duplex and held my heart. Although it was cold in the basement, I was sweating now, down my spine, between my breasts, in my armpits, and on my forehead, and I wiped the sweat from my eyes with the back of my hand so I could see.

I walked to the center of the room, listening, gazing, circling around to confirm what was already obvious—it was empty. There was no Ping-Pong table, no workspace, no TV lounge, no dartboard. The vast space was vacant of anything that would seem to warrant a ghostly call. Then I noticed a door at the far end, on the other side of the stairs from which I'd just come.

I waited, listening for a sign. I breathed in, out. A distinctive scent hit my nostrils, of dead mice and old socks. Maybe a minute passed. Maybe five. But there was only silence.

"Birdy?" I whispered. No answer. I slowly walked to the door, my pounding heart and my quiet footsteps the only sounds in the room.

It was a wooden door, with an antique brass knob. I turned the knob, opened the door, and saw some vague outlines of large cylinder-shaped objects and heard the *whoosh* of a roaring furnace. A string dangled in front of me, which I yanked. A light came on, illuminating a bare bulb and a room containing two furnaces, a water heater, a metal desk against a wall, and a floor littered with mouse droppings. I stood there for a moment, confused. Had Birdy really led me to this basement? Perhaps to this room? Or had I merely imagined that the sound this old furnace made was a voice, calling my name?

I was about to pull the light string and leave when out of the corner of my eye, I noticed a few cardboard boxes underneath the metal desk. They were tucked—almost hidden—against the wall. I went over to the desk, crouched down, and pulled the boxes toward me. Each of the boxes was labeled with a Sharpie marker: The top one read "HCS Bills 1995–2000." The middle one read "HCS Bills 1990–1995." And the bottom one read "Misc."

It appeared that these were Haven Circus Society documents that had been overlooked when the society had moved out.

I maneuvered the boxes until I was able to grab the bottom one and place it on top of the desk. It was an old cardboard box, torn around the corners, with no strapping tape holding it shut, the flaps closed but not sealed. I opened it up and brushed past a manila envelope, fingered through about a hundred circus flyers advertising "The Lawrence Brothers Circus" performing back in 1953, and dug through, at the bottom, some papers that appeared to be receipts and bills. I then picked up the manila envelope, which was heavy and thick with something, and examined it more closely. It was old, with a string tie and snap on the back, and on the front, some writing in pencil. The letters seemed strangely familiar, and I realized, with a chilling recognition, that they were in the same shaky block capital handwriting that had spelled the words "JUMP" in dust on the rocking chair in the nursery and "HELP" in pencil underneath the wallpaper on the dining room. And then my heart raced, blood rushed to my ears, and the envelope fell out of my hands, as I made out the words:

FOR LILY

33

WHAT WAS IN THE ENVELOPE

I STARED AT THOSE WORDS (my name misspelled, as it was), waiting for my heart to stop pounding and my hands to stop trembling. When they didn't, I unwound the flap string anyway, reached inside the envelope, and took out what appeared to be two documents, each one held together with a thick metal clip. From the yellowing color of the paper, and from its faint vanilla scent, it was clear that the documents were old, an observation that was confirmed by the heading on the first page:

> August 12, 1947: Prenuptial Agreement between Robert
> Shawcross and Beatrice Lawrence

The prenup . . . The document that Chas Lawrence had refused to steal from his girlfriend's legal firm. He said there were two copies, one at the firm, one at the house. I must have been looking at the latter. I breathed deeply, trying to focus, and continued to read. I skimmed the numerous pages of legalese until I found what I thought were the relevant passages and studied them carefully.

> Robert Shawcross hereby waives, discharges, and releases any
> right, title, and interest whatsoever that he may acquire in the
> property or estate of Beatrice Lawrence at any time hereafter
> by reason of the marriage.

> . . .

Income earned by a party during the course of the parties' marriage, from whatever source, shall not be deemed an asset of
the marriage, or marital property, but rather shall remain the
sole and separate property of the party earning the income.

. . .

Each party is fully aware that if one of them predeceases the
other while the marriage is still in effect, the present laws of
the State of Wisconsin would entitle a surviving party the net
estate of the deceased party. However, each party desires to
release any and all marital property rights and will receive no
such rights except through a separate bequeathal. . . .

The document was signed by the bride- and groom-to-be as
well as by a witness, Beatrice's father Edgar Lawrence, and filed by
the Haven legal firm of Lija, Michaels & Zukauskas. After skimming the pages and reading these pertinent sentences more than
once, I came to one undeniable conclusion: in case of divorce, Robert Shawcross received nothing. Not a dollar, a dime, or a single
Lincoln penny. In case of divorce, this legal document (and Edgar
Lawrence, who did not want his daughter to be taken advantage of
by the charismatic Bobby Shawcross, was my guess) made sure that
Robert "Bobby" Shawcross would not benefit from the Lawrence
Brothers' circus fortune, from Edgar's wealth, or from Birdy's hard-
earned money in any way.

I set down the prenup and examined the second document. The
first page, which was clipped to a lengthy last will and testament,
contained only a few sentences:

July 21, 1954: Codicil to Last Will and Testament of Beatrice
Lawrence Shawcross

I, Beatrice Lawrence Shawcross, hereby declare this to be a
CODICIL, executed July 21, 1954, to my LAST WILL AND
TESTAMENT, dated August 12, 1947.

I give all my tangible personal property to my husband,
Robert Shawcross. If he does not survive me, I give that property to those of my children who survive me, in equal shares,
to be divided among them.

I flipped through the 1947 will and found the bequeathal language it replaced:

I give all my tangible personal property to my children who
survive me, in equal shares, to be divided among them.

So, in 1947, on the day Birdy had signed the prenup, she had
also signed a will in which she'd left everything to her children (or
her child, as it had turned out), once again leaving Bobby out of seeing any of Edgar's or her money, in case of death as well as in the case
of divorce. But in 1954, several years after Edgar had died and the
year before the tragedy, Birdy had revised her will to leave everything
to Bobby.

*If I'd a done what he'd asked, she'd still be alive today. And so . . .
and so would that little girl.*

Chas Lawrence's words ran through my mind . . .

Bobby had clearly been considering divorcing Birdy. Maybe he'd
thought that by getting rid of all the copies of the prenup, he could
walk away with half of her estate. But when Chas had refused to help
him steal the one from the lawyer's office, he'd decided to focus on
getting Birdy's will changed instead.

To what end? Had he intended to kill her? Is that what Chas had
known or suspected? That if Bobby couldn't get half of everything
through divorce, he'd decided to get all of it through murder?

A chill ran up my spine and tiny hairs prickled on the back of my neck as I realized that whatever happened that night back in 1955, the newspapers had gotten it all wrong.

Between these documents and Chas Lawrence's fragmented recollections, it was clear to me that Birdy hadn't killed her husband and daughter in a bout of hysteria. She hadn't been unstable or evil.

She wasn't the villain of the story. Bobby Shawcross was.

34

GET WHAT YOU DESERVE

I FELT HIM BEFORE I SAW HIM. A coolness, an electricity, and the scents of cigarette smoke, whiskey, and something else, something sulfuric and metallic, faintly reminiscent of the Fourth of July. Bobby Shawcross was standing in the doorway of the furnace room, his wavy dark hair parted on the side and swooped over his forehead, his animal brown eyes peering deeply into mine, his full, wide lips, soft as a pillow, just barely parted, for a kiss, or perhaps a plea.

I closed my eyes, rubbed them hard. I told myself this wasn't real. I opened my eyes. Bobby Shawcross was still there.

This was no hallucination. He was right in front of me. And hadn't Ricarda Heller said there was a dark presence in the house? Hadn't I seen and experienced enough to know that it was true? Hadn't I been led to the photo album and all this evidence in the envelope? Here was my ghost. All this time I'd thought it was Birdy. But it must have been Bobby, haunting me.

"You're the one," I said.

Bobby smiled a gorgeous, dimpled smile. "Sure I am, baby. I'm the one. The one for you," he said in that singer-sexy Oklahoma voice of his.

He reached his hands toward me, but I pulled away. I clutched the documents to my chest, Chas's words playing in my mind like a song from the radio: *If I'd a done what Bobby wanted, my cousin and her little baby would still be alive today.*

"You're the one who's been haunting me," I said. "You led me to these documents, to the photo album." I tapped on the manila envelope, the words "TO LILY" facing him. "Is this some sort of confession?"

He tilted his head, squinting. He looked uncertain. "Whatcha got there, sweetheart?"

"It's Birdy's prenuptial agreement and her will. The will she changed the year before she died, leaving everything to you."

Bobby shook his head. "That damn prenup was all Edgar's idea. He thought I was some kind of a gold digger."

"Weren't you?"

"Damn it! Birdy was three months pregnant when we got married. I was doing right by her and our baby! But Edgar said the only way he'd leave Birdy anything was if I didn't have control of it. Said I'd gamble it away. But he did give me a good job. General manager. Which was just fine, until the circus closed down."

I took a step closer and said the words I knew, deep down, were true. "You killed her, didn't you? You killed your own wife."

His dark eyes were gazing into mine as if I were the only woman in the world, as if mine were the only opinion that mattered. "She jumped off a cliff," he said quietly. "Broke her neck."

"And you had nothing to do with that?"

It should have felt strange to be talking to a ghost, but he looked and smelled so real that somehow it did not, and I gazed at him the way I would have gazed at any flesh-and-blood human standing a few inches away from me. He seemed tired, suddenly, or maybe I was just now noticing it, like he hadn't slept in years. The light was fading from his eyes, and his shoulders were slack from carrying some invisible heavy burden. "Let me put it to you this way," he said, and his voice was tired, too, as if he were trying to make a joke, but it was difficult to put in the effort. "I had enough to do with it to last me an eternity to consider." Then he looked down at his chest and legs. "But she gave what she got pretty good, too. I can still feel where the bullet holes went in."

He was wearing his royal blue suit and white button-down shirt. Only they weren't riddled with bullet holes, and there was no blood anywhere. They were stylish and neatly pressed. Still, I knew that according to the newspaper reports, he had been shot about eight times.

"This one hurts the most." He pointed to a spot on his chest that must have been right where his heart was—the kill shot. Then he reached out and rubbed his finger against my heart. I felt a cold shock go through me. "You're hurting, too, aren't you, baby? I see you. You want something."

Tears stung behind my lids. I was filled with wants, with needs, and I felt like this wicked, seductive spirit knew them all. Peering into his dark eyes, I thought of the last time I had seen him, when I had been making love to Jack, and he'd inhabited Jack's body—or had seemed to, anyway. I felt a stirring of something inside me, something primal and sexual. I shook my head, to make the image go away. "You're wrong," I said.

"Sure you do. And it's completely natural." Was he trying to arouse me? Seduce me? It wasn't going to work, not after what I'd learned. "I've seen you around, here and there, seen what you do, where you go, how you look. A child. You want a child. Badly."

His words slashed my heart like a blade. "How do you know that?"

"Because I know you. And I know it hurts. That desire. I don't want to hurt you, baby. I might be able to help you. Help us both."

"Help me? How?"

His eyes were pleading and soft. "One thing you got to understand, I always loved my little girl."

"Loved her? Are you sure it wasn't you who killed her?"

"You don't know what you're talking about."

I spit out the words, "And your wife? Did you love her, too?"

I was trying to provoke him, but he was calm and thoughtful as he replied, "Sure I did. More than any other girl I ever met. Until she got stingy on me, tried to control me with her money, our money, really, or it shoulda been. But Amelia was the light of my life, the only thing I ever brought into this world that was good. She *saw* me. Just like I see you. She saw me the way I wanted to be, even if I wasn't that man back then. But I'm closer now than I ever was. I'm getting there. I'm changing. Funny. Who knew that you could still change after you was dead?"

He looked sincere, sad. Heartbroken, really. His eyes became glossy. "I didn't deserve Beatrice Lawrence. But in life, we get plenty of things we don't deserve." He smiled at me, a sad smile, and then he laughed. "You are so beautiful. You know that?"

I shook my head. I had been told something like this a hundred times in my life, by young boys, old men, teenage girls, directors both professional and lewd, fellow actors male and female, gay and straight . . . but I couldn't remember the words ever having meant more to me than they did now. When I felt so un-beautiful. "Your husband tell you you're beautiful? He appreciate how gorgeous you are? How special?"

"Of course he does," I said quickly, though I couldn't remember the last time Jack had said anything remotely like this to me.

"Uh-huh," Bobby Shawcross said, unconvinced. "Your husband. He deserve you?"

I let out a bitter laugh. "Most people would say I don't deserve him."

"I ain't asking most people. I'm asking you."

Did Jack deserve me? I had felt so grateful to him for rescuing me after my father's death, for taking care of me, for seeming to love me because of my weaknesses rather than despite them. But did I want to be loved for my weaknesses rather than my strengths? He always told me how he loved my curiosity, my childlike wonder, my imagination, my empathy and caring for others. But sometimes I felt he treated me more like a child than a partner. When we'd met, I'd thought—we'd both thought—that I'd needed to be taken care of as delicately as any orphaned bird. But was that true? Had it ever been true? I was thirty-seven and had survived the death by suicide of my father, the abandonment of my mother, and the loss of three unborn babies. Didn't that mean, deep down, I had managed to take care of myself? And if he had fooled me—both of us—into thinking that I couldn't manage without him, then maybe I did deserve more.

Would he have proposed to me after seeing me as Lady MacBeth instead of Ophelia?

"I don't know if he deserves me. I'm pretty sure he doesn't know me," I said, and the truth of it made me sad.

"Ain't that a shame," he said quietly, and I felt like his sorrowful tone said what his words did not: that Jack may not have known me, but he, Bobby Shawcross, certainly did. "So, what're you gonna do about it?"

He seemed to think I was still the woman he had fondled in the foyer, while his wife and daughter had been sitting in the other room. Yes, I had felt deeply attracted to him then, and I still was, on some animal, pheromonal level. But I also felt repulsed by him, now that I knew he was somehow complicit in their deaths.

"What am I going to do about what?"

"Your wet rag of a husband."

"What?" I barely managed to ask.

He smiled. "Don't look so surprised. You know what I'm talking 'bout. Don't you? You could leave him. But then you'd lose the house. You belong here. Out there's no place for you, baby. So then, you could . . . you know," he said, waving his arms, "*abracadabra*, make him disappear. I can help you, if you want."

I concentrated very hard on what he was saying. Was he telling me to . . . kill Jack?

"What are you talking about?" I whispered.

"There are ways to do it, so you won't even get caught. Poison. Shooting, if you do it right. You could always—"

"Stop."

"You ever thought about doing it?"

"My God! Of course not."

He nodded, untroubled. "It ain't hard. All you need is rat poison. At first a little, and then a little more. And then one night, more than a little, and then . . ."

Amelia had been killed by poison. Had Bobby been lying when he'd said I didn't know what I was talking about, implying he wasn't the one who had killed her? Had he poisoned both of them? Is that why Birdy had looked so sick?

"Stop!" I yelled, stepping back. What were the words Ricarda Heller had incanted? "Spirit, leave this house and cross to the other side!"

His smile was wry, as if he got a kick out of my spell. He stood closer to me and touched my hair. "I wish I could, darlin', but I can't. Not yet. Not until I make sure . . . let's just say I have some unfinished business here." He moved his hand to my cheek, cupping it tenderly in his hand. I closed my eyes. "Make sure he loves you real good, sweetheart," he said in a low, quiet voice. "Or just, well, make sure you get what you deserve." He stroked his thumb against my cheek. Our faces were only inches apart. And then I realized what that metallic, sulfuric scent was: Gunpowder. Brimstone. I opened my eyes, alarmed.

Bobby Shawcross was gone.

35

COMING CLEAN

I WAS DREAMING THAT JACK was at the foot of the bed, nudging my ankles and telling me to wake up, when I opened my eyes and found that he was at the foot of the bed, nudging my ankles and telling me to wake up. I immediately felt guilty for sleeping in, even though I had no idea what time it was. The blinds were shut, and some vague winter light was creeping through. I sat up, rubbed my eyes, and pulled the sheets and comforter over my tank top and heart-print pajama bottoms. I felt cold, and also sorrowful, because I couldn't remember the last time I had actually felt happy to see my husband.

"What time is it?" I asked.

"One. In the afternoon. Are you taking a nap, or did you never get up?" He looked like he was trying to maintain a blank expression, like he was trying to ask a neutral question, but it wasn't working.

The truth was, I couldn't remember. I didn't think I'd gotten up and gone back to sleep, but I wasn't sure.

"We need to talk. I'm going downstairs to make some coffee," he said, standing. "Want some?"

This was a loaded question, and we both knew it. I only drank coffee during the two weeks between the time I was menstruating and ovulating. Was this those two weeks? I hadn't been filling out my fertility graph, but I remembered we hadn't had sex since I'd peed on that stick. "Sure, I'll have coffee," I said. "Be right down."

I went to the bathroom. I washed my hands, brushed my teeth, and gazed into the mirror. My skin was dry and haggard. My cheekbones were prominent, and the cheeks beneath them hollow. The parts that were available to me now, if I were still acting, would be few and far between. Cassandra in *Agamemnon*, cursed to prophesy but never to be believed. Blanche DuBois. *"The Grim Reaper put his tent up on our doorstep!"* Yes, I could pull that off. I thought of my vision (yesterday or a few days before, I wasn't sure) with Bobby Shawcross. It was a bit of a stretch for him to consider me "beautiful," and it made me smile, until I thought of the rest of our conversation. I didn't want to think about that, or the fact that I'd had that vision—or whatever it was—at all. I touched my hands over my cheeks, down my neck, and over the sides of my body, still peering at my reflection, when I realized that I could see my ribs beneath my tank top. I lifted up the shirt and gazed at my torso. My hipbones jutted out. My breasts were smaller. I had become thin in a way that I knew was probably not healthy. When had I last eaten? I couldn't remember. *We need to talk*, Jack had said. I would go downstairs right now and have some buttered toast with my coffee, and then I would listen to whatever stern lecture I feared Jack was determined to give.

I put on an old sweater over my tank top, clean underwear, and my favorite pair of jeans. The jeans were now a size too big and fell down on me. I decided to have jam on my toast as well as butter, and I reached for a pair of skinny jeans that had always been too tight. They fit. I went downstairs.

Jack was sitting at the kitchen farm table, checking his phone and drinking coffee. I poured myself a mug and sat down in the window seat next to Olivier. I grabbed his brush from the basket on the floor and brushed him while I sipped my coffee. He purred sweetly while I ran the brush through his thick Persian hair and pet his sweet, grumpy-looking face. The actions made me feel calm.

Jack set down his phone. "I want you to know I've called a real estate agent." His expression was matter-of-fact.

"What are you talking about?" I asked, a surge of confusion and adrenaline running through me. I felt like I'd awakened from a nightmare only to find I didn't recognize where I was.

"We can't live here anymore. You haven't been working. As far as I know, you haven't looked for a new job."

"I haven't had time, but I will. I will look for a new job. I'll do anything. I'll file for a license in the state of Wisconsin. I'll apply for a teaching job in the district." Suddenly, it didn't matter to me that I hadn't felt ready to be around other people's children. I knew that I would do anything to keep this house. I would apply to be the assistant in a day care with twenty babies if it would mean not putting the house up for sale. "I'll apply today," I added, and I meant it.

"Right," he said, nodding, and his pretend belief in me was truly annoying. "Let me ask you something. What day is it?"

"I don't know. What does that have to do with anything?"

"You don't know the day of the week. Do you know the date?"

"Yes. It's mid—no, it's late November." I remembered seeing advertisements on the television for the Macy's Thanksgiving Day parade. I hadn't missed Thanksgiving. We hadn't missed Thanksgiving. Had we? Had Jack come home for Thanksgiving? Was it this week? Tomorrow?

"Okay, you know the month. You had one out of twelve chances of getting that right. I came home at one in the afternoon, and you were still in bed. Look at you."

"What about me?" I stopped brushing Olivier and ran my hands through my own tangled hair.

"Are you eating? When was the last time you ate? Look at your wrists!"

They were the bony wrists of a child. I brought my sweater down to my knuckles. I remembered my intention to make myself some toast, and I would. I just hadn't gotten around to it yet.

"Maybe I haven't been that hungry lately, maybe I haven't looked at a calendar. Anyway, I was about to make myself breakfast. What's your point?" I tried to sound strong and aggressive, but I felt as though I were being led into a trap.

"You're not fit to teach a classroom full of children," he said softly.

From somewhere far away, I felt the words wound me. I carried on. "I'll get a job as a server, then. I was always good at that."

He ran his hands through his hair, shook his head, and sighed. "I'm not explaining this right," he said. "I don't want to live here anymore. I can't live here anymore. We can't afford it. We never really could afford it, and with your not working, and the housing market getting worse and worse . . . and you can't buy me out. There's no way I can make it clearer than that. I've talked to a real estate agent. A guy at work's sister who's supposed to be excellent. It's done. Do you understand?"

I had earned mostly As at my private boarding school and at Northwestern, with the occasional C in a math or science class, but throughout my life, as I had tried to navigate the practicalities of the world—dealing with forms, banks, taxes, post offices, government officials, and medical professionals—people on the other end of those interactions often said the same thing Jack was saying to me now ("Do you understand?") very slowly, enunciating clearly, while looking at me as if they were trying to figure out if the lights were on. I had dealt with this underestimation of my intelligence dozens of times in my life, but never with Jack. Sure, we'd had our spats, disagreements, and frustrations before, but he'd never spoken to me quite like this. His eyes were wide, and his expression was open with a sort of fake kindness, as if he were trying to be patient with the actress who was "too pretty." The thought *I used to love this person* came into my head and then floated away.

"Wait! Just wait. I have some things I need to show you." I felt a sudden surge of hopefulness. I had evidence, after all. Jack just hadn't seen it yet. I simply had to convince him—he who was always so logical, so practical, whose belief system was based on the ideas that *There are no such things as ghosts* and *Whatever happens, there's a logical explanation for it, even if we don't always know what it is*—that my evidence was founded on facts and reality, so that he would understand I wasn't crazy. Once he saw the evidence, maybe he would see that my quest made sense, and he wouldn't make us sell the house until I had all my answers.

I went upstairs and retrieved the photo album from my bottom clothing drawer in the bedroom and the manila envelope from the bookshelf in my study. I brought them downstairs and set the items in front of Jack on the kitchen table.

"I didn't show you these before because I didn't think you'd believe me, but I don't have any choice now." My heart was racing; there was so much at stake. "I found them here, in the house. And I didn't just find them. I was led to them. The photo album was hidden in a cabinet in the third-floor attic. The envelope was in a box in the basement. The basement! You know I would never go into a basement if I didn't have to. It was—"

"Why not?" He asked me this in a sweet tone, as if he were merely curious. He had never asked me this before. It was our deal. I had told him, *I don't do basements, laundry, or Chinese food, and I don't talk about why,* and he'd always respected that deal. But now, it was as if the gloves were off.

I was standing beside Jack, and he turned and stared up at me, that same stupid fake-nice expression on his face. Had he always looked at me like that, had he always been so patronizing of me, and I'd just never noticed? Or was this patronizing attitude and fake-nice expression of his new?

I felt too shocked to answer, but then we both turned our attention to the task at hand. Jack began flipping through the photo album, and then he opened the envelope, which was lying face down, and quickly glanced at the documents there. "What is all this stuff?"

"This is the photo album of Birdy Lawrence." I showed him the last page and pointed to the picture of Birdy and Amelia. "In this last picture, you can see that her hair is balding, and she has a rash. She was clearly sick. And I think it may have been from poison. From a substance in rat poison called thallium. It's what Amelia, their daughter, died of. I think Bobby Shawcross may have also used it to kill Birdy. Or, I mean, to try to, anyway."

He didn't say anything, and so I kept explaining.

"This envelope contains two important documents. Their prenuptial agreement—"

"Prenuptial agreement?" he repeated.

"It states that if they divorce, Bobby doesn't receive any of Birdy's fortune. But Birdy's will, which was revised the year before her death, gives Bobby everything. See?"

Jack perused the items in silence. Finally, he frowned and asked, "How did you say you found these things?"

"I heard knocking. And someone calling my name. And the knocks and voice led me to them. There's a real ghost in this house, Jack! I'm so close to understanding it all. Just give me a little more time. Give me a chance to figure everything out. And then . . ." My voice trailed off as I tried to finish the sentence.

"And then what?"

And then . . . and then I would feel whole? And then I would put my ghosts to rest? I had always imagined this would be the house in which I would become a mother, but now, looking at Jack, who was gazing at me as if I were twelve and impaired, that dream seemed impossible to believe.

Jack turned the envelope over, which I had been hoping he would not do, for I had no explanation for what he would see there. "What's this?" he asked.

We both stared at the words in choppy block capital handwriting: FOR LILY.

I looked into his eyes. I didn't know what he saw in mine—fear, terror, hopelessness—but what I saw in his was a cool distance that was worse than anger.

"Sit down," he said, and I did. He put his hand on my shoulder. It felt authoritative, unwanted, the hand of an oppressive director letting me know who was in charge. "I'm worried about you. I want you to see someone. My work provides excellent insurance of every kind. I'm going to get the name and number of a good psychiatrist. You need to get back on your meds. And the sooner the better."

I closed my eyes, breathed out. I had known this would be his reaction. I picked up the envelope and brought it to my chest, so that the "FOR LILY" was pressed against me.

"Where did you say you got that envelope?"

I kept my eyes closed and answered, "The basement."

"Yes, the basement. You never answered me. You never told me why you won't go into basements. What you're afraid of."

A bird flew into my throat and flapped its wings there. The undead had led me to an unsafe attic, to a dark basement, but I had never been more scared than I was now, when I had the chance to brush this conversation off, or forge ahead, revealing myself to Jack, come clean, and perhaps save the dredges of our marriage. It took every ounce of strength I had to speak through those flapping wings. "My father didn't die of a heart attack," I said. "I found him in the basement. He died of suicide. Of hanging. With a rope. I cut him down."

My heart was pounding. My stomach was sick. But the bird was gone, and I felt proud of myself. I opened my eyes. I didn't know what I expected to see on Jack's face—sympathy, sorrow, love, admiration, sadness, pity—but I knew I didn't expect to see what I found there: a smirk. He shook his head and let out a chuckle without a hint of humor in it. "Unfucking believable," he said.

It took me a couple of seconds to understand his reaction. "I know I should have told you earlier . . ."

He stood up and paced around the kitchen. "There weren't enough things you were lying about, so now you had to lie about this, too? Your own father's death?"

"What? No, you don't . . . I'm not lying."

"Oh, so you were lying before, but not now."

"I didn't mean to."

"And your mother? I mean, when I met your mother, she told me your father had a heart attack. She was lying, too?"

"She doesn't know."

"She doesn't know."

"No, she doesn't know how he really died. I've never told anyone before."

"That's convenient."

He paced around, hands in his pockets, hands out, stroking his cheeks, hands back in his pockets again. "I said I wanted to sell the house—no, I said I was going to sell the house. And you pull out your best performance yet, so I'll feel sorry for you and give you more time? You know what that is? That's sick. You are sick."

He stared at me, angry and disgusted, as if he'd been promised a pretty princess, but instead had been given a repulsive witch. He seemed to be waiting for a response, but I was shocked into silence.

He just stared at me for a minute, that disgusted, angry expression on his face, and then he grabbed his car keys, wallet, and coat, and left through the garage door, slamming it behind him. A few moments later, I heard the car drive fast down our driveway.

I went to wipe my eyes, but I found I wasn't crying.

36

WHAT HAPPENED THAT NIGHT

I COULDN'T SLEEP THAT NIGHT. I tossed and turned for hours, waiting for something to happen. At one point, I fell into a short, fitful sleep in which I dreamed a violent dream I couldn't remember, and then awakened with Macbeth's words running through my mind, *Sleep no more, Sleep no more, Sleep no more.* I checked my phone. It was 3:00 a.m.

I pushed away the covers and stepped out of bed. I was wearing thermal leggings, a T-shirt, and wool socks. My legs felt unsteady, and my head felt grainy, but I was determined to go downstairs. I walked down the dimly lit hall, and then down the grand staircase until I stopped in the entryway underneath the black chandelier. As I stood there, even though there was no music this time, no Perry Como, no Patti Page, I sensed that something was different. I could feel it in the air, which was not the cold, desolate air of a run-down twenty-first century, long-abandoned haunted house, but rather the warm air of a mid-century home populated with people and furniture and art. I was in a different time, a different world. I turned to my left and gazed into the living room.

I wasn't shocked this time, wasn't the least bit surprised, to find the living room occupied with its previous inhabitants. I didn't bother rubbing my eyes or telling myself I was dreaming. I simply stood in the foyer, accepting that what was in front of me was somehow real. I had somehow crossed through a portal into the past.

Birdy was sitting on the couch, her back to me. I could see from behind that her hair was even thinner than in the last picture of the photo album and that there was a large bald patch at her crown. Bobby was wearing his shiny royal blue suit and black dress shoes, pacing up and down the room, smoking. Every so often he'd stop his pacing to tap his ashes into the hand-shaped ashtray on the round Scandinavian coffee table, or take a sip of his drink, which rested on a coaster on top of the piano. His pacing was unsteady, as if he'd had a couple of drinks too many. He didn't seem to see me.

Amelia was sitting in one of the orange chairs by the fireplace, wearing bunny-print pajamas, her brown hair in a ponytail. Her beautiful, wide-eyed, freckled face, and her bare feet, which swung back and forth, not quite reaching the floor, gave her the mien of an old-fashioned image of an angel. But there seemed to be something troubling her. Her eyebrows knit toward one another, and she rubbed her two thumbs together on her lap, as if engaged in some perpetual battle of thumb wars she seemed to be playing by herself.

"Is she going to be there?" Birdy's voice was quiet but forceful.

"Definitely not," Bobby said.

"How do you know?"

"Because I know." Bobby took a sip of his drink. "Listen, hon, I already told you. Frank's parties are imitant. Intimate." He paused, as if he was surprised that he'd slurred that one word, and then, after getting it right, went on. "Not antsville like Joanie's at New Year's. Just a dozen or so people. And none of them are people you . . . don't like."

Birdy picked up the teacup that was on the tray in front of her, sipped from it, set it down in its saucer, and said, "It doesn't matter. I'm not feeling well enough to socialize anyway. I've already called the sitter and canceled."

"You okay?"

"I'm tired. I have a headache. And my numbness and tingling are bad today. I feel like my feet have been walking on hot coals."

"I'm sorry, honey."

I was still in the foyer. I couldn't see Birdy's face, but I could see Bobby's. He truly did appear sorry. Pained, even.

"I went to see Dr. Grodin today."

"I know."

"What? How do you know?"

Bobby took a long drag of his cigarette and exhaled. "He called me."

"Why would he call you?" Birdy's voice was incredulous, irritated.

"He's worried about you, that's all."

"Well, I don't think he's worried enough. I told him I want lab tests run. He says it's all in my head. I want a second opinion. He tell you all that?"

"He did."

"And what do you think?"

"I think it's a good idea, darlin'. I don't like to see you in pain."

"What's the matter, Mommy?" Amelia asked. She was squeezing her bottom lip between her forefinger and her thumb, a worried expression in her big doe eyes.

"Nothing, honey. I'll be okay," Birdy said.

"You know what?" Bobby said, his voice animated and bright. "Let's forget about going to Frank's party tonight. Let's stay home. Birdy-boo, we're going to get you some more tea and put you to bed. Then you . . . you can just sleep, and you won't be in any more pain."

"I like that idea, Daddy."

Bobby turned to Amelia and smiled. "It'll be nice, right?"

Amelia smiled shyly, a closed mouth, slight smile, as if she didn't want to get her hopes up. "Yes."

"It's a little late for some sort of grand gesture, isn't it, Bobby?"

"Putting you to bed ain't no grand gesture." Bobby stubbed out his cigarette in the ashtray and sat down next to Birdy on the couch. He leaned in close. "I'll do whatever you want."

I could hear her sigh from the foyer. "You know what I want. I want you to get a job. I want you to stop running around."

"I will."

"Will you?"

"Yes, darlin', of course, I will."

He leaned forward and kissed her. Their kiss lasted a few seconds. I glanced over at Amelia, who was watching them, not taking her eyes off her parents kissing, making up.

They broke apart. Bobby smiled, touched Birdy's cheek.

"But, you know, Franky'll blow a gasket if I don't at least stop by for one quick drink. I won't go if you don't want me to, but we have some business. Possibly a job, like we've talked about. Franky's boss, you know that. And I want to keep things smooth between us."

There was a long, tense pause, and I saw Amelia's face tighten up, the wary hopefulness gone.

When Birdy finally spoke, it was in a flat, matter-of-fact tone. "A job," she said. It wasn't a question.

"Like we disc"—he couldn't quite get out the word—"like we talked about."

"Well, if you have to, you have to."

"Thanks, honey. I won't be out long. You gonna be okay?"

She turned her head toward Amelia. "We'll be fine, won't we, Butterfly?"

"We can relax and play Old Maid, Mommy," Amelia said. She appeared to be rallying at the idea of staying at home with her mother, just the two of them, and playing cards.

"That sounds relaxing indeed," Birdy agreed.

"Darlin', are you sure?" Bobby asked again.

"I'm sure. But, Bobby? Promise you won't make a fool of me."

Bobby shook his head and sighed, as if it were beneath either of them to even consider such a thing. He kissed her on the cheek and said, "I love you, darlin'. I won't be out late."

Bobby stood, and then Birdy went to stand, and Bobby helped her up. Now that she was standing, I could see that she was wearing a white dress and white open-toed high-heeled shoes. It was a beautiful dress: a swing dress with a gathered V-neckline, feminine half sleeves, a tight-fitting bodice, and an A-line flared skirt that hit mid-calf. It seemed familiar somehow, as if I'd seen a picture of her wearing it before. I went through all the photos of her in the album in my mind, but I couldn't remember seeing this one.

And then I realized, I hadn't seen it, I'd read it. This was the dress described in the *Haven Herald*. And Amelia was wearing bunny-print pajamas. And Bobby was wearing the cobalt blue suit he'd been wearing in the basement just the other day, an undead soul roaming the property fifty years after his death. His death suit.

And that's when I knew—this was the night everyone was going to die.

Bobby took a pair of black leather and cream knit driving gloves from his pocket, put them on, picked up the tray with the teacup and teapot from the table, and walked right past me. He went into the kitchen, and I followed. I stood in the arched doorway between the kitchen and the dining room and watched him. He turned on the kettle, took out the used teabag from the teapot, and put in a fresh one. He refilled the bowl of sugar cubes. Then he grabbed a bottle of Coca-Cola from the cupboard, cracked ice into a tall glass, and poured the soda into the glass. His hand was unsteady, and he spilled a bit and wiped it up. He set the glass and the rest of the bottle onto the tray.

Then he pulled out a stepladder—the kind that doesn't fold, two metal steps—stood on the second step, wobbling a little, and opened the cabinet above the sink. It was a cabinet Jack and I never used because it was too high to be practical. Bobby strained his arm, grabbed something, and brought it down.

I wasn't surprised to see it, not really. It confirmed what deep down I had already known, or at least suspected. The brown bottle had a cream-colored label that pictured a skull-and-crossbones with little rat ears, just like Ricarda Heller had seen in her vision. The name "Thall-Rat" was written in bold black letters. Still, even though I wasn't surprised to see the bottle, to read that label, that didn't mean it didn't hurt my heart to see it there, in Bobby's hands. I went over to him, reached out, and said, "Bobby, no."

But we were in the past, and he couldn't hear me, couldn't see me. And I couldn't touch him, either. My hand passed through his skin as if it were passing through air.

Bobby poured some Thall-Rat into the teapot, and then even more, and then, after a moment's consideration, even more. Then he got back on the stepladder and put the rat poison back in the cabinet. Clearly nervous, distracted, and inebriated, he didn't notice that when he closed the cabinet door, it didn't quite catch on the latch. As he climbed back down the stepladder, the cabinet door silently swung back until it was halfway open, the bottle partly visible.

He put away the stepladder and returned to the teakettle and tray. His face was grave but determined, as if the task at hand was distasteful but necessary. He poured the boiling water over the tea and the poison, and then lifted the tray.

Birdy was asleep on the couch now. Her eyes were closed, and her breathing sounded wet and crackling. Bobby set down the tray on the coffee table, and then he walked over to Amelia, who was playing with what appeared to be an Annie Oakley doll. He kissed her on the forehead. "I want both of you to turn in early," he said, though I was sure Birdy couldn't hear. Then, "I love you, little darlin'."

Amelia didn't look up, didn't acknowledge him. She was clearly upset that he was leaving after promising to stay.

"Don't I even get a good night?" he asked.

She held up her doll and said, "Night, Mister."

"All right. Guess I gotta be content with that. Good night, Miss Annie. Good night, Amelia. Love you, sweetheart."

He took his keys out of his pockets, jingling them as he walked, and then he left out the back door.

Amelia dropped her doll, crawled to the other side of the coffee table, across from the couch and her mother, and kneeled. She picked up the bottle of Coca-Cola, eyed the teacup and sugar cubes, and set down the soda bottle. Then she poured herself some tea, spilling a little onto the saucer. She picked up one, two, three sugar cubes, plunked them into the teacup, stirred the sugar into the tea, set down the spoon, and took a sip. "Ahhh," she said, smacking her lips.

I rushed over to the coffee table and kneeled beside her. "Amelia, honey, don't drink that!" I thought of Bobby's putting one dosage of poison in, and then another, and then another just a few minutes before, and I remembered his telling me, in the basement, "*It ain't hard. All you need is rat poison. At first a little, and then a little more. And then one night, more than a little, and then . . .*"

This was the night. Bobby had been poisoning Birdy for what must have been months, giving her *a little, and then a little more*, and this was the night he intended to finish her, having given her *more than a little*. The night after Birdy had told Dr. Grodin she wanted lab tests, that she was going to seek another opinion . . .

"Amelia, please, don't drink that!" I shouted, but she didn't hear me. I tried my hardest to knock the teacup out of her hands, to smash it into a million bits, but I may as well have been doing battle with the sky. I was seeing a vision I couldn't change. Defeated, I nonetheless whispered, "Please, Amelia, honey, don't drink that. Please."

My words didn't cut through space and time. She drank the whole cup and then poured herself more. She added sugar and drank that cup, too. She finished the last drop of the entire teapot, and then set the teacup on the saucer, where it tipped over on its side. After a while, she leaned back, hugging her knees, and groaned. I hovered my hand over her shoulder and traced the bunnies on her pajamas. The background of the fabric was pale pink, and the white rabbits were outlined in brown. They were in different positions. Some were sleeping, some were sitting up, their ears at attention, while others were hopping away. It occurred to me that she would always be eight, always wearing these pajamas. There was nothing I could do.

Tears came to my eyes and rolled down my cheeks. I buried my face in my hands.

Amelia groaned again. The sound woke up Birdy. She rubbed her eyes, sat up, and looked over at her daughter, on the floor, rocking back and forth. "Amelia? You okay?"

"I have a tummy ache."

"Here, lie on the couch."

Birdy guided Amelia onto the textured green couch, where she lay with her head on an orange pillow, her feet straight out in front of her. Birdy sat beside her stomach and rested the back of her hand against Amelia's forehead. "Amelia? My little butterfly? Are you okay? Are you sick?"

"It hurts, Mommy," she said. And then she seemed to fall asleep. Birdy didn't move. After a while, Amelia groaned, and creamy white froth escaped from her lips and dribbled down her chin.

"Oh my God, are you okay?" Birdy asked, fear causing her voice to break. Amelia didn't answer, just clutched her stomach, and groaned. "I'll be right back. I'm calling the doctor," Birdy said.

I followed Birdy into the kitchen, where she found her telephone book in a drawer, and then went to the phone, which was connected to the wall. She dialed numbers with a trembling forefinger, twirled the cord at a nervous pace, and said, "Hello? Is this Betty? . . . I'm sorry to be calling so late, and on the weekend, but I need to talk to Doctor Grodin. It's about Amelia. Sure, I can wait . . ."

Birdy had been glancing around the kitchen as she talked to whoever "Betty" was (Dr. Grodin's wife, perhaps?), and now her eyes alighted upon the clearly visible bottle of Thall-Rat in the open cabinet above the sink. She dropped the phone so that it floated to the floor, and then pulled out the stepping stool and climbed up it to investigate.

Birdy stood on the top of the two steps, picked up the bottle, brought it down, opened it up, sniffed it, and set it on the counter. She inspected the counter and found a few flecks of the poison next to the tea kettle. Then she leaned against the sink so that her face was to me. I was only a few feet away, and I saw the red rash all over her face and cheeks, her scalp clearly visible beneath her thinning hair. She looked as if she'd experienced a radiation accident. She glanced at the bottle again, while touching her damaged face, her straggling hair. And then, as if she were finally convinced that one plus one did in fact equal two, her brows furrowed, and her jaw clenched into an expression of rage. She stood there for a few seconds, her face bright red, and then she went to the sink again, this time with her back to me, and cried. The crying lasted for about ten or twenty seconds. Then she turned on the faucet, splashed her face with water, dried it with a dish towel, and turned around again. She let out a deep breath, as if she remembered she had a job to do, and picked up the phone. "Hello? Hello?" she said into the mouthpiece. But it was clear that no one was there anymore. She slammed the phone into the receiver and ran into the living room.

Amelia appeared to be asleep on the couch. She wasn't groaning anymore, though her hands were still clutching her stomach. Birdy lifted her into a sitting position and yelled, "Amelia! Wake up! We have to get you to the hospital! Amelia! Wake up!" She shook her gently, and when that didn't do anything, she stuck her finger down Amelia's throat. Amelia coughed. "Amelia, please, wake up!"

Birdy set Amelia back down on the couch, stood up, and ran out of the room and up the stairs. She returned with a patent leather purse. "Okay," she said, "I found my purse and car keys. Let's get you to the hospital."

But just then a low groan came out of Amelia's chest, her entire body shook with convulsions, and a stream of white foam erupted from her mouth. Her eyes rolled back and then became glassy.

"Amelia?" Birdy said in a panicked voice. "Amelia? Amelia?" She placed her head against Amelia's chest, clearly listening for a heartbeat, and then she pressed her thumb against the inside of Amelia's wrist, and when that didn't seem to work, her neck.

Birdy must have now understood what anyone looking at her daughter would have known.

Amelia was dead.

She let out a wail that was almost unbearable to hear. Even though I thought I knew what loss was like, I had never experienced the pain I heard in that scream. The wailing grief reverberated in my ears and felt like it would go on forever. The pain of a mother who has lost her child.

37

STAY WITH ME

ABOUT AN HOUR LATER, we heard a car pull into the drive.

Birdy had stopped crying by then. She was sitting with a gun in her lap, a gun she'd retrieved from the library, from an object that appeared to be a book, but which had really been a box with the gun inside. I had seen her open the chamber, spin it around, and close the chamber again, appearing satisfied. Then she'd sat back down, stroking her daughter's hair with one hand, holding the gun with the other.

When Birdy heard the rumble of Bobby's car, she walked out the back door into the backyard, and I followed.

Bobby stepped out of his robin's-egg-blue Studebaker, and I saw immediately from the way he moved that he was sober. And surprised. "Birdy. What are you doing . . . ?"

"Alive? What am I doing alive?"

"Up. I thought you'd be asleep."

"You monster!"

I didn't know if it was the word itself, the cold intensity with which she spoke it, or the gun in her hands, but Bobby stopped in his tracks, his face scared and shocked. "Beatrice," he said, pleading.

"You killed our daughter."

"What? What are you—?"

He began to hurry over the grass toward the house, but she pulled the trigger and shot him. The bullet pierced his right leg, and a bright stain spread on his royal blue suit pants. He fell on the ground, clasping his thigh in his hands.

"You don't get to see her."

Bobby was curled up on the grass, writhing in pain. "I didn't kill her! What the hell are you talking about?"

"I found the poison. You've been poisoning me. That's why I've been feeling so sick, why my hair is falling out. Right?"

"I never meant—"

"Well, tonight Amelia drank your tea!"

"Oh my God! Amel—!"

He started to get up, and this time Birdy shot him in the shoulder. She was a good shot. He grabbed his shoulder and collapsed again.

"You don't get to say her name."

"Oh my God!" he said. He was clearly in excruciating pain. Tears ran down his face. "What are you doing out here? We have to take her to the hospital!"

"It's too late. She's dead."

"Why'd you let her drink that tea? I gave her Coca-Cola, not tea."

Birdy shot him again, this time in his side. He howled in pain. He was moaning, sweating, writhing, bleeding onto the grass, but he wasn't screaming anymore. I don't know if he could. From his sweaty, pale complexion and glassy eyes, he appeared to be going into shock.

"You tried to kill me, and you almost did. But instead, you killed our daughter. For that, I'm sending you to hell."

She walked closer to him, and with both hands on the trigger, shot him in the chest until there were no more bullets, and no more writhing and moaning. Bobby Shawcross was dead.

Birdy didn't even bother wiping away her fingerprints. She just tossed the gun onto the grass and went back into the house.

She walked to the couch, sat beside Amelia, and held on to her. She was no longer crying. She was somewhere deeper and darker than tears.

"Amelia, Amelia, wake up," Birdy said in a hopeless voice, cradling her daughter in her arms. "Please, Amelia, wake up!" She clutched Amelia close to her. "Don't leave me, Amelia," she pleaded. "Stay with me, baby. Stay with me. Don't go! Stay with me!"

And that's when I saw her. Not her body, which was still on the couch, but her spirit, which was standing next to it, with those same doe eyes, the same high ponytail, the same bunny-print pajamas and white socks. Her death outfit. She stood there and met my eyes. It was clear that her spirit could see me.

"Amelia?" I said.

"Don't leave me, Amelia!" Birdy repeated, pleading. "Stay with me, baby. Don't go! Stay with me!"

Then Amelia's spirit spoke to me: *"And so I did."*

38

BIRDY'S LAST ACT

AMELIA AND I FOLLOWED BIRDY into the backyard, trailing behind her. We walked past Bobby's body, lying bloody on the grass, and by his spirit, standing next to it, watching us, but Amelia gave no sign that she saw either. She was focused on Birdy, on her mother, who was walking quickly ahead of us, as if she knew exactly where she was going. Over the lush grass, past the weeping willow with the tire swing, past the garden flourishing with spring flowers in bloom, straight to the edge of the property, to the cliffs.

A waning crescent moon and a million stars hung in the sky. We were standing next to Birdy now. I could see her thallium-ravaged face, streaked with rivulets of dried mascara-laden tears. She gazed up at the starry sky and then down at the flowing river below. I couldn't quite read her expression. Determination? Purpose? Was there fear in those dark eyes? I didn't think so. I wondered if I was seeing a hint of what she must have looked like back in her circus days, as she prepared to leap off the platform, flying without a net for the last time. I felt helpless, repulsed, and fascinated. Amelia, on the other side of her, looked sad and resigned.

Birdy took a step closer to the edge, tottering in her white heels. "Here I come, little butterfly," she said. "Don't worry, here I come!" She backed up a few feet, got a running start, and then sailed into the air. Her bare arms were stretched out beside her, her head and neck were curved gracefully toward the night sky, and her white dress shimmered and fluttered all around her. While she was held aloft for a second, it was easy to see where she'd acquired her nick-name, for she looked as natural as any bird in the sky, a beautiful white hawk perhaps, ready to swoop down to the river, dip her beak into it for a drink, and then sail up again. Except I knew there was no coming up. I heard a hard, battered sound. I couldn't quite see to the solid earth and the rocky river forty feet below, didn't want to, but I knew her body was splayed in an inhuman position, her leg abnormally behind her, her neck contorted and dangling to the side.

"That's how my mommy died," Amelia said. Her voice was quiet and solemn. "She flew after me. But she never came back. And she told me to stay here, and so I did. And we've been apart ever since."

It was like something from Maupassant. Only in this version, there were no hair combs and watch chains, only death.

I glanced at Amelia, but she was still staring into the abyss ahead of us.

Then there were sirens. And then everything disappeared.

39

IT WAS ALWAYS YOU

I WAS IN THE NURSERY. I didn't know if it was the same day, or the next, but I was in the present again, in my own time period, in a room that was nearly empty. I stood by the window, gazing out, and waited. After a few minutes, I felt her presence: not Birdy's of course, but Amelia's. It had never been Birdy's. *Some lady. We seen her in the window at night.* She'd never been a lady. Only a little girl whose mother had told her to stay with her—and so she had.

"Is that you, Amelia?" I asked.

"It's me."

I turned around and saw Amelia standing in the doorway. She seemed real, human, like Bobby had always been.

"It's you," I said. "It was always you."

"It was always me." She looked down, smiling shyly, and then gazed up at me, pleased.

I smiled at her. "You're so . . . beautiful!"

She ran up and flung her arms around me. I felt the pressure of her hug, warm this time, not icy cold like the hand from the bathtub. I wrapped my arms around her soft back. I felt a sudden amazement and wonder at her impossible presence, and something else, something new and unexpected. I felt as if a hole were being filled up inside me; that is, I thought this was what it must be like to feel whole.

*   *   *

I spent the next couple of days with Amelia. I read fairy tales from the Brothers Grimm aloud to her, played in the snow with her, and watched TV with her on the couch. She liked the movies of her childhood on Turner classics and those on the Disney channel. Thanksgiving had come and gone. Jack had had the long weekend off for the holiday and had asked me if I wanted him to come home, but I'd told him I'd be fine. He said he'd be spending the holiday with old friends in Chicago. Amelia, Olivier, and I had celebrated with rotisserie chicken, deli mashed potatoes, and store-bought pumpkin pie, though only two of us could eat. Certain channels were beginning to show Christmas movies. Amelia liked those the best. *Miracle on 34th Street. A Charlie Brown Christmas. Elf.* She'd only ridden on an escalator a couple of times herself, and she laughed and laughed over the scene in which Buddy tries to take one for the first time.

Sometimes we talked about what had happened between us. I struggled to piece things together. Had she been trying to scare me? "No," she said, then giggled. At times, she'd merely wanted to get my attention. The bath had been, well, a bath. And she hadn't attempted to terrify me by crawling up to me and wrapping her arms around my waist; she'd wanted to make me feel better, to comfort me. "And 'JUMP'?" I'd asked one night, when we were curled together on the couch.

"I was trying to tell you what happened to my mother, how she jumped and left me after telling me to stay."

"You never felt or saw her after that?"

"I think she did that thing that lady said."

I tried to imagine what she was talking about, and then I thought of Ricarda Heller. "She crossed to the other side?"

"That's it."

"So, you've been here all this time . . . with your daddy?"

"Yes, but he's not around a lot these days. He keeps going to the woods."

"The woods? What does he do there?"

"I think he wants to cross to the other side, too. He's ready to meet his Maker, to face whatever's next for him, is what he says. He's tired of being like this. Here but not here. Always awake. Never dreaming or resting. Neither alive nor dead."

I shivered over the existence Amelia described, and my heart broke for her then. What must it feel like to never sleep, never dream? This explained why she often poked me awake in the middle of the night. "*Wake up,*" she'd say. Or "*Wanna play?*" Or "*Watch this!*"

"And you? Do you want to cross to the other side?"

"I've tried. Lotsa times. To be with Mommy. But I don't think I can. Daddy didn't used to because he says Mommy put a curse on him and sent him to hell, and this is it. And once he told me that even if he could cross over, he never would, because he didn't want to leave me alone. But now, he thinks he can. Now that you showed up."

"Now that I showed up? Why's that?"

"You're the first person who's ever been able to see us. And you care about me."

I reached out and smoothed her hair, and then I raised my eyebrows as if to say she still hadn't answered my question.

"I used to be mad at Daddy," she said, staring up at the ceiling, as if she were thinking of something else. "I can't remember why. I don't remember what he did exactly, I just know he's the reason we're here, and Mommy's . . . there. I'm not mad at him anymore. Now I'm just sad. We both are. I mean, we were. Until you got here. And now . . ."

"And now?" I whispered.

"And now Daddy thinks you can take his place."

Goose bumps raised on my arms as I thought of Bobby's saying he knew I wanted a child. *Badly.* And then the words I hadn't understood at the time: *I might be able to help you. Help us both.*

"Daddy says the reason you can see us is that you're special. He says you're going to be a real good mama to me. Daddy says you're going to stay here and watch over me." She let out a sigh. "But Daddy says a lot of things." Then her eyes became pleading pools of need. "Will you? Will you be my mama?"

It came into my head to wonder what would happen after I died. How would she manage? Would she be trapped in this house forever, waiting for the next broken woman who desperately wanted a child to see her and adopt her as her own? Or would she someday be able to cross to the other side? Or would I need to find a way to stay with her forever myself—never sleeping, dreaming, or resting, neither alive nor dead, but rather imprisoned in some sort of nightmarish purgatory, like she was? I had no idea what I was getting myself into, but I felt I didn't have a choice. I touched her button nose and smiled at her worried little face.

"Yes," I said. "Of course, I'll watch over you. Of course, I'll be your mama. Yes."

40

GET YOUR LIFE TOGETHER

I WAITED TO CALL WHEN it would be happy hour my mother's time. As I was growing up, my mother had always had two glasses of Chardonnay at five o'clock, and her mood was always best after the first. I called at 5:45 in Oranjestad, 3:45 Central Time, hoping my timing would be perfect.

"Mom?" The word was unfamiliar in my mouth.

"Who is this?"

Jeez, how many daughters did she have?

"It's your daughter, Lilly."

"Lilly, what a surprise."

"How are you doing?"

Her voice softened as she said, "Frozen shoulder. I'm in terrible pain."

"I'm sorry to hear that. That must be terrible."

"It is, as I said. Thank you. But it will pass. Like everything else, pain is only temporary."

I didn't know how to respond. "Umm, yeah, good?" I managed. I paused, and then forged ahead. "So, Mom? I have a favor to ask you."

"I suspected. Usually, you don't call."

Usually she didn't call, either, but I let that observation drop. "I've never asked you for money before, Mom, but I'm in a bit of a pinch."

When my father had gone bankrupt and my mother had leapt off that sinking ship onto a ninety-foot yacht, I hadn't asked her for any help, and I hadn't asked for any help since—not for bills or rent, not even for my father's funeral. Well, I was asking now.

"What sort of a pinch?"

"Two hundred fifty thousand would cover the whole thing. But I'd take anything to help me get by."

For a moment, there was only a dry silence, as dry as I'd heard the air was on that small, beautiful, arid island. "What are you talking about?" she asked.

"Jack and I bought a house. And now he's leaving me, and I want to buy him out. Or if I can't buy him out, then I want to pay the mortgage for a few months until I can get back on my feet."

"He's leaving you? Why? What did you do?"

"I didn't do anything. We just grew apart."

I could hear my mother sip her wine. She didn't say anything for a long time. Maybe thirty seconds, maybe longer. "Did you know you were an accident?" she finally asked.

"What?"

"It was never my dream to be a mother. I had you by mistake. I was terrified when I was pregnant with you. And then, when you were born, I loved you, I really did. But as you grew older, I found that my instincts had been right, I just wasn't cut out to be a mom. Not everyone is. When men aren't cut out to be fathers, nobody berates them. When women aren't cut out to be mothers, they're seen as villains. Anyway, that's why we had nannies. So they could fulfill your needs, and I could fulfill mine. It worked out fairly well as far as I was concerned."

I thought of the nannies, Swedish, just shy of elderly, who had made my meals, dropped me off at school and picked me up again, bandaged my wounds and hugged me when I was sad, who had lived in the same wing as I had, and who had often been the ones to tuck me in at night. I loved them, all of them. And when it had seemed

I was getting to love them too much, there had always been some excuse to fire them and hire a new one.

"Why are you telling me this?"

"People fall in and out of love. Nothing is permanent in this life. Not love. Not houses. You need to let things go."

I tried to consider her saying that I'd been unwanted, loved, and then unloved as nothing personal, just the life span of a bird, a fluttering of impermanence, but I gave up. It sounded too much like an excuse for bad parenting wrapped up in Zen bullcrap packaging. I inhaled, exhaled, and did my best to forgive her. "It wasn't always easy, growing up without you, without your love," I said.

"In this life we learn from having motherly love, and we learn from not always having it. I do much better as a doting step-grandmama, I've found."

I hadn't wanted to use my trump card, but I'd known I would, if I had to, and it was clear I had to. "Then you'll be happy to hear my good news," I said brightly.

"Your good news?" She sounded skeptical.

The subject was too sacred for me to lie about. I would never say the words "I'm pregnant" when they weren't true. But I would tell her the truth, and in so doing, say the words that might make a difference. "I have a child."

"What? How is that possible? You sent me that email, it wasn't that long ago. You were going to do IVF. And now—you have a child?"

"Oh, I didn't give birth to her."

"I see." Her voice said she should have known as much.

"I mean, she's still mine."

"Uh-huh. Is this a legal adoption, Lilly?" I hadn't been prepared for that question, and it caught me off guard. While I was thinking of how to respond, my mother chuckled and said, "You and your strays. You were always bringing home the pets nobody wanted. That mangy cat your schoolmate's mom was allergic to. Or so she said. I think it was because that thing was so mean. And—"

"Rufus wasn't mean."

"—I'll never forget that one-eyed pug. The vet bills for that thing!"

"Sparky. My best friend."

"The point is, Lilly, it's wonderful you've taken in this child. It is. But it's not like this is my grandchild. Is it?"

"Of course she is," I said, but perhaps I'd waited a beat too long. Perhaps my acting skills weren't what they had once been. For even though I saw Amelia as *mine*, I couldn't quite see Amelia as *hers*.

My mom said, "Right."

"Mom, please, Jack is leaving. And I have a child. And we need to stay in this house, and I've never asked you for anything, and I'm asking now. Can you help me?"

The pause that followed reminded me of the pause in a courtroom on TV, before the sentence is handed down. Then she said, "One minute. Let me talk to Phillip." I heard voices in the background. Phillip owned at least two hotel and casino resorts, last time I'd checked, maybe more. I was pretty sure he was a billionaire, so my mom's refusal to change my life with two hundred fifty thousand dollars or less would be like a normal mom's refusing to buy her daughter a cup of coffee at Starbucks. She wouldn't do that—they wouldn't do that—would she? Would they? Then she came back on the phone and said, "I'll tell you what we're going to do."

My pulse sped with anticipation and excitement. "Oh my gosh, thank you!"

"We're going to fly you down here and comp you for a weekend in one of Phillip's resorts, all your meals included. And you can bring . . . the child, too. We'll fly her out as well."

It took me a minute to figure out what she was talking about. "You're going to fly us to Aruba?"

"Anytime you want."

I almost laughed, the idea was so absurd. I didn't need to eat at buffets, lounge in swimming pools, and spend money gambling; I needed a direct deposit into my account to keep myself and Amelia afloat. I forced myself to sound grateful rather than frustrated when I replied, "That's kind of you and Phillip, but what I really need is some financial help. And if you won't give it to me, then what about a loan?"

I could hear her take what sounded like the last sip of her wine. The tiniest hint of teeth clicking, the tiniest hint of a slurp. The voices in the background grew louder, as if there were more people now, and I heard classical music. Vivaldi. "Lilly, dear, I need to go, but you really must understand that attachment is the root of all suffering. You sound much too attached to this house, which, after all, is only a material object. It wouldn't be good for you if I helped you out, dear. If you lose this house, you'll buy a cheaper one. Or you'll rent. Or you'll live out of a camper. Or a tent. Like the birds and the trees, the Universe will provide for you—and the child."

My heart sank, and tears stung my eyes.

"The trip will be all-expenses paid. It's a chance for us to mend fences. And meet the child. Maybe after that, we can do more."

A cry choked in my throat. "Thanks," I said.

"You're welcome."

"I guess I should go."

"And, Lilly?"

"Yes?"

"Try and get your life together, will you?"

I wiped my tears on my sleeve. "I'll try, Mom."

41

THE CLIFFS

JACK CALLED TO SAY HE would be late, that he was going straight from somewhere to somewhere; I forgot the names of the small Midwestern cities as soon as he told me. While he was gone, I spent my days playing in the backyard with Amelia, watching TV with Amelia, reading aloud to Amelia. I rarely saw Olivier, but I knew he was around, as every day I had to refill his food and water bowls and clean his litter box. I was starting to eat more often, too. My appetite was back, and my anxiety was lessening, now that I had solved the mystery, now that I knew the cause of those unearthly disturbances, why things had gone bump in the night. A ghost had caused them. I was living with her. And she made me feel happy. Contented. Whole.

One afternoon, maybe it was the second day after I'd called my mom, maybe the third, I was downstairs in the living room, when I thought I heard a car pull up in the drive. I peeked through the plastic sheeting and then ripped it off the window to get a better look. Jack was hammering a sign into the snowy front yard. The sign read FOR SALE in black block letters on a white background, and next to it were the words HAVEN ACRES REAL ESTATE AGENCY. A blond woman's photo and a phone number were below the name. I watched as he stepped back to admire his handiwork, and then he headed up the unshoveled walkway, unlocked the door, and stepped into the grand foyer. I walked over and stood underneath the black chandelier. Jack said, "Hey."

"Hey." I gestured outside and said, "So . . ."

"Yeah. I stopped by the agency to fill out some paperwork. They were going to come by and put the sign in the ground today, but since I was on my way home, I told them I'd do it. I hope it stays put. The ground's pretty hard right now."

He took off his coat, which was dusted with snow, and walked into the living room, not bothering to take off his boots, which, I noticed, were new.

He glanced around the room and said, "I don't want to spend more than I need to, but it's clear we can't sell it like this. I've taken out a loan on my 401(k), and I'm going to hire some guys to finish the floors, paint the dining room, and fix the hole in that ceiling. That's the minimum that needs to be done."

We both looked down at the partially finished floors that I had stopped sanding about a month before. The tools and plastic sheeting still lay jumbled in a corner. I peered past the foyer into the dining room to see that while the wallpaper was gone, the walls were bumpy and bare, discolored in places where I hadn't quite gotten all the glue off. I had been planning on finishing everything eventually. I could see Jack stopping himself from saying, *I told you so.*

He sat on the couch, and I stood by the window, staring at the sign. "You made a final decision."

"Like I said, I didn't have a choice. I can't afford to pay the mortgage, and you can't afford to buy me out. We need to talk about . . . our future. Are you okay?"

I turned around to face him. "Why? What do you mean?"

"You don't look . . . well."

Amelia and I took a bath together every day, but it was hard to wash my hair in the bath, and I guessed it was getting a bit greasy. Maybe I hadn't brushed it. Maybe I hadn't brushed it for many days. It was the afternoon, and I was wearing thermal leggings and a sweatshirt, but that wasn't strange. Maybe I was a little pale, but I was always pale. I knew I had a pimple on my forehead, and I knew my lips were chapped. Had I brushed my teeth? I was almost certain I had brushed my teeth. If not that morning, then the night before.

"I'm fine. And you? How are you?" Jack seemed well rested, even though he'd been on the road for . . . I didn't know how long. Weeks? He'd gotten a haircut, and his eyes were bright behind his black hipster glasses. He was wearing new jeans, a new black V-neck sweater, and a striped T-shirt that peeked out underneath it, which I'd never seen before. He must have gone shopping with his 401(k) loan proceeds. I couldn't help but think that our time apart agreed with him.

"I'm doing great," he said, standing up and coming near me. As he moved, the air moved, and a scent wafted by, an unfamiliar scent. Sandalwood, maybe, and cardamon, and vanilla, and . . . oud? Was Jack wearing cologne? In all our years together, I had never once known him to wear cologne. It occurred to me that perhaps he was having an affair. I thought, *Good for you.* "So, listen. I think it's clear we're going in different directions here. I want a separation. Or, I don't know, I guess a divorce. I think we need to start thinking about where we'll go after we sell the house. I'll probably get an apartment near the main office."

The part about the separation and divorce wasn't a surprise to me. I felt like it was a conversation we'd already had, even though I couldn't remember having it. When I'd told him how my father had died, and he'd thought that I'd been lying, in my heart, that had been our moment of separation. I wondered if the woman Jack was having the affair with—if he was having an affair—was the blond real estate agent or a colleague from work, or some random woman he'd met online or at a bar or at a local coffee shop near a university campus. Whoever she was, or whoever she would be, later on, I hoped he would be happy. I had more important things to worry about.

I thought of Amelia, bound to this house by the word "stay," a dutiful daughter forever, and I felt that magnetic force I'd always experienced with this place, which was stronger now than ever. I finally understood the cause of that pull; it was the pull of a mother's love. Since Amelia had remained here, without her mother, it was as if the very walls of the house were making sure that if Birdy hadn't been able to join her, to watch over Amelia, that I would. It was no wonder I'd always felt I must.

"I don't want to sell the house, Jack. I can't."

Jack took a deep breath and let it out again. "I'm not going to fight with you today. If we don't sell the house, the bank will foreclose on it, and our credit will tank, and they'll kick us out anyway. Maybe you're willing to let that happen, but I'm not. We can't afford the mortgage anymore. Not with our debt. Do you understand? It's done. I know you love this house, but—"

"I want, I mean, I wanted, to be a mother here."

Jack looked startled, and then sympathetic. He walked over to me and put his hands on my shoulders. "Oh, Lilly. Honey. That's not going to happen. Don't you see? I'm not going to have a baby with you. And you're . . ." He stopped himself.

"I'm what?"

"Nothing."

"Tell me," I insisted.

He looked away. "You're not fit to be a mother."

I sucked in my breath with a cry. I don't know if I ever exhaled. I carefully removed his hands from my shoulders. I stepped back, away from him. No slap in the face, no kick in the gut, no knife to the heart could have hurt me as much as those words. *You're not fit to be a mother. You're not fit to be a mother.* They played inside my head, a dreadful refrain.

"Maybe," he said gently, "if you see a doctor, and go on medication, then maybe someday, you might possibly be able to be a mother. Who knows? But now?" A pause, while the words "*But now*" hung in the air, as if they were impossible to imagine. He began pacing around while I stayed at my sentinel at the window. "I've been making some calls. Checking around. There are some excellent places that can offer you help. Do you realize that you need help?"

My heart raced. I held on to it with my right hand to try to steady it while attempting to appear cool, calm, collected, as if I were not about to keel over, while my mind zapped along: *Your husband wants to lock you up.* And: *You're not fit to be a mother.* Yes, I realized I needed help. I needed help figuring out a way to keep this house. I needed money for food. I needed all the things a wife needs that Jack had not been able to provide for me: someone who loved me for my strengths, someone who understood me, someone who listened to me, who believed me, who saw me.

I had to think, had to clear my head. "I'm going outside," I said.

Jack's eyes narrowed in confusion. "In the snow?"

"I need some fresh air."

"Are you all right?"

"Yes, I'm fine," I lied. I'd so often lied to him about how I was doing, had told him what he'd wanted to hear. It didn't occur to me to do otherwise now.

I went to the mudroom, slipped on my winter coat and boots, and went outside, where it was lightly snowing. There, in the middle of the backyard, stood Bobby Shawcross, wearing the royal blue suit in which he'd been shot. His ghost suit. I hadn't seen him since then—since the night he'd died, since the night everyone had died, when Birdy had cursed him to hell.

He smiled when he saw me. A warm, loving smile. His smile said he was glad to see me. He understood me. Maybe even loved me. *Don't worry*, his smile said. *Everything is going to be all right.*

"Hey, beautiful," he said.

I heard the back door slam shut, and I turned to see Jack step outside, wearing his coat.

"Can my husband hear?"

Bobby laughed. "He's not listening. He never does. Don't worry. He can't hear a thing. He never could, could he?"

"No," I said, "he never could."

"You cold?"

"I'm not cold. I'm worried. He's selling the house!"

"Is he now?" Bobby said.

Bobby took my hand. I don't know if I led him, or if he led me, but we walked to the edge of the property, to the cliffside and its drop down to the river, which was beginning to freeze. When we arrived, I looked down at that icy river below, and it felt like home. Like I belonged there. With my dad. And Birdy. And my lost, unborn babies. All I wanted was to spread my wings and fly, to be released from all this pain and suffering and worry, and to join them.

You're not fit to be a mother. I thought of my own mother then. My example. She had never seen me perform, and I must have been four or five when she'd stopped hugging me when I cried, when she'd stopped putting a cool hand on my warm forehead when I was sick. What did I know about being a mother? Maybe Jack was right. Maybe I was unfit. A *raving lunatic.* There went that siren call again. *It would be so easy. You can leave all this pain and loveless-ness. Just go ahead and join your dad. You know you want to.* Maybe my unborn babies would have been better off without me. Maybe the entire world would be better off without me.

I lifted up one wing, one arm, and closed my eyes. I couldn't fly gracefully, like Birdy had, but I could still fly far away from here and be free.

But then I felt Bobby's hand grasp my elbow, and I heard him say, "No, baby, no." And then, "Amelia needs you."

Amelia. I pictured Amelia in that enormous old house, abandoned again, in the same way she had been abandoned by Birdy. I had promised to protect her, to take care of her. I loved her.

I turned around, expecting to see Bobby, but it was Jack grasping my elbow.

"What are you doing?" he asked. He seemed genuinely afraid. "Lilly, were you going to . . . jump?"

"Of course not," I said.

"You were, weren't you? This has gone too far. We need to get you some help."

"I'm fine. I just need a little time alone. To sort things out."

"You need to come with me. I'm not leaving this house without you. I'm taking you somewhere safe."

"He isn't taking you anywhere," Bobby said, a low grumble in my ear.

Jack's arm tightened around the tender spot in my elbow, which I could feel even through my coat. "Ouch, Jack, you're hurting me!"

But instead of loosening his grip, his grasp around my elbow tightened, and he swung me around so that he was standing between me and the edge of the cliffs, as if to keep me from jumping, or perhaps from falling. He tried to grab on to my other arm, but I pulled away.

"Stop it!"

Bobby was standing there, beside me, in front of Jack. "Are you listening to her? She told you to stop." Bobby took a step closer and added, in an animal growl, "You ain't taking her anywhere!"

I watched in disbelief as Bobby set one strong hand on each of Jack's shoulders—and pushed. Jack looked astonished as he lost his balance and realized he was falling backward. Our eyes met, one last time.

As he fell backward, off the edge of the cliffs, Jack yelled, "Liiiiiilllllllyyyyy!"

I stood there, paralyzed with shock.

The name—my name—echoed down the cliffs, bounced off the frozen river below, and jumped back up into my mind, where it echoed again and again, a thousand times. I knew the name meant purity, innocence, and beauty, and I also knew it was the most popular flower at funerals, as lilies symbolized restored innocence after death. Would Jack's innocence be restored? Had he ever been guilty to begin with? Of what? He didn't deserve to die. Would my innocence be restored after his death? Was I guilty? Of what? I'd always hated the way those mournful flowers smelled: saccharine sweet, biting, tropical, like a too-heavy perfume. They'd always reminded me of something used to cover up the scent of death.

"Jack!" I called down to him, sobbing. I peered over the edge and stared down, at his body, broken and lifeless, below. "Jack!" I screamed.

"He's gone," Bobby said quietly.

I turned and pounded on Bobby's chest. "What did you do?" I cried.

"I did what had to be done," he said.

Time blurred. I called 9-1-1. Paramedics came. Police interviewed me. They wanted to know what had happened, why we had been walking so close to those cliffs. "We were selling the house," I said. "We were talking about improvements we could make. We talked about putting a fence up. It's so snowy and icy. My husband slipped."

I broke down and cried again then. They were real tears. I felt horrible, devastated. I couldn't get that picture out of my head, of his lifeless body at the bottom of those cliffs.

When the police left, I made phone calls. I called Jack's boss, his brothers, our closest friends from Chicago. I told everyone there would be no memorial service; I didn't say it was because I couldn't afford one. Jack was going to be cremated, which I knew was what he'd wanted. I called the real estate agent. I told her that I couldn't bear selling the house now, with all the memories. She told me she understood and to call her if I changed my mind. At some point, someone must have come to take away the FOR SALE sign, because one day I looked outside, and it was gone.

The police returned again, and again. From the way they questioned me, it was clear that they'd talked to my coworkers at the library and had some concerns about my state of mind. I did my best to play the role of the perfectly stable and sane, if grieving, wife. I made sure to wash and brush my hair, apply light makeup, and wear the appropriate costume: corduroy pants, a button-down blouse, and a sweater. I made eye contact while we talked and dabbed my eyes with a tissue. They dropped the matter.

On their third and final visit, they told me Jack had been having an affair. "Did you know about it?" one of the officers asked me. It was clear they were watching to see how I would react.

The truth of it hit harder than I'd expected. "No," I told them, "I didn't know."

When they left that time, one of the officers said, "I don't think we have any more questions. Thank you for your time, Mrs. Bly. And sorry for your loss."

Loss. Lost.

Jack, too. Jack was now one of my lost.

42

OUR LITTLE SECRET

ON A COLD DECEMBER DAY, I finally got up the courage to do something I'd been thinking about and postponing for weeks. I knocked on the grimy door, half hoping the owner wouldn't be home, and needing him to be there and answer my final questions both at once.

Lorenzo DeMarcos opened the door and squinted at me. "What the hell do you want?"

"Please," I begged.

"I got nothing more to say."

He started to close the door, but I put my boot in the jamb and clasped my hands together, fingers as steeples, in the traditional sign of prayer. I hadn't been able to find my gloves, and my hands were freezing. "Please? Let me in. Just for a minute? You're the only one who can help me." Lorenzo DeMarcos was the sole living witness to what had happened that night, so many years ago. I had experienced "the triple-death tragedy." I felt and knew the truth of it. But I still needed—ached for—a living, breathing person to confirm what I had seen.

He looked at me for a second, then opened the door and moved aside. "Okay," he said. "I guess I can't let you freeze to death out there. But I ain't apologizing for the mess. I wasn't expecting no visitors. You can sit on this here chair."

Everything was covered with a thin veil of dust and cigarette smoke. Newspapers rose in piles on the floor. The rectangular pine coffee table was cluttered with a couple of dirty dishes, a Sudoku book, today's newspaper, and an ashtray filled with butts. An oxygen tank stood on a portable cart beside the navy corduroy couch.

I sat in the La-Z-Boy he'd pointed at. I didn't bother to take off my coat. Lorenzo was wearing a long-sleeved shirt and wool sweater vest. He kept the place chilly. "Where's your dog?" I asked him.

"He bit some bratty kid. They put him down."

"I'm sorry."

He looked up at the ceiling and blinked a few times. "Yeah, well . . ."

"My husband died."

He nodded. "Yup. Was in the paper."

I hadn't bothered to pay for an obituary, but there had been a notice of the accident. I glanced at the pile of newspapers, then at the one on the table, at today's date. It was almost Christmas, and it occurred to me that he didn't have a tree. Of course he didn't. Why would he?

"Coffee?" he asked.

I hesitated, wondering about the cleanliness of his mugs, about the taste of his old man's drip coffee. But I thought it would be rude of me to decline, and so I said, "Sure."

The living room, dining room, and kitchen were all one room. He walked over to the kitchen counter and returned with two piping hot mugs of black coffee. I took a tentative sip. It was delicious. I took another sip. He sat on the couch and looked at me expectantly.

"Thank you," I said. "For the coffee. And for talking to me." I paused, not knowing how to begin. The last picture of Birdy and Amelia, clutching each other, floated before my eyes. "I found a photo album," I said.

"A photo album?"

Start at the beginning. It was Jack's voice in my head, always reminding me to start over, start from the beginning. Be logical. *Once upon a time.*

"Sorry. Remember the day we met? When you told me about the relative who worked as the caretaker before you? I met him. His name is Chas Lawrence. He's still alive, living at the Golden Oaks Nursing Home," I began.

And then, it all flowed out. I told him everything I'd learned . . . the prenup, the will, the photo album, the poison. I told him what I suspected. I told him enough about my experiences in the house to make him raise his eyebrows, more than once. "I know it sounds crazy, but I saw them, just like I'm seeing you now," I said. "Sometimes, I don't know if I'm losing my mind, if I lost it long ago, and I'm living in some fantasy world, or if I've just entered some reality no one else can see."

For the first time, for as long as I could remember, I wasn't trying to appear sane. I didn't care how I sounded. I wasn't acting. I wasn't lying. I was just pouring my guts out to another human being.

I don't know how long I talked. But it was long enough for Lorenzo DeMarcos to light a cigarette, smoke it, stub it out, and drink an entire mug of coffee.

"I need to know," I said finally. "You were there. I know you lied to the reporters, way back then. If you'll just confide in me, I won't tell anyone. I won't . . . judge. Because . . ." And here was the crux of it. ". . . I'm not sure I'll survive if I don't find out what really happened. If someone else doesn't confirm it."

Lorenzo stared at me in silence. Then he glanced over at the oxygen tank. His gaze shifted back to me and ultimately landed on his hands, old and gnarled, with yellowed fingernails, which were resting on his thighs.

"He never said it out loud," Lorenzo said. His voice was rough, gravelly, from smoking or disuse, I wasn't sure. Then he paused for a long time, so long I was afraid he wouldn't continue. I waited, sipping my coffee, which was lukewarm now, silently praying he would go on.

"He never told me that he was gonna kill her, that he was poisoning her. When he asked me to buy the Thall-Rat, he said it was for a rodent problem he was having. We lived right by the woods, a course I believed him. I didn't know nothing about the prenup or the will, but I ain't surprised. Bobby never woulda divorced Birdy without getting half her money. And I guess that whole business musta been the reason Chas decided to get the hell outa there. I always thought he'd quit because Bobby was secretly running around behind Birdy's back. Not that I cared about that part of it. A guy has needs, right?" He chuckled grimly. "Besides, like I said, I got paid extra for those errands.

"I drove Birdy and the little girl around, too. It was only after Birdy started getting sick that I put two and two together.

"I confronted him. I'm not a monster. Never killed anyone, 'cept during the war. And I didn't like the thought of being involved in that kind of thing. I told him I'd go to the cops if he didn't stop making her sick. It was the first time I ever stood up to him.

"We was in the car. I was driving. He was in the back seat. He told me he didn't know what I was talking about, and even if it was true, if I ever ratted him out, he'd say I was in on it. I was the one who bought the poison, after all.

"I shut up after that. He was right. I did buy the poison. At the hardware store, clear as day. And I'd done some other things the cops didn't need to know about. I looked at Bobby in the rearview mirror, and whaddyathink he did but wink at me? That's right, Bobby winked at me. He had this way of making you think you were the only one that mattered, even when he was lying or screwing you over. I saw him do it to dames. I saw him do it to Birdy, to Amelia. Hell, he'da probably tried to do it to God Himself if he ever got the chance. And here he was, doing it to me.

"I'll never forget that wink, and then him saying, 'It's our little secret.'

"And it was, our little secret. I've lived with what I done for fifty years. Never told nobody. Until now. Now that I'm near gone, anyway. I don't much like those doctors, but they're right about one thing. It may take a while. But that smoking? It'll get ya."

Relief washed over me, but mixed with it was a sense of sorrow and longing, for as it turned out, it was no great pleasure to be right about something so sad. Bobby Shawcross had indeed tried to murder his wife, and his daughter had died in the crossfire. And he had somehow implicated not just Lorenzo DeMarcos, but also me. *You'd like that, wouldn't you, baby? I can help you. I see you. I know you.* I had fallen for his lines, done what he'd wanted me to do, like a million girls before me. And now, here we were.

"You seem like a nice lady," Lorenzo DeMarcos said. "You should move to a house without so much suffering, so much history. Somewhere warm. You know where you should go? Florida. Even the circuses ended up there. That's where I'd go if I could. Florida."

43

GHOST MOTHER

MARY JAMES AND I SAT in the dining room, finishing our tea, while Olivier lay curled on my lap. I wrote a check, dated it December 17, 2009, and passed it across the mid-century wooden dining table, which had replaced the old IKEA one.

"I guess that settles it," she said. "Thank you."

"No, it's I who needs to thank you. Everything looks beautiful."

"It really does." Mary stood up to leave. The architect was a tall woman with long, wavy silver hair who worked out of a Milwaukee firm. Carmen Alvarez, the Director of the Haven Historical Society, had recommended her to me because Mary's expertise and passion was to restore Romanesque- and Tudor-style homes across the Midwest. It had taken almost a year, but between her, the contractor and his team, and the interior designer, the house—my house, Amelia's house, the *Lawrence Mansion*—was now restored to look just the way it had on April 14, 1955, before everything had gone wrong.

"I'll call you after the holidays, to have my team come up and take some photos, like we discussed, if you're still willing."

"Sure," I said, standing up and placing Olivier on the wooden chair with the turquoise seat cushion. I smoothed away some cat hairs from my dress.

Mary looked at me and smiled. "And seriously. Maybe you wouldn't mind being in a few of them? In that outfit?"

I laughed and ran my fingers through my hair, as if to say, "This thing?" I was wearing a long-sleeved satin emerald-green dress with a sweetheart collar and black pumps, something Grace Kelly would have worn in a movie in the 1950s. I now owned about a dozen dresses like this one, as well as a few vintage cropped jeans, skirts, and sweaters. I had purchased them on eBay and online stores that specialized in retro clothing, but I only had one credit card now, and I paid off the balance each month. My hair was cut into a shoulder-length bob that I washed and curled every other day, and I was wearing pink lipstick and mascara. I could be the mom in a TV comedy about a bunch of kids growing up in the '50s—or I could pose for the "before and after" photos in an architectural or design magazine.

"I can do that," I agreed.

We hugged goodbye, and then Mary James put on a parka over her jeans and sweater and walked out into the December day.

I closed the door behind her, and, just as I had over a year before, when Jack and I had first bought the house, I walked through my domain, starting with that grand foyer, and that striking black chandelier. The lacquer had faded over time, and some of the crystals had been missing, but now it was restored to perfection, and it was glorious. I admired it for a moment and then moved on.

I stepped into the living room, where the hardwood floors gleamed. It was like going back in time. The Scandinavian coffee table with the wooden legs and frame and the glass interior circle had been sanded and finished, and now it looked as good as new. There was a muted yellow couch with angled arms, and two pink round armchairs next to the fireplace, where a fire was blazing. An elegant grand piano stood in the corner, which I played almost every evening: showtunes and hits from the '50s—Sinatra, Sam Cooke, Patsy Cline—to which I sometimes sang along. Above the fireplace hung a circus poster of Birdy, The Flying Bird-Girl, from the Lawrence Brothers Circus back in the '40s, and which pictured Birdy wearing a glitzy orange leotard on the trapeze.

I walked through the archway into the library, went to my new record player, found what I was searching for, and took the record out of its sleeve and placed it on the turntable, before carefully setting the needle down.

Bing Crosby sang "I'll Be Home for Christmas" in that smooth, rich, wistful voice of his.

Opening the French doors, I gazed into the conservatory, which now housed an herb garden as well as some potted plants and teak furniture. The restored glass roof was covered with snow. Dampened sunlight trickled in through the glass walls. It was beautiful outside, a winter wonderland, every branch coated with sparkling white.

I walked through the mudroom and hearth room and into the kitchen, which was updated with stainless steel Wolf appliances. They were state-of-the-art but gave off a retro flair with their red accents and knobs. I loved being in the kitchen, making coffee, omelets, and real food for dinner, including homemade soups and casseroles, which I prepared from scratch using recipes I found online.

I refilled Olivier's water bowl, poured myself a glass of water, and went into the dining room, where Mary James and I had just sat. It was a gorgeous room, now that the ceiling was not only repaired but restored, down to the original oak inlaid carvings, and the walls were papered in a vintage design of yellow roses on a pink background. Olivier was still lying in the chair where I'd left him. I scratched his head. He lazily opened his eyes. I walked into the foyer, where I'd started, and went up the stairs, my heels clinking on the newly finished floors.

I stood at the top of the stairs and breathed in. It was so comforting, so peaceful, to stand there for a minute, taking it all in, knowing that every room was restored, repaired, painted, furnished.

That things I couldn't see were humming with steadfast efficiency and energy. The electrical wiring had been upgraded, the furnace and roof had been replaced, and a new air conditioner had been installed. These were all things the contractor had said I'd needed, and to each of them, I'd said, "Yes, of course, go ahead." Landscapers and painters and stonemasons and asbestos experts and driveway fixers and electricians and plumbers had come and gone, and in the end, the house purred like a contented Persian on catnip.

Jack had always told me he'd had excellent insurance, and as it turned out, that had included excellent life insurance. There had been two in-person interviews with an insurance investigator, who had asked many of the same questions the police had asked. Then there had been a follow-up phone call with a different insurance agent, and some paperwork I'd needed to fill out.

Three weeks after the police had closed their case, a check had arrived in the mail for $1.5 million. Ever the caretaker, Jack had even taken care of me beyond the grave.

The first thing I'd done, once the check had cleared, was to pay off my credit cards. I'd gone online, had made the transfers, and had watched my debt vanish from an astronomical amount down to zero. I'd stared at each screen, each "Current Balance $0," as if I'd been staring at a crystal-blue lake, those zeroes as relaxing as calm waters. Then I'd closed two of the accounts, had cut up the cards, and had felt the weight of stress and shame from decades of debt melt away.

I stood at the top of the stairs and gazed out the window of the landing, beyond the refurbished orange velvet divan, and into the backyard. Snow was lightly falling, just like it had about a year before, the day Jack had died. I had scattered his ashes underneath the willow tree. It had snowed, and rained, and been windy, and sunny hundreds of days since then. I didn't know where the ashes were anymore. If they were still on the ground, or if they were in the air, or if they were already in soil, making new plants, new grass, new life. But his spirit wasn't here, clinging to the house he'd never wanted in the first place. I had never felt him, anyway.

The actor in me, skilled at memorization, recalled lines from the funeral poem on Edgar's memorial card, and I imagined hearing them in Jack's voice:

> *When I am dead, my dearest,*
> *Sing no sad songs for me;*
> *Plant thou no roses at my head,*
> *Nor shady cypress tree:*
> *Be the green grass above me*
> *With showers and dewdrops wet;*
> *And if thou wilt, remember,*
> *And if thou wilt, forget.*

It was funny the way memory worked. When I thought of Jack, when I missed him—and I thought of him and missed him every day—he came to me in fragments. I remembered sitting at a table with him and another couple, Sunny and Ranj, our closest friends in Chicago, drinking wine and listening to blues. Jack had his arm around me as Sunny whispered something in my ear that made me laugh. Jack squeezed me close to him. My entire body had been happy, as if the liquid in the wineglass had been contentment, and I had been swallowing it down. I remembered a Lake Michigan boat tour he'd taken me on, to view the skyline, how his blue-gray eyes had shimmered against the background of the turquoise water. I'd felt myself being drawn into them, and I remembered thinking, *How lucky I am that I get to grow old with this person.* I thought of his proposal. He'd gotten on one knee in the botanical garden and had been so nervous, he'd dropped the velvet box that contained the diamond engagement ring. "Will you make me the happiest man in the world?" he'd asked. Later he confessed that he'd been afraid I'd say no, but in fact, I'd been waiting for him to ask me. I loved him. From the first day we'd met, I had loved him.

I could almost feel the stubble on Jack's cheeks, the scent of his neck. I could almost hear him calling my name. . . . There was an urgency in his voice. *Liiiiiillllllyyyyy!* I pushed the memory out of my mind.

As Bing Crosby crooned that he'd be home for Christmas, if only in his dreams, I went into the room I had used to think of as the nursery, and which I now thought of as Amelia's room. Starburst wallpaper lined the walls. A canopy bed, with a pink comforter, fluffy pillows, and stuffed animals faced the door. And of course, that old Mission-style rocking chair was here, now reupholstered with a daisy-patterned seat cushion. That's where I found Amelia, rocking back and forth in her forever bunny-print pajamas, her thumb rubbing against her bottom lip.

"What's wrong?" I asked.

"I was just waiting for you. Did you finish with the arch . . . with the lady?"

"Yes, we finished. Everything's done. What do you think?"

She threw her arms out in front of her, as if to gesture at all the delights of her room. "I love it!"

"Can I sit down?"

She scooted over. I sat on the chair, and she sat on my lap, and I stroked her ponytailed hair.

"I wanted you to feel at home."

"I always feel at home here. This is the only home I've ever had."

"Well, now I feel at home here, too. I love living in this house the way it's supposed to be."

"So, you'll stay with me forever?"

I poked her in the tummy. "Silly. It's not how the house looks that would make me stay with you forever. But yes, of course I'll stay with you forever." Forever was a long time, but I didn't see the need to complicate things to an eight-year-old.

"Just the two of us."

I hadn't seen Bobby since that night, since the night Jack had died. Amelia said he'd gone into the woods, and then had disappeared. Had he *crossed to the other side*? What sort of other side had been waiting for him? Had he been able to wink at God, trick Him into doing Bobby's bidding, like Lorenzo DeMarcos had said? Or had he gone to the otherworldly hell where Birdy had meant to damn him? Even after everything, sometimes the words came into my mind: *Forgive him.* (Was that a prayer, or was I talking to myself?) And: *Forgive me.*

"Just the two of us, and, well, Olivier, of course," I said.

Olivier had become less frightened of Amelia over time, for although he didn't venture near her, he no longer disappeared or arched his back and hissed at the sight of her. He had followed me up the stairs, and now he lay at the top of the landing, front paws forward, sphinxlike, Amelia and I in his line of vision.

"I was waiting for you for a very long time."

The way she said it, it was clear she wasn't talking about my time downstairs with Mary James. "I know," I said. "That must have been hard."

"I waited a million years for a mommy."

"It sure must have seemed like it."

She had waited over fifty years for a mother. She must have been so lonely. I thought I knew what that was like.

"I waited a long time for you, too, you know," I said.

She looked at me with those big doe eyes, surprised. "You did?"

"A million years."

Amelia held on to me, gripping me tight.

I felt the heaviness of the past, then, the length of my time without her, the fierce longing I'd once felt to have a child, to be a mother. It turned out that falling in love was both a dark tunnel and a soft feather bed. It was both falling into darkness, feeling the fear of the unknown, and landing on soft, feathery contentment. But it was something else, too, something I'd never imagined. A weight in your heart that steadied you, that made you feel whole, but that also held you down. Love was a tunnel; love was a feather bed; love was a shackle. *So, you'll stay with me forever? Yes, of course, I'll stay with you forever.*

Sometimes I dreamed of driving down Lake Shore Drive in the Jag with my dad, the convertible roof down, the wind whipping through my hair, the sun on our faces, feeling free.

"I thought you were dead," I'd say.

My father would shake his head and laugh. "I'm not dead. That was just a dream."

And I'd feel so happy, so joyful, buoyed by a sense of freedom, that life with all its promises and possibilities was still ahead of me.

When I'd wake up, it always took me a few minutes to remember where I was, who I was. *This Lilly. An angel of death with clipped wings.*

So much of my previous life was fading from my memory.

"We're together now," Amelia said, tightening her grip on me. "Together, together, together. Thank you for all you did to stay with me. For all you did for me."

What had I done? Had I done anything? I could no longer remember. Besides, wasn't that what mothers did? We sacrificed everything for our children. Well, mothers who were cut out to be mothers, anyway. "I would do anything for you," I said.

And it was true. I would stay in this chair, rocking back and forth with her, allowing her to clutch me tightly, so that the squeeze of her soft hands around my waist became uncomfortable, almost suffo-cating, and even then, even now, I wouldn't tell her to stop. I would hold her, hug her, trace those bunnies on her back, sing to her when she asked me, play with her when she asked me, read aloud to her, even when I was tired. Even when I was exhausted.

I had always known I was going to be a mother in this house. I had hoped I would be a good one. And now I was.

I started to stand. My stomach was growling, and I wanted to make myself lunch. "Mommy?" Amelia said.

"Yes, my butterfly?"

"Stay with me," she said.

"I was just going to—"

"Please, Mommy, stay with me," she said.

And so I did.

ACKNOWLEDGMENTS

I am greatly indebted to my agent, Henry Dunow, for being the best reader I could have. He pushed me to make this book better every step of the way and gave me suggestions and advice for which I am immeasurably grateful. I thank the entire team at Union Square & Co., especially my editor Claire Watchel and executive editor Barbara Berger, whose encouragement and expertise have been invaluable. I am forever grateful to my husband, Louis Wenzlow, who has been the most incredible (and tireless!) reader and editor for me. My daughter, Alice Wenzlow, has given me excellent advice and has been my greatest inspiration. (I love you, bunny!)

For helping me at various stages of this novel, I thank my readers Nina Clements, B. K. Loren, Hunter Loushin, Jules O'Donnell, Jessica Rippel, Viki Siliunas, and Kristen Wells, and especially Jeff Vintar, who read multiple drafts and gave me crucial suggestions, which have helped to make this book what it is today. I thank the following people for sharing with me their knowledge and expertise: Treasa Bane (library); Dean Case (vintage cars); Mike Lelivelt (work); Lija Siliunas (law); and Jennifer Brown (cats). (Any/all mistakes are my own.)

I thank my colleagues, students, and friends at my University of Wisconsin campuses, and at the University of Iowa Summer Writing Festival. I'm especially grateful to Dan Emerson, John Markestad, and Dr. Marc Seals from the former and to my riot grrrl squad at the latter whose writings and friendship keep me going: Amy Margolis, Juliet Patterson, Sarah Saffian, and Suzanne Scanlon. My classmates at Oberlin College and the Iowa Writers' Workshop continue to inspire and support me, and I am particularly indebted to my writing teachers, living and deceased, including Peter Cameron, Frank Conroy, Susan Daitch, Stuart Friebert, James Galvin, James Alan McPherson, James Salter, Elizabeth Tallent, Diane Vreuls, David Walker, and David Young, along with Connie Brothers and Deb West, all of whom taught me lessons that continue to influence my writing. My San Pedro friends and classmates are a constant source of encouragement to me: thank you, dearest friends! I also thank Becca Rodriguez of Curate for her friendship and hard work on my behalf, Nina Lorez Collins and Mona Susan Power for their friendship and support, and the Etzweiler family and Anna and George Grayhek for their friendship and hospitality.

I thank my family, especially my brother, Dean Dwyer, and my cousins, Michael Dwyer and Gary Minkin, for their love and encouragement.

The memories of my parents, Richard and Sharon Dwyer, and my grandparents and ancestors, are continual guides and inspirations to me.

I am grateful to the many authors of ghost stories and haunted house books who paved the way for me, especially my constant, Henry James.

Finally, I thank you, my readers. Life is short. I am grateful to you for spending this time with me and my story.